CW01674425

The Mainstay

The Topaz Files: Book 3

Richard Robinson

SpellBound Books

First Published by in 2025 by SpellBound Books

For Millie and Daisy – for whom I'll keep one foot in front of the other.

One

If the man had calculated his distances correctly, this awkward situation need never have occurred. However, as it was, a rather plump man dressed in a rubber Batman costume was on the floor and in severe pain. He had seriously injured his legs, knees, and stomach and was crying out in agony.

There had been a significant and humiliating misjudgement.

The wardrobe, his launch pad, had toppled forward and was now rather precariously balanced on the edge of the bed, with one of the doors gaping open and knocking against the bedpost. This noise was almost a rhythmic accompaniment to the other cries and howls elsewhere in the room.

On the bed, a woman was screaming. Only seconds earlier it was laughter, but now it was quite clearly panicked screaming and an urgent flailing of tied arms. She was dressed in slightly under-sized Wonder Woman attire; her legs were her only free limbs, but any attempts to release herself were fast becoming fruitless. This was the worst imaginable result for both Batman and Wonder Woman, and now they were helpless.

Less than 100 yards away, eighteen-year-old Sam Jacobs was mowing the lawn of a rather grand townhouse. It was his third lawn of the day. It was nearly lunchtime, and he was tired. He'd been telling his university friends that he was developing a 'lawn-mower's waddle' and was becoming oddly transfixed on keeping his mowing blades super sharp. The waddle, he believed, was a professional affliction that came from mowing whilst walking and avoiding the spraying of loose grass and moss. He'd decided it was most unattractive and needed rectifying, urgently.

As his petrol lawnmower pootled around the corner of this finely manicured garden, he was lost in his thoughts. Sam felt out of place in this coastal village in the north coast of Ireland. He knew his birth family came from somewhere in Ulster and thought he might feel some kind of connection. But he was miles from his real home and the pull of Ireland wasn't evident yet. He also felt out of sorts in university generally. His tiny circle of new acquaintances at university were probably hungover from last night's pub action or from enjoying the student craic, something completely outside Sam's comfort zone.

However, at the princely fee of £15 a lawn, his wallet was much fuller than normal, and this cheered him slightly. He wasn't skint and he could begin to plan a little.

His new-found lawn-mowing career was a result of his disastrous attempts to budget during his early months at university. He had swallowed up his entire overdraft and student loans on clothes, take-aways, and visiting the cinema. The resulting financial pickle meant lawn mowing was his first tentative step towards economic stability, and the staggering amount of second homes and holiday lets in the area meant it could be a gift that kept giving.

With the grass needing emptying from the lawnmower, Sam switched the engine off and stood, hands on hips, surveying the scene. It was a cooler-than-usual late summer's day, he noted. Ballycastle, nestled in County Antrim and a growing hot spot for the tourist trade, had been enjoying a rare late-season heatwave. But, on this particular day, the holidaymakers and locals were probably enjoying the relief of a temperature below 23 degrees.

As the engine noise finally abated, he heard cries in the air. He turned and tried to assess where it was coming from. His initial thought was that this was a seagull. They had an odd way of sounding human occasionally, but after listening harder, he could make out a desperate-sounding female voice. In need of a distraction, and always keen to help, Sam decided to investigate.

He prised open the wrought-iron garden gate, which led directly onto the street and listened again. Above the sounds of a passing tractor, it seemed the yells were coming from the largest house on the street, and they were now more frantic than ever. The female shrieking sound was worrying him. He didn't want to intrude on some domestic argument, and certainly didn't want to put himself in danger. But, as the adopted son of a fireman, he focused on the direction of the cries and followed them, just as his dad would have done.

He sprinted the short distance towards the house and checked both sides of the street for help. With the tractor long gone, the road was deserted. It was a residential road that led directly down into Ballycastle's main shopping area, but motorists would need to be a resident or have a reason to drive up the hill to the big houses. This was a rather exclusive *cul-de-sac*. So, this little emergency was probably left for him to deal with, he decided.

The house in question was a turn-of-the-century stone mansion with a large, high hedge around the perimeter. It looked newly renovated. Sam checked around the outside of the house for smoke, but there was no sign of fire. As he jogged through the open front gate, he swiftly found the main door and tried the handle. It was locked. He ran around the back of the building and looked for another way in. The shrieking was louder, and he picked up the first sounds of a male voice.

At the back of the house, Sam was faced with a key code system. But the sounds of distress seemed to be coming from the third floor of this enormous townhouse. Did he simply break in? He rapidly decided against that possibility and with no other plausible way in, he shouted up to the woman.

"Can you hear me?" he shouted. There was a brief silence and Sam heard the two voices again, this time talking to each other. But he couldn't make out the conversation.

"Yes," came the response. "Thank God. Can you call for help?" the woman said. She sounded stern but panicky.

"Are you hurt? What's the matter?" Sam replied.

"Just get an ambulance, please. Now," the female voice shouted down.

Sam searched his pockets for change, momentarily forgetting that 999 calls were free. He vaguely remembered seeing a phone box down the road but having left his wallet with his rucksack in the other garden, he had no coins and no phone card. There were still no other signs of life nearby.

"Hold on. I'll get help. I'll ask next door to borrow their telephone. I'll just be a minute," he shouted up.

"Shit. No, don't involve anyone else. There's a telephone in here. I'll tell you the entrance code." This was a male voice. It was equally unfriendly but clearly desperate. Sam now knew there were two people up there, but he was still no clearer about what he was dealing with.

"OK. I'll come up," Sam called back, trying to sound calm.

There was a brief silence before a few muttered words were exchanged again.

"2968. Then press the hash key," the woman shouted. She sounded relieved now. The man had gone quiet. Perhaps they were buoyed that Sam was about to rescue them? But what on earth was going on?

After inputting the code into the key system, the door sprang open, and he was faced with a lavish kitchen painted a duck-egg grey. He noticed expensive-looking modern artwork, state-of-the-art white goods and two bottles of champagne, possibly empty, on a large kitchen island.

Sam made his way through the kitchen into the hall and quickly found the stairs. After running up two flights, past a series of elaborate landscape paintings, large white sculptures on wooden stands and a few ancient full-length portraits, he was soon on the top floor and a landing with five doors.

"Hello?" he said, breathlessly, trying to work out which door to try.

"Yes, in here. Third door from the left." The sternness had gone from the woman's voice and had been replaced with an almost vulnerable tone. Sam tentatively edged towards the door and opened it.

He took an anxious deep breath as he ventured into the room but, as he'd come this far, he continued. He was immediately hit with a mixture of embarrassment and awkwardness as he became fully aware of the situation. This wasn't what he'd envisaged at all, and he was instantly hit with the notion that many of his friends would find this unspeakably funny. He didn't.

He'd walked into a really bad dream, with Batman clearly in pain and Wonder Woman wriggling and tied up with blue rope to the bed. Sam studied the two characters as he pushed a wardrobe up off the edge of the bed and upright. Batman was lying about three feet away from the right-hand side of the bed and within touching distance of a large rectangular window, half-shaded by a Venetian blind. As Sam bent down, he could see pale blue eyes through the Batman mask and the beginnings of a salt and pepper beard poking out of the bottom. Both of his knees looked badly damaged as he had fallen onto a wooden floor. There was a nasty cut on his left leg and bruising where his stomach had caught the end of the bedpost. Batman was in agony. Sam held out his hand and Batman gratefully clung on and pulled himself onto the bed. The sounds of his anguish made Sam wince.

"Be careful with him, young man," said the woman. She had

re-adopted her rather formal school-matron tone and Sam didn't like it much. He hadn't looked at her properly yet but had decided she might have too much flesh on show, so kept his distance.

"What's your name, boy?" the woman asked. She had a soft local accent but with a formal edge.

"Sam Jacobs," he replied, somehow feeling that he was about to be lectured about his appearance or for lateness. There was silence for a few seconds as the man regained some of his composure and Sam noted a few odd looks between the two. This was only natural, he thought. This must be an incredibly embarrassing moment for them both.

"OK, Sam, it's very kind of you to help us," the man began, coughing to clear his voice first. He also had a local accent, perhaps Belfast area, and was now desperately trying to sound gathered and in control.

"In the next room, there's a desk phone. If you wouldn't mind, please pick it up and dial 130. Ask for Andrew and explain that they need to attend the Garden House. That's the name of this property. Don't say any more."

Sam moved to leave the room, but as he did so, the man called back. "Sam, could you help me untie my friend first?"

Sam didn't want to get involved in the untying business. This meant he'd have to look at Wonder Woman. But he gritted his teeth and ploughed on. He forced himself to glance over at the woman tied to the bed and looked at her arms shackled to the headboard. She looked uncomfortable.

Wonder Woman was a good deal younger than he had envisaged, with a mass of curly light brown hair, verging on auburn, and wearing thin frameless spectacles. Her costume left very little to the imagination and her freckled breasts were largely exposed, with only a fraction of the fabric guarding her modesty. She didn't seem bothered by the exposure. Otherwise, the woman was pale skinned and was wearing the red costume immaculately, with long blue boots, a gold-trimmed corset and expertly applied make-up.

She was a beautiful woman and Sam blushed a little as she noticed him looking at her. He looked down and away instantly.

Sam thought about other things to stop his redness from becoming too obvious. How old were they? He put Wonder Woman in her late twenties, maybe early thirties. Batman was in his late forties. Batman certainly hadn't put in the same effort. He'd opted for just a pair of flimsy blue briefs, a cape and the trademark mask. It wasn't a pretty sight, and his belly spilt over his briefs with a mass of tufted hair around his chest. There was a large tattoo on his left leg, but Sam couldn't make out what it was. However, as he continued to untie the woman, Sam was unnerved by the caped crusader's fixed stare with his vivid blue eyes.

He hurriedly removed Wonder Woman's shackles, still blushing, and ran into the other room. This was a well-used office with walls lined with books and a computer set-up on a large mahogany desk. The phone sat to the right of the desk and open in front of it was a Filofax. He moved that to one side and dialled 130.

"Yes?" Came the instant reply.

"I have a message for Andrew," Sam replied.

"This is Andrew. Go on ahead."

"Can you come to Garden House right away? There's been an incident."

"We'll be there," Andrew responded. "And who is this?"

Sam had no idea how to respond and decided to put the phone down, rather than have a long, drawn out and probably awkward conversation. He half expected the phone to ring back instantly, but when it didn't, he headed back into the bedroom.

Batman and Wonder Woman were now sitting facing each other on the side of the bed, with the woman assessing Batman's injuries. She seemed to do so with great care and affection.

"It's better than it looks, Sam. I'm sure I'll be fine." Batman smiled.

"That's good to hear. Well, shall I be on my way then? I've called Andrew." Before Batman could reply, there was a noise downstairs. Sam ran to the window and watched as a large anonymous black people carrier pulled up. Surely this couldn't be Andrew already?

The tinted windows gleamed in the afternoon sunlight. All signs of a car make and model had been removed. As two men left the vehicle, they slammed the doors behind them and marched around to the back of the property. They didn't look up. The crunch of the shingle path was audible three storeys up. It was at this point that Sam heard smashing glass downstairs, closely followed by thundering footsteps up the staircase.

"Who in God's name is that?" Wonder Woman shouted.

"I think I can answer that. They'll be my men. Well, men that work close to me." Batman sounded apologetic.

"Jesus Christ," the woman continued. "We didn't need more witnesses. I really don't want to be in the middle of this." She looked genuinely horrified.

Sam reviewed the situation, if only to take his mind off the scene. My men? What had he meant by that? Why would they smash through the door? Sam was sure he'd left the door open. Then he remembered seeing some milk bottles by the back door. Perhaps they'd just been clumsy and broken them, but how did they get here so speedily? Why did Wonder Woman look so scared?

Sam wasn't entirely clear about what was happening, and this was making him anxious. He wanted to get out and finish the lawn. He was due a decent payday and he'd become diverted. Now everything was moving far too fast; he was wondering whether he should have helped them at all.

Suddenly, with the sounds of people heading up the stairs, Wonder Woman stood up and silently pushed Sam into the wardrobe, as she did so, she smiled at him and whispered, "Stay very quiet. This is for your own good, Sam."

She closed the door shut and Sam, with his heart rate now sounding like a full military band in his head, bent down and sat on the floor of the wardrobe. He hated being confined, and something stank in there.

Through crack in the door, he continued to watch. The bedroom door was opened and two men walked purposely into the bedroom. They were wearing sharp business suits but looked strangely unkempt. One, with a small rucksack on his back, had a walkie-talkie.

Sam wasn't sure who they were and didn't much care. He concentrated on staying quiet, keeping his breathing faint, and watched the scene unfold. The two superheroes had also gone quiet and Wonder Woman, who was directly in Sam's eye-line, looked extremely concerned. There was an odd normality to the suits, Sam thought. They looked absolutely at ease with the situation. As if this was a normal occurrence.

"Hello? Yeah, this is Andrew. We'll need the other black people carrier to The Garden House, 149 Primrose Grove in Ballycastle. Just get here," the man switched off the walkie-talkie and pointed at Wonder Woman.

"You need to make yourself scarce," he demanded. "I need a chat with your man. My mate will speak to you in the other room, sweetheart."

She smiled sarcastically and kissed her hand and placed it on Batman's face. No words were exchanged. Batman simply continued to look down. Sam registered the look of relief on her face as she headed away from the scene. The other man followed her out.

Andrew then reached into his rucksack and pulled out a smart Polaroid camera and began snapping the scene.

He seemed to pointedly ignore Batman, who seemed to be getting very anxious about the photography.

"There is no need for that, Andrew," Batman said. "What do you need photos for?"

"There was no need for any of this, was there?" Andrew replied. "But from our perspective, this was quite useful. Because you're a prize prick and this will get you ousted immediately. Photos are just our wee insurance policy."

"Ousted? By whom? I doubt that. You don't know what you're talking about," retorted Batman, sounding infuriated.

"Oh, come on, Phil," Andrew continued. "You're half-naked with some local call girl, or whoever, and we now have photographic evidence. Did you really think we can hush this up, too? You're an absolute liability. Your coke habit, prostitutes, and the continual screw-ups. Your nice guy image is just a façade."

"Whatever. I need medical attention. And stop calling me Phil. It's Sir or, at the very least, Mr Bradley to you. Have some respect." Andrew burst out laughing in response.

"Respect? Look at yourself. You're finished. You called me here to do what? Clear up after your messes again? Jesus. You're deluded." Andrew continued to laugh.

"George," Andrew shouted to his colleague, who was in the next room with Wonder Woman. "Get the girl out of here. Bung her a few quid for a taxi and make sure she's decent. Alright?"

"Dead on," George called back. "Leave it with me."

Sam watched nervously and felt his left foot slowly beginning to fall asleep. The pins and needles were making his leg tremble slightly. He knew this was not an ideal time for pins and needles.

"Andrew?" A voice shouted up the stairs. "Are you here?"

"Yes, I'm here, top of the stairs," Andrew responded.

"You told him?" Batman whispered. "For God's sake, man. After all we've done for you? You fecking Judas."

"Shut up, Phil. I'm sick of running after you. It's making me look like your poodle. He had a right to know. You're making the rest of us all look bloody ridiculous. Just imagine what would happen if the press found out about you? They'd have a field day," Andrew responded, the words almost spat from his mouth.

When the door opened, Sam could make out a large man wearing a fishing hat, thick green gilet, and brown utility trousers with loads of pockets. He had his back to Sam.

"You've ordered the other people carrier, Andrew?" The man asked.

"Yeah."

"Well, don't let him freeze. Get a few of the space blankets around his legs and shoulders. It's a wee bit chilly in here. I'm guessing you're cold, Philip?" the man continued. Andrew vanished.

"That's very kind of you. It's certainly parky with the front door open. It's quite unseasonal. Are you not angry with me?" Batman replied.

"Angry? No," the man responded. "I think we're past that. It's a question of quiet acceptance now, I guess. You've put at risk all the careful foundations we laid. We need to accept that you will not comply."

"Comply?" Batman repeated. "You gave me the tasks; I found the people you needed, and I undertook any other demands to the letter. You've got exactly what you wanted from me. All I want is a little fun."

Sam could see Andrew placing the shiny silver space blanket around Batman's shoulders and another over his legs.

"Oh, I can see that, but your fun is now getting out of hand. The business empire is suffering," the man responded. "Better now?" He asked, as the space blanket was applied. Batman nodded.

"It won't be long before our more anonymous people carrier arrives with the blacked-out windows. Until then, I'd like you to consider this. Very carefully." The man in the fishing gear walked over and shut the door. Andrew and George were nowhere to be seen. Sam suddenly wanted to cough, but somehow held it in. He continued to peer through the crack.

"Consider this exact moment the end of our working relationship. You know this can't be tolerated. But remember, your wife and kids will have etched on their brains that their husband and father was fresh from committing adultery and dressed as Batman when he...."

The man pulled out a small pistol and fired a bullet through Batman's head. Batman, with a surprised look on his face, slumped onto the bed. The blood splatter shot all over the space blanket, with mere fragments hitting the wall behind.

"...died," the man concluded, calmly.

Sam watched as the gunman pulled a handkerchief from his gilet and wiped the pistol from top to bottom and placed it in the hand of the dead Batman. Sam wanted to scream but he had to call on every ounce of his resilience not to make a single sound. He had never been more shocked or afraid in his life.

"Andrew. Get in here now. As you can see, the embarrassment for poor Philip was far too much. I gave him the choice and he took the coward's way out. Are we clear?"

"Perfectly," Andrew replied, with no shred of shock or concern in his voice.

"Make sure the people carrier brings a body bag. Tell them they have a clean-up job and that we say nothing until I'm good and ready. We may need to move him."

"Absolutely. I'll speak to the boys. It'll be no bother."

"Grand. I'm going back to the lake. I've not been here. I'll leave you to sort this out and get the place spotless. Make sure Wonder Woman has her story watertight. If you can't, well, we'll deal with her another way too."

"She'll be fine. I'll make sure she's on the right wavelength," Andrew added. "Maybe I'll give her a lift home and avoid the taxi. She'll be nice and easy."

The man nodded in response and patted Andrew on the shoulder. The room fell quiet, and Sam watched as Andrew covered Batman's body in the space blanket and laid him down on the bed, ensuring the pistol didn't move from his hand.

As the man in the fishing hat partially shut the door, there was another conversation. Sam tried hard to listen in. He heard mention of money, a business transaction, and another woman's name. But nothing stuck in his brain as panic set in. He could feel cold sweat on his forehead, his hands were shaking, and he wondered what might happen next.

Sam knew what was at stake. He couldn't move an inch. A single muscle move could cost him, but as the horror of what he'd just witnessed slowly permeated his consciousness, he felt himself getting tearful. He felt his eyes well up and he had a desire to just burst into tears. But he couldn't.

For two hours he watched on from the wardrobe. He saw the second black-suited team arrive and place Batman in a makeshift body bag and carry him out of the room. He saw Andrew and George strip the bed and mop the floor, bleach the walls, and disinfect everything. He listened as Wonder Woman laughed as she was finally let out of the back door and was led to Andrew's waiting car.

Sam left after waiting for nightfall. After listening hard for every possibility of life remaining in the house to disappear. He opened the wardrobe door, breathed in the heady mix of antiseptic and bleach and stepped gingerly over the still-wet wooden floor. He was soon out of the back door and back to his things in the adjacent garden.

He was still shaking when he went to take the mower back to the garden shed; still struggling to comprehend what he'd seen when he collected his £15 from Mrs Mott, the elderly lady who wanted her nice lawn trimmed before she went to visit her sister in Donegal; and still hearing the noise of that silenced pistol in his head when he got back in his Vauxhall Nova to make the trip back to his student halls in Coleraine. He was jumping at every shadow, every noise and wondering why nobody had asked about the friendly English lad who called Andrew to the scene. How long would he have to keep looking over his shoulder and fearing the worst?

Two

It had been raining on and off all morning at Knock Road RUC Station in Belfast. Large puddles had appeared in the gated back yard which normally, during the summer, the staff would use to relax and chat about life, the universe and everything. An old adage tells us that there are only seven types of rain in Belfast – Monday, Tuesday, Wednesday... -and now that the heatwave was apparently over, it seemed that this late summer was to be no different. Rain was simply a fact of life.

With the yard deserted, the only one foolish enough to take the air was Chief Inspector Orla Massey. She would avoid the forced summer socialising in the yard like the plague. Only during the peaceful, slow drizzle did she want the air and the solitude. She was a solo act. A loner.

She stood staring up into the grey morning skies from the relative dryness of the porch, leading to the metal cages which surrounded the entire building. She'd already been through half a packet of Superkings, and it wasn't even 11am. Chain smoking was a sign that Orla was vexed by a case. This one had been grinding her gears for about six months, and it was a particularly savage episode.

A young family from Ballymacash emigrated to New Zealand for a fresh start. They'd sold their home, auctioned off any useful possessions to make money for a new life and said goodbye to friends and family. However, they didn't say goodbye to the husband's 87-year-old mother, who was suffering from Alzheimer's and was left in the kitchen of the sold home with only two cases of baked beans and a tin opener for company. The house, which she'd owned since just after WWII, was actually in her name and they'd sold it from underneath her.

When social services and a safeguarding team arrived at the house, she was barely alive and the new owners, a young family who were excitedly moving into their dream home, were not expecting to find a confused old lady trapped in the kitchen, half dead. Orla had been working to locate the family and bring them home to face justice. But they had seemingly vanished off the face of the earth. New Zealand Police provided records of the family landing in Wellington and going through customs in June of that year, but since then the trail had gone cold.

It was becoming almost unbelievable that no one seemed aware of their movements once they'd left the airport. Their bank accounts were closed, no communication with the wife's sisters or nieces, and no obvious sign of the two young children starting new schools in NZ. The lack of a lead had shattered Orla's confidence and left her, instead, focused on a few paramilitary cases of punishment beatings and extortion rackets where, of course, no one knew anything about anyone involved until a reward was mentioned and then, ironically, grandmothers were sold to provide information. This was the norm.

As she stood smoking, she pulled out her diary and rifled through appointments. There were divisional briefings at 12 noon and 2pm, including one with Eric Rogers from the RUC's Paramilitary Squad, a man with a legendary ego and possibly the most chauvinistic individual to ever draw breath. Then at 4pm, she was off to Thiepval to meet the recently resurrected Young Communicators Unit, now under the leadership of Declan McNally, a man who had become a rare friend despite her wrongly accusing him of being a mass murderer. But that was another story altogether. He liked a pint, and Orla liked a pint, too. Their friendship was solid.

As she briefly considered her transport back from Thiepval after a night in the mess bar, a young trainee PC poked his head around the corner of the porch.

"Ma'am, there's a call from Sergeant McClellan. He's asking for you specifically. Shall I say you'll call him back?"

"No, I'll take it now. I'll be there in two ticks. Just tell him to hold on." Orla put out her cigarette on the grille of the cage and sighed. Surely someone else could listen to Bob McClellan and his rural bullshit.

Routine calls were becoming a large part of Orla's job in recent months. But she knew this was largely her own fault, as she'd found it so hard to trust other people. In the rest of the UK, a Chief Inspector's principal job was to manage several inspectors. Orla often reminisced about her short time as a Chief Inspector back in Derry, where she handled the three inspectors who ran the patrol shift in the city and local rural areas. This is where she'd made her name. However, she missed being active. She'd yearned for the frontline and Knock Road gave her a portion of that back.

It was a posting that made her the most senior active investigations inspector in the whole of Northern Ireland and the most senior female officer in the RUC. But this also made her a target and a scapegoat. Plus, being a policewoman meant success was far from guaranteed.

"Bob," she began, gritting her teeth and expecting a series of farm equipment robberies or another spate of domestic heating oil thefts. "How can I help?"

"It's a biggie. Phillip Bradley, the NUC MP for Causeway East, is dead. He's committed suicide. He's been found in a derelict house in Ballycastle."

"Phil Bradley? Are you sure? And what makes you think it's suicide?" Massey wasn't expecting this.

"I'm as sure as I can be without a post-mortem. The gun was in his own hand, with no defensive wounds, but he also had a broken left kneecap and bruising around his legs and torso. Those are slightly odd injuries for a suicide."

"You're not joking," Massey responded. "Any hallmarks of a punishment beating?"

"Nah, don't think so. They looked like impact wounds, not blunt force. Say, from a fall or a trip. You haven't heard the best of it yet, Massey."

"What?"

"He was dressed as Batman. Cape, blue trunks, mask and fancy boots." McClellan cackled slightly and Massey just widened her eyes and shook her head. There was little left that could surprise Orla Massey in the Northern Ireland. But a Unionist MP, with a slightly unconvincing track record, killing himself dressed as Batman was a new one, even by her standards.

"Where's the body?" she asked.

"It's on its way to forensics now. But it was found in a disused gamekeeper's cottage near the seafront, next to Ballycastle Golf Course."

"Anything useful from the scene?"

"Hardly anything. There was no sign of blood splatter, and the room was clean. So, he could have been moved, I guess. Or maybe he flew? With those legendary superpowers!"

"Sergeant McClellan. Three things, if it was a suicide, why would anyone move the body? Secondly, Batman doesn't fly. Thirdly, has anyone contemplated the fact that if he was dressed as a superhero, this might be a sex game gone wrong?"

"Sex games? I wouldn't know anything about that, Massey. But I'm thinking it's been moved to protect whoever Bradley was with before his death."

"Okay, fair enough, Sergeant. I'll take it from here. Send me the paperwork."

"One more wee thing, Massey, if you don't mind? Before I sign off."

"Have you been watching Columbo, McClellan? Before I lose patience, tell me everything. I don't need any jeopardy or a dramatic build-up." Massey was toying with him now.

"The Belfast Gazette is sniffing around the story already. Rosie Jones, from their news desk, reckons she's got photos of the body. They'll be running it tomorrow."

"Photos? You fecking what? How? Who let a journalist into a crime scene?"

"Not me, Massey. But I'll investigate. I'll report back."

"Please do. And post their balls to me in a jiffy bag. What culchie idiots do you have up there?" Orla didn't wait for a response; she slammed the phone down and stormed to her desk. She lit another cigarette en route. McClelland would need to clear that mess up, and she had no time for niceties.

"Ma'am!" a trainee PC on reception called out. "We have a call from the Belfast Gazette. They need an urgent word."

"Tell them I'm unavailable currently. And tell them if they print anything whatsoever without my express permission, I'll unleash the hounds of hell on them. And yes, tell them that verbatim."

Orla just about made it to her desk without blowing a gasket, where a fax was already sitting in a buff-coloured folder for her attention. She skimmed it. It contained a few scene photos of where the body was found and a couple of close-ups of the mess that was Philip Bradley's face. She noted the complete lack of splatter marks anywhere near the body and realised that it had unequivocally been moved.

Whilst Massey's famously quick temper had shown itself in abundance to Sergeant McClellan, she also knew this was exactly what she needed. She made a mental note to ring Bob tomorrow and be nicer, maybe even apologise, as she knew one day she'd probably need him onside. She cringed slightly at the thought of calling his team culchies. That seemed, even for her, a mite unfair.

But she needed this case. She needed something to get her teeth into. Something big. A case to make her forget her empty life and her growing belief that she was on a slow passage to spinsterhood. She'd even recently taken on a cat, a rescue Tom she'd called Georgie, after her favourite footballer.

At 39, Orla had two long-term relationships, one of each. A boyfriend whom she'd loved since her schooldays. Someone who she'd nearly married on holiday in Gretna Green when drunk on Buckfast. But with or without alcohol, she wouldn't have regretted marrying him, not for a single second. She worshipped the bones of him, and she'd have been proud to have been his wife.

Sadly, it was a relationship that ended after nine years when he moved to England to join the RAF and where he married someone else, almost instantly, and had umpteen children, again very quickly. As a Protestant, that was almost unheard of. He now lived in a sprawling rural idyll in Cornwall and sent her Christmas cards with 'family updates' that made her want to angrily set fire to things.

She had a one-bedroom studio in run-down Garmoyle Street, Sailortown, in Belfast. It was one of the few remaining properties in this once thriving district. But she had vivid dreams of living next to the sea, somewhere, with Georgie. Maybe in nearby Holywood or somewhere more vibrant, like Portrush or Portstewart. But then she'd be overrun with awful tourists and nosey locals.

She then fell for a colleague, Cheryl McManus, the real reason she left Derry.

A same-sex relationship just about cemented her reputation as the black sheep of the family. But that didn't last either. They both drank so heavily that they were almost driving each other to alcoholism and other forms of addiction. Orla decided her career had to come first and so she ended it in the worst way possible.

She achieved this feat by moving to Belfast without telling Cheryl, taking all the furniture and white goods aside from a temperamental fridge. It was on the fridge that she left an orange post-it note that read, "This isn't working, sorry." It took Cheryl a good few minutes to realise she didn't mean the fridge was malfunctioning.

Afterwards, unsurprisingly, Cheryl took the break-up very badly and moved to Scotland. But Orla knew, if she hadn't ended it, one of them would have died. They were putting Baileys on their cornflakes and vodka in coffee, just to get through the day. Massey had then been branded a predatory lesbian by the entire RUC, which she wouldn't have minded, but she wasn't entirely sure whether she was gay, straight or just fell in love with a person rather than their plumbing. It was all a touch hazy for her. She just wanted someone who understood her and who she could love completely, without killing herself in the process.

So, with the buff folder in her hand, she walked into the Knock Road main office and summoned two of her most trusted inspectors, Simon and Marie. Both were clever, in their own ways, and both brimmed with enthusiasm just as Massey liked them. In fact, the minute she walked into the main room, they scampered towards her like obedient spaniels.

"Simon, Marie, I'm pleased you're keen. We have a major case on our hands. I need your support. I'll brief you straightaway, and we can go through an action plan."

"No can do, Ma'am," Simon replied, with a worrying twinkle in his eye.

"What?"

"Marie and I have been commandeered by Eric Rogers to undertake a re-investigation. He says it's a top priority as this is two RUC officers murdered in paramilitary explosions. I'm sure he said he'd mentioned this to you?"

"He did. Yes. They were absolute tragedies." Massey replied, biting her lip so hard that she half-expected to cover Simon and

Marie in blood from the trauma. She was involved in the original investigations but had forgotten about the request from the loathsome Rogers.

"It's a month-long investigation, at least. Sorry Boss," Marie chimed in. "Couldn't you use the CIDs in Woodbourne or Strandtown? Eric's case is monopolising all our time here." Marie seemed genuinely keen to support, and Massey tried desperately to hide her growing frustration. So, she compromised by simply walking away, saying nothing and plotting Eric Rogers' torture methods in her head. It would involve electrodes, car batteries, and his nether regions.

"Ma'am!" The trainee PC called out again. The second time in almost twenty minutes. He was pushing his luck now.

"There's another call on line two for you. It's from Declan McNally. He's going to meet you here at 5pm instead. He has a meeting near City Hall. Shall I say that's fine?"

"Jesus Christ. Yes. Tell him I'll meet him at Robinson's at 5pm. Now, no more interruptions, unless they are absolutely vital."

"No bother, Ma'am. Message received. Oh, hold on."

"What now?"

"I've got a wee fax for you, too. It's a picture of a fella in a Batman costume. He seems to be looking straight at the camera. It looks like a polaroid. From the Belfast Gazette's newsdesk. I'm guessing you want that. Am I right?"

"Looking at the camera?" Massey replied.

"Yeah. Maybe a bit of an awkward smile, too. He's sitting on a bed."

"Holy Jesus and Mary. Show me that."

Three

Jones was a 19-year-old MI5 officer, just over a year older than Sam Jacobs. That was quite young for a career in espionage. It had been quite a challenging career journey so far, too.

He was of average height, had averagely brown hair, and was averagely attractive. But this rather uninspiring biography was bolstered by his significant IQ, a mind that had somehow developed itself into an open-access storage facility and the ability to utilise his high-functioning autism as a superpower, or that was what he told himself.

He had been with MI5 for less than a year and had been balancing this blossoming career in espionage with an equally promising relationship he'd built with a fellow officer, Jenny Richmond. The two had met in the secretive Milton College in England, a specialist covert communications training centre, and their talents were spotted. They were selected to be part of the Young Communicators Unit in Thiepval Barracks near Lisburn, Northern Ireland. It had become a home from home.

Their basic training had been cut short by the horror of two bombings in the Limehall and Lennoxville areas of Belfast, which massacred all but two YCU members. Their role in the Topaz mission had seen them fast-tracked into active service. It was a cataclysmic rise from obscurity to notoriety that Jones was still getting his head around. Perhaps that's why he had developed an Olympic standard drinking problem, but felt he still needed the practice.

Jenny Richmond, on the other hand, had always been a good deal more ambitious than Jones. But her steely determination was tempered by imposter syndrome. In her mind, she'd never be good enough and this astonished her partner, bearing in mind she'd taken down Joseph Armstrong, a significant scalp, on board a shipping container off the coast of South America. She shot him through the head at close range, at the same time effectively saving Jones's life.

Armstrong, acting as a foil to the equally murderous Stephen Finch, was the man ultimately responsible for the two bombs and the murder of eight YCU recruits in Limehall and Lennoxville – as well as the killing of Finch (a Russian sleeper agent), a rogue MI5 officer, a policeman and two innocent crew members on the shipping container. It was an unnervingly impressive kill-list and Jenny was pleased she'd been the one who consigned him to history.

These facts, their brief history and an unswerving belief that they could ace anything together, had drawn them back to Thiepval and the YCU. A team that was rising from the ashes and today was day one. YCU was reborn.

"Ladies and gentlemen, if you could put your Everything Books away and focus on my direction for five minutes, thank you," Virginia Curry, the YCU stalwart, in her most formal voice, announced across the Briefing Room in Thiepval. The Everything Books were a YCU operative's best friend. It was a pocket-sized almanac which contained almost every conceivable useful piece of information and fact. The discerning spy would never leave home without it.

"I hope you all enjoyed your resilience and orientation tests yesterday. You all did very well, and I'm pleased we have a strong and promising cohort. A sixteen-mile hike in the dark without navigation devices is a fantastic introduction, as I'm sure you'll all agree?" There were amused noises and harrumphing amongst the recruits. It had certainly sieved the wheat from the chaff. The resulting sleep deprivation exercise had brought the numbers down even further. What was left was the hardcore.

"There will be a full debrief on this later and you will be given some time to recover. However, for now, you will need to listen to me and understand future arrangements." Virginia, with her half-moon glasses perched on the end of her nose, looked across the fourteen exhausted faces of the Young Communicators Unit. This was something she'd done probably at least fifteen times before, but none since the bombings, a tragedy caused by Finch, one of their own. There was an air of anticipation, amongst the tiredness, from the recruits.

"You will be divided into two groups. These will be called Delta and Echo. All of your challenges, programmes and missions will be devised and explained by the YCU Chief. He is Declan McNally. Mr McNally will identify himself to you now." McNally stood up and half-smiled at the group. The Derry-man was wearing his rather unseasonal long leather trench coat and brown trousers. His normal stubble had been replaced by a rather splendid grey and red-speckled beard and his thick NHS glasses had been upgraded to a pair of round spectacles that wouldn't have looked out of place on John Lennon.

Virginia, in a flowing orange summer dress, re-organised her notes and pushed her glasses back onto the end of her nose. "Team Delta, you will be under the leadership of Jenny Richmond. Jenny, could you please stand up?" Jenny stood up and smiled at the group. She was donning the normal Team Topaz grey hoodie and black joggers; her long, frizzy, red hair was tied back in a ponytail. She was still showing the signs of a tan from her time recuperating in Bermuda. As ever, she looked effortlessly cool.

"Team Echo, you will be coordinated by Jones. Stand up, please, Mr Jones." Jones, likewise, in grey but sporting a t-shirt rather than a hoodie and ripped black baggy jeans rather self-consciously saluted the group and sat down quickly. He'd been given one of Virginia's trademark disappointed looks for opting for scruffy ripped jeans at the introduction meeting. Jones looked slightly haggard after a heavy night in the Bunch of Grapes, a pub just down the road in Lisburn. There had been a Guinness promotion, and he had needed very little persuasion.

"There are also other members of staff here at Thiepval that are here to support you. Isadora Brown, seated to my left, will support Mr McNally in assessing your progress and will flit between the groups, offering strategic advice on your key projects."

Isadora, in a grey jumpsuit, waved enthusiastically at the group and smiled at Jones and Jenny. She was in a good mood. Thiepval was unfinished business, and this felt right.

"You also have a three-strong technical team who will be based in the Quartermaster's Department. This is opposite the refectory, near Briefing Room Beta. This will be led by Mr Singh, who will issue you with your handhelds and other equipment needs later in the session. He has two assistants, Tom Marsh and Carl Kelly. One will be assigned to each team, Delta and Echo, to support all missions and challenges as technical liaison. Please identify yourselves."

Mr Singh, Tom and Carl all stood and acknowledged the groups. A be-suited Mr Singh was still extremely excited by his new role at Thiepval and hadn't stopped smiling in months. He'd have time and space to develop his ideas and new inventions in the Quartermaster's Department (QD), whilst having a team of guinea pigs to test them in the field. This was also a direct route to his idols in GCHQ and Thames House. It really couldn't get any better than this, in Mr Singh's world.

However, Tom and Carl had spent much of the same time guilt-tripping Mr Singh into letting them join the group at Thiepval and they were, after much deliberation, given modern apprenticeships at the barracks to assist with technical requirements. It was a compromise. These were roles roughly in line with the YTS-training scheme of the 1980s and their pay would be no more than beer money. The qualification itself, not that it mattered to them, was far below what they'd expected from Milton College. But they were keen, if a little naïve. It was a move described by Jones as 'like letting two toddlers run around on a minefield,' but Mr Singh believed they showed genuine promise. Only time would tell.

Virginia, who was getting infuriated by a group of three recruits who had been whispering and chatting throughout the introduction, banged her hand loudly on the table in front of her and startled the less-focused trio. She looked astonished they had the energy to chat like teenagers.

"Right. I must finally introduce myself. Many of you will know me from Milton College and you will see me here from time to time, acting as your pastoral support. To be clear, this does not mean I am your mother, grandmother, or maiden aunt. I am here to deal with genuine issues and to support you as you make your way here. You are our first cohort in a few years, and we want you to succeed, but this isn't a given. Work hard, focus, and give us your best. Otherwise, you'll be back home as quick as a flash."

McNally, sitting three seats along from Virginia, produced a clipboard and read aloud the names of Teams Delta and Echo. They filed off one by one to be met by Jones and Jenny in the two briefing rooms. Jones winked at Jenny as she marshalled her group away. He was loving the competitive element and had been gently goading Jenny in describing the sweetness of his likely victory.

Day one was going to be a soft landing after their rather hellish hike from the airport. They would learn basic ciphers and signs and Mr Singh would talk them through the use of the handhelds. He'd updated the technology further to allow them to send and receive spoken messages, up to a maximum of ten seconds. It was a bit like a portable answering machine. Tom and Carl had spent the last few weeks using this technological advance to send each other rude words. For example, Tom had been delighted to be awoken in his dormitory room to a recorded message of Carl shouting 'arse' in a variety of hilarious regional accents.

Earlier in the day, McNally had briefed Jones, Jenny, and Isadora on the basics of the first mission. This would take place in two days' time. This early knowledge and sight of the challenge, but not the evidence pack, would enable Jones and Jenny to run through some low-level rudiments in these early days. They remembered being baffled by McNally's challenges as YCU newbies and this early heads-up was appreciated.

McNally had explained that it was a relatively simple *aperitif* task and there was even some discussion about whether he'd gone soft on the YCU after the tragedies of the past. He would give the groups a full briefing pack of evidence to coordinate an exchange somewhere in County Down. The first team to contact the as-yet-undisclosed target would take the spoils.

However, he'd added a little spice to the challenge by throwing in a few red herring ciphers and asking a few friends to pretend to be angry locals near the exchange point to further throw them off the scent. Jones and Jenny knew the basic premise of the test, having undertaken them before, but would be as clueless as the rest of the group when faced with the briefing pack. It would be an intriguing start.

After the getting-to-know-you sessions, Jones, Jenny, and Isadora had planned to meander down to the Bunch of Grapes for a few pints after enjoying a carbohydrate-heavy meal at the refectory. But during the session de-brief and caffeine-fix, McNally had other ideas.

"I'm off into Belfast to meet Orla Massey. It's just a few pints and a chat; she's decent craic and she has her finger on the pulse locally. You're welcome to tag along."

"When you say, 'tag along', you want me to drive, don't you?" Isadora smiled. Isadora had become the designated driver back at

Thiepval and wasn't bothered. She enjoyed rallying the pool cars, generally beefed-up Land Rovers, around the rural roads.

"You know, I hadn't thought of that, but that's a brilliant idea. I'll take you up on that, aye! We'll leave here at 7pm, but no pre-loading at the mess bar. I want a semi-sober meeting with Massey." The team nodded and headed back to their new dormitory bases.

Even by 4pm Jones was still looking the worse for wear. Their new Delta and Echo charges hadn't slept after enduring a gruelling series of tests, but yet he still felt totally off his game. It was, perhaps, the mixture of Guinness, Harp Lager, Bushmills and then a pre-bed port and brandy that had done the damage. Although suspiciously, Jenny seemed fresh as a daisy, and she'd matched him almost drink for drink.

"I'm not sure I'm up for another session in Belfast. I need to get my head down. I might have overdone it last night. My liver is practically screaming in pain," Jones admitted, looking pathetically over at Jenny, who was writing up her notes from the day on the table in their shared quarters.

"No shit. Look, why don't you sleep for a few hours? We're not out until 7pm and maybe you'll be back on form?"

"That's a plan. I'll have forty winks and see what the evening brings." Jones threw himself on the bed and was snoring loudly within thirty seconds. But Jenny had other plans. She nipped out of their quarters and through to the refectory. The main cafeteria area, full of blue plastic chairs and white MDF tables, was empty, aside from a few squaddies drinking tea and chatting at the far end of the room. She turned the corner and headed through to the mess bar, where she noticed McNally smoking one of his cigarillos and sipping what looked like an espresso. It probably had whiskey in it, she thought.

She raced back through the cafeteria and into the admin offices opposite the Briefing Rooms. The area was clear of personnel. Virginia had left for the day. The QD team were doing, well, whatever they did in their new home, maybe playing Kerplunk or

Hungry Hippos, and she now simply needed to find McNally's paperwork. She needed a little head start. She needed to beat Jones.

In the third office, she noted a long trench coat hanging from the door. It looked slightly newer and less weather-beaten. This was a moment of realisation. Did McNally really own two virtually identical coats? After taking that fresh knowledge in a little, she carefully rifled through the paperwork on his desk and hastily came across two maps. Both led to a location in Rathfriland. McNally had marked a spot near what looked like a church or community centre. This had to be the meeting point for the exchange. She flicked through a few of McNally's notepads, all numbered and carefully handwritten in his extraordinarily detailed script but found nothing obvious. These all looked like notes of meetings and reminders, rather than concrete plans for the task. Maybe he had the more detailed notes on him?

It was then, as she walked out of the admin offices and headed towards the small library, that the guilt hit her. This wasn't a Jenny Richmond plan. This wasn't her style at all. She had been drawn to the dark side by a nagging urge to do better than Jones. She was cheating and this was simply not cricket, as her dad used to say. She could almost hear his voice. Even worse, if Isadora found out, she'd definitely tell McNally and probably Jones too. But Jenny couldn't re-bolt the stable door, so she decided that, after a little research into Rathfriland, she would try to forget this ever happened and go back to Jones.

Maybe she'd lay next to him on the bed for a while and ensure he was okay? Maybe she could wake him up in a special, loving way. Perhaps this would assuage her guilt a little?

The library was liberally stocked with reference and non-fiction books, a slightly larger section of maps, and then a tiny rack of fiction and biographic books. The latter were mostly collected and donated by Virginia and her husband, the ex-secret service bigwig Sir Charles Curry. They had often promoted the virtues of a good book for escapism when on a challenging mission.

However, she found a reference guide to County Down and found a useful description of Rathfriland. The village was a typical McNally destination. It was an interesting little community with a big slice of history. She could almost see McNally's clues and ciphers laid out in front of her already.

She promptly spotted that Patrick Brontë, the father of the famous Brontë sisters (the authors Charlotte, Emily, and Anne) was born nearby in 1777. He lived there until a local vicar paid his way to Cambridge University in 1802. While studying at Cambridge, he changed his name from Brunty to Brontë. He preached and taught at Drumballyroney Church and School House, between Rathfriland and Moneyslane. There was a little church just outside the village, which locals called the Brontë Church. Bingo! This was where the exchange would take place. Bloody hell, Jenny thought, you've combined the dark arts of cheating with your own slice of personal brilliance.

It was now time to get back to the dormitory and resume doting girlfriend duties. But Jones was so tired and hungover, he'd probably be sucking the light bulb off the ceiling by now, she thought.

Four

At the Hunter's Arms in Ballyramsey, the landlord 'Wee' Joe McCartney was heralded by the local gangs as a sympathiser. Someone who would turn a blind eye to illegal activities, perhaps keep some illicit goods in the cellar, maybe let the nearby Strabane paramilitary units have meetings in the function room and even organise fundraisers to help the cause. He was a good old boy.

The only issue with this generosity of spirit was that he needed to keep the tills ringing. He needed to make ends meet, to pay the rent to the brewery that owned the pub and, much more importantly, to pay for the upkeep of his three children who attended the local Catholic grammar school. His wife had left three years ago when the pressure to 'sympathise' became too much, but the kids didn't want to move to England with her. They were happy at the pub with their Da and their wee friends. But Wee Joe was almost penniless. He'd come to the end of his savings and the brewery had hiked up their tenancy fees.

Therefore, after a few late-night drinks with a friendly stranger who seemed to take a real interest in Joe's bills and challenges, the sympathetic landlord was invited to a meeting in a roadside café on the A5. Here he met a newly promoted DCI called Orla Massey. Firstly, she bought him a few buns and a cup of tea, then a toasted cheese sandwich and a packet of Worcester Sauce-flavoured Taytos. And then, just before he left the café, she bought him entirely. His names, his telephone numbers, dates of meetings and his promise that he'd tell her everything. In return, he got a regular fee as an informer and a new, plain clothed police friend, who would visit the pub to receive Wee Joe's tip-offs and to give the landlord some words of comfort about the ongoing safety and security of his three kids. That was his real weakness. As long as his kids were safe and Massey kept the money coming, he'd tell her absolutely everything. And he did.

At around 6pm, just before one or two locals normally arrived for some post-work pints and jollity, Wee Joe was contacted by someone from a local paramilitary gang. They didn't give their names; they never did. But they would be in the function room for a quick meeting at 6.45pm and they'd just want five pints of lager and a few packets of crisps. He would leave the refreshments on trays in the room and then leave them in peace. This wasn't unusual. The local groups didn't keep minutes, conduct 'any other business' or have a structured meeting schedule. The meetings just happened when they were required, and the Hunter's Arms was ideally positioned for that. It was nicely out of the way.

Wee Joe kept half an eye on the identities of the people using his function room, and their car registration plates and knew he could hear a good percentage of their conversations from the gents' toilet, which backed onto the function room. He had a little notebook in the pocket of his purple cardigan, and he kept that pad safely under his pillow at night. The bolthole in the gents was riskier, though.

He'd only taken advantage of the listening point in the gents once before, which had led to a sting operation led by Massey. His tip-off had prevented the ambushing of a works van heading from Larkin's Catering Butchers in Roundhill. He'd saved the lives of those eight workers in the van but accidentally condemned the Larkin's Security Guard to death. The guard was wrongly fingered as the informer, and he was shot as he left home for work three days after the ambush was foiled. Joe had been lucky.

Things felt different at the Hunter's Arms today. There were only two cars in the car park, and initially he had recognised none of the five faces that he'd watched walk into the Function Room. There was a huge fella with a suitcase. He wasn't a local man or, at least, Joe had never seen him before. There were three stooges, all dressed in suits without ties and all buzzing around the huge man like flies around shite. Finally, bringing up the rear, was a young man in jeans and a green Thin Lizzy tour t-shirt. Now, he looked vaguely familiar. But this could be as a resemblance to someone else. Joe had been the landlord since the mid-1980s and had seen plenty of people come and go.

He waited patiently for the five men to go into the room and sit down. His two regulars then showed up and he served them two pints of Beamish and some dry roasted peanuts. They would happily chat away whilst Joe pottered around. He would sweep the green baize on the pool table, wipe down the dart-board blackboard and maybe restock the cigarette machine. All these jobs gave him a good view of the Function Room. But his cleverest move, albeit also his most dangerous, was to hang his bar towels on the rotary washing line to dry, which was positioned exactly outside the back window of the room where the meeting was taking place. He'd then sneak a few looks inside. This was his plan today. He waited for about ten minutes, swept the pool table and dandered outside with his bar towels and some clothes pegs.

As he pegged the first one onto the line, he dropped a few on the floor and used that clumsy moment as an opportunity to look inside. With one curtain partially closed, he could see they were already preparing to leave. That was a bloody quick meeting, he thought. He decided it wouldn't do any harm if I took a quick slash in the gents and discreetly listened to the end of their chat.

He carefully shut the gent's cubicle door and placed his ear against the listening hole.

"Lads, that's two dead in two days. We need rid of George's body. I don't care how, but this is no one's fault but his own. No-one in my business sells photos to the press. Andrew, you're sure no one else was part of this betrayal?"

"About as sure as I can be, Boss. But I never expected George to sell our polaroids to the paper. He's been absolutely loyal, and I trusted him with my life."

"Wise up, Andrew. Money talks. Someone got to him."

"True enough, sorry Boss."

"Look, it's a good job we're paying someone on the staff on the paper. Very bloody lucky. I knew it would pay dividends in the end. Now, stick the body in the boot of your car for the moment. Contact Bennie and he'll find a means of disposing of it. Understood?"

"Yes, Boss."

"You two, you need to clean this mess up. The landlord here is one of us, so I hear. But let's not take the piss, aye? Make it look clean."

"Absolutely, Boss." The voices tailed off.

Wee Joe rushed out of the toilet, picked his bar towels off the grass near the rotary washing line, and headed back to the pub. Sweat trickled down the back of his white shirt. This was bad. Someone had been killed in his Function Room and, as he began chatting to one of his regulars about an earlier horse race, his brain did a loop-the-loop. There were three goons in his room, the same room that someone had booked for a christening for next weekend, they were cleaning up blood and God knows what else. A life has been lost, here, in little Ballyramsey. Wee Joe knew this was more than hateful – it was utterly incomprehensible.

As he poured another pint of Beamish, this time for himself, he watched as the two cars backed out of his car park. He heard the shingle spit and pop as they hurriedly pulled onto the main road.

He looked into the early evening sun, wondering whether something divine might give him a shove towards his next step. Instead, he wandered back over to the Function Room and pushed straight through the double doors into the main area, decked out with two long tables and rows of chairs. He immediately noticed that one pint glass was still full. Jesus, they didn't even give the poor bastard a drink, he thought.

He then walked over to the far side of the room and saw wetness. There used to be an old darts oche, a long plastic mat, which remained from when the function room was used for local darts tournaments. That mat had gone. And the walls in that far corner were wet. There was also a fresh smell of detergent.

He couldn't phone Massey now. He needed to lock the doors of the room, hold his nerve, and wait until after closing time. Unless the regulars left early, and he could make a telephone call in relative safety. As he paused once more to survey the scene, the scene of utter nothingness, that he knew was absolutely everything, he spotted a piece of white card on the floor near one of the long tables. He bent down to pick it up. Maybe it was an old cardboard beer mat from the christening last week that he'd missed when he tidied up. Since the wife left, he seemed to spend his whole life tidying something.

But no, it wasn't a beer mat. It was a polaroid photo. A feint black-and-white photo of an unmade bed. That's all. Just an unmade bed. Remembering the word polaroid from his brief foray at the listening point, he stuck it into his back pocket and felt his anxiety pique again. What if they came back looking for it?

He locked the door of the Function Room and slapped himself around the face twice to regain his composure. Massey would know how to deal with this. For now, it needed to be business as usual.

Joe strolled back into the public bar; two more regular faces had arrived. The younger one, nicknamed Tadpole, as he was half Polish and half Irish, smiled knowingly at him.

"Fancy a smoke outside, Joe?"

"Aye, I do. I've been wanting to take the air for a wee while. Let's walk."

As the pair walked outside, Tadpole patted Joe on the shoulder.

"Joe, I've got a boot-full of something that I think you'll be keen to see."

"What?" Joe replied.

"Come on, big fella. Come and take a look."

Joe followed the young man to the back of his small white Yugo car. The car, with plates from the Republic, seemed to be held together by rust and good luck. As the man unlocked the boot, Joe wanted to close his eyes. His heart rate hadn't recovered, and it was still broad daylight.

"Okay, it's 100 bottles of Cif Lemon from Poland. Toilet cleaner. My brother thought you might like to buy them, for the bogs and so on. They're kosher. They just call them Cif over there, rather than Jif. Me brother says Jif means foreskin, or something, in their lingo."

"I'll take them," Joe replied, feeling totally exhausted suddenly and needing to end the conversation.

"Pay me in pints, for tax purposes!" Tadpole smiled.

"Naturally," Joe responded.

As they turned to walk back to the pub, with Joe beginning to feel light-headed with all the turmoil in his head, he heard another voice.

"Here, Joe, you didn't find anything in the Function Room, did you? We're missing a scrap of paper." It was one of the goons. Joe didn't hear the car arrive back, worryingly.

"No son, nothing. I haven't cleaned up in there properly yet though, I just took the empty pint glasses back." He threw the goon the keys for the Function Room.

The goon smiled as he caught the keys. Joe sensed he was nervous.

"Be my guest, take a look. I'll be in the bar if you need me."

"You're a trooper, Joe. I'll bring the keys back in a wee minute. I'll have a wee nosey."

Joe had no idea how the goon knew his name. Maybe he'd just heard the locals chatting. He was fairly sure the goon trusted him. After all, even the huge bloke, their boss, sang his praises. But he knew he had to hide that photograph straightaway. So, he walked back through the main doors and into his private kitchen. He stuck the kettle on. He needed hot, sweet tea. Thinking on his feet, he emptied all the sugar out of his blue and white striped Cornish-ware sugar pot and put the polaroid in the bottom. He then hastily re-filled it, ensuring it was covered.

The sound of the bell on the bar sounded and Joe ambled back behind it. The goon was there, standing next to the smiling Tadpole.

"Nope, nothing there. Maybe it dropped out of my pocket somewhere. No dramas Joe, but if you happen to find it...?" He threw Joe the keys back as he spoke.

"Thanks. Aye, I'll let you know. I'll be cleaning in there later. One for the road?"

"No, I'm grand. I'll be on my way. Thanks, big lad."

Joe watched as the goon disappeared out of the front door and he breathed a slow sigh of relief.

"I'll have one." Tadpole said, eager to be compensated for his sale.

"Of course, you will! One pint of bog cleaner on its way!" Joe smiled and poured the man a pint of Killarney Mild, a beer so unpopular he couldn't shift it for love nor money. The young man looked like he thought about complaining and then had second thoughts.

Out of the corner of Joe's eye, he saw the youngest of his sons, 12-year-old Sean, heading towards the back door. Jesus, he thought, if they ever found out about my double life.

Joe waved to Sean half-heartedly, who waved back whilst

seeming to empty an entire tube of Smarties down his throat in one gulp. Joe went back into the kitchen and shut the door firmly behind him. He sucked in the air gratefully, breathing in through his nose and out of his mouth. He would bide his time before he made any moves. He just had to act naturally, before calling his RUC insurance policy. But that would come later, when the pub was empty.

Five

Orla Massey was late for her meeting with McNally at Robinson's Bar. McNally had grown accustomed to her atrocious timekeeping, and he normally used this waiting period as a bit of a pause. He would order a whiskey and cogitate over his day. McNally, much like Massey herself, had always been a loner, but YCU had forced him out of his comfort zone. A troubled career in the British Army had made him untrusting and a bit brusque, but he was working on himself.

Tonight was different, though. He had a full table. Jones, Jenny and Isadora would expect craic and banter after any serious police talk was out of the way. Even Jones had found a second wind and was already onto his third Harp. Jones knew he'd been as white as a sheet earlier and was annoyed that he'd not been at his best during the induction day.

After exactly forty-five minutes of small talk and occasional watch-checking, Massey strolled in through the front door and made a beeline to their table. Jones spotted her surprise that McNally had brought guests, but she seemed content enough. They were all well-known to each other.

Massey looked smart in a navy trouser suit. Her shoulder-length brown hair had some blonde highlights, and she'd applied some subtle makeup. Jones hadn't seen Massey look so, well, feminine, before. But he then admonished himself for registering that thought, as he'd always been taught that women can look and wear what they want. It was just she looked a little more relaxed than he remembered her. She was always a little feisty and challenging when they'd worked together on the Finch case.

"Right, lads, what are we all having?" Massey called over. This was a good start, Jones thought.

"We're alright, I think, we've just bought a couple of rounds. Get one for yourself and you can catch up," McNally replied. "We've been waiting for you. Very patiently."

She returned moments later with a pint of Guinness and what looked like a whiskey chaser.

"That bad?" McNally asked.

"Yeah. It's just people," she began. "They're everywhere and half of them only exist to piss me off. Present company excluded; I hope? You've got nothing outrageous to tell me? That's not why you're all here?"

"Christ, you really have had a bad day, Orla," McNally said.

"I brought them all out because I think it would be good to acquaint everyone with the fine hostelries of Belfast. Nothing else. We'll probably go to the Crown after this, maybe a few in Whites Tavern before ending the evening back at the Bunch of Grapes."

"You'd best excuse my paranoia then. But I swear everyone at Knock Road is plotting against me. I've now got a suspicious death on my hands, but with no real team to support me, just a few PCs, and some pretty bizarre evidence."

"No team?" McNally enquired. "For a suspicious death? How so?"

"Bloody Eric Rogers. He's reviewing a few paramilitary murders of RUC officers. He's taken both of my inspectors, a sergeant, and the best part of my investigation team. The bastard will be crowing when I don't get a result, too."

"Use us!" Isadora, sitting to Massey's left, called over. "We can be your investigation team tonight. We've all signed the Official Secrets Acts and your secrets are ours, too. This could be like therapy."

"Ah, I don't know. It would be madly unprofessional. I have standards to uphold," Massey responded, being only partially serious. The drink had made her smile and drop her guard. "But I can tell you that they'll be a Belfast Gazette headline tomorrow about the suicide of a prominent NUC politician. And I'll bet you all the tea in China that it was murder."

"Really?" Jenny said. "A NUC politician?"

"Yeah. I've already said too much," Massey added.

"Let's hear more. Is he involved in the peace talks? Is this another case of shutting up an MP before they give too much ground to the nationalists? Or vice versa?" Jenny was already hooked.

"Good question. I don't think so though. I think this particular MP was involved in other things. I just can't work out what yet and who'd want to kill him. Early days still. We haven't even looked at the body yet."

"Hold on," McNally interrupted. "So, what makes you think it was murder? If you've not seen the body and it's a suspected suicide?"

"I'll need another drink before I go into that." Massey downed her chaser and gave the glass to Jones. "Fill that up and we'll talk more. But if I can prove it's murder, I might get some of my team back. Suicide doesn't need major resources, even when the victim is well known."

Jones had already downed his glass and was ready to head back over for a refill. Fortunately, the bar was half empty and their table was quite a distance from the rest of the punters. They wouldn't be overheard. So, Jones rushed to the bar and grabbed Massey another chaser.

"Right now, you've got to promise me you'll keep this to yourselves. I know you're all sneaky beakies, but I can't be seen to be blabbing about this stuff."

"I'll give you their word. They know you'd terrorise them if they let anything slip," McNally replied.

"You're not joking. I'd crucify them. Where was I? Okay, the politician was wearing a fecking Batman costume. It was a single shot through the head and no splatter. And he'd clearly been moved. Why would you move a suicide?" There were a few smirks at the mention of a Batman costume, but this was a life lost. They quickly reined it in.

"Perhaps to protect the other party? In this case, maybe Robin? Seriously, could this have been a sex game?" Jones asked, just about holding onto his composure.

"I'd thought of that. But if this was some kind of bizarre sex game gone wrong, wouldn't you have given him some dignity? The man had a family. Kids. Their Da is going to be on the news in a Batman costume with his brains hanging out." Massey was already swigging at the chaser.

"How the hell did the local rag get the photo? Did they get to the scene first?" said Jenny, just finishing her first drink and looking worriedly at Jones' umpteenth pint in an hour.

"Another good question. And another one I can't answer. I don't have a clue. But if I find out that one of the plods from Ballycastle let them in, there'll be hell to pay. But I just can't believe they'd be that stupid and the Belfast Gazette hardly has a huge news team. It would be a major coincidence for a photojournalist to be available and on the scene. I just don't know."

Over in the corner of the room, a young man with a semi-acoustic guitar started to set up his music stand and fiddled with a small amplifier. The twang of him tuning his guitar penetrated the smoke-filled bar.

"Let's listen to this fella for a couple and then head down to Whites. We can continue this there. I don't think they have music on a Tuesday," Massey half-shouted as the rest of the group craned their necks in to hear her words.

As Jones and Jenny disappeared to the bar with McNally in tow, Isadora was left with Massey minding the table. After a couple of moments of awkward silence, Massey leaned over to Isadora.

"I was sorry to hear about your awful injury at London Docklands, Isadora. But I hear you got the bastard?"

"Jenny killed Joseph Armstrong. I think it gave her a degree of closure, but being back at Thiepval with the YCU, that's a real buzz. It feels like we're making things right for the Alpha and Beta teams."

"I blame myself for some of that, you know," Massey responded, staring into her glass.

"What? Why?" Isadora replied.

"I spent so long believing McNally was involved when you were stuck up there in that damn storage facility on The Europa. If I'd have stopped being so bloody stubborn and listened to Charles Curry. I'm so sorry, Isadora."

"No, I won't have that, Massey. You have no reason to apologise to me. It was your support that enabled us to track down Finch. Let's just draw a line. Move on."

"Well, that's very kind of you."

"Not at all. You know, I don't aim to be in this chair forever. I can take a few steps now. I'm having weekly physio at the Barracks. This is just a blip. We need to be a team and I'm up for anything. My God!" Isadora paused and laughed, pointing over at Jones and Jenny by the bar.

The guitarist had started to sing 'Whiskey in The Jar' and they were dancing and shouting along enthusiastically. Jones, with his pint in his hand, pulling his rather ungainly rhythmic shapes and Jenny being her normal graceful self.

"If the rest of the world could see how much fun we have here, they wouldn't avoid this place like the plague. Belfast is a beautiful, friendly wee city. It's just them 'uns that cause the problems,"

Massey explained, smiling and looking over as the impromptu dance floor welcomed more hardy souls.

"Them 'uns?" Isadora replied quizzically.

"Have you not heard that? You've been around here for years; this is part of the lexicon."

"It's passed me by, clearly." Isadora replied.

"You need to get used to it. I hear nothing but 'them 'uns get to march up and down our streets whenever they want; them 'uns are trying to foist a foreign culture and language on us; them 'uns kicked off the latest round of rioting'. Young people here honestly believe they have to be violent to get heard. But it's always them 'uns. Believe me."

"I'll bear that in mind. And are we them 'uns, Massey?"

"No, Isadora, we're us 'uns. But you're very English and that complicates things greatly. Shall we just get another drink?"

"I'll have a diet coke, thanks. I'll stay here and watch Jones making a dick of himself. It's fascinating stuff."

Jones clapped loudly as the guitarist finished the song and seamlessly moved onto 'The Irish Rover'. Again, the dance floor swelled, and jolly locals shimmied and shouted as the music took hold.

"Right," McNally shouted to Jenny and Jones. "I'm going to have a feg and we'll move up to Whites. I can't believe how much we got out of Orla tonight; she's been very open."

"Maybe it's the drink talking?" Jones replied, before spotting something over near the front door of Robinson's.

He watched as Massey moved away from the bar and headed towards the front entrance. She'd been queuing for a drink, but something or someone appeared to have pulled her away. As he watched her, he saw a figure in a black biker's helmet standing by the entrance. As she approached, the man opened the visor and mouthed something to Massey. She nodded, gave him some kind of direction, and then moved back to the table. Her face changed to something far more business-like.

Jones grabbed Jenny off the dance floor and joined Isadora and Massey. Massey, looking slightly perplexed, took a huge swig of her pint and steadied herself.

"We have another body," she said, rapidly, as if rationalising the news as she spoke. "It's another man. It's been badly mutilated. That was one of the Desk Sergeants on his way home passing on the message."

"Shit. Where was it found?" Jenny replied.

"It's been discovered by a dog-walker up near the old Control Tower at Ballyhalbert. It's an old RAF base, converted into a caravan park. The body was wrapped in a rubber mat. Again, a single shot to the head, but someone has tried to conceal the identity." Massey knocked back the rest of her pint.

"How?" Jenny asked.

"Unclear as yet. We need to get up there," she continued.

"Now? What? We've been drinking for the past two and a half hours. Won't this cause problems?" Jenny asked.

"I haven't, I'll drive. I'm as sober as a vicar," Isadora piped up.

"Good, good. You're a dote, Isadora. Who else is coming?" Massey looked across at Jones and Jenny.

"Okay," Jones replied. "I think we'll all come. I'll grab McNally."

"Yeah, let's all race to see a badly mutilated body. What a wonderful way to end the evening." Jenny added, before running to fetch her jacket. She meant it.

Six

Ulster University had several sites in Northern Ireland and further afield. However, nestled away on the banks of the River Bann and with views to the North Coast and County Donegal hills, the Coleraine campus had something special about it. At his arrival, it hadn't felt like a university town to Sam Jacobs; it felt like a quiet, safe space for him to undertake his studies and mow a few lawns.

Sam, like many young people at the end of sixth form, had no clear idea of his next steps. He pondered psychology, film and journalism, travel and tourism, as well as teacher training as potential study options.

Although inspired by their hard work, he didn't draw a great deal of vocational inspiration from his adopted parents back home in Ash, a village on the Surrey-Hampshire border. His dad was a Station Officer at a large fire station in Guildford and his mother was a Revenue Clerk for Waverley Borough Council in Godalming.

He'd been adopted at five, but he remembered little about his birth family, as there were other brief stays with foster parents prior to the adoption. That made things blurry. He had been given a note from his mother, a copy of which he carried with him almost constantly. It was scribbled on London Posthouse Hotel headed notepaper. He guessed this was her last duty as his mother, writing him a brief note explaining the circumstances of the adoption and then getting the next flight home once the handover was complete.

He'd been told she was an alcoholic with manic depression, cut adrift from her own family, and she felt she'd only let down her child. There was never any mention of his real father, but he often wondered whether he was some kind of salesman. But this was purely an inkling that had taken root in Sam's brain and grown over time, as there was no logic or evidence to support it.

Sam was blessed with a sibling. That was his youngster sister, Emma, ten years his junior, who was adopted from the same Irish birth mother, but years later. History clearly repeated itself, he'd decided. But whilst he knew this was an odd set of circumstances, he'd also felt reassured that his birth mother must have seen the Jacobs as a safe pair of hands, if they were entrusted with her second child too.

Sam's adoptive mother had been told she'd never have her own children. They were loved and treated wonderfully, but Emma was still a little young to be told she was adopted, as she was only a tiny baby when it happened. But when the time was right, Sam knew they would explain everything to Emma sensitively and transparently.

Sam's adoptive parents were always his mum and dad, he'd never known or wanted anyone else. He didn't yearn for his birth mother, but he often wondered about her and perhaps that thought process had dragged him back to Ireland when the chance arose. But this was a gentle pull rather than a desperate yank.

He was very proud to be part of the Jacobs family. William and Rosie Jacobs worked hard, and Sam knew they'd really struggled when his father had first left the Army. He'd served in Northern Ireland during the worst of the Troubles but still loved the place and the people. He'd made friends for life, but there were horrors he couldn't block out.

Sam could remember the bad days after his father's discharge from the army. William, or Bill, Jacobs would sit in front of the television, endlessly smoking and watching boxing videos. That seemed to go on for months and months; and Sam could still remember the terrible rows as they became more and more desperate for money. That was before he landed his first civilian job, as a trainee in the fire service.

All of that seemed like a distant memory now, as they soon found their groove as a thriving young family. Bill had recently bought the family's first brand new car, and they had even been on a proper foreign holiday to Lloret-de-Mar in Spain. It was hot, Sam had burnt his alabaster skin almost instantly and been horrified by the resulting explosion of freckles. This was a normal life with normal challenges, and that normality made Sam content.

Emma, Sam's sister, utterly adored her older brother and sent him little postcards to make up for the loss of him not being around the house and making her laugh. She missed him dreadfully. He was also still coming to terms with student life and the lack of his little friend who followed him around at home. He could do nothing wrong in her eyes.

He'd chosen a BA (Hons) course in Film Studies as a major and Psychology as a minor route. He decided that mixture would give him options and he certainly enjoyed watching films. That was as far as his decision-making had taken him. But he knew his father's military career, serving in Northern Ireland, Gibraltar, Cyprus, and Germany, wasn't for him. But he did have an impressive contacts book in Ireland who he'd been calling uncles and aunties for years.

It was this contacts book he'd been staring at whilst sitting in his single room in his student halls. Running his finger down the names of his dad's friends and their families, those who'd watched him grow up and knew he was studying nearby. He was looking for someone with whom he could feel comfortable chatting through the horror of Batman's death. Someone who'd listen and not immediately drag him to the nearest police station. But no-one immediately stood out.

He'd barely slept since it happened. Repeated flashbacks of watching Batman slump onto the bed had kept him awake. The horrible noise of the splatter hitting the space blanket and the blankness of his dead eyes. But there was one thing that really upped the ante for him, a thought that piqued his anxiety further and made him want to disappear. That was the fact that Wonder Woman knew exactly what he looked like, and someone had heard Sam's voice on that telephone.

He kept expecting the big man in the fishing hat to burst through his student door. He winced every time the payphone rang, which happened all too often. He was dreading someone suddenly knocking on his door with an ominous message for him. Surely, telling the police would make this worse? He needed someone to confide in. The late evening darkness made it worse and somehow, as the heavy rain pelted against his bedroom window, he felt isolated and vulnerable.

He had an Uncle Colm, up in Newry, maybe he could call him? He was always jolly and supportive. But no. Sam dismissed that option almost as soon as he'd thought of it. Colm would be drunk by now.

Over in the corner of his room, Sam had brought with him a black-and-white television and an old top-loading video player. It had to be tuned by hand and the aerial had been replaced by a coat hanger. He'd often located a decent reception for BBC One and UTV, but less so on Channel 4 and BBC Two. A variety of positions around the room hadn't established perfect signal quality, but it was functional for his needs. The video worked perfectly though, and he'd be watching taped episodes of Top of the Pops, The Young Ones, and Shooting Stars later and then, perhaps, be brave enough to meet a few course mates at the college bar for last orders. That was if his anxiety had lessened.

He sat on the edge of the bed and gently tuned his television, looking for BBC One. He might catch the end of a comedy. He needed his spirits lifting. Instead, he stumbled against the Northern Irish regional news on UTV Live, the calendar programme after ITV News at Ten.

"Reports are emerging that Phillip Bradley, the Northern Unionist Coalition MP for Causeway East, has been found dead in a house in Ballycastle. The RUC is currently offering no confirmation of the cause of death, but local reports suggest that the death is not being treated as suspicious. Over to James McMillan in Ballycastle for more."

Sam Jacobs went cold. This had to be Batman. He couldn't imagine many other deaths in Ballycastle, and the notion of him being an MP seemed right in Sam's head. The report continued with the on-scene reporter broadcasting live from Ballycastle. The journalist, in a green cagoule, was dripping wet and was being almost blown off his feet as the harsh Atlantic Sea winds almost got the better of him.

"I am told that his death was reported to the RUC late yesterday evening, when a local estate agent found a body in the holiday let behind me."

Sam swiftly realised this was miles away from the location. The beach-side holiday home, which looked a little dilapidated, was a world away from the high-end mansions where he'd seen the shooting earlier.

"The identity was confirmed early this morning. He was a married man, with two small children and with his mother and father living locally in Ballymoney." The reporter steadied himself, as the breeze nearly blew the microphone out of his grip.

"Philip Bradley, at just 46, was seen by many as a future Unionist Leader in Northern Ireland. He was charismatic, personable and someone who wasn't afraid of looking for compromise on

controversial issues. His death will be a savage blow to his NUC party and to the Unionist cause in the province. Whilst the RUC is not currently commenting on the death, local sources tell me that this is not being treated as suspicious, and no witnesses are being sought. We expect more from this story in the coming hours, but this has saddened a close-knit small community in Ballycastle, a village which is not used to the limelight and will not welcome it. This is James McMillan reporting from Ballycastle; back to the studio."

"*Thank you, James.*" The UTV Live host rustled her papers and continued onto her next story, an unexploded pipe bomb found near a Primary School in Crossmaglen.

Sam re-tuned. He found a sketchy signal from BBC Two and caught the end of a conversation between Radar and Hawkeye in M*A*S*H. But he couldn't focus. His whole body was cold and shaky, and his heart rate had quickened. He knew he needed to tell someone that this death wasn't suicide. Sam was intelligent enough to know that 'not being suspicious' meant exactly that. The big man, the man who had killed Phillip Bradley in cold blood, had somehow covered his tracks so well that the local police had already written this off as a suicide. That seemed wrong, but maybe this injustice would keep Sam out of trouble, he thought.

Sam felt nauseous suddenly, he'd only eaten a ham and cheese Ginster pasty and a king-size Snickers all day but needed to be sick. He rushed to his little *en suite* toilet and vomited into the lavatory. As he pulled his head back and moved to the sink to wash his face and hands, he heard a knock on the front door. Sam froze again.

"Are you in there, Sam?" He recognised the voice instantly. It was his neighbour in the student halls, a Nigerian student called Oladele, or Dele, for short.

"Hold on Dele. Give me two minutes," he called back.

"I'm walking down to get a hot chocolate from the café. The rest have gone to the bar. Do you want to come?"

"Yeah, I need a change of scene," Sam called back. He wiped his mouth with a flannel and splashed his face with the cold water from the tap. He could still see his hands shaking, but the wave of sickness had gone. He needed to get out. He grabbed a black bomber jacket and met Dele outside the front door.

Dele was a giant of a man, at least 6'6" tall, with a thick black beard. At nineteen he could easily be mistaken for ten years older, but he had only recently arrived in Ireland, and everything was fresh to him. Sam enjoyed being the one to show him the ropes. As Sam and Dele walked out from The Oaks, across the road and past the 24-hour garage, they spotted The Kabin, a café which had the largest menu Sam had ever seen.

"You are quiet, Sam. Were you sleeping? Did I wake you?"

"No. I've just had an odd few days. How are you settling in?"

"The room is too small; so far the food is very bland, and the course seems very slow to get going. But I like it here. The people are friendly."

Sam only vaguely listened as Dele talked about his experiences of campus life. He found himself looking at parked cars, checking out pedestrians as they passed the pair *en route* to The Kabin and even stopping to look behind him. He still felt cold and anxious.

"What are you doing, Sam? You seem edgy." Sam couldn't tell Dele what was on his mind. They barely knew each other, even though there was already a bond, but this was a subject too far.

"I've had too much caffeine. A few too many cokes and a couple of coffees always make me paranoid," he fibbed. "I'm sure a hot chocolate and one of their traybakes will sort me out."

"Caffeine is bad for you. I don't touch it. Because caffeine is a stimulant, it is common to experience increased alertness, increased blood pressure and increased breathing rate. How can that be enjoyable?"

"You're right, Dele." Sam pushed through the entrance to The Kabin and was immediately met by two RUC officers and a third, perhaps a plain-clothed officer, sitting drinking tea and eating plates of sausage, chips and beans. What locals called a *cowboy supper*. Sam felt his blood pressure rise again.

In the background of the café, the radio played loudly. It was BBC Radio Foyle, the Derry-based broadcaster. Their half-hourly news service was going through headlines.

"The NUC Leader, Bryan Campbell, has been the first to send his condolences to the family of Phillip Bradley MP, who was found dead in Ballycastle earlier today. Mr Campbell praised Phillip Bradley's constituency work, his commitment to unionist values and his recent efforts to forge closer cross-community links in the Causeway and Glens area. Mr Bradley leaves a wife, Saoirse, and boys of 8 and 10."

This news was following him about, Sam thought. It made his brain ache. He felt guilty and scared.

"A man died? That's sad. Ballycastle is quite close, isn't it?" he said.

"Close enough," Sam replied. "I was working there earlier today, too. I was mowing some lawns and doing a bit of gardening."

"You were near where that man died? That's exciting."

"I don't know about exciting, Dele. Anyway. Let's change the subject. What are you eating?"

"I want a hot chocolate and something sweet. Shall I buy you the same? Maybe that'll help you refocus. Why do you want to change the subject? Did you see something?"

"Of course not. What made you ask that? Yes, I'll have the same as you. A traybake and a hot chocolate. Although you realise this is our summertime? And we are wrapped up warm and drinking hot chocolate."

"This isn't summer," Dele responded. "I'm not sure I'll ever get used to the Irish weather. I'll be wearing this thick coat all year; I'll never be able to blend into the background here." He smiled and then disappeared off to the counter to order.

Blend into the background? Sam thought. That's an idea. It was then that it dawned on Sam. He had to tell someone what he'd seen. He had to explain what he'd witnessed in that mansion and ensure the family knew the truth. But he could do it without giving away his identity. He would use the payphone down the road from the student halls and ring the local RUC station. He'd make an anonymous call. Then, his conscience would be clear, but he'd not face any reprisals. There are thousands of students in Coleraine. He'd not be found.

When Dele arrived with a massive slab of a rocky road for himself and a fifteen, a local delicacy, for Sam, he spotted that Sam's mood had changed. He had an approach he could live with. He licked the marshmallows and whipped cream off the top of his hot chocolate and started to plan, in his mind, what he'd say on the call.

Meanwhile, Dele, who had taken one of the paper menus from next to the till, pulled a biro out from his inside jacket pocket. He scored across 'rocky road' and wrote 6.5 next to it.

"What on earth are you doing?" Sam asked.

"I'm going to try every menu option in here, give it a mark and then I know what the best option is every time I come in. I'll allow some variance because there'll be specials and different cooks, with different levels of competence. But I think, otherwise, this is foolproof."

"So, the rocky road? What do you think?"

"I've awarded it 6.5 Deles."

"Deles?"

"These are my personal units of quality. For example, this hot chocolate is an encouraging 7.25 Deles. It's a little hot and the ratio of marshmallows isn't consistent. I'm aware you had many more of them, too. Otherwise, it was good."

"Do you want to try my fifteen? Give it the once over?" Sam offered.

"No, that is yours. That is an Ulster thing, isn't it?" Sam nodded. The recipe's name derives from the fact that the traybake is made with 15 digestive biscuits, 15 marshmallows, and 15 glacé cherries, which are combined with condensed milk and desiccated coconut. It was Sam's dad's favourite and reminded him of home.

"I would find it hard to score something badly if I knew you'd enjoyed it. And you look as if you are. Congratulations on that," Dele smiled.

"Thanks, I think," Sam responded, wiping coconut flakes from his face.

"Okay. Let's enjoy our hot chocolates in relative silence for a while and let the flavour take hold. I will leave you to your thoughts."

"Again, thanks, Dele."

Sam sat and slowly sipped his drink. He was aware that he was about to make the most important call of his life but was slightly distracted by Dele's quality scoring system. He liked Dele's need to have a full understanding and a system. He was a fantastic much-needed diversion. The fresh air, the company and the calories had done him good, he decided, and finished the rest of his fifteen in one bite.

As Dele slowly sipped his hot chocolate and considered life, Sam decided to make the call straightaway, hoping he'd sleep soundly once his conscience was clearer. He pulled on his jacket and patted Dele on the shoulder.

"I've got to make a quick call from the telephone box. It's a family thing. Give me five minutes."

"Okay, Sam. Are we eating more here?" Dele responded.

"I don't think so. But be my guest if you want to indulge in more delicacies from the menu."

Sam walked out and paced up the street, past the university library and the small convenience store and up towards a row of small alms-houses. They looked, perhaps, two hundred years old and full of character. Sam was strangely calm as he opened the stiff door of the red telephone box, with the default smell of urine and a vandalised local phone book in situ. However, he noticed the number for Coleraine RUC Station was amongst the 'useful numbers' listed on the wall, along with the local hospital, churches, Citizen's Advice Bureau and the lifeboat station.

He threw fifty pence in the slot and dialled the number. It was answered almost straight away.

"Hello, Coleraine RUC, can I help?"

"Yes, I'd like to give some information concerning a reported suicide I saw on UTV tonight." Suddenly Sam shivered. His body reacted to the fear of where this telephone call might lead him. He waited for a response.

"Go ahead, young man. Although, if you're talking about Philip Bradley, I'm not sure any cause of death has been released yet." The PC responded in a rather matter-of-fact way. Sam guessed they might get regular tip-offs or odd calls from loonies.

"Okay, whatever. But I know Mr Bradley didn't kill himself."

"I'm sorry? How would you know that...?"

"I know because I was right there," Sam interrupted. "He was shot at point-blank range by a big man wearing fishing gear. It was in a townhouse in Ballycastle, and Mr Bradley was wearing a Batman costume."

The RUC officer went quiet. Sam realised the Batman costume hadn't been released to the media, so they knew he had vital information.

"I'm going to need you to give me your name, son," the policeman asked, making notes as he spoke.

"This is totally off-the-record and anonymous. I'm sorry. It's far too dangerous for me to reveal my identity." Sam felt his anxiety rise.

"Alright. Let me get the Duty Sergeant on the line. Hold on a wee minute." The telephone beeped as the officer tried to transfer the call.

Sam began to feel incredibly uneasy. There was a man waiting to use the telephone right outside the door. He was wearing a light blue towelling house coat, navy pinstriped pyjamas and impressive leather moccasin slippers. He was standing a few feet from the telephone box, and Sam wondered what he could hear. He carefully looked over his shoulder at the man, who stared right back at him and took a sip of tea from the mug he was holding. Sam was desperate to end the call but needed to hold his nerve. This would be over soon.

"Hello, this is the Duty Sergeant. I believe you have information concerning the death at Ballycastle, but you're not prepared to give your name?"

"That's right," Sam replied.

"Understood. Tell me what you know."

"I know he was shot at point-blank range by a big man wearing fishing gear. It was in a really plush townhouse in Ballycastle, and Mr Bradley was wearing a Batman costume. He was with a lady with auburn hair in a Wonder Woman costume, but she was escorted away. The big man talked about the end of their working relationship."

"Working relationship? Are you sure? Who told you to say all this?" the Sergeant asked.

"Told me to say this? What? No-one! I was there. I saw it all. This isn't the kind of thing you make up." Sam felt his anxiety turning into anger but kept his voice low to avoid being heard by the pyjama-ed man outside.

"Okay, son. You're saying that you witnessed Philip Bradley being murdered? You were in the room?"

"That's right."

"And what were you doing in the room?"

"Hiding. Mr Bradley was injured. I was working nearby and heard their cries for help. He'd fallen off the wardrobe. He'd injured his knees. Wonder Woman was tied to the bed. There were other people there too. They wrapped him in a space blanket and shot him."

There was silence from the Duty Sergeant. Sam had revealed more information the media hadn't reported. Maybe the policeman would believe him now, he thought.

"There was another conversation too," he continued. "But I couldn't quite make it all out. There was something about money, a business agreement maybe, and a woman's name. But it was muffled, and I was so scared." Sam felt his heart rate increase again, as if reliving the moment.

The beeps started sounding for the end of the call and this sound interrupted his thoughts.

"Look, I'm sorry, I've told you everything. I hope you catch him."

The fifty pence dropped into the silver machine and the line was dead. He'd told them almost everything. Perhaps that was enough. Even so, the panic and fear made him question everything he'd said as he pushed the telephone box door open.

The man in the pyjamas, steaming tea in hand, slipped past Sam into the small red box and Sam exited back towards The Kabin. He'd done his civic duty. With the weather still unseasonably cold, he pulled his hood up and walked back to Dele.

His hands were still shaking when he pushed open the door to the café.

Seven

Jones sat at the back of the Land Rover in the middle with his head between the two front seats. Isadora, now fully used to the vehicle's adaptations enabling her to drive, drove at speed, and Massey was giving directions. Jenny, sitting to his left and McNally to his right, were watching out of the window. It was a cool summer's evening, and the roads were empty.

The thought of visiting a badly mutilated dead body in the Northern Irish countryside was bringing back painful memories for Jones. He remembered clambering through the long grass in Limehall and finding the remains of the Alpha Team after they'd been murdered by Finch. He took one look at Jenny and guessed she had similar thoughts.

"How much further?" he asked, as they came to a turn in the road. In truth, Jones had nodded off briefly during the journey and was just getting his bearings back. He had no clue where he was.

"It's just up here. There'll be a track on the left in a minute leading to the caravan park," Massey replied and, as if on cue, the Land Rover was greeted by a young-looking RUC officer with a notebook.

"I'm really sorry," the young officer explained, "this route is now closed to traffic. You'll need to go back the way you came. There's been an incident."

"Good evening, Officer McIlhinney, if you could let us pass, please," Massey responded, ducking down to enable him to see her face in the window.

"Of course, Ma'am, straightaway. No bother," he stammered. "And these other people? I've been asked to keep a note of who enters the site."

"They're with me, Stewart. They're all sneakies. We'll deal with this later. Just write DCI Orla Massey plus four."

He smiled nervously as he caught Massey's eye in the passenger seat.

Officer McIlhinney pulled back the police tape and Isadora drove through. Despite being summer, the route was muddy, and the deep tyre tracks obvious.

Ballyhalbert was a quiet coastal village in County Down, on the east coast of the Ards Peninsula. Residential homes had recently been constructed next to a small harbour and there were also hundreds of caravans, some static and others with electric hook-ups for touring holidaymakers.

The village played a major role during World War II. It protected Belfast and the eastern half of Northern Ireland as it was home to the RAF, Army, Navy, and United States Army Air Force personnel. Since then, the airfield had been sold off to developers and then came the caravan park and the construction boom. There was little evidence left of its wartime backstory.

The site of the body was shielded by a large white tarpaulin and the area had been taped off. There were two RUC scenes of crime officers forensically combing the area. They looked nonplussed by the arrival of Massey's group.

"Do you know this area, Declan?" Massey asked.

"Aye," McNally responded. "I know it well. I had a cousin who had the contract to mend the houses close to the sea whenever the storms came. Even with the sea defences, there's still plenty of damage and debris. So many caravans here now, but it retains its rugged charm," he continued.

"Like your good self, eh?" Massey replied. "Anyway, let me just go over there and take a look. You can join me once I've got a situation report."

She opened the car door and walked over to the site and Jones could see her chatting with one of the officers. She pulled back the temporary sheeting covering the body and seemed to be examining the victim's head. Before too long, she waved them over to the scene.

The vehicle was parked on a muddy track that had the remains of concrete underneath, and the first row of caravans was probably about a hundred yards away. The Irish Sea was visible in the distance, past the old Control Tower and further down towards the harbour. The crashing of the waves against the shingle beach, with the wind picking up too, immediately brought Jones to his senses. There was the continual cawing of gulls and other summer visitors, and that added to the slightly unnerving atmosphere.

Jones could see a washing line in the distance and a few rows of parked cars. He guessed the RUC cordon and activity in a nearby ditch would have set tongues wagging. But the spot itself was isolated, three or four feet down in a drainage ditch that would have flooded when the sea breached the defences. Whoever dumped the body would have known this out-of-the-way spot.

"Are you alright with this?" Jones asked Jenny as she squeezed out of the back seat and joined him.

"I shot a man in the head about three months ago and covered you in his brain matter. This doesn't bother me that much. I'm just tired and ratty. What about you?"

"Oh, I'm fine and dandy. This has shades of Limehall though, doesn't it? It all feels eerily familiar." The thought of that terrible scene with bodies strewn across the wasteland often replayed in Jones' mind. The steps he made as he found the bodies and the look of abject horror on one of their blast-damaged faces, the one closest to the old stables.

If Jenny was feeling it too, she was hiding it well. "Yes, I guess so. But we've both grown up since then. As Virginia would say, we just need to put our big girl pants on." She grabbed his hand and squeezed it.

"She's right," McNally interrupted. "I've seen more dead bodies than I care to remember. After a while, they all look the same. I just try not to picture them with kids or with their parents. It works for me."

"Jesus," Jones said. "That's wedged in my brain now, cheers McNally."

They joined Massey at the site and McNally was the first to walk gingerly over to the body and pull back the sheet covering it. There was a stiff sea breeze that was making the edge of the tarpaulin flap loudly.

"No touching the body and stay behind McNally," Massey called over. Isadora was still manoeuvring herself over to the scene, and the others knew well not to offer her any help. She wanted to manage things herself, but she was also careful to stay back and not get too close to the scene.

"Well, this looks like a single shot to the head from point-blank range," McNally said, in hushed tones. Almost in reverence to the deceased in front of him. He walked two paces to the other side of the body and looked at the victim's hands.

"No obvious defensive signs. But he was a Thin Lizzy fan. It's a tour t-shirt from 1980. I saw them on that tour in Leisureland Ballroom in Galway. They were class. Anything in his pockets?" McNally asked.

"Nah, nothing at all," Massey replied. "But we'll check to see if his fingerprints are on file. I don't suppose you recognise him?" She shone a torch purloined from one of the SOCOs into the face of the victim.

"My God," Jenny said. "How can you recognise anyone with that horrific injury? It's blown half of his face off."

"No," McNally said, after a pause. "These youngsters all look the same, with all that hair, and most of his upper head has gone. Poor wee bastard."

The victim was probably early twenties, Jones guessed. He had unkempt blonde hair and the first signs of stubble. What interested Jones, though, was the rubber mat in which he'd been wrapped. The mat had been deposited to the left of the body and was waiting to be forensically examined.

"This looks an awful lot like a darts oche," Jones announced.

"Bloody hell, Jones. You and your pub knowledge. Who'd have thought it would come in useful?" Jenny said, walking over to join him.

Massey pulled out a pen and used the end to turn the mat over. Sure enough, there were measurement marks on the mat which indicated how far the thrower should stand away from the dartboard and the brand name Wimnau.

"He's right. It's a bloody odd thing to wrap a body in, though. I can't imagine anyone would seek one out. It would have to have been convenient to where the victim was killed." Massey speculated. McNally nodded in agreement.

"There is no shortage of pubs around here, but I doubt too many would have a dartboard. You don't see many now. This is certainly an angle worth pursuing. Will you get the resources now?" McNally asked.

"Yeah. My gut tells me I have two murders now. Phillip Bradley and whoever this poor fella is. I think they outrank a serious case review. But I could still use your help. It might be an interesting project for you, although technically it's police work."

"I don't see why not. And if this is a paramilitary death, MI5 would have an interest. We'd be ahead of the game," McNally said. Jones, Jenny and Isadora tried to hide grins of excitement.

"Anyway, thanks for bringing me out here. Why don't you lot

get back to Thiepval and we can talk tomorrow? McIlhinney can take me back to Knock Road. There's plenty for me to do here."

"Yeah, we'll head back," McNally replied. "I think we've seen enough."

"We'll speak to you in the morning," Jones called over. "The new recruits have a physical training session first thing, and I'll be damned if I'm going to skip my Ulster Fry for that nightmare."

Isadora, who had spent most of the past five minutes getting herself out of the car, into her chair and then manoeuvring herself to about ten feet of the scene, now had to do the same in reverse.

As the doors of the Land Rover slammed and McNally bagsied the front seat, the group could see a driver in a white Volvo in conversation with McIlhinney by the cordon.

"That's a local journalist. Someone has tipped off the local rag," McNally said. "Nothing ever good happens when the press is involved, mark my words. Especially around here."

The group made their way back to Thiepval in relative silence. The excitement of being involved in a double murder gave them all something to think about, but the bleakness of the past half hour and the sea air had muted the atmosphere. There wasn't even the mention of a nightcap from Jones.

Eight

Opposite the double doors that led to the two briefing rooms was a large store cupboard. The front-end door opened out to the entrance to the YCU offices and the briefing rooms, and the back-end door gave access to the main corridor leading to the cafeteria and mess bar.

For years, the store cupboard had been simply that, a large storage space for things as varied as the two table tennis bases, some physical training equipment and a mobile bar, turntables and lights for the occasional barracks disco. These had been moved to an outside storage facility next to the NAAFI Shop outside. In its place was Mr Singh's new HQ, a world away from the mildew-infested, musty and ramshackle lair in Milton College. It had even enjoyed a paintjob with new magnolia walls and gloss green entrance doors.

After almost a fortnight on site and with the first of the two containers from Milton arriving at Larne Port, absolutely crammed with Mr Singh's hoarded treasures, the Quartermaster's Department or QD was taking shape.

It was an L-shaped room with Mr Singh taking the larger rectangular section, with his shelves and cupboards full of resources, peripherals and junk, and Tom and Carl had two desks in the square bit on the end. They were happy. They'd even brought a record player over for Carl to ensure his air drumming skills didn't suffer. They'd spent the past two weeks undertaking a full inventory, or stock take, of Mr Singh's possessions but had struggled to identify about 40%. They would occasionally call over and request clarification.

"What's this, Mr Singh?" Tom would shout, with a large mechanical box covered in wires in his hand. "Oh, that's a spare engine for a Ferris Wheel," Mr Singh would reply nonchalantly.

Other interesting discoveries included part of the penguin enclosure locking mechanism from Chester Zoo; two stainless steel tea strainers; an industrial ham-slicing machine; the rudder from a Lancaster bomber; fourteen Sindy doll heads; a bag of sand from Broadstairs beach; some mahogany veneer for a 1950s kitchen cupboard; nine ribbons for a defunct Olivetti typewriter; and the back axle from a Triumph Dolomite. And this was just the first container. Tom and Carl had given up trying to rationalise any useful function for most of these carefully squirrelled-away items. Mr Singh would just shrug and point to a random location where they would be stored in perpetuity.

There was only one vital piece of the jigsaw missing. Mr Singh's truly remarkable technician, Wendy Watson, who was stuck in Milton College for another month, invigilating the signs and ciphers tests for the year twos and the surveillance exams for the year three communication students. She had been so excited to join the team, but the College Principal had made her a financial offer she couldn't refuse for this extra month of support as they continued recruiting for her successor.

In the meantime, she would communicate with the team by handheld and Mr Singh would occasionally fly back to Milton to undertake guest lectures and work on departmental strategy. Tom and Carl had prepped a desk for Wendy already and knew if they hadn't, Mr Singh would have filled the QD to the brim with meaningless rubbish and there'd be no room left for her.

On this particular day, Mr Singh seemed chirpier than normal. Not only had he got his new lemon-yellow Capri successfully shipped over from Cairnryan Port, but he'd also adapted the wall-mounted colour television in the QD to receive clandestine Bangla TV. But that wasn't all.

"Gentlemen, I have some Indian delicacies for you to start the day," he announced. He pulled a small white paper bag from the right pocket of his brown warehouse jacket and pulled out two fresh-looking samosas.

"Wow!" the two lads chorused, whilst sniffing the air like demented Bisto-kids, taking in the highly spiced fragrance.

"I didn't realise you could cook, Mr Singh," Carl said, taking one of the samosas and taking a large bite. Tom did the same.

"Well, I can't really. But like with anything, I'll give it a go. These are made from Sunita's recipe, my eldest sister. She's quite the cook. But I have an ulterior motive," Mr Singh explained.

"These are delicious, and not too spicy," Tom remarked. "I'm hoping this will be a weekly treat now. Hold on. Ulterior motive? What do you mean?"

Mr Singh bent down and switched on the nearest computer terminal and watched as it booted up. "Wait, two ticks," he said, as the machine slowly whirred into life.

Before too long, Mr Singh's patented RangeFinder 200 GPS system appeared on the screen. There was an instant blue light flashing on the screen, indicating the location of something or someone.

"Oh dear," Mr Singh said. "I'm going to need some sparkling mineral water. Could you pop over to the NAAFI, Carl?"

"Of course. But why?" Carl responded, staring at the screen and noticing nothing was moving. There was just a stationary blue blob. Mr Singh didn't respond. He pushed an Ulster Bank £5 note into his hand and ushered him on his way.

"Oh, and Carl," he called out as he left the room. "When you get the water, drink about half a pint. Don't ask why, just do it."

Carl didn't respond. He was good at doing as he was told, especially relatively straightforward tasks. Fetching and drinking were certainly in that ballpark.

Tom was intrigued. He walked towards the screen and saw the blue dot move slightly.

"Hold on. Is that blue dot me?" Tom asked.

"Walk to the other side of the room, could you?" Mr Singh said, and Tom complied. He strolled over to the far side of the QD and back again and Mr Singh watched as the blue dot mirrored that manoeuvre, moving very slightly on the screen.

"What was it? Where is the tracker?"

"It's a new little invention, with little being the keyword. Hang on. I think Carl has started drinking the water." Mr Singh pointed at the screen and a pink dot appeared.

"How has he activated a GPS with water?" Tom said, staring at the screen as Carl's dot slowly made the journey back from the stores.

"Okay, okay. Any second now. Wait," Mr Singh replied. Carl's dot picked up pace and soon he arrived back at the door of the QD with two bottles of sparkling mineral water, Mr Singh's change and two Wham bars plus a box of Animal biscuits.

"They've bloody got Animal biscuits! At the NAAFI! Literally arrived this morning. It's mind-blowing news. I'm almost giddy," Carl excitedly half-shouted.

"Okay, that's smashing news, Carl, I'm sure. Now, don't eat anything else at the moment if you can try to stop yourself for a few minutes. Please look at the screen." Mr Singh pointed to the two dots.

"I present to you the Personal Exposure Application. It works in the body for about nine hours, or thereabouts, and will give a strong harmless GPS signal indicating an individual's location, hidden in a delicious foodstuff," Mr Singh beamed, proudly.

"I'm confused. Two questions, if I may, Mr Singh?" Carl asked.

"Carl, I know the answers to these questions. I can take an intelligent punt at what you're about to ask, if that's alright with you, Mr Singh?" Tom interrupted and Mr Singh nodded his assent.

"It's called Personal Exposure Application because the GPS device is hidden in a pea. Hence the acronym. They are staple foods in a samosa, and you wouldn't taste the device because of the spices. It only lasts a maximum of nine hours because the body will expel the device using the normal channels," Tom explained, looking over at Mr Singh.

"Absolutely correct, young man. Top marks." Mr Singh clapped his hands in admiration.

"What?" Carl shrugged. "Normal channels?"

"You piss it out, Carl," Tom responded, looking frustrated.

"Only one slight correction to your assumptions, Tom. That is that the device won't taste of anything. It is totally flavourless. I have designed it so that the tiny receiver will be activated by acid. Your stomach acid will work nicely to achieve that."

"And that's why you sent me over to the NAAFI because you guessed my pea was stuck in a tooth," Carl guessed.

"Stuck somewhere, certainly. Maybe in your gullet or something. But it was dislodged and activated when you drank the fizzy water. Then bingo, your pink dot appeared on the screen," Mr Singh tapped the screen as if to make his point.

"You're a bloody genius! What's more impressive, is that the samosa means you can't see it, taste it and you won't have any clue that you've just swallowed a GPS receiver. It's really clever, Mr Singh." Tom shook the smiling inventor's hand.

"Yes. The same could apply to a Cornish Pasty or cold meat pie of any description. I just happened to have my sister's recipe to hand. However, there is only one issue with these PEAs, gentleman." Mr Singh looked slightly sheepishly at his two protégées.

"That is, I'm going to need them back. So, when you use the lavatory, please take these with you." Mr Singh handed Tom and Carl a stainless-steel tea strainer each.

"That's really grim," Carl said. "And won't people look at me oddly when I use the urinal?"

"Use the cubicle for privacy, Carl. Please," Mr Singh replied, shaking his head in disbelief.

"I'll then use my microscope to make any required changes, and we can use them again," he continued. "After fully cleansing them, of course."

The lads pocketed their tea strainers and walked back to their desks to progress their stock-taking.

"Bloody lovely samosas, though. Can I eat my Wham bars now?" Carl asked.

Nine

As Orla Massey's red Mazda ploughed through the morning rain, she divided her time between missing the puddles which had accumulated on the street and dodging the potholes. The road had been due for repair for many months and the rainwater was hiding some of the deeper holes.

It had been raining in Belfast for most of the previous night, and it felt more like a dismal winter morning rather than late summer. She had hit traffic on Castlereagh Road and again on Knock Road itself at Shandon Park, near the golf club. On a normal day, Massey would have cursed her way to work. She riled easily and other drivers were always an inconvenience, especially the parents driving their children to school and getting in her way when they should be walking.

Today though, she used the time to run through her thoughts. In fact, the extra ten minutes added to her journey gave her time to fully unpack the past few days and to prepare a briefing for her team, most of which would be released back from Eric Rogers' internal investigation, she guessed. But he'd try to cling onto as many as possible, such was his superiority complex.

After the Scenes of Crime Team had left Ballyhalbert, the body was taken by private ambulance to Queen's for a post-mortem. Massey had filed most of the initial paperwork by 01.00am back in the station and implored the team at Queen's to send her the early indications urgently. RUC Officer McIlhinney had then driven her back to Sailortown and the comfort of a large glass of Malbec and a fag. Barely a word had passed between them.

She'd been carrying around of tin of pilchards in her work bag for Georgie, her rescue cat, who looked as if he'd barely moved from the sofa since she'd left the previous morning, and she was grateful for the furry warmth of his company. He was just grateful for the pilchards.

As she finally swung into the station car park and past the metal gates, she had made a few decisions. Firstly, she needed to use her team of informants from across the divide to see what they'd heard about Bradley or the young man in the ditch at Ballyhalbert. Whoever was involved didn't seem too bothered about the furore and spotlight of the deaths. Bradley's death had made the main news bulletins in London and Dublin and there would be a statement made in the House of Commons later. But this was murder, she was convinced. The suggestion of suicide was barking mad.

Secondly, if the two deaths were connected, which was a big if, then she'd need to look into Bradley's back story. But suggesting a link would ensure she'd hold on to both cases and most of her team. So, she'd need to be innovative in her thinking. Finally, she would send that darts mat for analysis. Something would show up, aside from blood and tissue. She needed to know where that lad had been killed. The why would come later.

Approaching the front door, she saw Eric Rogers leaning against the reception desk. He was signing in and smiled when he saw Massey enter the building.

"Morning Orla, you look like a drowned rat. Still raining?"

"Yes, does it ever stop?" Massey replied, struggling for small talk.

"I heard about the second body last night. Your head must be spinning. I've released Marie Bristow back into your team. I know how challenging a murder investigation can be. You'll need all the resources you can get."

"That's kind of you, Eric. But I'll need a few more than Marie. Has this been cleared upstairs?" One sergeant wasn't going to be enough for a double murder, she thought.

"Oh, haven't you heard? You'll need to get used to calling me Sir, I'm afraid."

"What?" Massey felt her shoulders rise.

"The Super has taken a leave of absence. We're talking three to six months. I've been asked to step up temporarily. I'll be Acting Superintendent. I trust you can stomach that?"

Every core of Orla Massey's body screamed no. An overbearing, obnoxious, egotistical man running the show was the last thing she wanted. It was the very reason she'd left Derry. There were too many senior RUC men at Orange Order or Freemason's Lodges and treating the constabulary like an old Protestant boys' club. Worse still, Rogers was ex-Special Branch and Flying Squad. Yet another Englishman looking down from his high horse on the mere mortals of the RUC and Northern Ireland generally.

"I'm a big fan of transparent, inclusive recruitment processes," she replied sarcastically.

"Now, now, Massey. Let's be fair. This is only a temporary thing and I've known the Super for years. It was a natural choice. I won't impinge on your workload or time, or not much anyway. I'll just need a good briefing, and we'll rub along just fine," he smiled. She knew he'd be enjoying this moment.

"Congratulations, Eric. I'm sure you'll have a few drinks to celebrate at the Lodge later. Maybe you'll see the Super there too? Anyway, I have work to do." Massey pushed through the double doors into the main office.

"I'll ignore that comment for now, Chief Inspector," he called after her. "I'll have you know I've not been to the Lodge for years.

That was out of order. But I won't be afraid to use all the tools at my disposal if you need reining in."

Massey ignored him. She'd had her say for now, but the anger of being passed over for an interim promotion just simmered gently. The only reason she hadn't thrown all of her toys out of the pram was the possibility that, had she been promoted instead, she'd have to hand over both of her new cases to someone else. She wanted the challenge of the murders and the operational buzz but hated the obvious chauvinism of the decision-making process.

"Twat," she said, under her breath.

Massey, unusually for a Chief Inspector, didn't have her own office. Instead, she had an unremarkable open-plan zone. A bolt-hole. She had a few blackboards, a row of numbered hooks with case-file clipboards attached to them, and three brown filing cabinets. There was no hiding place from her team. They were literally a few metres away from her and she relied on communal briefing rooms for any confidentiality whatsoever.

"Boss," Marie Bristow called over. "We might have a wee breakthrough on the Bradley case. But it's a little mysterious."

"Okay, Marie," Massey responded, perhaps louder than she'd planned. "Let's hear it." The room, with around eight or nine officers milling around, suddenly stopped and they fell silent.

"McClelland's boys took an anonymous call last night. About 9pm. It was from an English lad, clearly nervous, who claims he was in the room when Bradley was shot."

"Interesting. And why do we believe him?" Massey said, still half-heartedly leafing through some files in her in-tray.

"Because he described the Batman costume, the space blanket Bradley was wrapped in, and even gave a description of the killer. None of this was released to the press." Bristow was reading from her shorthand pad and a few of the rest of the team took notes as she spoke. "Oh, and he also mentioned a female companion who was dressed as Wonder Woman."

"Christ. This sounds genuine." Massey looked up at Marie and stared at her momentarily as she swiftly re-ordered her thoughts. "Do we have a full briefing from Coleraine or Ballycastle, yet?"

"Yeah, it was the Duty Sergeant who took the call. We have the transcript of the conversation. One other thing, he reckons the lad was in a phone-box, as the line cut off mid-sentence and there was beeping. We should be able to get the telephone number and then we'll have a location."

"If he saw the shooting, he's in grave danger," Massey said. "We need to get hold of him urgently. I'd hate to think what some of our paramilitary friends might do to an English kid who witnessed a killing."

"We're assuming it's paramilitaries are we, Boss?" Bristow asked.

"We don't assume anything, Marie. You know that," Massey countered. "Right, team, let's prioritise locating this wee lad and we need to listen to any whispers about this or the Ballyhalbert body. Has anyone heard anything so far?"

There was a brief silence before a younger officer stood up.

"One of my informers has cancelled on me. Ma'am. It's the first time he's done it. He's over in Ballyramsey. I think you know him yourself." Informants' names were never spoken in open meetings, sometimes codenames were used, but Massey knew exactly who the young man was talking about. Wee Joe McCartney at the Hunter's Arms. She knew him well.

"I normally meet him at his place of work, late. But he's told me he's busy," the officer added.

"It might be nothing," Massey, thinking out loud, replied. "But I think I know where he'll be this evening and we can just carefully check in on him. Leave this with me, will you?"

"Absolutely, Ma'am," he replied, before sitting down and looking a touch relieved.

"Boss, if the anonymous caller was in Coleraine, he might be a student at Ulster University. There are bloody hundreds of them. Bound to be a few from England, don't you think?" Bristow added. Bristow, with jet black hair in a short pixie-style and in a black trouser suit and turtle-neck jumper, was always eager to impress. There were precious few female role models in the upper echelons of the RUC and Massey knew Marie Bristow was a fangirl and even played on it a little.

"Get on that, Bristow. Speak to admissions, find out who they have from England, and see if the Duty Sergeant can narrow down an accent. It's an angle whilst we wait for Tech to get back to us on the phone-box number."

"I'll call them now," Bristow replied, eagerly.

From out of the corner of her eye, Massey saw McIlhinney coming through the double doors with a manila file in his hand.

"Ma'am. I think we might have a name for the body at Ballyhalbert. A Mrs Pauline McCool from Strabane has reported her son, George Michael McCool, missing. He was living at home, only 19-years-old and has vanished completely. She's distraught."

"Okay, McIlhinney, give me her details and we'll call on her. Do we know anything else about him?"

"She says he works at Maddison's Scrapyard with his dad and brother. He's not had a single sick day since he joined from school but has every Thursday off. She says he's not the sharpest tool in the box and is constantly skint. To be fair, I couldn't get a word in edgeways when she called. She speaks at one hundred miles an hour."

"Alright, Bristow, when you've finished speaking to the University, take McIlhinney to meet Mrs Jennings and tease out of her whether he's likely to be in one of the paramilitary groups or what have you. Tell her it's a missing person's report. Get a photo."

"Okay, Boss," Bristow replied, with the desk telephone receiver still in her in hand.

"We need a name for the anonymous caller within 24-hours to get him to safety. Do I make myself clear?"

Everyone in the room nodded, and the hubbub of the investigation room took over once again. The sense of urgency was immediately palpable, so much so that Massey opted against another extended fag break and raised McNally on her desk phone. She had decided they'd be going on a little trip tonight.

TEN

Day three for the YCU at Thiepval had been tough going for the recruits. One of the Sergeants from the 39 Infantry Brigade had been brought in to put both Delta and Echo through their paces on the Physical Training Field behind the Barracks. It was gruelling in the heavy rain, with packs that grew heavier and heavier as the rain soaked them through.

A few were running out of steam but had been hauled to their feet and propelled back to undertake laps of the yard. Amongst the early stragglers were Carl and Tom, who had been told that they needed to up their fitness levels to meet the requirements of the job. This was a tissue of lies created by Jones, who watched their torture from a bench in Briefing Room Alpha as he slowly demolished his morning fry. However, as the hours ticked by, Tom appeared to be revelling in the challenge and was nearing the front. Even Jones was impressed.

In the same room, but with croissants and jam instead of the usual massive carb-feast, Jenny and Isadora were running through the challenge that McNally had set. The two evidence packs had been handed to the teams early in the morning, and Isadora was advising on logistics, strictly impartially. Jones had picked an Irish rugby fanatic called Niall as his deputy and Jenny a scarily fit Scottish woman called Ailsa. She was leading the pack as they approached the final half-hour of the fitness task and appeared to have barely broken a sweat.

There were plans in place to leave at 12.00 hours, giving them an hour after the PT hell had finished. Jones was feeling quietly confident but was bemused by one cipher that mentioned 'Squire Hawkins and black magic'. Jones and Jenny were slightly ahead of the game, as they knew the inner workings of McNally's mind. He had taught them well and, therefore, with some exceptions, the pair could happily work out the methodology to his ciphers. They knew, at least in these early days of YCU, he'd used a simple substitution cipher and then rely on the team's common sense to reach a conclusion about the target.

In cryptography, a substitution cipher would be a method of encrypting where units of plain text can be replaced with the ciphertext, in a defined manner, with the help of a key. These would be letters, numbers, or symbols. But as the Delta and Echo were still learning, the units were more likely to be single letters, pairs of letters, triplets of letters, mixtures of the above, and so forth. The teams would have to work out the key first, in the briefing rooms, and then decipher the text by performing the inverse substitution process to extract the original message. It was simple, in theory.

Jenny already knew the location, as she'd cheated and was feeling horribly guilty about it. Jones was unaware of this but certainly knew something was up. But he was enjoying her current over-affectionate persona. She'd assuaged her guilt further by basically unpicking the ciphers with Jones within earshot and then it would be a simple race for the two teams to the Brontë Church in Drumballyroney.

But Jones wasn't listening. Not only was he still mopping up the remains of his late breakfast with soda bread, but he also had one headphone in. He was facing away from Isadora and Jenny. This meant that he was literally half-listening to Jenny as she slowly revealed her hand, but also listening to Troublegum by Therapy? A local band that were as loud as they were exhilarating. This absolutely ended any possibility that Jones was going to pick up any clues.

With PT ending and Ailsa already in the showers before prepping for the task with Jenny, Jones went looking for Niall. He found him, rather charitably, helping Tom carry Carl off the field. Carl was exhausted and in a bad way. At least he now knew that air-drumming was not meaningful exercise.

Within half an hour, both teams were in their respective briefing rooms and going through the ciphers, route logistics, and researching the meaning of the unlocked codes. Both Jenny and Jones were impressed by their young charges and Isadora had already noted the emerging talent of Delta's Ailsa, who had virtually completed the cipher challenge single-handedly and with little input from Jenny. So, it was no surprise that Delta left in their Land Rover Snatch and headed out into the mid-afternoon sun. The rain, for once, had cleared up and even the Mourne Mountains were clear in the distance as the blue sky emerged.

Jones stood over Niall and their Echo team as they poured over the evidence pack. They had worked out the key for three out of the four codes and there were literary references. With Jenny already knowing the Patrick Brontë link, the first cipher, which decoded to 'The Maid of Killarney 1818', was hurriedly researched as a book and then Delta pinpointed the author, Mr Brontë himself. They were in the lead.

Echo had stumbled. They started looking at pub names, nicknames of famous politicians and then poems, before finding the book by Patrick Brontë. But he came from Haworth, in England, surely? The Brontë sisters were of Northern English heritage. Jones, in a rather foolhardy move, decided this was a McNally red herring and pushed the team onto cipher two. Even though, at one stage, the birthplace of Mr Brontë was about an inch from his index finger in the Encyclopaedia Britannia.

Both teams de-coded the words 'Captain Moonlight' which Delta linked to Rathfriland as the birthplace of a well-known New Zealand bushranger, but Niall focused instead on his crimes and execution. Captain Moonlight was a masked and cloaked bandit who robbed a bank in a small Australian gold town in 1869. He started looking at gaols.

It was at this stage that Delta disappeared off to Rathfriland in their Land Rover and decided they would complete the final clues en route. They took a few handheld communication devices to stay in contact with base.

Echo spent the next half hour trying to decode a cipher which McNally had reversed. It was the same key, but with Z-A rather than A-Z. This was a typical McNally move, and both Jenny and Jones bit their tongues whilst their team worked it out. However, once completed, the phrase 'Inis Glas' revealed itself. Delta, by this stage sitting in a roadside café, looked for every possible anagram with no obvious winning combination. Luckily for them, this was a red herring.

Niall jumped on the clue straightaway. With his basic level of Irish language, he translated this to Green Island, with Greenisland being a town not far from Carrickfergus. This cheered all five of Team Echo dramatically, with their presumption that Niall's Irish language knowledge had revealed the location.

They hit the road and decided they would head towards Carrickfergus. They had no idea what connected Captain Moonlight to Greenisland but felt that the remaining ciphers would make the difference. Jones, in a moment of rashness, but trying to give Niall some confidence, found there was a historic gaol in Carrickfergus that closed in 1850. This was now part of the Town Hall complex. That was the agreed location.

Delta had long given up on Inis Glas and had moved onto the final cipher in the pack and this was the location to find the target.

The cipher de-coded as 'Squire Hawkins black magic'. With Jenny already knowing the location, she guessed that this was a monument of some kind and Ailsa, who had brought a range of Irish History books for reference, handed them out amongst the team to find more detail.

One of the other members of Delta, Rebecca, found the reference in a tour guide of County Down: 'Squire Hawkins, the well-known practitioner of black magic, is buried in the Drumballyroney Church graveyard. No other local burial ground would accept his body and even at Drumballyroney the horses would not pull him up the hill to the graveyard. His coffin had to be carried instead.'

This meant his grave, at the so-called Brontë Church, had to be the location of the final cipher, hidden by McNally. They drove there at speed. Jenny was letting the excitement get the better of her and simply expected Jones, who she desperately hoped had been eavesdropping on her earlier conversation with Isadora, to show up at the same location. This was his thing, she thought. He's the brainbox.

Back in Thiepval Quartermaster's Department, Mr Singh was watching two coloured dots on a screen going in varying directions. Tom and Carl sat with Isadora and watched as Delta edged closer to the target whilst Echo were headed the wrong way. The GPS in the Land Rovers, installed by Mr Singh over the past week, was paying dividends.

Isadora was confused. "I just don't get it. Jenny explained exactly where she thought the clues were leading, with Jones easily within earshot. Where on earth is he going?"

"He's only supposed to be guiding and supporting, isn't he?" Tom replied. "Maybe he's showing them how to fail gracefully by simply following their ideas and hunches. That's very Jones, don't you think?"

"That's just about plausible, I guess. But I've seen Jones play Cluedo, Frustration, and even Battleships. He hates losing. If this is him being professional and playing fair, I'll be flabbergasted but impressed." Isadora watched as the Echo Team dot edged closer and closer to Carrickfergus.

It was at this moment that Virginia walked in. She'd just arrived back in Thiepval from a pamper day at a local hotel and spa. She looked radiant and knew it. She'd be listening to the conversation from her office.

"Isadora, I'm with you on this. If I'm hearing this right, Jenny and Delta Team have undertaken a challenge that was supposed to take about five hours in less than two. McNally's ciphers are hard. Either Jenny is harbouring some kind of genius in that team or something odd is going on."

"Look," Carl chimed in. "The Delta Team is already at the church. This will soon be over."

"Crikey. Give me one of the handhelds, Mr Singh. We're going to have to even this up and then conduct a bit of a post mortem." Virginia was unmistakably riled. Mr Singh handed her one of the HQ handhelds and she radioed Jones on channel 14.

"Jones, are you reading me? This is Virginia."

"Go on ahead, Virginia. I'm hearing you loud and clear."

"Where the hell are you going? Talk me through the rationale for your current position."

"Well, Captain Moonlight was a robber and went to jail. Another code was Irish for Greenisland. So, we are looking for jails near Greenisland," Jones explained.

"I see. And the other clues?"

"Patrick Brontë, the author of The Maid of Killarney, comes from Haworth in England. I even studied Jane Eyre at Sixth Form. It's an obvious red herring, as the book has an Irish name and he's the father of the Brontë sisters. They're famously English. We've not sorted the final cipher yet."

"Okay, Jones. I can see your thinking. Can I politely suggest that you might like to look again at the birthplace of Patrick Brontë? And perhaps also the origins of Captain Moonlight?"

"Oh. We're a million miles from the answer, aren't we, Virginia?"

"Not quite a million. But your competitors have rather stolen a march on you. There'll certainly be a Steward's Enquiry. I wouldn't want Team Echo to lose heart so early in the proceedings. So, please re-evaluate your approach based on my suggestions." Virginia then signed off before Jones could thank her.

Jones hastily grabbed a rather tatty Reader's Digest guide to Ireland and located the pages marked for Patrick Brontë and Captain Moonlight. Immediately seeing his error, he asked Niall to turn the Land Rover around and head back towards Newry. Jones was perplexed that Virginia had made the call. How had he got it so wrong? Even if this was purely a moment of brain-fog, how did Delta make the connections so swiftly?

"Okay," Jones shouted to the rest of the team in the back of the Land Rover Snatch. "We now know Brontë and Captain Moonlight were born in Rathfriland. This is a lesson learned from poor research and observation. Let's sort this final cipher."

One of the team at the back grabbed hold of the paperwork where they'd decoded the key and started work on the cipher. Jones already knew this had something to do with black magic. So, once Squire Hawkins was de-coded, another quick scan of the Irish history book revealed he was indeed famous for black magic.

As the Echo vehicle sped furiously towards Rathfriland, Jones had a horrible sinking feeling. Jenny would be celebrating this evening. He'd have to deal with her gloating. From being shit hot at this, Jones had a worrying feeling he was just shit instead. He knew Jenny was easily his equal, but he had an odd feeling about this.

"I've got it." One of Jones' Echo Team announced at the back. "He's buried at the local church. There was some mystery about how he got there. It's all blah, blah, blah, otherwise." They were probably 18 minutes from the dead drop in Rathfriland.

"Shall I put my foot down, Jones?" Niall asked.

"Yeah, I think that's probably a good idea," he replied.

In the churchyard, Jenny was surprised to find the whole place deserted. There was a new-looking shingle car park and a wooded fence around the old burial grounds, but it was eerily quiet. She had half expected to see either Jones or McNally by now. Neither were evident. The sun was getting hazier as the afternoon marched towards early evening and the bird song quietened as the team looked for a dead drop from McNally. As they scanned the perimeter of the cemetery, its location wasn't immediately obvious.

Isadora, Virginia and the group back in the QD were watching closely as Jones' dot hurtled closer to the dead drop location and they awaited news of Jenny finding the final cipher on site.

"Do you know where it is, Virginia?" Mr Singh asked. "Will they find it easily?"

"I've got an idea where McNally may have hidden the dead drop. I think they'll probably spend too long looking for the gravestone and they'll struggle to locate it. The grave is actually unmarked. But inside the church, there is a larger memorial for the Hawkins family. They owned the village at one point. I'm guessing he's squirrelled it away in there somewhere."

After all five of the Delta group and Jenny had circled the cemetery a few times, they opted to re-evaluate. Ailsa and the rest of the team went through everything again, clue by clue, cipher by cipher.

Jenny walked to the centre of the graveyard. There was an unmarked grave with a high pointed metal fence. The stone laid in the centre was cracked in the middle, in the shape of a cross. This looked more by accident than design.

"This has to be it. If someone was into the dark arts of black magic, wouldn't you want a protective fence around them?" Ailsa said, looking hopefully at Jenny.

"That makes sense, and McNally is a devious man. But nothing here reveals a name. We've been through every nook and cranny of this monument." Jenny, now beginning to doubt herself, sat on a low wall nearest the church. The rest of the group followed suit.

As the last member of the team, a small young-looking chap with curtained hair, sat down, the door of the church slowly opened. And there, in full religious attire, was the local vicar. He didn't see the group at first and was about to light a rolled-up cigarette he'd pulled out of his trouser pocket.

"Hello," called Jenny. "Your Grace....?" The vicar looked down at Jenny from the top step and smiled.

"There are three types of people that get called Your Grace. A Duke, Duchess and an Archbishop. Sadly, I am none of those. But you can call me Kevin. How can I help?"

All of Delta stood up, as if choreographed, and walked towards the steps leading to the church.

"Well, it's a long story. But we are doing a quiz. We're stuck on one answer. It's about the grave of Squire Hawkins," Jenny explained.

"I'm afraid you're at quite the wrong church and actually in the wrong village. This is Drumballyroney Church. You need St Mary's at Rathfriland. It's about five miles down the road." Kevin pointed down the road, back the way they'd came.

"Drat," Jenny replied, carefully. "We'll head back there. I was so sure we'd come to the right church."

"It's a simple mistake to make. We have lots of people coming here, interrupting services, looking for Brontë facts. Go to St Mary's and ask for the Reverend James Newell Osterberg."

"We're so sorry to have bothered you. We'll be on our way. Thanks for the help," Ailsa said, as they strolled back to the Land Rover. Kevin waved them off. He looked busy.

It took them around eight minutes to get to Rathfriland. It was an undoubtedly quaint Northern Irish village, and there was certainly more life than at Drumballyroney. The church itself was covered in climbing pink roses and there was a young verger on a ladder. Jenny guessed he was changing a light bulb in the entrance porch.

"Is this St Mary's Church?" Jenny called up. The verger, having been too lost in his thoughts to notice the group walking towards him, was slightly shocked and hurried down the ladder.

"We've come to see the grave of Squire Hawkins. Kevin, the vicar at Drumballyroney Church, suggested we speak to you about it. Are you the Reverend James Newell Osterberg?" Jenny smiled. The verger burst out laughing and then corrected himself a little, before smiling back at the group.

"I don't know where to start," he chuckled.

"What's funny?" Jenny replied, still smiling but struggling to see the humorous side.

"Well. First of all, there has been no vicar at Drumballyroney Church since 1970 and it was then deconsecrated in 1976. So, I'm not sure who Kevin is."

Jenny managed "Oh."

"Secondly, the grave of Squire Hawkins is unmarked in the centre of the cemetery back at Drumballyroney. But you'll find a family memorial inside, near the old entrance hall. It's a ticket office now, as it's a live music venue."

"Is it? I see," she replied with an embarrassed shrug.

"But best of all, James Newell Osterberg is the real name of Iggy Pop. I'm quite a devotee of The Stooges, but he's not known for his religious work." The verger laughed again. "I think you've been had! I'm very sorry."

"Drat," Jenny said again, and the team followed her back to the car.

"I think McNally is having a little fun at our expense. He's a huge Stooges fan," she explained to the others. "But, I probably should have realised it had been deconsecrated in the 1970s. Good research makes the team work. We'll learn from this."

They drove silently back to the Drumballyroney Church. As they manoeuvred the car back into the Brontë church car park, they saw a second Land Rover Snatch come into view. Echo had arrived.

There was a collective slamming of doors and a crunching of gravel as the two teams congregated in the middle of the parking area and faced off. Jones was the first to speak.

"Good afternoon, Delta," he smiled, desperately trying to look as if everything was smooth and that he hadn't just driven for forty minutes in the wrong direction. "Have you cracked it yet?"

"It's in there," Jenny replied. "I'm guessing you've worked out all the other ciphers?"

"Kind of," Niall answered before Jones could fathom a response. "We might've over-thought a few of them." Niall's Dublin accent almost made the mistakes sound jolly.

"Well, it sounds like we're on the same page now. But if Jenny Richmond is looking confused after being here for a while, there's a problem," Jones added. "It's the last piece of the puzzle, right?"

"Yeah." Jenny's guilt was front and centre in her thinking. "Look, Jones, can I grab a private word with you? Just for a second?"

"Of course. Hold on," he replied, turning to Niall and his group. "Team, scout that big memorial there, the one with the railings. I'll only be a minute."

Jones and Jenny walked to a bench surrounded by a few magnificent Horse Chestnut trees. There were the beginnings of a cool breeze, which made Jenny's pony-tailed hair flap as she walked ahead of him to the seat. Delta sat on the low wall near the entrance and Echo looked around the already well-searched graveyard.

"I have an admission to make," Jenny began, already looking forlorn. "I cheated. I searched through McNally's stuff whilst you were sleeping off that mega hangover the other day. This location was listed, and I did some research on the Brontë Family."

There was silence as Jones looked everywhere around the graveyard, avoiding Richmond's gaze. But he wasn't annoyed at all.

This explained today's issues. It helped him make sense of things. He just wasn't ready to admit that. As he digested the news, they sat and he watched his team scour the grounds. Jenny broke the silence.

"I'm really sorry. Don't hate me."

"Why would I hate you? I just don't get it," Jones said, quietly. Finally looking into her eyes. "Why did you need to cheat? You're one of the cleverest people I know. This kind of cipher is your sweet spot. You're good at this."

"But not as good as you," Jenny replied, moving a little closer to Jones on the bench.

"Rubbish. Jesus, you're madly frustrating sometimes, Jenny. You know that?"

"Frustrating?" she said.

"Yeah. You're like a million-piece jigsaw. You're insanely complicated and you don't see your own unique skills until they are presented in front of you."

"You're calling me complicated? Wow!" Jenny sat wide-eyed for a second, before reverting back into apologetic girlfriend mode. Jones was easily the most complex character she'd ever met. But now was not the time to bite back. "I don't understand, Jones. Aren't you annoyed with me?"

"Of course not. But you didn't need to cheat. You had this task in the palm of your hand. What made you do it?" he asked.

Jones felt a little disappointed, but there was no anger or hate. Jenny was his best friend, his confidante, and his girlfriend. He was more concerned that she simply hadn't told him.

"I needed to beat you. I wanted you to think I was a challenger. You have a unique brain, a photographic memory and this amazing recall of facts and information. What am I? I've always played second fiddle to you. And Isadora, for that matter." Jenny looked over in the distance, towards the deserted road into the village.

"We'd be nothing without you. You saved my life when you shot Armstrong. You came to my aid when I was trapped on the

General Eduardo. You shaped a mission that rescued me and let our relationship blossom. You're the reason we're back with the YCU, not me. But, much more importantly, this isn't about us. It's about them." Jones nodded over at towards Echo who were fruitlessly checking the large memorial and Delta, who were happily chatting in the late afternoon sunshine.

"It never feels good enough. I never feel I'm quite at Jones or Isadora level. But you're right about this being about them, not us. I'm sorry." Jenny turned and looked at Jones. She avoided an obvious show of affection in front of the teams, but she looked deep into his brown eyes.

"Why don't we talk about this later? And I'll not tell a soul, especially your team. But never think you're anything less than inspirational, Ms Richmond. Please. You're my hero." Jones held her gaze and smiled warmly.

"You just said something really lovely, and you're not drunk. Thank you." Jenny looked away and waved over to her group.

Jones smiled and watched as she re-composed herself. She slipped back into professional mode, but he wondered whether McNally and Virginia were already aware of her clandestine research methods. That wouldn't go down well at all.

"There's a Hawkins family memorial near the entrance hall inside. The last clue will be somewhere near it. Let's gather both teams at the bottom of the steps and we can have a race to the finish. I honestly know nothing about this final aspect," Jenny confessed.

As they walked away from the bench and headed towards the entrance to the church, Jones wondered whether Jenny was simply lacking confidence or whether this was something more. He cast aside that thought process after hearing her announce the plan to Delta and Echo.

"Ladies and gentlemen. We have decided to share the context of the final cipher. There will be a scrap of paper in the entrance hall attached to the Hawkins family memorial. Ailsa and Niall, you two can go in and find it. Report to us out here when you locate the last instruction."

The two team leaders sprinted into the church and, within seconds, Ailsa returned with a pink envelope. She raced back down the steps and presented it to Jenny, who tore it open. The paper inside had just one sentence written in McNally's perfect script. It said 'John McCredy McAlery liked peace and quiet'.

Eleven

The beauty of McNally's cipher test was that he really didn't need to be around to watch it unfold, especially with Jones and Jenny coordinating things. So, for once, he could take a few hours off and prepare for the task finale. He opted to take in a football match at his beloved Cliftonville Football Club, a pre-season friendly. This would enable him to mix business and pleasure.

A morning call from Orla Massey asking for a quiet chat threatened his plans, but much to McNally's surprise, Massey suggested they meet for a few drinks at the football ground's social club. She had seemed far less than interested when he'd briefly mentioned the friendly at their group meeting at Robinson's Bar.

Her odd keenness to see the match was still in his thoughts as McNally walked the two-mile journey from Belfast city centre to Cliftonville's home and stopped off for a pint at The American Bar in Dock Street. This was close to Massey's flat in Sailortown and he had half-expected to see her.

Cliftonville F.C. held a special place in McNally's heart. He was following in his father's footsteps by supporting them and had travelled to North Belfast for as long as he could remember to watch 'The Reds', even though his local club was Derry City. With Derry being Cliftonville's opponents, he felt duty-bound to attend, even though he knew it would be a sparsely attended affair and nothing more than a final warm-up for the season.

The rationale for his attendance was simple. The two teams rarely met, as they were in different league set-ups. Derry, nicknamed the candy stripes on account of their red and white striped shirts, were the anomaly. They were a Northern Ireland-based team but played in the Republic's League of Ireland competition, as opposed to the Northern Ireland League. McNally remembered very well how sectarian issues had led to the club almost folding in the 1970s and battling to join the South's more prestigious league. They'd done well since those difficult days, and he was full of admiration for them gaining a foothold in the League of Ireland. But he had long pinned his colours to Cliftonville.

Cliftonville were based at Solitude, Ireland's oldest football ground. It was hidden amongst a residential area north of Belfast City Centre. The main entrance and turnstiles, located at the rear of a red-bricked main stand, were at the end of three Victorian terrace streets, Cliftonville Drive, Cliftonville Parade, and Cliftonville Street.

The imposing main stand, on the south side, dominated the ground. A steep seated tier of 1,000 seats gave a good, elevated view of the pitch. To the front of this 1950s stand was a narrow standing area with a limited amount of shelter from the regularly inclement weather. To the right of the main stand, in the south-east corner, was the two-storey social club with its sheltered viewing balcony and with the players and official dressing rooms directly beneath. This was known to fans as the Whitehouse.

There, sheltering from the late summer sunshine, was Orla Massey. She was wearing a grey hooded jacket and jeans whilst holding a pint of lager and smoking a cigarette. A small crowd had built up, including a few shirtless lads holding a tricolour. Everyone else appeared to be in the red and white or red and black of the two clubs. She looked uneasy but gave McNally a half-hearted wave as she saw him carefully squeeze past the pint-holding spectators in front of her.

"Well, this is a turn-up!" he said, when finally reaching her. "I had no idea you were a football fan. I was thinking more wrestling or bare-knuckle fighting would be your bag."

"Don't take the piss. This is work, Declan. I'll explain in a minute. I'd appreciate your support on something, but we've got a bit of time." Massey kept looking over his shoulder to an area of the ground called The Cage.

McNally followed her eyes. She was clearly waiting for someone.

"Work? I'm here for the match. Well, mainly," McNally replied.

"Get yourself a pint and, for God's sake, take off that bloody trench coat. You must be sweltering," Massey continued.

McNally stared down at his battered leather jacket through his round glasses and shrugged his shoulders. The coat stays on, he thought, as he strode up the steps into the bar for a Guinness. The white emulsion paint was peeling from the concrete steps and weeds were poking through the gaps. The sun was still warm after a glorious day and McNally considered that any oomph would soon disappear from this friendly fixture, as the players toiled in the above average temperatures.

It was as he made his way back down the steps, avoiding a young fan who was blowing soapy bubbles through a tiny green plastic hoop, that he noticed Massey was looking animatedly in his direction. Police officers have literally no in-built covert surveillance skills, he thought, as he avoided her eyes and slowly headed towards her location. As he did so, the black and red shirts of Cliftonville made their way onto the pitch, and there was a small ripple of applause. This would be a gentle kick about before the game started in earnest in around twenty minutes.

"What's the drama? Can you make it any more obvious?" McNally asked.

"No time to explain now. He's here," Massey replied.

"Who is?"

"Let's go over and I'll introduce you."

McNally, with his full pint of Guinness, followed Massey as she navigated through the fairly meagre crowd towards an almost empty area of the ground. There, standing with a teenager, was an older man, maybe in his early-sixties, with greying hair and gold-rimmed glasses. He was reading the match programme and seemed to be totally unaware of the two guests heading in his direction. The man was wearing a short-sleeved Cliftonville replica shirt, and the teenager to his left wore the same, albeit perhaps a season or two newer.

Massey positioned herself to the man's left and McNally stood behind in the next row of the standing area.

"Good evening, Joe," Massey began. The man looked up from his programme and the blood seemed to immediately drain from his face. He folded up the booklet and tucked it into his back pocket.

"Mother of God! Are you trying to get me killed, Massey? Do you have any idea who attends these games and the influence they have?" Joe replied, a look of horror spread across his world-weary face. "Son, disappear over to the social club and get yourself a can of coke and some crisps."

"But, Da! The game's about to start," the lad replied looking disappointed.

"You'll do as you're told. I won't be long. You can keep the change." The teenager looked down at the mound of change handed to him, as if weighing up whether it was worth his while and sloped off. "Good lad," Joe called after him.

"This is insanity..." he started. But Massey interrupted him.

"You missed your appointment. That is very unlike you. Oh, hold on, where are my manners? Joe, this is McNally, a colleague, and this is Wee Joe McCartney, the landlord at the Hunter's Arms in Ballyramsey. He's a good lad."

"Delighted, I'm sure," Joe responded, staring at the pitch, and not looking at either Massey or McNally. He was absolutely petrified, McNally observed.

"Now, I have two dead bodies and one of them was wrapped in a darts oche. What can you tell me about that?" Massey asked, as a stray ball from one of the Cliftonville players narrowly missed McNally and hit the advertising hoardings behind.

"Wise up. Not here. Please. I was going to ring you. But I get the feeling I'm being watched. Things have changed at home." Joe looked to his left at Massey briefly, as if imploring her to stop and then turned his attention back to the pitch.

The Derry City team strode onto the pitch and, again, there was a little ripple of applause and cheering. They were noticeably well-supported, and Joe used this distraction to quickly explain more to Massey.

"Some unfamiliar faces are using the function room at the back. Some young 'uns too. They're all very civilised and keen to use my hospitality, but it doesn't feel right. These aren't the local fellas."

"New people? Are you sure, Joe?" Massey was doing all the probing whilst McNally listened from behind, eyes entirely focused on the pitch.

"I'm absolutely sure. But that dead body. He wasn't wearing a green t-shirt, was he, Massey? Was it a young lad?"

"Do you know him? What did you see?" Massey asked.

"I'll tell you. But I can't have you crawling over my pub. They'll kill me. Talking like this, here, it's absolute madness. They know who you are, they know who I am. You have no idea who you're dealing with."

"What are we dealing with, Joe?" McNally finally broke his silence.

"That's the thing," he replied. "The local committee, the lads who've been coming in for years, they're fighting for what they believe in, and they punish those that fall out of line. They're dangerous but familiar. But this was something else."

"What do you mean?" Massey said.

"There was a big fella. Looked like he'd been fishing or hunting. I couldn't hear it all. He just smelt wrong. There was something evil about him. I don't know how it happened, but I'm fairly sure the green t-shirted lad was killed in my function room. I reckon that's my darts mat. I'm one missing, anyway."

"We're going to need access to that function room. Scenes of crime will need to be in there, combing through the room, looking for evidence." Massey knew this would cause a problem. She checked Joe's face for what his response might be.

"I know. I've been thinking about that. I've not touched it. It's been locked and unused since it happened," Joe responded, almost with a sense of inevitability in his voice.

"I just needed time and to let things pass. Come in plain clothes. Black the windows out or something. No-one can know I've spoken to you. Absolutely no-one. If someone sees police swarming over my place, I'm a dead man," he continued, his face etched with fear.

McNally handed his untouched pint of Guinness to Joe. For the first time, Joe turned and looked at him. "It'll take more than this, you know. I've got a family and a virtual gun to my head twenty-four-seven. I can barely sleep."

"Report a burglary tomorrow, Joe," Massey said. "Tell your regulars that someone stole the bar takings and nicked one or two other items. Something major from the function room. Make it a couple of thousand pounds, at least. That'll give us an excuse to search the pub. Will that stop the locals from talking?"

"No! You're the RUC. The locals don't want yous anywhere

near the place. They believe they fight their own battles and deal with their own problems. RUC doesn't represent them. But why am I telling you? You know all this," he replied. "If there's been a break-in, they'll want to support me and sort it."

"Right enough," Massey agreed. "So, what do you suggest, Joe?"

"You're supposed to be the experts on stealth, for feck's sake! I'm a wee pub landlord. Look, I reckon your forensics can come in plain clothes very early in the morning and with luck, they won't be spotted. We're quite isolated, so if you're in and out promptly, we should be fine. But one screw-up, and this is over. Understood?" Joe shot a look at Massey, looking for affirmation.

Massey nodded. Another ball headed up from the warm up below. McNally threw it back down onto the pitch.

"What about Philip Bradley? Did anyone mention that killing? What did you hear?" Massey asked. She realised that the longer this conversation went on, the more risk Joe faced of being spotted by unfriendly forces.

"I heard plenty. It was that big fella. I reckon he's involved in both. Your man in the outdoors gear. I heard him say *'two dead in two days'*. Whether he was talking about your man Bradley, I don't know."

"Go on," McNally urged. Joe seemed to be holding something back.

"I've got a wee listening post in the gents. I heard them say that the young lad sold photos to the press. Polaroids. I'm guessing that's why he was killed. But it was all so matter of fact and fecking evil." Joe carried on. "I heard the name George. He must be the dead lad. Poor wee bastard."

"That tallies. Jesus Christ, Joe," Massey responded. "This is a goldmine of information. You should have called us. This is exactly the intel we needed."

"Aye. So, you better look after me, Massey. I have a family," Joe responded. "My wife may have left me, but I still have one of the boys living with me and those wrong 'uns would easily find the other two. I'm a sitting duck."

"Understood. But would you recognise the big man again?" Massey felt a wave of excitement rush through her. Wee Joe had started to unlock everything. But she couldn't use it. Joe was an informant and a bloody important one. He wouldn't want to be on the stand, he still had much more value.

"Not a chance. I didn't see him clearly. But I'd recognise his voice. He had a heavy accent, like a mixture of Cork and American. I also saw one of his goons. Another young lad, black suit, dark hair with a teardrop tattoo on his neck. I'd not seen him before. But the tattoo stuck with me."

"You're a gift that keeps giving," McNally added, chirpily.

"Aye, well, I'm pleased I could help. You'll be seeing me right, Massey? That pub is losing money hand over fist otherwise."

"Leave it with me, Joe." Massey patted him on the shoulder. "We'll make sure you're alright financially, of course. Also, one sniff of danger, ring me and we'll swoop in."

"I was worried you'd say that. I don't want you lot swooping in. Now, please let me enjoy this match and disappear. The lad will be back in a second, and I don't need the questions. God knows who he talks to at school. Go now." There were no goodbyes. Joe looked exhausted, and his face was ashen from the ordeal.

As they walked away, the referee blew the whistle for the start of the game and McNally and Massey slowly headed back to the standing area near the social club. The Cliftonville faithful appealed loudly for a penalty within seconds when one of the Derry defenders scythed down their striker in the box, but the referee waved play on, and order was soon restored.

Massey looked back at Joe, with his son now back by his side. He was staring intently at the game. She knew she should have waited and lessened the risk, but she now had the potential for forensics from the pub function room. This was the mother of all breakthroughs, but forcing things was often her biggest weakness. She pushed that to the back of her mind, for now.

"We struck gold there. But forensically, it's going to be difficult. That pub is pretty rural but there are local houses full of busybodies," she whispered as they found a gap in the crowd.

"The MI5 forensic team would be in and out of there in an hour, and nobody would suspect a thing. It's what they do. I'm just not sure about the legal parameters. Leave it with me a few hours and I'll speak to an old colleague in Palace Barracks."

"That's good of you, Declan. Just don't let Eric Rogers get wind of it. I'm not even sure he'd be happy with you being here. I'm guessing you heard about his promotion?"

"Virginia did. She knows pretty much everything. Is he going to cause you grief?"

"He already is. His ongoing existence is a constant bind. Anyway, I'm going to head-off, unless you fancy another pint before I go? I have to write this up and speak to my team soonish. Joe's been very helpful, but I need to find actual usable sources who can back this up."

"Understood, but it's nearly 8pm. Hang about for one more, keep me company. The whole gang will be here soon. Jones, Jenny and you can meet the new Delta and Echo teams, assuming they have the brainpower to work out the last clue of a cipher test, I set them," McNally smiled.

"I'll hold on for an hour then. A cipher test? How exciting! I love a clue. Test me."

"Well, once successfully translated, the final clue was 'John McCredy McAlery liked peace and quiet' and your new-found interest in football should help you."

Massey picked up her pint glass, studied it, and took a large swig. It was nearing the bottom, and there was a dead fly amongst the dregs. She was running through her internal Rolodex of local trivia, but she'd drawn a blank. Peace and quiet? She had little other option other than to admit defeat.

"How bloody frustrating. I give in. Buy me a drink and you can educate me," Massey shrugged.

"Come on. What's the name of this ground, Orla? You've lived around here long enough to know that."

"Oh. It's Solitude, isn't it? Of course! And I'm guessing John McCredy McAlery was the first manager or something? Hence him liking peace and quiet? He liked the ground?"

"Close. He owned the ground and the house before it became a football club and constituted the club. It was a cricket club before. But you've got it, yes. The answer is Solitude. John McCredy McAlery was born in Rathfriland, their starting position," McNally explained.

"You clever swine! That's actually really tricky. I can't believe you beat me."

"Your head is focused on a double murder. I wouldn't feel too guilty. Delta and Echo just need to check their history books and they'll be here soon for a quick drink and sandwich before they go back to the Barracks. This is a fairly basic test. You'll be surprised how difficult it gets."

As the pair headed back up the steps to the social club, Cliftonville took the lead when a deep cross from the wing was headed past the stranded keeper. McNally was animated enough to raise a fist in triumph.

With the excitement of the opening goal and the queue building in the social club, the pair hadn't spotted that Wee Joe McCartney had other visitors now. Two men, neither of them dressed to watch a football match, more for a wake or a business function. They were smiling, but their motives were unclear to the casual observer.

They were gone soon enough, and long before Massey had been served at the bar, but Joe's already dour demeanour was now plumbing new depths of anxiety. A half glance back from McNally would have seen the second of the two visitors chatting happily to Joe's son.

Moments later, the two Land Rovers pulled into the Solitude car park within a few minutes of each other. The two men in black smart suits unknowingly passed by the front of Delta's vehicle as Jenny, the first at the venue, was reversing into a space. She missed them by a fraction of a second.

The two teams were tired and relieved the first task was over and were delighted by McNally's unusual generosity and bonhomie at his favourite club bar. Sausages and sandwiches greeted them, along with a couple of congratulatory drinks.

Twelve

Georgie had spent the best part of thirty minutes clawing at Massey's brand-new Dunne's duvet in an attempt to get some attention and secure his breakfast. Orla was exhausted after a late night at Solitude and then a few beers on the way home at the American Bar. Even her cat's cupboard love wasn't winning through. He was cute, but he wasn't irresistible.

The bright white walls of her tiny Sailortown flat were almost encased in the summer sunshine piercing through her silver Venetian blinds, but that wasn't a big enough pull to leave the comfort of her duvet. She could still taste the red wine nightcap she'd half-finished last night and she could smell the stale odour of the cigarette she'd smoked out of the living room window at 01.00am. She could have easily rolled over and slept until lunchtime.

When the moment finally came to shake herself out of her slumbers and head towards her kitchen for coffee and her first cigarette, the sound of the telephone interrupted her thoughts. It was 07.00am and the voice at the end of the phone was Eric Rogers, the man who, inconveniently, was now her boss.

"Massey, Eric here. I hope I didn't interrupt your breakfast." His voice was as welcome as a punch to the face.

"No, not at all. I'm just going through my notes from the two murder investigations. I had an interesting meeting with an informant last night," she partially lied. Orla was now only in a short fawn dressing gown, and talking to Rogers made her feel exposed. "I'll be in the office by 8.30am and I can give you a full briefing."

"That would be useful," Rogers replied. "But I have an update for you, too. Our mutual contact, Jube Spencer, is flying in this morning. He's been asked to join a meeting at Hillsborough Castle about the Philip Bradley episode. The Secretary of State has convened it."

Massey was unaware that Eric Rogers knew Jube Spencer, and they seemed unlikely bedfellows. Jube was the former Belfast-based MI5 liaison who had been promoted to lead 'the Seekers', a logistics and surveillance unit of the security service based in East London. Massey imagined them to be fellow freemasons or perhaps weekend golfers. That was the only obvious link she could establish. Jube was ruddy-faced and likeable. Eric was anything but.

"Who's representing the RUC at this briefing?" Massey responded.

"I've suggested you attend. I have a diary clash. It's a meeting with the Chief Constable about the internal investigations. It's a massive pain, as I would have liked to have gone. It's certainly in my wheelhouse, liaising with senior government figures." Rogers was clearly bruised by being left off the guest list. Massey guessed the Chief Constable ordered Rogers to invite her, as he was completely out of the loop on the murders. But that was a hunch. This was more likely his way of saving face.

"It's fine, I'll attend. I'm just a little confused about why the Secretary of State wants to be updated and his rationale for involving MI5. Any ideas?"

"The mysterious death of a Member of Parliament was always

going to raise a few eyebrows in Westminster, Massey. That's just how it works. If you're convinced it's a murder and it's connected to the other young lad that was killed, they'll want an overview. That's only natural."

All of his bluster was just guesswork, and Eric Rogers clearly knew nothing, she concluded. Despite that, he continued chuntering on about his previous glorious exploits with the great and the good in England, and she purposely switched off and let him disappear down his various mindless rabbit holes. Englishmen have an annoying habit of believing everything important happens there and she couldn't stand the arrogance of it. Eric was a microcosm of this nonsense.

In closing her mind to his rambling, she unpicked Jube's visit and planning. Massey had worked closely with Jube in the past and she was sure he wouldn't show up for a gentle briefing about a suspicious death, parliamentarian or not. No, that was massively unlikely. Likewise, neither would the Secretary of State want a chat about such trivial matters. There was much more to this.

She made a mental note to ring Jube later and castigate him for not informing her of his visit. Once she'd knocked him off his stride, she could ask him whether MI5 could send local forensics to the pub in Ballyramsey to get analysis from the function room floor. Jube was a pushover, and Massey was quite difficult to say no to. The deal was as good as done.

As this plan permeated, Massey realised Rogers was still talking and she pulled her dressing gown tightly around her again. Even his voice made her cringe.

Out of the corner of her eye, she noticed Georgie was sitting on the litter tray, eyes closed in deep concentration. His deposit would not be a helpful addition to her morning chores. Ironically, just as Georgie had proudly moved away and clawed at his litter tray to cover his seemingly bigger-than-physically-possible present, Rogers finished his speech.

"I appreciate the update, thank you. I need to get myself into the office, Rogers. I'll see you soon."

"Yes, I'll see you upon your arrival. Oh, and you'll need to get used to calling me Sir," the Englishman replied, a little tersely. Massey hung up and completed an eye-roll worthy of an Olympic medal.

Georgie had created a foul smell, and Massey had suddenly gone off the idea of breakfast. She would grab a tea and a bacon bap from the garage on the way in, as she needed some four-star fuel, she decided. She poured a mound of cat biscuits into Georgie's green bowl and sprinted upstairs to the shower. 'Call me sir? Kiss my hole,' she muttered as Georgie munched contentedly.

After a long shower and then taking roughly five minutes to flatten her short, cropped brown hair with mousse and apply very limited make-up, she attempted to leave the flat. She made it past the corner leading to her parked car three times, only to discover that the cat had followed her a hundred yards up the road and needed escorting back. It was a busy road, and she could do without Georgie on her conscience for the rest of the day. She picked him up and he licked her chin.

Twice, she picked Georgie up, gave him a stern ticking off, and left him back at the doorstep of the flat, hoping he'd get the message. The third time, she gave up and put him lovingly back upstairs, knowing full well that the litter tray couldn't get any worse after his earlier pungent discharge. That could wait.

She grabbed her sunglasses from her black handbag and looked up into the sky. The morning haze had lifted and what remained was a solitary long and feathery Cirrus cloud that seemed to be acting like a white highlighter above the Belfast skyline. In contrast, there was the slightly unnerving sound of a pneumatic drill a few streets away and a wood pigeon that seemed to be stuck on constant repeat. She needed to get to work now. She walked quicker, more purposefully. A bit like her 'I'm very busy, feck off' walk at work. Her colleagues generally got the message.

Fiddling for her keys, she opened the door of her little Mazda, removed the remains of yesterday's morning bacon bap from the passenger seat and checked her hair and make-up in the driver's side vanity mirror. Then, from nowhere, she saw a brief flash of fluffiness in her wing mirror. "That little bastard! He must have got out of the kitchen window again," she said. "Bucking hell. Will he not get the message?"

She opened the door of the car and swung her legs around to get out. She yelled his name and glanced at her watch, frustratedly. She was going to be late, maybe she'd skip her roadside breakfast.

As she manoeuvred herself out of her seat and made to climb onto the pavement, she gently knocked the keys in the ignition with her left knee. That was all it took to detonate the bomb hidden under her car. She saw a burst of vivid colour, a deafening booming sound which seemed to bounce off the houses in the street, followed by a horrific shattering of glass and the acrid smell of petrol.

She had been thrown far away from the car, but it had rocketed forward and smashed catastrophically into an old brown Ford Cortina. That was now alight and the awful smell of burning rubber had created a noxious plume of smoke above the tonnes of distorted metal laid bare in front of her. Even the tarmac on the road of the quiet suburban street seemed to be on fire. It all seemed to happen so slowly, so meticulously, and yet so bloody violently.

Then it was quieter, aside from the sound of her heart beating in her head and a car alarm a few hundred yards away.

It was all over in a few seconds, and she was almost instantly unconscious. The last thing that she registered was her lack of petrol, how the car couldn't ignite fully, as the tank was empty. Somehow her brain functioned, but she knew she'd been horribly injured and she could feel blood on her legs and midriff.

When she came around, she found that she'd been thrown about six feet into the front garden of a nearby house. Her navy business suit was all but ripped from her shoulders and she could feel glass debris in her face and embedded in her hands. There was more wetness around other parts of her body. She briefly wondered if this was more blood, urine or whether someone had just watered the lawn. She desperately tried to process what had happened to her, tried to conjure up what she needed to do next, but lost consciousness again.

It was a long half hour before the ambulance arrived. When Orla Massey regained consciousness again, she was holding the hand of an elderly woman wearing a beautiful, white-beaded necklace and a patterned summer dress. A poodle was sniffing around the back door of the ambulance. A paramedic was checking her blood pressure and feeling for her pulse.

"Ah, there she is. She's awake now. You poor wee thing. What a hateful surprise for you and all dolled up for work, so you were," the woman said.

"You've been extremely lucky," the paramedic added. "In fact, I'm not really sure how you survived that. We'd normally be picking the body parts up at this stage. Not being insensitive, love."

"It was Georgie," Orla managed. "He saved me."

"I think she's hallucinating," the old woman, still holding her hand, whispered. "There was no-one here at all when I arrived."

There was the sound of police cars heading towards the scene with sirens wailing. She guessed there were maybe two squad cars, a duo of loud sirens, and it was quite unnerving. The sound was shrill and piercing and all she wanted was peace. She wondered who it would be. Which colleague would see her ripped clothes, cuts, bruises and her utter despair?

At no point did her brain think about who had placed the bomb under the car and attempted to kill her. It was whoever possessed the evil that Wee Joe McCartney so feared.

And with that, Orla Massey drifted off again.

Thirteen

It was 14.00hrs when the YCU Management Team at Thiepval were called into Briefing Room Alpha. There was an odd hush and a few nervous smiles, and, at the back of the room, McNally was pouring boiling hot water into a polystyrene cup from a large silver tea urn. He passed the first cup to Virginia, and he then poured another before they took their seats at the top of the table.

The call had gone out to the team only twenty minutes earlier to assemble and no-one was quite clear what the briefing was about. Every pore of Jones' body screamed bad news. It was like an icy cold tap on the shoulder that made him almost unable to function until this feeling of growing inevitability had passed. He sat between Isadora and Jenny on the left-hand side of the long rectangular table, wondering who had died or what tragedy had hit.

Mr Singh, Tom and Carl, sitting on the other side of the table, had spent the morning working with Isadora on the analysis of the first cipher test. Carl had bought snacks and Mr Singh was poised with a newly purchased notepad.

As the ongoing awkward hush was poised to become intolerable, the double doors of the briefing room swung open, and two figures walked in. Eric Rogers, in full RUC uniform and his peak cap tucked under his arm, and Marie Bristow in a Massey-esque black trouser suit and white blouse. Jones, scanning the room, realised that Virginia and McNally were already aware of the update as they both looked incredibly stern, even angry, but there was a hint of emotion too.

"Everyone," Virginia announced, standing up. "This is Acting Chief Superintendent Eric Rogers. He has asked to join us today and explain some upsetting news. Afterwards, the Quartermaster's Department can leave us as we have some operational detail to discuss." Mr Singh nodded, and McNally showed Rogers and Bristow to the two seats at the other end of the table. Marie Bristow had clearly been crying, Jones could see that. Rogers sat down for a moment and then, as if needing to undertake a formal presentation, instantly stood up again and placed his hands behind his back.

"Today, at approximately 07.35, DCI Orla Massey was involved in a car bomb explosion near her home at Sailortown in Belfast. Initial reports suggest the device was placed under the driver's seat and, as a single woman living alone, there is no doubt she was the target. There is a team examining the scene and we are expecting a full report by lunchtime tomorrow," Rogers explained.

McNally interrupted: "The operational detail is secondary, Rogers. Is Orla alive? You seem to have skipped that detail." McNally was noticeably furious. Marie Bristow responded.

"The DCI is in Belfast City Hospital. She is in a serious but stable condition. She has a broken pelvis from where she was thrown from the vehicle and some significant shrapnel and blast injuries. She's drifting in and out of consciousness and isn't out of the woods yet." Bristow's voice was full of emotion, but she remained calm and professional throughout. Rogers put his hand on Bristow's shoulder from his standing position and moved to the centre of the floor again.

"Has anyone claimed responsibility, yet?" Virginia asked. "Orla is a very high-profile RUC officer, and she must have been high on target lists. I hate to say it, but she has enemies. A stack of them."

"You're quite right, Mrs Curry. As the former lead on Paramilitary investigations, a position I've vacated to take on the Acting Chief Superintendent role, I am aware of a number of possible terrorist organisations that would have targeted DCI Massey in this manner. But none has claimed responsibility yet."

"They would have done by now. Surely?" McNally interjected. "They would have been delighted with this attack. It's incomprehensible that no-one has come forward yet. Have the press got hold of it?"

"Radio Ulster and one of the commercial stations have picked up on the explosion in Sailortown, but we've asked them to hold off on the detail currently until we can reach Massey's parents in Derry. But it'll be on the evening news, across all channels. That's a cert," Bristow replied.

"Okay. I think we'll pause there," Virginia intervened. "Mr Singh, we will leave the three of you to go back to your duties, whilst we discuss some operational detail. We'll keep you updated."

Mr Singh nodded again and turned to Rogers and Bristow. "I am so very sorry to hear of this news. Please pass on my best to DCI Massey and everyone at Knock Road when you're able. She is a very courageous officer." With that, the QD team left the room, Carl returning briefly to pick up a small white bag of cola jellies he'd left on the table.

McNally strode over to the double doors and shut them behind the QD team.

The white walls of the briefing room and the long rectangular polished table seemed almost clinically clean as the sun shone in through the blinds. It wasn't a day to be cooped up inside and deep in conversation.

"Rogers," he began, "it's not normally my style to do this, and especially with an audience, but I want it placed on record that I blame you and your narrow-minded approach to policing for this catastrophe." McNally was pointing directly at Rogers and his anger was clear.

"Massey is damned lucky she wasn't killed today. Who knows whether she'll pull through yet, and yet you were so focused on resources for your damn internal investigations that you left her like a sitting duck."

"I beg your pardon?" Rogers responded. His face was glowing red and Bristow, to his left, put her head down and looked at the floor. Avoiding all eye contact.

"Firstly, I made this trip out of courtesy, and I did not come here to be reprimanded by some retired spook who, I might say, appears to be aware of confidential RUC matters that are totally out of his remit." Rogers was bristling with anger.

"Catch yourself on, Rogers! Can you hear yourself?" McNally shot back, with his eyes glaring at the uniformed man.

"Declan, please," Virginia implored, grabbing hold of his arm.

"No. This needs saying," he continued. "I'm not retired, and neither is it out of our remit. One call to Clive Gentry at Palace Barracks, and MI5 will crawl over Massey's case. I dare say your Chief Constable would also be keen to understand why a highly respected DCI didn't have round-the-clock protection during a double murder investigation."

"She didn't have protection, Acting Chief Superintendent?" Bristow queried, looking surprised. "Why not? I thought all senior officers, ranked DCI and above, had protection."

"That is beside the point. It is not my duty to explain myself to...." Rogers began.

"It's hardly beside the point," McNally interrupted. "Explain why she wasn't afforded such protection? Was it, perhaps, that as the most senior female officer on the RUC, she wasn't considered important enough?

"That's nonsense," Rogers spat back. But McNally wasn't going to let this go.

"Does DCI Geoff O'Meara have protection? At the Derry station? He's a friend of mine. Shall I ring him and check?"

"Of course, Geoff has protection. He's working on the Bogside. That's a flashpoint and car bombs and pipe bombs are ten-a-penny. We have to be vigilant there." Rogers was growing more and more annoyed by this line of questioning.

"There? But not here? What about your DCIs in Newry, Antrim, Armagh, Newtownards...? Shall I go on? Where was that vigilance today at 07.30am in Sailortown? Perhaps, if you'd had been willing to share intelligence with the security service, Massey wouldn't be drifting in and out of consciousness now. This was on your watch." The room fell silent again. Rogers was looking flustered. McNally knew he was right. Isadora, Jones, and Jenny watched on in horror.

"Do you even have a full briefing of the Philip Bradley and George McCool murder cases? Do you have the merest inkling of how significant this could be?" McNally asked. "I was with Orla at Solitude last night. Immediately prior to this attack, I probably know more operational detail than either of you do, Rogers. No offence, Marie."

"None taken," Bristow replied.

"Massey was due to update me this morning actually, it was all planned. I could hardly have predicted the blast. And, for the avoidance of doubt, the intelligence services at Palace Barracks would have been fully briefed at a meeting at Hillsborough Castle later today. The Secretary of State has called the meeting, Jube Spencer is flying in, and Clive Gentry will be in attendance. Orla Massey was going," Rogers explained.

"That didn't strike you as bloody odd, Rogers? You didn't think that was worthy of a little more of your valuable time to consider? Because, from where I'm sitting, someone in Whitehall has decided that the Bradley murder is an issue of national security and well beyond the realms of the understaffed, underperforming and, clearly, under-fecking-supervised RUC!!! Jesus Christ, Eric! What were you thinking?" McNally was shouting and even as he stood, finger pointing at Eric Rogers, his head was shaking in disbelief.

"Just imagine if she'd died... Rogers!" McNally added.

"Right," Virginia intervened again. "Let's take this down a notch or two. I can see you're upset by this attack, and I think I can speak for all of us here, including Acting Chief Superintendent Rogers, that we need to work collegiately to bring those responsible to justice. Not just for this horrific attack on Massey, but also the two murders."

"Of course," Rogers said, quietly.

"Can I ask that you two gentlemen sit down?" Rogers, now quietened, and McNally, who was still fired up, paused hostilities for a moment and sat at either end of the table. Virginia thanked them both when they resumed their seats.

"Orla told us you were struggling with resources," Jenny calmly entered the conversation.

"We're always struggling with resources, young lady. But I'm under a great deal of pressure to supply clarity on a series of internal investigations as well as overseeing the Knock Road day-to-day operations." Rogers was grateful for a more sympathetic line of questioning.

"We have six suspended officers, fourteen on long-term sick, and I have politicians on all sides expecting miracles. The internal investigations are just another opportunity for both sides to castigate the RUC in the press. But even I can see, perhaps undue prominence was placed on those investigations with a double murder on the books," he continued. Sensing a small climb-down, Virginia jumped on this.

"Perhaps we can help here?" Virginia offered, oozing diplomacy. "We have four fully trained field officers in this room now, all with full clearance and with a decent understanding of the case. Let's be honest, if Jube and Clive are discussing this today, this is likely to become an MI5 led operation, with support from the RUC. MI5 lead on issues of national security, you know that?"

"Yes, of course," Rogers replied. "I've worked hand-in-hand with Jube Spencer for years."

"So, why don't we take a plan to the Hillsborough Castle meeting and show we're working in collaboration already and ahead of the game? I'm guessing you'll be in attendance now, Acting Chief Superintendent Rogers, in Massey's absence?"

"I'll need to check with the Chief Constable, Mrs Curry, but I presume so," he agreed.

"McNally, can you raise Clive Gentry and get the green light that we can supply immediate operational help? He'll be keen to utilise the expertise of the three young officers at our disposal, I'm sure, along with your good self, McNally. We can build this into our YCU scheduling. I'll roll up my sleeves, a little, too."

"No bother," McNally responded. "I'll call him after this."

"If you're in agreement, Acting Chief Superintendent, maybe Sergeant Bristow could give us a briefing on the current case detail and maybe McNally can share his thoughts on last night's meeting at Cliftonville? Does that sound doable?" Virginia, with her usual guile, had brought the tension down significantly. But she knew McNally hadn't finished.

"I can see that such a collaborative approach would have merits," Rogers replied, holding onto the last semblance of his seniority.

"That's very magnanimous of you, Rogers. But I warn you now, no matter what our friends figure out at Hillsborough later, if I discover Orla wasn't given protection because of her gender, sexuality, or worse, some kind of negligence on your behalf, it will not be white washed. I'm watching you now."

"I think you've made all that very clear, Mr McNally," Rogers responded, now hunched forward at the table. "Sergeant Bristow, as Mrs Curry suggested, maybe you could run through the current position."

Jenny, Isadora, and Jones, pulled their chairs around a little to face Bristow as the meeting moved in a more workmanlike direction. Jones knew that the notion of Massey's gender or sexuality leading to a lack of protection would have, rightly, fired up Jenny and Isadora. But his brain was trying to think about the national security angle. He would bide his time and ask at the right moment.

"Philip Bradley, a high-flying unionist politician with a young family, was found dead in a seaside holiday rental in Ballycastle. He was in a Batman costume. So far, Forensics have evidence that the body was moved. But we don't know from where or why. He sustained a single bullet wound through the head, which initial reports suggested was self-inflicted, but DCI Massey is convinced it was murder."

"What made her come to that conclusion?" Jones asked.

"Well, it was just a theory until the call came. There were no defensive wounds at all. He was wrapped in a silver space blanket, and he was still wearing the Batman outfit. We all thought it a was sex game or something," Bristow continued.

"Hold on, what call? You said a call came?" Jones said.

"Yeah, we had an anonymous call from a telephone box in Coleraine. A young lad with an English accent. The Duty Sergeant reckons he was a Londoner. He explained, in great detail, that he was on site when the murder of Philip Bradley took place. He described the costume, the space blanket, and even gave a description of the killer and another occupant of the room, who was dressed as Wonder Woman."

"Sweet Jesus, have you traced this lad yet? Or a description of the killer? Because if this lad saw the killer, he's got a massive price tag on his head," McNally asked, suddenly very interested. Bristow pulled out her notebook.

"We have a team in Coleraine working on tracing the caller,

but we've drawn a blank so far. I'll get an update on that when I get back to the station. In terms of the alleged killer, he was a big man in fishing or outdoors gear. That's all we've got."

"Okay, I might be clutching at straws a little, but Massey and I met an informant last night. He was absolutely petrified. He described the George McCool killer as being a big fella in hunting or fishing gear."

"This informant saw the second murder take place?" Jones asked.

"No. He heard the suspected murderer and a few accomplices talking about the killing," McNally explained. "They mentioned two deaths in two days. This has to be the Bradley shooting. The informant thinks he knows where the shooting of George McCool took place, but security service forensics will need to be arranged, as the informant fears that any obvious police activity will lead to his own death."

"Do we know why George McCool was killed?" Isadora asked, before Jones could ask another question.

"The informant reckons that George McCool sold the photo of the Philip Bradley crime scene to the newspaper. It was a Polaroid. This must have cost him his life. This is what Orla and I were told last night. Massey was also convinced that the media don't know the photo was taken at a different location to where his body was recovered. They don't know he was moved."

"She'd made some bloody useful strides since we last spoke," Bristow said. "This is valuable stuff."

"Absolutely. She was building the case in her mind. The body was moved. The Polaroid is of the scene of where the killing actually happened, not the Ballycastle holiday let. It all fits." Bristow was furiously writing notes whilst pulling the strands of evidence together.

"You're really not going to tell us who that informant is, McNally?" Rogers chimed in. "He's one of Orla Massey's paid informants?"

"Yeah, he is. But he's in great danger too, so, no, I'll not confirm his identity yet. Not until I'm assured of his safety. He's the key to this, I'm sure."

"But he's our informant, McNally," Rogers insisted.

"Give me 48 hours, Rogers. And let's confirm the forensics. Then, we'll talk about the informant and an approach to ensure his ongoing cooperation and safety."

"We know George McCool was killed in a pub, though, right? He was found wrapped in a darts oche mat. Do we know the location of that pub?" Jenny asked.

"It could be a pub. But it could equally be a youth or social club, working man's club, who knows? We don't have a location though," Bristow replied. "There were no forensics on the mat. Mainly because the mat was covered in petrol, this suggests that they were planning to burn the body but were disturbed." McNally knew exactly where the pub was and was getting more and more concerned about Wee Joe McCartney. But there was no way he'd let slip his name to Rogers, that much was clear.

"Can anyone explain the link to national security to me? Why are Jube and Clive involved? The Secretary of State? What's this all about?" Jones finally asked. This was looming large in his thoughts. "Is this a stupid question?"

"Not at all. But it's all guesswork, son," Rogers replied, somewhat cagily. "The murder of an MP in the United Kingdom will always have some security service involvement, but, any more than that, your guess is as good as mine."

"Acting Chief Superintendent Rogers doesn't know." McNally countered. "Neither do I. But I have a hunch. My suggestion is that the late Philip Bradley MP was involved in something major. It could be organised crime. Maybe he was paid to create connections for drugs or human trafficking. Those are both possible, but equally, it could even be collusion with a foreign power. The Russians, maybe. That would certainly pique Clive's interest.

You don't kill an MP, especially in a Batman costume, unless things have fallen apart spectacularly."

"So, what are the next steps? What are the key tasks?" Virginia asked, trying to bring the briefing to a close.

"The DCI was trying to do three things. Find and protect the wee English lad who allegedly saw the killing of Philip Bradley, work out what groups George McCool was allied to, and identify his local network. She was also asking questions about Bradley's business associates." Bristow read from her notepad.

"We have a plan then," McNally responded. "Rogers, I'm coming with you to Hillsborough. I'll check with Clive that he's okay with that. Bristow, can I suggest you stay with Jones, Jenny, and Isadora and look at how we can assist your team?"

There were no more arguments. Rogers, with his tail between his legs, nodded at McNally and brushed down his epaulettes as he stood to leave.

"I will instruct a few of my officers to act as a security detail at City Hospital. I'll visit her myself on the way back." Rogers' ethos had changed. The prim, confident, and egotistical senior officer had listened, but it was far too late now. Massey's worst-case scenario had only just been averted and that was simply due to luck and a tenacious ginger tomcat.

Virginia switched the tea-urn back on and watched as Eric Rogers left the room. She now had ten spirited YCU recruits to train almost single-handedly, knowing full well that her new leadership team would be pulled into a complicated double murder investigation.

FOURTEEN

Sam Jacobs had endured another restless night. He'd watched film after film in preparation for his first assignment on film noir and it really hadn't inspired anything at all. He'd started watching the films within the core syllabus in chronological order, beginning with The French Connection and Shaft (1971); The Godfather (1972), The Friends of Eddie Coyle and The Long Goodbye (1973), and then, finally, Chinatown (1974).

He had no doubt that all of them were skilled neo-noirs that, in some way, enlarged the culture's notion of what crime cinema could be. He just wasn't sure whether he actually enjoyed them or what the genre meant to him, which was at the root of the assignment. He wrote far too many vague notes and then momentarily fell asleep whilst rewinding the video of the Maltese Falcon, which he'd actually been looking forward to watching.

His brain was somewhere else. What hadn't helped was the UTV News, after the ITV News at Ten, had led on a car bomb explosion in Sailortown. A senior female officer had been seriously injured, but no-one had yet claimed responsibility for the attack. His paranoia was already on high alert and the phone call to the team at Coleraine RUC had done nothing to lift his mood. There was no closure at all. If anything, it had made him feel worse. He somehow felt anything to do with the police, no matter how vague, must have something to do with him and the death of Philip Bradley.

The next day, after meeting Dele for coffee in The Kabin, he was planning to mow a few lawns in Ballymoney before heading back to the University for a tutorial with his lecturer. Dele would be with him, too. They'd buddied up for the classes and had opted to do the tutorials together.

It was a sunny morning and the walk down to the café was brisk. He could feel tiredness in every step, and he knew that if he shut his eyes, even for a second, he'd fall into a deep sleep, so coffee was the order of the day.

Dele had put a message under his door to say he had a parcel to pick up from the newsagents on Abbey Street and he'd meet him at the café afterwards but when he arrived there, the place was already heaving, and there was no sign of Dele.

He grabbed the last remaining table outside The Kabin and stared at the menu with limited interest. There was an Ulster Fry with the addition of veg roll as a special. There were beans on toast with cheddar and there was a large bap filled with egg and bacon. He opted for the beans and ordered a large filter coffee. Dele would take an age to order anything, and Sam would probably have a 'breakfast dessert' of a traybake whilst his friend savoured and scored every bite.

When Dele finally sauntered into view, clutching a large yellow box, Sam knew that there was something up. His demeanour was edgy, even shifty, and once Dele recognised Sam, he sped up, racing to get to him.

"Sam, I think we need to talk urgently," Dele said, breathlessly.

"No time like the present," Sam replied, attempting a smile.

"I think you might be very angry with me. That only occurred to me once I'd walked away from the officers. But I'm used to being polite and helpful to the police and they were so nice and interested," Dele explained. Sam looked at him wide-eyed and at once expecting the worst.

"They were asking if anyone had seen or heard about the death of a local politician. There were two uniformed lady officers. I explained that my friend had heard all about the death and was working nearby. I knew you'd want to help."

"You gave them my name?"

"Yes. Also, your room number. Was that the wrong thing to do?" Dele looked at Sam with such a pleading face that Sam was loathed to say something too unforgiving.

"I would really rather you hadn't," was the best Sam could muster.

"Do you want me to go back and tell them I've made a mistake? That my facts were incorrect?"

"Leave it, Dele. Abbey Street is a good mile from here, it would be a long walk to just explain a mistake. Plus, I have lawns to mow this morning. They can come and find me later and I'll explain you were mistaken." Sam smiled, but inside, every part of his body was running at a million miles an hour. He was paranoid, sweaty, anxious and a bit peeved, but was too polite to let it show. Dele was just being, well, Dele - thoughtlessly nice and helpful.

"No, I wouldn't need to walk down to Abbey Street. It's fine. I'll talk to them now. They're just behind you."

As Sam turned, two young RUC officers were walking towards the café. They clocked him chatting to Dele and walked towards him.

"You told them you were meeting me here?" Sam responded, almost in shock.

"Of course. It seemed very urgent. I didn't think you'd mind."

The café owner, a large man with a black apron and a white shirt, emerged with his beans on toast and coffee. Sam half-thought about walking away, but the lure of the breakfast, especially with the mountain of cheese, and the need to ensure Dele wasn't offended was too great.

"Are you Sam Jacobs?" one of the RUC officers asked.

"Yes, that's me," he replied, his mouth on autopilot.

They pulled up the spare two chairs of the table of four and watched as Sam devoured a sizeable chunk of brown bread with the beans spilling over the top. A stringy piece of cheese had attached itself to his top lip.

"Your friend here tells us you were in the vicinity of the death of Philip Bradley. Can you explain where you were?" The officer, the smaller of the two with quite judgemental eyebrows and mousy brown hair tucked underneath her cap, had already retrieved her notebook and had licked the end of her pencil.

"I was mowing a lawn nearby," Sam replied in an act of nonchalance worthy of an Oscar. "It's a little side-line I have."

"I see. Please go on," the young officer urged.

"I was working at the top of Primrose Grove, and I heard some commotion. As I explained to my good friend here, I was aware of a black car on the scene, and I then went back to my mowing."

"You didn't say anything about a black car to me, Sam. This is fresh news. How exciting," Dele interrupted. Sam shot him a look which screamed '*just shut up*'.

"Are you sure this was at Primrose Grove? The body was found in a holiday let at Cushendall Road in Ballycastle." The young officer turned to her equally junior colleague, who was taller with straight blonde hair and gold-rimmed spectacles and nodded. She walked a few steps away and made a call on her police radio.

Sam's heart rate skyrocketed. He looked at his watch. He was due at the first house in Ballymoney at 11.30am. He had an hour to get back to his room, find some old gardening clothes and get on the road. He wondered whether there was a way of reversing out of this awkward cul-de-sac.

The blonder officer returned and put her police radio on the table, next to Sam's coffee. He could hear a little interference in the background, so it was clear the radio had been left on, purposefully.

"Tell us about your course, Sam. What brings you to Coleraine?" The first officer asked.

"Well, it was the course, I really liked the syllabus." He tried to sound calm and casual. "I have some local connections too. My father served out here in the 1980s and my family were keen for me to get a good degree, but with some local contacts, in case I needed some help."

"That's him, I think," came the voice at the end of the radio. "Bring him in, Siobhan."

Sam was aware of his predicament. His voice, his accent, and his manner had given him away. The game was up. He took his last mouthful of breakfast and grinned at the officers.

"I have a few gardens to mow and a tutorial. Could I come in later?"

"Sam, this is purely voluntary. But if you're the young man who spoke to our Duty Sergeant a few days back, you're in grave danger. We suggest you come with us. Immediately. You can plan to reschedule tutorials once we get you somewhere safe."

"Danger?" Dele asked, looking concerned. "Why ever would he be in danger? I live next door to Sam. Am I in danger, too?"

"We'll station a few officers around the university, to monitor things. But Sam will need to come with us now." The first officer's eyebrows had now settled in a regular position. Sam took a huge swig of coffee, grabbed his bag, and stood up.

"Okay," Sam said. "You make quite a convincing argument, officers. I'm all yours."

Sam thought his anxious brain was about to burst. But something inside was gripping onto this, entirely fake, easy-going manner. He wondered for how long. He'd seen a man killed, for God's sake.

He walked back towards a side street where their car was

parked and shook hands with Dele. Dele looked a little confused and unhappy, but smiled at Sam, and wished him all the best.

There was no small talk as the police car weaved its way towards the station. Sam was sitting behind the driver, the blonde officer, who looked a good deal shorter without her cap. He stared quietly out of the window.

Stuck at a set of lights near the town centre, he felt like a small child with the excitement of sitting in a cop car. But bizarrely, Sam felt totally numb as he stared out at the passers-by, bemused, but numb. Yes, he was caught up in a truly bizarre situation, but surely the RUC would ensure he'd be safe now?

The car headed down a narrow lane punctuated by speed bumps and turned off into a deserted courtyard next to a large red brick lobby. Two male uniformed officers marched out from the lobby and opened the large steel gate.

Before too long, Sam was escorted into a small interview room and a civilian member of staff offered him a hot drink. He wasn't going to refuse a cup of tea. But, as two plain clothed officers walked in, one with frizzy red hair and the other an average-looking bloke with a big smile, he finally grasped the enormity of the situation. He was going to have to tell them everything.

"You're probably wondering what's going on, aren't you, Sam? Well, before we go on, let's introduce ourselves. I'm Jenny and this is Jones. We're both English, like you, and we are working with the police to support this murder case. This must be very worrying for you."

"Well. Yes. You could say that," Sam said, quietly. "What happens to me now?"

"You're safe. That's the main thing. But we really need you to explain about the call you made from the telephone box. That was you, wasn't it, Sam?"

"Yes," he replied. "But this is the reason I made an anonymous call. I didn't want to get caught up in this mess. I'm new at university and I just want to get on with it. I don't want any trouble."

"We understand that," the male plain-clothed officer responded. "But the sooner we have a full statement and your safety secured, we can ensure your life gets back on track. For what it's worth, we're really sorry you got caught up in all of this."

"Could you tell us what you saw and heard, Sam? Let's start at the beginning, where did this incident take place?" Jenny said, calmly.

With Jenny sitting opposite, looking concerned and sympathetic and her colleague also putting Sam at ease, the façade disappeared. Sam, for the first time, let his emotions get the better of him and he began to slowly sob.

"It was in a posh house in Ballycastle. I think it was called The Garden House in Primrose Grove," Sam managed, in between quiet sobs.

"Very good, Sam. Now take your time and tell us what you remember," Jenny gently urged.

"I was just a few metres away. It was one shot to the head. He died straightaway and I saw it all. I just..." Sam stammered, "I just can't get it out of my head. It's wedged there. That look on his face. The blood."

"You're doing brilliantly. Now, just focus on trying to remember as many details as you can," Jenny said, briefly putting her hand on his arm. "What did he sound like?"

"Sort of, American. Like a cross between an American and an Irishman, maybe. But with such a deep voice. I was sitting in a wardrobe, watching from the crack in the doors. His voice echoed around the inside of the wardrobe. But he was so matter-of-fact, so calm."

"Do you think they saw you in there?" Jones asked.

"No, I waited for hours to come out. I got my lawnmower from a few houses away and drove to my room in Coleraine. But Andrew, he heard my voice on the telephone when Philip asked me to call him. I was the only Englishman there. The rest were all local, Andrew, George, Philip Bradley and the woman in the other mask. It was only the big man in the fishing gear who sounded different."

"Andrew?" Jones repeated. "You heard that name?"

"Yeah, he was the chap I was asked to call when I first arrived at the house. He then turned up with George and the man in the fishing garb."

"Righto. Useful stuff, Sam. What about Wonder Woman? What do you remember about her?" Jones continued.

"She had hair like yours," Sam said, pointing at Jenny. "It was poking out from behind the mask. She was really pretty and didn't have much on. It was really awkward. I had to untie her from the bed frame. She was wide-eyed and really weird."

"Weird?" Jenny repeated. "Explain that."

"I can't really describe it any better. She seemed off-colour, kind of edgy, and was shaking. She clearly had feelings for Philip Bradley, as she was nursing him and calming him down. But something wasn't right about her," Sam continued.

"I owe her my life, though. She was the one who told me to get into the wardrobe. I'd have been killed, I'm sure, if I hadn't followed her instructions. I kept expecting them to open the wardrobe, especially when they cleaned the room."

"Cleaned the room?" Jenny wrote '*Wonder Woman = drugs?*' in her notebook and continued the questioning.

"Yeah, two blokes came in. They drove a people carrier of some description. They took the body away and then cleaned the room, the floor mainly, from top to bottom. It stank of bleach. One of them briefly opened the door of the wardrobe, but I curled up into a ball amongst some carrier bags and shoes. Somehow, they didn't see me." Sam was regaining a little strength now and had wiped away the moisture from his reddened eyes.

"Is that everything?" Jenny said, quietly. "Is that all you can remember?"

"There was a conversation between the man in the fishing hat and Andrew, I think. But I just can't remember it. Something about money, but that might have been to pay for the people carrier to arrive, I don't know. They said the words 'business transaction' and there was definitely a woman's name. I was focused on not being heard, not breathing too loudly. So, I can't be certain."

"Okay, Sam. You've done really well. Just take another deep breath and think hard. You can't remember the name mentioned? Anything about the business transaction?" Jenny smiled over at Sam.

"I've been over this in my head. I've barely slept. I just can't drag anything else to the front of my brain. I'm so sorry." Sam wanted to weep again, even to dispel the terrible butterflies in his stomach. But instead focused around the room. Jenny nodded and continued to write notes.

In the far right of the room was a large black screen. Sam hadn't seen one of these before and was unaware that behind it were two other attendees. They were watching the interview unfold. One was Sergeant Marie Bristow, who was now leading the investigation for the RUC in Knock Road and the other was Isadora Brown, the other field officer co-opted to the case.

The interview, which continued for just under two hours, revealed that Sam Jacobs was not only aware of the shooting, the location and could give a description of the killer, but was also aware of George McCool, the other victim, and Andrew, a new name for the investigation. As Jones and Jenny, in their friendliest of guises, persuaded the young man to give more and more away, a forensics team was on the way to The Garden House in Primrose Grove and a photo-fit was being prepared of Wonder Woman. Things were now hotting up.

The woman's name, the business transaction and the money. This was another avenue of enquiry. But Sam seemed very sketchy about that. The team asterisked that part of the notes and added it to the intelligence log.

Arrangements were then made for Sam Jacobs to be placed into a safe house, but he would need an officer who could act as liaison and support him as the investigation continued. Sam Jacobs was a vulnerable witness, and the team knew that his identity could leak easily with just a few questions asked to Primrose Grove homeowners with extensive gardens.

The biggest question was who they were guarding him against. And that made life very difficult. Sam knew too much, and that made him a terribly vulnerable young man. He needed to be out of harm's way.

Fifteen

Hillsborough Castle, a Georgian country house in County Down, has been the official government residence for the Secretary of State for Northern Ireland, as well as the home from home for the British monarch since 1924. Hillsborough had played an important role in the Peace Process in Northern Ireland since the 1980s. American envoys and negotiators, with the peace talks beginning to take shape, used it as a grand guest house and meeting venue.

Since the 1970s, the castle also acted as a political retreat and hosted several important negotiations as part of the Peace Process. In 1985, the Anglo-Irish Agreement was signed in the State Drawing Room at Hillsborough Castle by British Prime Minister Margaret Thatcher and Irish Taoiseach Garret FitzGerald.

However, whilst the Castle, with its sweeping grounds and manicured gardens, oozed class and serenity, it was also an absolute nightmare for the MI5 based out of Palace Barracks. The security detail at Hillsborough had to be robustly strengthened, with bulletproof glass fitted throughout. There was an increased military presence around the perimeter and occasionally snipers would be dotted around the curtilage. Even the heavily guarded helipad, installed to ferry important visitors in and out more safely, was such a target that all the roads would be closed all around the village and heading into Belfast to prevent anti-aircraft fire. With the peace talks blowing hot and cold, this expensive security remained in place with the Secretary of State almost permanently in situ.

The man in charge of these arrangements was Clive Gentry, an impressively muscular black man, with an enviable taste in tailoring and a reputation for commanding the NI team with an iron fist. His number two, currently seconded to the Seekers in Balfron Tower, was Jube Spencer, a man who had acted as MI5 liaison in Belfast for almost ten years and was rightly respected for his knowledge and for being politically savvy. Finally, the Secretary of State himself was Conor Steele, the only Conservative politician the Prime Minister had found with strong links to Northern Ireland, as his parents came from Lisburn. But that, as the Whitehall bubble readily admitted, didn't mean he knew anything about the Troubles or the spiky political nuances which didn't seem to be going away anytime soon. Being a nice man with Irish parentage had earned him the shitty end of the stick, cabinet-wise.

These three men, as well as a young female assistant, sat drinking tea around a wooden table in the pleasant Hillsborough gardens. Steele had lit a cigarette and, with the heat of the day at its peak, Clive had removed his expensive-looking herringbone jacket, and revealed a white shirt that was so tight it could have been sprayed on. Jube, on the other hand, was munching through a small packet of TUC biscuits that he'd found in the guest entrance to the Castle. The birdsong was so loud that he was having to crane his head to hear the diminutive Steele quietly explain the detail.

"You see, I knew Philip Bradley quite well. Our politics were quite similar, so to speak, as Unionists. He'd made me feel quite welcome here. Our families were even quite chummy. It's been a dreadful shock."

"Yes, I'm sorry to hear that, Secretary of State," Clive began.

"Conor, please. I think we'll dispense with the formalities."

"Very well, Conor. But I'm afraid there are a few more shocks coming your way. Hence this rather ad hoc meeting. Jube has most of the details. But Philip has been quite open to new friendships, especially if money is involved."

"My word, Clive. What are we talking about here?" The petite, grey-haired politician clearly wasn't yet used to high-level MI5 briefings. They rarely led to good news.

"Let's wait a few minutes before we give you the full picture. We have two more guests appearing yet. Acting Superintendent Eric Rogers from the RUC and an old friend of ours, Declan McNally. His is a rather complicated story. Jube, do you want to take this?"

"Yes, Clive." Jube's broad Belfast accent had softened, over the years, to something more refined. But as the only local in the group, he was delighted that McNally was on board. "Declan McNally is leading the Young Communicators Unit in Thiepval. He's a Derry-born ex-SIS field officer who was pensioned off about eight years ago to work in a training position. He's now back, with full clearance, in a strategic leadership role. He knows his stuff."

"And why is he here, Jube?" Conor asked, sipping his tea.

"He's assisting the RUC, or that's the plan. Their resources are stretched now that Orla Massey is hospitalised. She's currently in a serious condition in City Hospital after being the victim of a car bomb attack in Sailortown. She's shit-hot, the lynchpin locally. We need her back soonest," Jube explained.

"Yes, I'd heard that. That's tragic news. Has anyone claimed responsibility? How is she?" Steele replied.

"No news on either front, Secretary of State. But temporarily losing Massey compounds an already tricky situation. Eric Rogers has a sinking ship at Knock Road RUC station. There's huge absenteeism and recruitment has fallen through the floor. People want danger money to work for the RUC. So, with this being an issue of national security, it has been suggested that the security service takes the lead. With Palace Barracks entirely focused on the peace talks and paramilitary skirmishes, McNally is the only show in town."

"What about the YCU? Won't they suffer?" Jube was surprised the politician had even heard of the rather secretive training unit.

"We have Virginia Curry leading the line at Thiepval. She's an old hand and played a huge role in setting up the unit. And there's a wee team there. All trained field officers. You might have heard about them from the Topaz and Wild Flowers missions. They won't suffer." Jube paused as he heard the crunching of shingle and footsteps heading towards the group.

Eric Rogers, with his silver RUC cap badge gleaming in the sunshine, marched towards the table with purpose. Behind him, slower because of his injured left leg, was Declan McNally. He wore his long trench coat and a brown roll-neck jumper, brown slacks and a pair of beige shoes. He took off his round glasses and rubbed them against his trouser leg. A ring-bound shorthand notebook was wedged into his top pocket.

All three men stood up to greet the arriving pair. Only the assistant remained seated and poured more tea.

"Acting Superintendent Eric Rogers, Declan McNally, meet the Secretary of State for Northern Ireland, Conor Steele." Clive motioned to each, as they appeared next to the table, and they shook hands in turn. Eric seemed to undertake some kind of court bow; McNally couldn't help but smile. Jube continued his briefing.

"I've already explained some of the detail to Conor, but effectively we are dealing with an issue of national security. Philip Bradley had been on our radar for some time, but nothing was provable, nothing stuck to him. His death, especially in this manner, suggests he was up to his neck in it."

"I'm sorry, Jube, but I'm still a little lost here. What exactly was he up to his neck in? We seem to be circling the issue without diving into it, so to speak," Conor Steele asked.

"I'm not sure where to start." Jube pulled out an A4 pad from a leather document wallet and scanned his notes before continuing. "I think we are all aware that the paramilitary groups have long had to take entrepreneurial approaches to fundraising and income generation. Yes, the Republicans get millions from our American friends at NORAID, if perhaps under some false pretences, but bingo at the Supporters' Clubs and passing the hat around in pubs will not go far in an armed conflict, no matter what side you're on. Therefore, there has been a growing issue of organised crime masquerading as paramilitary activity. Both illegal, of course."

"Aye, but this isn't new, Jube. This is almost established practice nowadays," McNally interrupted.

"Absolutely, but we are now seeing drug shipments from all over the world, arms caches from Libya and the US and worse, those consignments aren't even fuelling the conflict in these shores."

"Are you saying that Northern Ireland is becoming a hub for organised crime at unprecedented levels? Is that the headline?" Conor attempted to summarise.

"Partially. What I'm trying to underline is that not all money raised by or on behalf of a paramilitary organisation will find its way into the organisation's coffers. Increasingly, in recent years, terrorists have used their status, connections and skills in creating and developing criminal organisations and structures. These arrangements provide the resources for comfortable, and sometimes very extravagant, personal lifestyles. This is where Philip Bradley comes in." Jube shut his pad and pulled out a small pack of photographs. He scattered the images across the table. Each image appeared to be a building, apartment, shop, or venue.

"These, we believe, are all connected to Philip Bradley. There are 34 properties of interest, including the very property he was found dead in, the holiday let in Ballycastle. We believe this is a global property portfolio worth upwards of £43m and with more stashed in offshore bank accounts across the world."

"Why didn't we know about any of this, Spencer?" Rogers was picking up each photo and examining it almost forensically. "Are we actually sure of the illegality of this? I mean, one is allowed to have a property portfolio."

"We can't go around accusing a dead man, the victim, of being some kind of fraudster," Rogers continued. "I'm well aware of some of these properties. They are luxurious, the absolute top end of the market. But we had no intel that these were part of any criminal networks. Bradley was a family man. I'd even attended fundraisers with him for the local hospice."

"That's the point, Eric. This is a tangled web. We have no way of absolutely proving these all link to Bradley, but there is a single company, operating out of the Turks and Caicos Islands. It's called Mainstay Holdings. Philip Bradley has a luxury yacht berthed at Bangor called The Mainstay and his main property in Millisle, also near Bangor, is called Mainstay Barn. It has seven bedrooms, a large outdoor swimming pool and access to a private beach."

"But there's more," Jube added, lowering his voice. "There is a growing belief that Bradley was playing both sides and none. That he, or someone close to him, set up organised criminal groups in both loyalist and nationalist areas and was using known faces to act as go-betweens."

"Tell me your most wanted people locally, Eric," Jube continued.

"That's easy enough. Marty Kenny, Joe O'Kane, Paul McHugh, Terry Raphaelle, Johnny Wilcox, and the late Kenny Reid's daughter, Caragh. Are you saying these are connected to Philip Bradley? A unionist MP?"

"Terry Raphaelle is a murderer. We'll take him out of the equation. And he's been seen in Kingston, Jamaica. We'll not be getting him back to Belfast this side of the millennium," Clive added.

"Okay, except for Raphaelle, there is a possibility that all of these have been influenced or have been engaged by Mainstay Holdings. It could be financial, it could be via suppliers, or he could be the key man that links them all. This is one hypothesis." Jube looked around the table, with a look on his face suggesting he'd made his point.

"So, why was he killed?" McNally asked, still looking at the property photos.

"There are two possible answers to that question, McNally," Clive began, taking over the presentation. "This is why this is a matter of national security. If Philip Bradley is the man, we think he is and he was as greedy as most criminal players, he'll be looking to expand. He could expand south into the Republic, and their criminal networks utilise the Irish American connections, or he could expand into the rest of the UK, and where is the big money coming from into London at the moment?"

"The Russians and the Saudis?" Conor Steele answered.

"Exactly," Clive responded.

"The suggestion is that this was one deal too far for Bradley? That he got greedy and associated with the wrong group? Perhaps did the dirty on one of them?" McNally asked.

"I think that's the size of it. Also, Bradley had weaknesses and when you're trying to muscle in on new networks, the big players find those weaknesses straightaway. We have an informer who tells us Bradley had a coke habit. He utilised his various houses across Ireland to be entertained by escorts and prostitutes. This, whilst his reputation suggested he was a family man with a wife who still works in the local primary school as a teaching assistant."

"I wonder how much she knew. Where did she think this money was coming from?" McNally said.

"Hold on. We can talk to Saoirse Bradley. This is police work, not security service work." Eric suddenly announced, finding confidence from somewhere. "I understand any potential links to international organised crime is well above my pay grade, but the rest of this detail should be handled by my team, in situ."

"That would be lovely, Eric," McNally fired back. "But you actually pulled most of your frontline team into dealing with an internal investigation, in the mistaken belief that this would help clear up the tarnished reputation of the RUC."

"Is this true, Superintendent Rogers?" Conor asked.

"Ask him where the protection officers were for DCI Massey too, when the car bomb went off in Sailortown," McNally added, twisting the knife further.

"I admit, we have scant resources at the moment. Hence the lack of protection officers and asking the local MI5 team to assist with this investigation. I am very grateful for the support from Mr McNally and his young team. But we have to be the leading agency on the ground."

"Eric," Clive responded. "I don't want to appear harsh or downplay the significant role of the RUC during the Troubles. But the deal is done. I have already spoken to the Chief Constable, who we are meeting again later tonight, and he's fully accepted the plan for this to be an MI5-led operation. He knows you don't have the resources to be the leading agency. So, let's talk sense. We simply need investigative and administrative support from Knock Road for the Bradley murder and its connection to George McCool's death. However, the media and general public will see this as an RUC operation, so you'll still need to be front-facing, Eric."

"All the accountability, none of the decision-making. That'll be interesting," Eric responded sarcastically. Clive stopped and stared at Eric, prompting the slim, fifty-something to hold up his hand in apology. Clive's ability to produce a gut-churning scowl had earned him plenty of plaudits.

"Conor," Clive continued. "We will also need to green light enquiries in London relating to his parliamentary affairs."

"That's way above my head. You'll need the Home Secretary

on board. But I hear Imelda Phillips is a passionate supporter of your team. I'm sure you'll get her blessing," he replied.

"There is one final knotty issue," Jube added, directing his point to the Secretary of State. "Northern Ireland is a house of cards at the moment. If the unionist majority politicians here suspect for one moment that we are investigating one of their high-flying MPs, especially around organised crime, we will lose any ground we've made with peace talks. The republican movement will see this is a major win. Even though we suspect he's playing both sides."

"But the RUC and MI5 are seen locally as a protestant force. There are suspicions they whitewash issues relating to loyalist crime. If we cover it up, it'll create further divisions," McNally explained.

"Agreed. But from a diplomatic perspective, we will need absolute bulletproof evidence and present this as a crime. Solve the murder of Philip Bradley and then perhaps unpick the organised crime elements once they reveal themselves through diligent collaborative working. There doesn't need to be a sectarian trigger to this. If we're careful," Clive clarified and then stood up and stretched. This added further pressure to a set of shirt buttons that were hanging on for dear life.

"I think thorough communication will be our friend here. I'm meeting all sides in the next few weeks, plus the Americans and religious leaders. I could do with no muddying of the waters. Have we gone public on Bradley's death being a suspected murder?" Conor was now beginning to clock watch and clearly wanted to move the meeting on.

"Massey was buying time with the media. But eventually, the murder investigation will be obvious. It's best if it's on our terms. Plus, in the past day, we have placed a witness in protective custody. This is going to creep out if we're not careful," McNally said.

"Eric, what say you front up a press conference, using a script we write? Just a statement, no questions. We'll explain we are exploring all avenues of enquiry, and we've ruled out nothing. Maybe ask the public for any sightings of cars and vans around the Ballycastle property. But try to keep it relatively light," Clive suggested.

"I'm clearly in your hands, Clive." Eric responded, a little disconsolately. "I'll talk to my media team later today and I'll ask them to liaise directly with Palace Barracks?"

"Very good," Clive replied. "This is a team approach. Although we'll lead, we'll pool together our resources to minimise any risk to the delicate peace talks. McNally, is there anything else you need from me?"

"A hotline to GCHQ, the Seekers, and Palace Barracks' operational support. I will need the RUC to liaise with the Bradley family and for security service forensics to lead on another sensitive angle we've uncovered," he replied.

"You can have whatever you need," Clive confirmed. "But I have forty staff over here and they are almost totally absorbed in other missions, especially with the cousins crawling over our every move. Ireland is almost the 51st state at the moment. Utilising your proven experience will take a load off and avoid transatlantic interference."

Clive, Conor, and Jube were all standing poised to leave the meeting, with only the female assistant and Eric still looking settled.

"I think that brings things to a close, everyone. I suggest we talk often, but only through cleared communication channels." Conor started shaking hands with everyone, and Eric finally got to his feet.

With Clive and Conor remaining near the table and Eric now striding off at pace, McNally walked back to the car park with Jube. The two had some catching up to do.

"So, who have you lined up to assist you?" Jube asked. "I'm

guessing Jones, Jenny and Isadora are crawling all over this, like excited puppies."

"You'd be correct. They have already been working on this for a few days. Virginia is managing the YCU like a beaut. We are firing on all cylinders. But there are so many leads here, we're going to need support."

Jube put his hands behind his back, letting his red and yellow school tie flutter in the wind. The crunch of the shingle and the birdsong punctuated their slow walk to the car park.

"I have your back, McNally. You know that. But there is something about the Bradley stuff that stinks. Maybe I'm losing my touch, but I just can't put my finger on it at the moment." Jube was deep in his thoughts as they arrived next to their respective vehicles. McNally in a Land Rover and Jube in a pool car, a Rover.

"I get someone wanted him dead if he was forcing his way into new territories. I also buy the theory that his fingers are all over the properties, the investments in the Turks and Caicos Islands, and the crime networks. Mainstay Holdings feels like the logical front. What I can't fathom is why now and why Philip Bradley?"

"Think on it, Jube. You're here for 48 hours. Bradley will not get any less dead. Talk to me when it hits you," McNally replied.

"I will, indeed. I'll pop and see Orla too. That was a damned shame. Take care, McNally."

With that, McNally slammed the door of the Land Rover. Looking down into the console between the two seats, he saw the red LED of the handheld flashing. He immediately picked up the small black box and pressed receive.

"This is Jones. We're at the RUC Station in Coleraine. We've been interviewing Sam Jacobs. You're going to want to hear this."

"Fire away, Jones," he replied, fiddling with the car keys and watching Jube drive off towards Hillsborough village.

"Two things. Firstly, we've been told the Knock Road plods have concluded door-to-door enquiries at Ballycastle, up near the Bradley murder scene. Two of Sam's lawn-mowing clients say they've been visited by blokes wearing smart clothes asking questions about him. They claimed they were police. One of the Primrose Grove residents gave them Sam's business card."

"Shit. That's not good. Did the residents give a description of them? The suited fellas?"

"One was Andrew, definitely, with the teardrop tattoo. The other was nondescript, young and dark-haired. Both with local accents. They scarpered from one house when the residents asked to see a warrant card. They thought they left in a dark blue hatchback, maybe a VW Golf."

"Alright. That's useful stuff. Is that it, Jones? I need to get back."

"No, that was just the entrée. The main course is the station's recent anonymous call. It's a female voice. Local accent. Says she knows who killed Bradley and might go to the media unless she's paid for the information. We reckon this might be Wonder Woman."

"Sweet Jesus. What makes you say that? Are you sure she's not another nutter?"

"She told the duty team here that she ushered a young man into a wardrobe. That's the only thing she'll admit before we talk about money. I'm guessing she doesn't know we have Sam Jacobs in protective custody. We are on the cusp of something. But she didn't leave a contact number. We are waiting for her to ring back. She wants to speak to the man in charge."

"Aye, well, I guess that's me now. It's a waiting game then." McNally started the engine and switched off the handheld.

Sixteen

With Virginia Curry in temporary charge of the YCU, Carl and Tom had been called into action to invigilate a series of written tests. Isadora had been coaching them in surveillance techniques out in the field and this was to see whether the groups had fully grasped it all. Carl and Tom walked up and down the two briefing rooms, checking on the recruits and trying not to giggle as yet another in-joke surfaced.

The YCU's surveillance training module taught the recruits how to undertake various forms of surveillance in order to gather the best evidence from crucial intelligence. Isadora Brown's first-hand experience ensured it was relevant and delivered to best practice standards. She was a stickler for detail, and the recruits learned this quickly. This was not high school or a jolly. Even though she was now engaged on the Bradley case, her tentacles were all over this module and she eagerly awaited the results.

The module focused on understanding the difference between anti- and counter- surveillance and how to identify or disrupt foot or mobile surveillance that might be deployed in the field, using choke points, surveillance traps and other methods. In truth, Isadora loved showing off her skills and, even though the wheelchair limited elements of her mobility, she was still the best in the business. Ailsa, who was fast becoming the darling of the YCU, excelled during the practical workshops and was expected to ace the written tests too.

A few yards down the corridor, Mr Singh had been working on developing the next stage of his prototype PEA. Carl and Tom hadn't seen him for days outside the QD. They knew something interesting was afoot. The pair has 'passed' their own tiny devices soon after the original field tests and, although Mr Singh was clearly delighted, there would be countless further stages of testing and development.

Therefore, after the silence, came the proclamation. When the exam had finished, Mr Singh called the pair into the QD, to their respective stations, and presented them with yet another delicacy. This time, encased in a rather splendid gram flour batter, was Mr Singh's sister's onion bhaji surprise. The surprise, it turned out, was that one contained a large red chilli and the other a second-stage PEA, with some added extras that Mr Singh was excited to trial.

Carl didn't need asking twice. He ripped open the white paper bag and gorged on the spicy goodness of the bhaji with gusto. Tom, with a little more nervousness, nibbled at the snack before taking large bites. He swallowed the remains whole, and they were both given water to ease the process through.

"So, what's the deal this time, Mr Singh?" Carl asked, wiping his face with a napkin.

"Just go about your business as normal. Come back here at lunchtime, prior to taking your lunch, for a full de-briefing."

"Is there anything to worry about?" Tom remarked, remembering that Carl got the PEA stuck last time.

"Nothing whatsoever. As I said, go about your business. I have other things to do now. Please excuse me."

Mr Singh walked over to the corner of the QD and turned on the radio. As there was no live cricket, he tuned into a current affairs programme, grabbed the jar of Mellowbirds and switched the kettle on. This was the most relaxed they'd seen him in days. Perhaps ever.

Carl and Tom scurried back into the briefing rooms to report to Virginia. She'd been back at Milton College overnight to liaise with Wendy, whose arrival was imminent. Virginia had also completed a large piece of academic work for the principal, thus enabling her to fully concentrate on the YCU. She was dressed in one of her more floral summer dresses and had her glasses tucked in her hair above her head.

"Boys," she began in a rather school matron voice. "I need you to construct a session on the use of the handhelds. We have twenty-four of the current design and they will be useful as the recruits learn the ropes. It only needs to be ten minutes long, and you can take one group each."

"No problem, Virginia. We'll speak to Mr Singh and get the handhelds ready for circulation. I'll construct an itinerary list," Tom explained.

With her desk phone beginning to ring, Virginia hurriedly disappeared into her office and shut the door.

"It's elevenses," Carl announced. "Or perhaps pre-dinner nibbles time. I'm not sure what they call it over here."

"Greed?" Tom replied, smiling. "Let's head over to the NAAFI stores and you can feed your sweet tooth. You must be keeping that place afloat."

Thiepval was unusually hot and very busy. Against the backdrop of a warm cloudless summer day, large military vehicles were being filled with supplies ready for an operation or scenario-planning exercise. Uniformed men, perhaps two or three times the size of Carl, were lifting huge wooden ammunition boxes into utility vehicles and carrying long wooden and aluminium poles to be strapped onto the roofs of other awaiting vehicles. It was a hive of activity.

They nipped past the military vehicles and past the training ground where another team was cutting the grass with a gang mower.

"How fast do you reckon a mower could go on a motorway?" Carl asked, as they headed towards the shop.

"Oh, good question, mate. With modifications, I reckon they'd get it up to 60-70mph. But they'd have to take the blades off," Tom replied.

"Without a doubt. Imagine a gang mower Grand Prix. That would be phenomenal. BBC Grandstand would be all over that. Nigel Mansell, heading into the first corner of Brands Hatch on his souped-up lawnmower, it would be a hell of a spectacle."

"*There's nothing wrong with the lawnmower... except it's on fire!*" Carl chuckled as he did his best Murray Walker impression. Tom exploded with laughter in response.

Carl, still smiling from the last conversation, was now focused on the shop. He was hoping no-one had suddenly gained an interest in Animal Biscuits, Wham bars or, his new love, cola laces.

The shop itself was alive with soldiers stocking up with chocolate, fizzy drinks and traditional biscuits like bourbons and custard creams for their time away. One officer walked out with a whole crate of Irn-Bru and an enormous tub of vaseline, which raised a snigger between Carl and Tom. But he was in luck; all of his favourites were in stock, and he even treated himself to a large bag of roast beef flavoured Monster Munch.

"It's literally an hour before lunchtime. Do you really need all this stuff, Carl?"

"If I pace myself, I won't run out again until tomorrow. But it's going to be a precarious balancing act." Carl had already stuffed an entire Wham bar in his mouth and was struggling to speak. Tom grabbed his arm and pulled him safely back through the waiting queue of military vehicles.

"I wish you could successfully chew and walk at the same time. You're a liability, sometimes," Tom said, beginning to feel like Carl's carer. This was an all-too-familiar thought process.

"We're due back at the QD before lunch. We may as well head there now and we can then go through the afternoon's to-do list prior to the next round of tests."

Carl didn't respond. He nodded knowingly. Aware that the Wham bar limited his communication possibilities.

When they appeared through the double doors into the QD, Mr Singh was wearing a pair of unfathomably small inspection glasses as well as some large headphones. He was concentrating on a moving GPS blob on a computer screen. He removed the head-gear and settled down in front of his technicians.

"Well," Mr Singh began. "There is good news and bad news."

"About the trial? Were you looking at our locations using the GPS?" Tom asked, staring over his shoulder at the screen.

"The good news is that the trial was a total success. The bad news is that there is already such a thing as lawnmower racing. It's actually a semi-professional pursuit and people fix up ride-on mowers," Mr Singh smiled. "They can hit 70-mph easily."

"How the hell did you know about that conversation?" Carl looked confused.

"Tom, go into the corner of the QD and listen to my radio through these." Mr Singh instructed. Tom did as he was told and put the headphones over his head. They looked like relics from a Spitfire pilot's kit.

"Carl, tell me, how many handhelds did Virginia tell you we had in stock? When you met her in her office?"

"Twenty-four, Mr Singh," Carl replied.

"My word!" Tom shouted. "I can hear you very clearly. Have you seriously put a tiny microphone receiver in the PEA? How is that even possible?"

"A mixture of science, engineering and genius. The only problem is that Carl's incredibly chewy bar is now going through his digestive system at the same time as the receiver. That might kill it. I did mention eating the bhaji *before* lunch, I should have stipulated before any kind of food, knowing Carl's insatiable appetite. Not to worry though, I have a few more that are ready to test."

Tom looked over onto Mr Singh's workbench and next to a soldering iron were two pea-shaped objects. There was even a tiny tin of Humbrol bright green paint, probably purloined from an Airfix kit.

"It's a bloody good job I didn't say anything iffy," Carl responded. "Not that I would, of course, being such a stickler for professionalism." Tom stared back at him in disbelief.

Ignoring him, Mr Singh continued. "This will revolutionise how we undertake surveillance on targets in the field. The only problem is... the microphone signal only lasts a matter of hours. And it's quite an expensive piece of kit. I need to think about how we extend its life," he said, thinking aloud.

"There's another issue too," Tom interrupted, holding up the small tin of green paint. "It says here, highly toxic do not consume. Danger of death."

Mr Singh picked up the paint pot and studied it, his inspection glasses now wedged at the very end of his nose.

"Oh, you're right. Now that's quite a pickle. Go and get yourselves some lunch and Tom, come and see me if Carl starts to projectile vomit or passes out with convulsions. That'll be the clue that something's wrong."

"A clue?" Carl said, as Tom led him to the refectory through the double doors.

"Make sure he drinks plenty of water," Mr Singh called after them as they headed out.

"Blimey. Is Mr Singh completely sane? Is he some kind of nutty professor?" Carl asked.

"I can still hear you, you know!" Mr Singh shouted from the QD. "I'm as sane as you are, Carl Kelly."

"Oh bugger," Carl said, quietly.

In the Barracks mess, a few hundred yards away from the Quartermaster's Department, Jenny and Jones were waiting for

Isadora to arrive with the Land Rover. McNally had called the entire team together at Knock Road RUC HQ and wanted to brief the assembled troops on the progress of the investigation.

However, Jenny was being unusually touchy-feeling with Jones. She was being outwardly affectionate, and this made him worry that something wasn't right. As he pushed the salt pot around the plastic-coated MDF table, he began to overthink, in his regular fashion. This simply wasn't her style, he thought. She had always been loving, but deplored public signs of affection. Something was up, Jones thought. As he watched Jenny reading the horoscopes in the Daily Mirror and shake her head disbelievingly, he decided that the conversation needed to happen.

"So, what have you done now?" Jones began, perhaps unhelpfully.

"What?" Jenny replied.

"You've been, how do I say, much nicer than normal recently? It's odd. The only other time you've done this is when you broke my grandfather's old beer mug, the ceramic one. It's like a need to overcompensate, a guilt complex."

"Jesus, Jones. Your brain. Can't I take care of you a bit? You're my bloke."

"Oh, come on! Taking care of me is not your thing. Every time I say 'I love you,' you reply, 'That's great,' rather than saying the same in response. I hold the emotional keys to this relationship. Suddenly, I'm being looked after? You don't even like people holding doors open for you."

"You cheeky shit!" Jenny half-shouted back. "I thought I was the emotional one. You've only ever said those three little words twice and mostly drunk."

"Really? Well, tell me I'm wrong then? The reason we work so well together is that I've been brought up by women who have explained the need for a balanced and equal relationship. I don't ask for anything, we're a team. A bloody good one. I'm not your bloke. I'm that fella you knock about with and that you secretly love and care about. We're equals."

"Ok. You've made a series of valid points," she replied, putting the paper down and moving in her chair to face him. Here it comes, thought Jones. Jenny had a habit of looking deeply into Jones' dark brown eyes when she wanted to have a serious chat, and she was now staring into them like she was looking for something important. Soul searching, maybe.

"I cheated," she started.

"With who?"

"No, you daft bastard, not that kind of cheating. I wouldn't have time for that," Jenny smiled nervously.

"So, what do you mean, then?"

"You know what I mean. During McNally's cipher tests. I feel terrible about it. I'm so ashamed. I know we discussed this outside the church, but I feel like an absolute nutjob. I just want to put things right."

Jenny continued to stare at Jones, almost appealing for forgiveness. He paused momentarily and felt the anxiety drop. This wasn't a big deal. He thought this had been discussed and they'd moved on. But she obviously hadn't, so he would need to handle it carefully.

"Well, I understand that. It was very un-Richmond-like. But I forgave you. This is ancient history. I couldn't hold a grudge with you. Is that really why you've been so nice?" Jones conjured up his most sympathetic look.

"Maybe," Jenny answered.

"You don't need to be. We're totally fine. But I bet you've not told Isadora. She'd judge you harshly for this. She'd be far worse than me."

"I've not told her, Jones. But I think Virginia knows. I have a meeting with her on Friday and she gave me one of her disappointed looks in the corridor the other day. I feel dreadful about it all. Have I let you down?"

"Jenny. We work in espionage. That's what we do. We cheat; we lie. Isadora will only hate it because you broke the rules. Virginia will be annoyed that you broke into McNally's office. And McNally, well, who knows? But I'd expect the worse."

"Yeah, you're right. I'll prepare myself. But we're good? You promise?" she asked.

"I think it's hilarious and I've quite enjoyed all the attention. It's proved that you're normal and fallible, but brilliant at the same time. I just don't understand why you bothered. You would have aced the cipher challenge anyway."

"No, I wouldn't. Your brain is otherworldly." Jenny finally looked away as two uniformed soldiers, in lime green berets, pitched up on the table next to them. They had two enormous breakfast baps and bucket-sized mugs of tea. Jones was suddenly hungry again.

"You realise..." Jones started, in hushed tones. "That your bravery and quick-thinking on board the General Eduardo saved my life? That I wouldn't be here without that intervention? Jim Shiels too. You saved us both." Jim Shiels was a freelance agent, normally attached to the Irish Security Service (known as J2), who was kneeling in front of Joseph Armstrong before Jenny made the kill on the shipping container.

"But I don't want all that fuss and bother. I love that I saved your life, don't get me wrong. But I'll never have the same unique mind, and I wanted, for once, to challenge you."

"We've discussed this. You're going over old ground. Honest," Jones responded.

Jenny, who had long finished her hot chocolate in a white polystyrene cup, took a swig out of it again, if only to punctuate the conversation. Jones knew that this was the kind of intimate chat that would be more suited to her regular mentoring sessions with Virginia. That they were far too close for his objective view to really cut through.

"Let's move on, shall we?" Jones added. "We're working on

another mission now. The YCU stuff can take a back seat for a little while. Maybe we can discuss all this competition malarkey once we've solved a double murder? Frankly, I'm beyond excited." Jones stood up as he saw Isadora enter the room. She was indicating that the car was out at the front.

"One more thing," Jenny said, grabbing Jones and pulling him close. "I do love you. I just think it's so obvious that I don't need to tell you all the time. I mean, let's be honest, who else would have you?"

"Back to earth with a bang!" Jones responded. "Normal service is resumed," Jenny added, and they walked slowly over to Isadora, who was already looking impatient.

"You took your time," Jenny shouted over to Isadora. "We were supposed to be leaving twenty minutes ago."

"Virginia caught me. There's been a problem at City Hospital. Two unknowns broke into Orla Massey's room last night. Eric Rogers is looking into it, but Special Branch was supposed to be providing close protection and they were nowhere to be seen." Isadora held open the doors as the two walked past towards the car park.

"That's odd," Jones remarked. "Is she okay?"

"Apparently, she was none-the-wiser. She's still on quite a high dose of sedatives and was either fast asleep or counting pink hippos. But this is certainly pretty worrying."

Seventeen

After a full day of cloudless, balmy weather, the Belfast skies were beginning to close in. Over in the distance, towards the Mournes, a mass of black clouds was heading into the city and the temperature had dropped a few degrees. Thoughts of beer gardens, after-work pints and a trip to a few hard-to-reach hostelries had been high on Jones' agenda, after Isadora drove from Thiepval at warp speed.

But rain was now imminent, and as he stared out of the window in Knock Road station assessing the weather, Jenny noticed him losing focus. She pulled him back from the window and gently onto the chair and handed him a small briefing pack held together with treasury tags. Their clearing-the-air conversation had nicely reset their relationship.

Jones had spent the past twenty-four hours being briefed, and it was becoming monotonous. Firstly, on the double murder timeline, then interviewing an understandably scared Sam Jacobs before finally running through the core strands of the investigation with Sergeant Marie Bristow. His brain was filling up fast and, whilst he loved the challenge and intrigue, he was feeling like what his grandmother described as 'a plod'.

His current role was cloudy, at the very least. He, along with Jenny and Isadora, had YCU contracts provided by the security service, but they were operating within an MI5 structure. With MI5 responsible for protecting the UK, its citizens and interests, against threats to national security. They had effectively, and unofficially, been seconded over to MI5 in Northern Ireland to underpin the rather fragile Palace Barracks team and the RUC staff shortages.

Nevertheless, he was now sitting in an RUC station with a team of police officers awaiting the start of another briefing. They'll be going through plans for the next stages of the investigation, and it all felt muddy but, in true Jones style, he felt it was a case of rolling up his sleeves and getting stuck in.

Sam Jacobs was awaiting transfer to a safe house and McNally had asked the entire investigation team to meet at Knock Road, Belfast.

"Right. Can I have your attention?" Marie Bristow began. The murmuring and muttering around the eight-strong team stopped. "Most of you know we are being supported by three MI5 officers in dealing with this case, and the leadership of the investigation also has a new face, Declan McNally." There was nodding around the room and the uniformed officers looked calm, despite clearly being ill-prepared for an influx of MI5 field officers in their squad room.

"They will introduce themselves to you as the investigation moves on. However, outside these walls, this is an RUC operation. I hope I make myself clear? The involvement of MI5 is one hundred per cent confidential and any leaks will be treated as gross misconduct. Understood?"

Those assembled nodded. Bristow had just supplied clarity in a manner Massey herself would be proud. The only difference was Bristow's slightly squeaky South Belfast accent just wasn't as terrifying as Massey's Derry-tinged orders. McNally then stood up.

"Okay, folks. Welcome to Operation Mainstay. Let's have a wee look at the blackboard here. We are working on a series of knowns, a few assumptions and some dotted lines. Turn to the front page of your packs. The man in the image is Philip Bradley. He was a family man, with a wife who works in a local primary school. He has significant hidden wealth and some vices that suggest there is more going on behind the scenes. We will need to have a hoke about in every aspect of his life. We need to find out where his vast fortune comes from. MI5 will lead on this, but we'll need police support in undertaking some interviews."

There were more nods and a few glances exchanged by peeved RUC officers who clearly didn't welcome the MI5 leadership role. McNally continued.

"We presume Philip Bradley was killed by a criminal network intent on removing his influence, or perhaps the family influence. This is our main line of enquiry, but we cannot totally rule out a sectarian element." There was now some furious notetaking around the room.

"We know his body was moved, and we have reliable evidence that the individual responsible for his killing had a possible Irish-American accent, was around 5' 9" tall, and was wearing outdoor gear - maybe associated with fishing or hunting. There is a photofit on page two. It's not that detailed but it's a start. But we need more."

"There were three other *known* witnesses. A thirty-something female with strawberry blonde hair, dressed as Wonder Woman. Our eyewitness suggested she was tied to the bed in the Garden House property and the witness released her. Bradley, we are told, was injured from a fall from a wardrobe." McNally paused as a few officers sniggered slightly.

"One of the other two witnesses is also dead. He's George McCool, a 19-year-old from Strabane. He worked at Maddison's Scrapyard with his dad and brother. He was found with a single shot through the head, much like Bradley, but this time covered in petrol in a sluice ditch in Ballyhalbert. He is not known to have paramilitary links, but he was almost certainly in The Garden House when Bradley was shot."

"However, the likely location of the Bradley murder has been cleaned so thoroughly that forensics could only find a single blood sample from the scene and some fingerprints on smashed milk bottles. Those fingerprints were Philip Bradley's and we have confirmation that the house was owned by Mainstay Holdings Ltd."

"That, aside from the clean-up team, leaves us with Andrew. Massey was told by a reliable informant that Andrew has a teardrop tattoo on his neck, but this isn't confirmed. We have no other details for this individual, but we are yet to interview the McCool's properly. We've simply had a wee chat with the mother, Pauline, who appears unaware of any reason for her youngest son to be involved. We need to test that theory. We believe George McCool was executed in a pub near to his home, as retribution for selling copies of polaroid photos of Bradley's murder scene to a newspaper."

"Have we got access to those photos yet?" Jenny asked, rifling through her pack, looking for them.

"No," Bristow replied. "But we expect to have them by close of play today, along with any other evidence from the Belfast Gazette they've been concealing. They've actually been very cooperative. But we expect the photos to confirm the location of the killing at Garden House in Ballycastle. What else is on those polaroids, we don't know."

McNally continued the briefing. "The murderer is most likely the man with the outdoor wear, Irish-American accent and using the same gun and same MO. MI5 forensics are visiting that property overnight and I will need an undercover surveillance team to assist with that. Is that in hand, Sergeant Bristow?"

"Yes, we have a team lined up to ensure this operation remains under wraps," she replied.

Jones interrupted. "What decision was made about the call from Wonder Woman? The strawberry blonde on the bed?"

"I think Jones is referring to the call received earlier today. Turn to page four of your briefing pack and you'll see a transcript of that conversation," Marie Bristow explained. "A woman claiming to have eyewitness information but wanting to be paid was received in our Coleraine incident room. However, she did not leave any contact information. The call has been traced through to another phone box, this time outside a bed-and-breakfast in Kilkeel. We await a further contact. There will be no payment. Acting Superintendent Rogers has made that clear and MI5 would take a similar stance."

"So, what do you need from us?" Isadora asked, sitting at the back of the squad room.

"We will need to look at three key questions. Why was Philip Bradley killed? By whom? And is there a bigger geo-political reason why this death is important? Those are the key themes for the MI5 team."

"My team," Bristow began, "will need to look at the George McCool death, put the pieces together and look at the identity of Andrew, the other likely witness. We will also deal with taking a witness statement from Wonder Woman if we can get hold of her. But I guess MI5 will want to join that too?"

"Absolutely," McNally answered. "Joint working is at the heart of all of this. This is not a take-over, it's a partnership. I think that brings this session to an end. We will meet again tomorrow afternoon to talk through progress and Sergeant Bristow will remain the contact here at Knock Road. Is everyone happy?" There was more nodding before the group dispersed. A few of the uniformed officers headed straight to the canteen. Others sat reading the notes.

McNally wandered over to Jones, Jenny, and Isadora. They looked ready to leave. McNally looked baked in his thick trench coat and Jones recognised the stale odour of his cigarillo habit.

"I'm pleased I caught you all," McNally began. "Miss Richmond, you and I need to talk about your dirty tricks with YCU. It surprised me a bit, I have to say. I wouldn't have thought dandering into my office to find the answers to the ciphers was your thing. But let's draw a wee line under that for now. There will be a forfeit at a moment of my choosing." McNally seemed half riled and half amused. For a man leading a double murder investigation, he had lost none of his dark humour, Jones noticed.

"Forfeit?" Jenny repeated. "That doesn't sound good. I know I did the wrong thing, but... how did you find out?"

"You'll have to get up mighty early to catch me out, Richmond" he continued. "Anyway, that can wait, I need you to head over to Saoirse Bradley and interview her straight away. You can tell her you're from the security service, as he was an MP, and she'll expect special treatment. I want to know more about their relationship, what she knew about his apparent vast fortune and his vices. We need to work out if she was implicated in any way."

"Okay," Jones responded. "We'll head over there. What are you up to?"

"Jube Spencer and I are meeting the President of his political party, the Northern Unionist Coalition. We're using one of the private rooms at The Europa Hotel. I'm trying to get a measure of the man, his standing in the party and any skeletons."

"Right, let's crack on then. Does everyone have handhelds?" Isadora asked. There was a quick confirmation from everyone, before McNally vanished towards the car park. Today was going to be make or break for lots of the key facts, Jones decided.

"Topaz is reborn," Jenny said, as Isadora jumped into the adapted Land Rover and headed through the reinforced metal gates of the police station compound. Isadora and Jones smiled a little as Jenny reminded them of their former Topaz moniker and decided they were back on manoeuvres for the first time since the horror of The Last Hurrah Operation.

Jones stared out of the window from the back seat and tried to regulate his thoughts. Operation Mainstay was an exciting mission and one that would ultimately unmask a murderer and eliminate a national security issue. Maybe he wasn't a plod after all.

Isadora drove at speed along the road between Belfast and Bangor. The clouds were still threatening above, but the rain had held off. They were looking for Mainstay Barn, a sprawling property near Craigboy Road, as Millisle Road seamlessly became Donaghadee Road. Within half an hour, the Land Rover had made it past Bangor and heading along the coast road and they were looking for the turn off. The sea, reflecting against the last embers of summer sun, looked light green and even from the back seat of the car, Jones thought it looked chilly. Holidaymakers' cars lined the side streets, leading to the perfect-looking bays and beaches. They were the lucky few, tourists and locals that recognised these hidden treasures in a part of Ireland, still mired in violence and tension.

"Hold on," Jones shouted, over the loud mixtape Jenny had put on the stereo. It was one Jones had curated himself and he was loath to switch off 'Loaded' by Primal Scream. "Slow down. Those large green gates look like the entrance to somewhere grand and bloody secure."

Isadora took her hand off the accelerator wand on the right side of the steering wheel, and the Land Rover edged past a series of large country houses set back from the road. Jones had seen the large clay stones and green gates in the distance whilst the other two had been singing. As they pulled up in a small layby, they could make out a large wrought iron sign displaying the name 'Mainstay Barns' with two large white Italianate statues on either side.

"Wow," Jones exclaimed. "Barns...plural. There's more than one in there. Pull up to the gates and we'll see if Saoirse Bradley is home."

Isadora indicated and swung the car up the narrow-tarmacked driveway to an entry console. She reached out and pressed the entry button. There were the sounds of angry guard dogs in the distance, and Jones noticed the entire property was secured by a large chalkstone wall with more artistic statues dotted around it.

"Hello, can I help you?" A quiet voice came from the console.

"Good afternoon, we are assisting the police with the enquiry relating to the death of Philip Bradley. I wonder if Mrs Bradley is available for a brief chat?" Isadora explained. The green gates slowly opened, and the Land Rover was carefully manoeuvred into the compound behind. The dogs, two large Dobermans, were called back into the house and vanished through a green side door.

There were two large, converted barns, with palm trees reflected against tall windows and a black-painted timber frontage. The nearest barn had dark green features, including porcelain planters full of colourful geraniums and asters, and the shingle leading to the front door was flecked with green pebbles and surrounded by green glass lights. A quick look to the barn further away revealed it was almost entirely the same, aside from a terra-cotta theme, with urns dotted around the exterior, that set the two apart. Security cameras, an unusual addition, were in evidence around the area.

"Classy," Jenny said, admiring the renovations. "Look, there's another one, a third, just behind. It looks like they're still working on that barn."

As Isadora applied the handbrake, Jones saw a small blonde woman emerge from the open door of the closest property. Initially, he thought it was a child, but as she walked closer, he guessed she was in her early thirties. She was no more than five feet tall, in bare feet and wearing a cropped black t-shirt and white Capri pants. She was holding a cordless phone and looking agitated.

"Hi," she called over. "I don't want to be rude, but I had no idea someone was coming from the police today and I've already made plans. But I guess I can be late." She had a northerly burr to her Irish accent, which gave way to the gentlest southern brogue.

Jones immediately placed this as a County Armagh tone, because of his grandmother's love of Gloria Hunniford, the TV presenter. But, if this was Saoirse Bradley, she was an extremely elegant woman who had crammed all that elegance into a very petite frame.

Isadora, who was still sitting in the driving seat as Jenny retrieved her wheelchair from the boot, called back, "I'm really sorry about that. I thought our colleagues had called ahead. We'll try to keep it brief. Are you Mrs Bradley?"

"I am," she answered. "You'd better come through. I'll put the kettle on. Sure, just make yourself at home in the front room." Saoirse Bradley disappeared back into the house, making barely a sound as she did so.

"She's not what I was expecting at all," Jenny said, placing the chair in front of Isadora. "What were you expecting, Jen? A woman in black with a veil?" Isadora replied, pulling herself onto the seat.

"Nah. Just not that. She's incredibly beautiful. Don't you think, Jones?"

"Oh no," Jones replied. "I'm swerving that question. I've given you honest answers before and we didn't speak for almost a week. She's a grieving woman and she has a lovely house. That's all I'm saying."

"Coward," Isadora smirked. She was now making her way from the Land Rover to the front door and staring down at the green polished glass stones that gleamed as they made their way up the path.

The interior of the house had thick stone walls and dark wooden doors with antique locks and latches. There were stone paving slabs along the corridor leading to the open-plan main lounge area and dark wooden floorboards in the rooms themselves. There were glass-fronted bookshelves, fully stocked. Saoirse Bradley, or perhaps her late husband, were big readers and fans of literature. There were also little Italian-themed trinkets and ornaments around the room.

Up on the right-hand side of the room was a depiction of Christ crucified and opposite this, a framed silver Virgin Mary image that looked to be hundreds of years old. Jones sat on a sofa with prominent ornately carved mahogany arms and features. Jenny sat to his left and, on the right, Isadora remained in the wheelchair. She'd been having a few back problems recently and was grateful for the respite. Saoirse Bradley soon arrived in the room with a silver teapot and four small china teacups with saucers.

"What happened?" she asked Isadora, motioning to the wheelchair.

"Bullet to the spine," she answered, shrugging her shoulders. "I'm going to get out of this, though. It's getting better." Mrs Bradley nodded sympathetically.

"Firstly," Jenny began. "Can we offer our sincere condolences for the loss of your husband? It must have been a terrible shock."

There was no reply initially. Mrs Bradley pursed her lips as she poured the tea into all four cups and looked as if she was attempting to force out an answer. Emotion hung over her, but she also appeared resolute as Jones tried to work her out.

"Well, he was a cheating bastard. Obviously. But he was a good father, the children worshipped him, and he provided for us all. It would be wrong for me to say otherwise."

"Did the fact that he was with another woman at the time of this death surprise you?" Jenny asked. Jones was surprised with her line of questioning; it seemed almost too brutal as a starting point.

"No, not at all. When the Superintendent called me and explained the circumstances, I was terribly upset, and it's taken me the past few days to regain my composure. But he's cheated before, and we've patched things up. I guess his good points balanced out the bad ones, and since he's been in Westminster, I've hardly seen him, anyway." She poured milk into all four cups without asking and handed out the tea. Jones couldn't see a sugar bowl and accepted his fate.

"There was an initial report that he'd killed himself..." Jenny started to explain, but Saoirse Bradley interrupted.

"Never," she said. "That would never, ever happen. He loved life and I knew that was wrong. He was lots of things, but he wasn't a quitter. But, when I heard he'd been murdered, that seemed remarkable too. Whilst we had our differences, Philip was well-liked. He was just so kind to everyone." Mrs Bradley took a handkerchief from the top pocket of her Capri pants and wiped away a tear. The rawness of it all was still close to the surface, Jones surmised. But there was something more. Something seemed to be lurking in her background as she spoke. Jones couldn't put a finger on it.

"No enemies at all?" Jenny countered. "He was a pretty vocal unionist MP, who absolutely denied any kind of framework for peace until relatively recently. Didn't that rub people up the wrong way?"

"It did. Yes. But things change. In the past eighteen months, he's been the one bringing the unionists into the peace process. He began discussing the art of the possible, asking what the unionists would be prepared to give up for peace. He's been a leading voice for compromise. I was dead proud of him."

"What about outside politics?" Jones ventured.

"You're all English? Jesus!" Mrs Bradley snapped, hearing Jones' voice for the first time. "Is the RUC on strike or something? Hold on, I haven't even asked to see warrant cards. You could be journalists for all I know, landing on me like this. I can't believe I've been so lax."

"Calm down, we're not the police, Mrs Bradley. We're from London, from the security service. This is the highest possible priority investigation because of your husband's role at Westminster." Jones fumbled through his wallet and found a rather dog-eared identity card, and Isadora and Jenny did the same. Isadora joined the conversation and underlined their role.

"You are under no obligation to speak with us," Isadora explained. "We have no powers of arrest, and if you prefer to speak to the RUC, that's not an issue. But we are simply trying to get to the bottom of the two murders."

"Two murders? You're connecting them?" was the response. Jenny shot Isadora a look. This wasn't supposed to be revealed.

"No, no. It's more of a resource issue. We're helping with both, but we can't rule anything out." Isadora hurriedly clarified. Jones, sensing the unease, brought the subject back to Philip Bradley's business dealings.

"You were telling us about his work outside politics. You have a wonderful house here and two more nearby. What did Mr Bradley do before politics?" Jones asked, carefully.

"Oh, you see, this is the mistake everyone makes. I'm disappointed you didn't do some proper homework first. Philip was a mere draftsman when we met, not even a trained architect. He designed these wonderful barn conversions with local help and had a brilliant eye for home décor. But that's as far as it goes."

"But correct me if I'm wrong Mrs Bradley, but don't you own a string of properties across Ireland?" Jones continued.

"The money that you've discovered is mine. I'm Mainstay Holdings Ltd. My father was Kenny Reid, you'll have a chunky file on him back at the office, I've no doubt. He was killed by the Lower Belfast Brigade of the Loyalist Enforcers about five years ago. His business dealings were split equally between me and my sister Caragh. She lives over in Andersonstown. We're estranged."

Jones looked over at Isadora as the pieces of the jigsaw slowly slotted into place. Why the hell hadn't Massey or Eric Rogers worked this out? Jones thought. How was this missed? Especially with Philip Bradley's immense public profile.

"Okay, I can see the pennies aren't dropping. Let me help you out here. My father, the late Kenny Reid, was a Republican freedom fighter, or that's what he wished to be known as. Yous lot will call him a terrorist or a paramilitary. I don't care, really."

Jones sipped more of his tea and realised the conversation had taken a dramatic turn. They were taking tea in the seaside opulence of Mainstay Barns with the daughter of a big-name paramilitary leader.

"I'm the black sheep," Mrs Bradley resumed, after taking a quick sip herself. "I married a protestant politician and have since been written off by my family and friends. Excommunicated, if you like. I'm as good as dead to them. But I still keep my faith. My husband and I accepted our religious differences."

"And yet you inherited half of your father's estate?" Jones, still stunned, clarified.

"Oh absolutely. But they tried very hard to get the Will changed. They even tried to kill me off. They threw the kitchen sink at me to get their hands on his money. But I held firm. Daddy simply forgot to change the Will. Hence the massive security here and keeping away from the big city." Saoirse Bradley put her cup back on the tray and smiled matter-of-factly.

"So, yeah, I'm a businesswoman with a property empire and investments in Ireland and further afield. This had nothing to do with Phillip. He was my husband and was a dedicated politician."

"Understood," Jones confirmed, "loud and clear."

"I'm pleased we cleared that up. But, let's be honest, I know the RUC couldn't give a damn about me and my family. I had a foot in both camps. Therefore, I was left to rot whilst this nightmare unfolded. Philip didn't have enemies at all. In fact, I think my own family preferred him to me towards the end. But I have a large pound sign hanging over my head." She poured herself more tea and composed herself.

"It really should have been me that was murdered, I was the real target for my family and their Republican friends. But that doesn't help you, does it? I still have no idea who killed him."

There was silence as the facts unfolded, and tea was consumed.

It occurred to Jones that Saoirse Bradley was a ghost. A woman who had somehow survived this sectarian blitz of division but had lost everyone and everything. Well, aside from her children and that fortune, which seemed to Jones like another millstone around her neck. Yet, here she was, politely drinking tea and grieving the loss of her husband, who had been cheating on her and perhaps using his father-in-law's dirty money to fund a coke habit. She'd not mentioned that, interestingly. This was a tangled web, Jones thought.

There would be another half hour of chit-chat and smaller, yet still useful, revelations before they made their excuses and started the half-hour trip back to base. Mrs Bradley almost seemed sad to see them go and stood at the front door of Mainstay Barns and waved them off, like some kind of doting, yet stunning, auntie.

Jones, first back in the car, with Jenny navigating Isadora, made the call to McNally on the handheld. He picked up the call immediately.

"Jones? What news from Saoirse Bradley?"

"We've been barking up the wrong tree. She's the one with the money, she's Mainstay Holdings Ltd and the secrecy is due to her connection with a known paramilitary family."

"Really? Which family?"

"Saoirse Bradley was once Saoirse Reid. The daughter of Kenny Reid and sister of Caragh Reid, over in Andersonstown."

"Mother of God! You've got to be kidding?" McNally exclaimed. The Reids had only been mentioned in passing days earlier in Hillsborough. "Why didn't we know this? Eric Rogers must've known, surely?"

"No idea," Jones said. "I can't believe Orla Massey was in the dark too. It seems inconceivable."

"I'll ask them both, believe you me! But I'm guessing it's not happy families between the Reid's since their father's death?"

"Apparently not, McNally. Saoirse Bradley reckons her family have tried to kill her on numerous occasions. But the Reid family connection opens up a directory of potential killers, doesn't it?"

"Absolutely. I've just left this meeting at The Europa with Jube and the NUC President. It's not at all what we were expecting. Philip Bradley, until the past six months, has been absolutely whiter than white. Almost untouchably professional, efficient and a brilliant constituency MP. The President of the NUC was fawning over him."

"Do we believe him?" Isadora chimed in, having manoeuvred the car onto the main road.

"Aye, I think so," McNally answered. "The President was aware of Bradley's recent indiscretions with drugs but reckons something or someone triggered this. That this was wholly out of character. What about Mrs Bradley? Did she give you any leads?"

"Aside from her entire family and a who's who of republican freedom fighters that wanted her dead? I think you might describe those as leads, but I'm new to this," Jones noted, with a large dose of sarcasm.

"Alright, Columbo. But I think we need to force things a little. We need to get our noses to the ground and sniff out who might be on the long list. I'll speak to Bristow about their meeting with the McCool family and I'll meet you back at the Barracks." McNally, in his usual manner, didn't sign off. The handheld simply went dead.

"I'm not sure how," Isadora said, having adopted her normal rallying style on the main road. "But we seem to have done the opposite of narrowing down our suspect list."

The journey back to Thiepval took place at a ferocious pace, as everyone tried to understand what they'd just heard. Jenny played Jones' 'His N Hers' Pulp cassette loudly and they sang along to 'Babies'. This was a useful respite from the Operation Mainstay headache and the growing list of questions.

EIGHTEEN

Sam Jacob's hasty relocation to a safe house situated just outside Belfast and away from prying eyes had resulted in him being forced into the wilderness. Or that's how he saw it. He was in a tiny cottage in Eden Vale, on the towpath next to the Lagan Navigation and accessible only via an isolated lock-keeper's path on the very outskirts of Belfast.

If Sam had been holidaying with his parents and little sister, this would have been a relaxing rural retreat away from the hustle and bustle of city life. As it was, Sam was alone and scared witless. The protection officer, sitting in a silver Ford Fiesta only yards away in a small clearing, looked half asleep and seemed to have a never-ending supply of sandwiches. He was hardly poised and ready for action.

The main double window on the front of the two-bedroomed cottage had a view over the canal, or that's what Sam assumed it was. He'd never heard of a navigation before. There was a long single steel bar running alongside the water to protect the walkers and joggers on the towpath. Greeting the visitors was a variety of wildfowl which gracefully glided up and down the water and foraged in a large reed bank only metres from the cottage's front door. He could hear the cawing and hooting of birds, the rustle of the wind as it blew through the stubby fledgling ash and rowan trees, and he could see the quaking pine trees and conifers further down the towpath. It was one part beautiful and the other part utterly terrifying, as every noise represented a risk. Every sound was the big man, in his fishing hat and green gilet, looking for Sam. Only it wasn't. It was another light gust of wind gently changing the view from the window.

The cottage itself was stark. The kitchen was a triumph of budget-end white goods, cooker and kettle, with a toaster unfathomably hidden in a cupboard. The zero-style crockery and cutlery wouldn't have been out of place in a 1960s cottage hospital. The two bedrooms were identically white with pastel yellow duvets and a single MFI-style wardrobe with three drawers. The only bathroom seemed immediately cold when you walked in and had an intriguing avocado-coloured suite and a shower that was controlled by rubber suckers placed over the hot and cold taps.

His current solitary existence was only punctuated by the television in an otherwise liberally furnished room. There was a brown sofa and matching armchairs and, in the corner, a pine table and four dining chairs. The only interesting piece of artwork was a large framed black-and-white photo above the entrance to the kitchen. This was a cityscape of Londonderry, entitled 'The Walled City'. Nobody had attempted to scrawl out the 'London' element of the city name, so Sam guessed this was perhaps a recent addition to the decor.

As he stared out of the window, watching the hazy orange sun slowly dip behind the conifers, he was aware of another car pulling up. He guessed this was a change of personnel, and maybe Sandwich Man (as he'd nick-named him) was at the end of his shift. But as the car pulled alongside the Fiesta, he began to doubt this was anyone from the police. The car in question was a 1985 Ford Capri Mk III with four headlamps, a black slatted grille, and with a black rear spoiler. It was resplendent in canary yellow and was shining immaculately.

Sam watched as the driver's door opened and a woman, probably in her very early twenties, stepped out of the car and banged on the door of the Fiesta. Sandwich man sat up in his seat, brushed the breadcrumbs off his navy-blue police-issue sweater, and opened the window. Words were exchanged. The woman didn't seem happy, but the conversation seemed professional, and Sam peered out of the window as she strolled towards the cottage.

She wore an oversized long red and black-striped jumper (seemingly channelling Minnie the Minx), a micro-skirt with a thick leather belt, black ripped tights and platformed Doctor Martens, also in red. Her hair was jet black and had been manipulated into two shoulder-length pigtails. She had a full face of dark make up. Her Ray Bans were still wedged on the top of her head, and she looked more likely to be heading to an alternative club or a Nirvana concert than to Sam's little cottage. But here she was, knocking at the door.

Sam sped away from the window and looked through the hole in the front door. He had received instructions not to open the door unless the protection officer had agreed it was safe. Sandwich man, still sloped back in the seat of his Fiesta, flashed the car's headlights at Sam and gave him the thumbs-up. Carefully, Sam opened the door.

"Hello Sam. I'm Wendy Watson. I'm from the security service. Before you say anything, I realise I'm probably not what you were expecting. And, if I'm honest, I wasn't expecting this assignment either. But shit happens."

Wendy, who had now stepped through the porch and into the tiny living room, had a small black rucksack on her back and swiftly took it off and laid it on a pouffe in the centre of the room. Sam was immediately transfixed by her. He felt himself blushing, embarrassingly.

"I've gathered together as much food as I can. I have six cans of

Harp Lager, pizza, some hob nobs, a pint of milk which is out-of-date today, four tea bags and a box of chocolate Animal Biscuits I stole from a friend. Well, I say friend, he's an imbecile who had the hots for me for a while."

Sam looked down at the stuff and grabbed one of the cans of lager. He noticed a large mobile phone in a leather pouch. He'd not seen one before.

"You're not saying much, kid. Are you alright?" Wendy ventured.

"I'm bored and a bit worried," Sam admitted, trying not to blush at Wendy again, who he'd taken quite a shine to.

"Boredom, I can help with. I've got a Sega Mega Drive in the Capri. We can play that until our eyes fall out, if you want. I'm brilliant at it, though. So, don't get disappointed if I thrash your arse." Sam instantly smiled at Wendy's words. He was very keen on the Mega Drive idea.

"You have no reason to be scared. I'm here now and the protection officer is outside, and he's armed," Wendy said in her most reassuring voice.

"Armed with sandwiches? He's been eating them since we got here. That's why I've called him Sandwich Man." Sam replied.

"Oh, I like that. That's a great name. Are you hungry? I've got a frozen pizza here. Is pepperoni OK for you, Sam?" He smiled again and eagerly grappled at the pizza box. All this panicking was hungry work.

"You don't look like someone from the security service," Sam began. "No offence, but you seem a little, er, leftfield to be here protecting me."

"Leftfield. Yeah. I can go with that." Wendy laughed, pulling her jumper down beyond her fingertips for comfort. "But let's get one thing straight. I'm not protecting you. I'm here to chat and to take your mind off things. Seamus, out there in the awful Fiesta, with the sandwich addiction - he's protection. I'm actually a technician. I work in labs normally, but this is day one for me here in NI. It's a new job and I'll do as they tell me. I sailed into Larne Harbour earlier today on the ferry. I brought the Capri too. You like it?"

"Oh, I adore it. It's a hell of a car. But can we eat pizza and play Sonic now?" Sam asked, his spirits lifted somewhat.

Wendy, who was actually far more nervous than she was willing to show, smiled and headed to the kitchen. She opened one of the cans of lager for herself and took a long pull of it. She would try to build some camaraderie between them. But being personable for an entire night was going to stretch her people skills and she doubted her Jiu Jitsu moves were at the level that she could take down a gun-toting criminal.

Back at Thiepval, the Topaz team of Isadora, Jones, and Jenny had decamped to the bar at the barracks. The sun had now all but vanished, and the initial coolness of the early evening had given way to a warming breeze as the temperature surprisingly notched up a few degrees. Jones was famished and was looking forward to a few cool ones.

As they entered through the main double doors, he was surprised to see Tom and Carl sitting with McNally and Marie Bristow at a corner table away from the empty bar. As the trio walked over to join them, McNally stood up and pulled a few more seats to the table. These were unlikely bar-room companions, Jones thought.

"Okay, Sergeant Bristow and I have been thinking about how best to infiltrate the local information at the heart of this case," McNally explained.

"Local information?" Jones clarified.

"Aye. We know victim number two, George McCool, lived in Strabane and was well known in that area. But we have another, as yet surname-less, second witness or suspect. The fella we believe is called Andrew, with a tear-shaped tattoo."

"Understood. But why are Tom and Carl here? Aren't they YCU technicians?" Jenny queried. Tom and Carl watched on, both with pints of lager, Carl looking slightly wide-eyed from his sudden escalation into operational duty.

"Indeed," Bristow confirmed. "But your friends here are completely anonymous. They have no links back to the RUC and that's dead handy for us." McNally was nodding confidently, but Jones was wondering whether he'd actually spent any time with Tom and Carl. Had he remembered their last foray into sensitive operations at the Black Bull in Ruislip, where they were nearly beaten to death by Stephen Finch?

"Can't you use us?" Jenny asked. "We're fairly anonymous round here, too."

"There would only need to be one loose lipped RUC officer and we'd be in trouble. They've all seen your faces," Bristow answered. Jones and Jenny knew she was right. But that didn't stop Jones inwardly cringing at throwing Carl into any operational role.

McNally took the reins. "So, with Wonder Woman still off the radar since her call yesterday, our only other opportunity is to gather more intelligence from the scene of the second murder. This, confidentially, is a pub called Hunter's Arms in Ballyramsey. The landlord 'Wee' Joe McCartney has been an informer of Massey's for the past few years. The pub is used as a local meeting venue for paramilitary groups. His life relies on this information staying totally private."

"Wee Joe will tell his locals that he's off for a few weeks to have his tonsils removed or something. We'll fly him somewhere nice, with his son. The brewery will send in two temporary managers to run the pub in his absence. This is where Tom and Carl come in. Carl has experience of working at The Jericho in Milton and Tom handled himself really well undercover in the Templeman Building."

"Do you feel confident about this, lads?" Jones asked Tom and Carl.

"Well, we've only known for about twenty-five minutes. But on the face of it, I think we can pull it off. Mr Singh is working on a prototype in the QD, but we can ask him to help us rig up the pub with microphones and receivers," Tom explained.

"Yep. Eyes and ears everywhere. That's the ultimate aim," Bristow agreed. "We need as much intelligence as possible. The MI5 forensic team will be finished in the function room this evening and we will then liaise with Wee Joe to formulate the plan. This is the only potential spanner in the works."

Three soldiers in civvies walked into the bar, about six feet away from the group, and therefore, the conversation soon tailed off. A small balding man in a red waistcoat arrived behind the bar to serve the newcomers.

"You are going to have to be very careful. When the pub is open, you'll need to focus on being barmen and serving the locals. Nothing else. You're going to arouse a certain amount of suspicion because you're English. But, if you play it calmly and carefully, they'll get used to you. Especially if this is very temporary," McNally explained. "Just don't do anything stupid or bring attention to yourselves."

There was a momentary silence amongst the team as the plan sunk in.

McNally and Bristow disappeared back to the YCU rooms, and both said their goodbyes to the group. McNally slapped Tom and Carl on the back, as if thanking them for volunteering, and he was gone. The chances are, he'd be back later to join the others for a drink. Isadora pulled herself up onto a bar stool and ordered drinks for herself, Jones, and Jenny.

"Lads, can I get you a drink?" Isadora called over to Tom and Carl, as the red-waistcoated barman sidled over to take the order.

"Two lagers, please Isadora," Carl replied. "Have you got any snacks?"

"Only nuts and crisps," the barman replied. "We have plain, salt and vinegar, smoky bacon and Worcester sauce crisps. Oh, and we have these wee bags of bacon fries."

"Two bags of bacon fries!" Tom and Carl chorused together. Isadora glanced at Jenny in dismay, who shrugged her shoulders.

"If you two act like this on the mission, you know they'll kill you, don't you? This isn't a game. You can't behave like toddlers," Jones reminded the lads, picking up on the vibes from Jenny and Isadora.

"We won't let anyone down," Carl responded. "I have almost no idea what's going on. I didn't entirely listen to what Mr McNally said, but I can run a bar. So, in my head, if I don't know what I shouldn't be saying or doing, I'll be safe."

"That sounds insane. But he's got a point," Tom agreed. "Carl's only dangerous with information. But you have my word, we will be on our best behaviour. It's just a shame Wendy's not here. She'd have loved this. The undercover work, setting up the microphones and receivers around the bar, she'd have been in seventh heaven."

Jones took a sip of his first pint of the day. It was a rather late to break the ice at 7.45pm, but he kicked back and attempted to relax as the plans circled in his head. Around him, Jenny had started on the vodka and orange, whilst Isadora was abstaining, ordering a Club Lemon to ease her thirst.

A few hundred feet away from the bar, Virginia Curry was sitting outside on the patio table next to her office. She had finished marking the test scores from the recent YCU module exams and now needed some relaxation. She poured herself a small gin and tonic, kicked aside her linen slip-on espadrilles and picked up her Ngaio Marsh novel. She'd had a banging headache for most of the day and was grateful for the peace. She'd have one drink before disappearing to her quarters for an early night, she thought.

It was then that her handheld buzzed into life. The red LED light blinked, and she instantly pushed the receive button.

"Virginia? This is Wendy. I couldn't raise anyone else. I'm really sorry to disturb you so late."

"Go ahead, Wendy. How are things with Sam?" Virginia was eyeing her glass of gin and tonic, wondering whether she'd need to suddenly dash out.

"Absolutely fine. But we've been chatting, and he's just remembered something which sounds pretty crucial, and I thought I'd tell you straightaway. Maybe you can pass onto McNally?"

"This is exactly why you're there, lovely. What's he said?"

"Sam said he was mowing lawns all the way round Ballycastle, especially the large houses in Primrose Grove. He was very well organised and gave every one of his clients his contact details."

"That's okay. We're aware of his cards. We have someone stationed in his student halls. If they try to ring him, we'll be able to trace them, and it'll give us a lead."

"No, that's just it. He also gave them a booking form. His parents are listed on there as emergency contacts. Their address and telephone number are printed on the form," Wendy explained.

"Goodness me. That's certainly a concern," Virginia sounded alarmed. "This means Sam's parents are now at risk. We need to sort that."

"But that's not the worst of it. I gave him my new Nokia mobile phone to ring his parents. Just to check in, like. There was no chat about the case. It appears Sam's little sister hasn't arrived home from her swimming lessons tonight. His father went to collect her, and she'd already gone." Wendy sounded fraught and Virginia fell silent for a few seconds.

"Virginia, please tell me that someone from the RUC has already been in touch with Surrey Constabulary? This is all covered? They had someone watching them? A family liaison officer?" Wendy asked.

"Oh God, Wendy, I really don't know." Alarm bells were now ringing in Virginia's head. "I don't know the procedure.

Leave it with me. I'll ring you back on the handheld when I get answers."

Virginia downed her drink in one, put her shoes back on and raced to find McNally and Bristow. This suddenly felt horribly wrong.

Nineteen

Jube Spencer had spent the day with Clive Gentry, the MI5 head honcho in Northern Ireland. They had discussed Saoirse Bradley's leadership role in Mainstay Holdings and the NUC's ringing endorsement for her husband. Philip Bradley seemed cleaner than first thought, but there was still more digging to do.

The seed corn of Mainstay's accounts was probably dirty money. Kenny Reid's inheritance to Saoirse was unlikely to be just the profits of his skip hire company or his small bar on Donegal Road. These, as Jube and Clive both knew, were probably fronts. The Reid Family hardly shied away from their criminal lifestyle. They were just never caught and punished. That inheritance must have funded Saoirse's property empire, but how clean was it now?

This made the pair discuss whether there were links to other significant security threats. Had they missed something? Why had Philip Bradley been killed? Why was there such a desperate need to hush-up any witnesses? This didn't seem the style of the most prolific crime families. Both Jube and Clive believed they were dealing with a big-name killer. Someone who couldn't afford to be found but, conversely, seemed to float about easily.

Clive disappeared back to Palace Barracks late in the afternoon and Jube had thought about a walk around Belfast City Centre. He would need a light coat and maybe an umbrella. He was jaded after a long day and was hoping a constitutional would give him fresh impetus. He'd planned to exit The Europa Hotel, head past the glorious Grand Opera House and then cross over the road and stroll towards City Hall, but he was stopped in his tracks when a call to his bedroom came.

"Mr Spencer, this is the hotel switchboard. I have a call for you."

"Very well, put them through." Jube sat on his desk chair and grabbed a notebook.

"Jube? This is McNally. We have an issue. Is this a secure line?"

"Talk to me Declan," Jube replied, sensing the urgency.

"The wee lad, the witness to the Bradley shooting. His young sister has gone missing in England. She's no-showed at home after an after-school swimming lesson. We may need to escalate things."

"Eric would have that detail covered, I'm sure. There'll be local police liaison dealing with the family if the young lad is in a safe house."

"Not according to Sergeant Marie Bristow. She's with me now. She can find no file notes relating to any liaison with the Surrey Constabulary. In fact, there's nothing relating to contact with Sam Jacobs' family at all."

"That can't be true." Jube shook his head and ran through a quick list of options. "Okay, McNally. I'll speak to Thames House and see if we can line up a local MI5 field officer to chat to the family. This is very unusual, though. This is a police matter."

"Surrey Police are absolutely aware of the disappearance. The lad's parents have telephoned the local station to report the missing child. She's eight years old; she shouldn't be out alone. But I don't believe they are aware of the link to the murders."

"I'll see if I can get hold of Eric or his Chief Constable and shake a few trees. If I get nowhere, I'll set Clive on them. Keep me informed, McNally. Let's not give up hope that she's simply got lost or is round a friend's house." Jube put the receiver down and thought for a second.

He walked over to the full-length mirror next to the wardrobe in his bedroom and saw that the vein in his forehead was throbbing. This was his telltale sign of stress. Jube could deal with violence, terrorism, and even the barbaric nature of war. But harming kids? That was his tipping point.

He half-sprinted round the bed to his leather briefcase and pulled out a small black contacts book. Written in pencil, towards the back, was the personal telephone number of Eric Rogers. A man so difficult that even calling his home repelled Jube slightly. But he put that to one side and dialled the number.

"Good evening, Belfast 762, Rogers speaking." Jube had never heard such a formal telephone manner in his long career.

"Hello Eric. Apologies for the late call. This is Jube Spencer. Can I ask you a quick question? It's a tad urgent."

"Go ahead, Spencer. I'm just about to have dinner though, so please keep it short," Rogers replied.

"When Coleraine RUC transferred Sam Jacobs to a safe house, did your team make his next of kin aware? His parents?" Jube inquired.

"Well, he's just over eighteen. We have no need to. I'm sure the boy would have been asked to make them aware himself. Why? What's happened?"

"We believe his sister may have been abducted. I'm wondering whether you liaised with Surrey Police to cover this eventuality," Jube was already suspecting the worse. Rogers had dropped the ball.

"Crikey." Rogers began. "How long has she been gone?"

"Unclear. She was due home earlier from swimming. She didn't show up."

"Well, as you know, that doesn't even merit a mis-per operation at the moment. She needs to be gone twenty-four hours, as per protocol. The local police can watch things. She could be with friends for all we know."

"She's a vulnerable eight-year-old, Eric. Her brother, who witnessed a murder, listed his parents' address and telephone number on his booking forms. Do I really have to paint you a picture?" Jube was beginning to lose his temper; his vein throbbed. He reached down into the mini-bar and pulled out a miniature bottle of Bushmills and poured it into his bedside glass.

"Yes. That's concerning," Rogers admitted. "Very well. I'll contact Surrey. I know their Chief Superintendent. We were at Hendon together. How much do I tell him? As your lot are running the show now."

"Tell him that her brother is the sole witness in a high-profile murder. That'll probably cause a flurry of activity in Surrey Police HQ. Isn't this obvious? It doesn't seem to have ruffled your feathers at all, Eric."

"You just caught me at a bad time, Spencer." In the background, Jube could hear a dog barking. It sounded huge but could equally have been a whippet with a deep voice.

"Shut up, Sejanus! Down, boy. Sejanus, stop! Bloody dog. I'll ring Surrey now, and I'll ring you back at your hotel afterwards." Eric Rogers ended the conversation, clearly still fighting with the family pet.

Jube Spencer picked up his glass and swirled the whisky in the bottom before taking a short swig. The burning sensation in the pit of his stomach warmed his body. As he did so, and he filed away Eric's incompetence, he tried to put himself in the shoes of the murderer.

'I've killed a man, someone with enough profile to cause a stir,' he thought. 'I've then killed one of my goons who sold a photo to the press. That's got to be a warning to the others to keep schtum. Do we ignore that one? Is that a distraction?' he said to himself.

'So why would you kidnap a child? The sister of the only

witness? Is he trying to bring the witness out into the open?' he considered. 'No, that can't be it.'

Jube paced up and down, undertaking an almost military turn at the end of the sofa, and circled the room again.

'Is he looking for profile? Perhaps to show he has the reach and influence in England? But why? Or maybe they think Sam heard more than he did? The woman's name? The business transaction? That might make more sense. Yes, that seems sensible.'

Jube sat back down on the bed and took another pull of his whiskey. He never drank alone normally, but he had to quell that throbbing in his temple, and things just wouldn't add up. This whole drama seemed too pre-arranged. The two murders, one very high-profile, the police swooping in and whisking Sam Jacobs to a safe house and now the possible kidnap. It all seemed like a purposeful drama.

Jube waited for Eric Rogers to call back and confirm the transfer of intelligence between the RUC and Surrey Constabulary, but his brain continued working at a feverish pace. An idea was shaping. Maybe a ghost was at play here. Perhaps the confidence from the double murders came from the murderer, knowing he simply couldn't be caught. Ghosts can't be imprisoned or detained. They can come and go as they please.

As he sketched out ideas in his notebook, it occurred to him that Saoirse Bradley had married a protestant unionist for love and thus crucified her relationship with her notorious family. But somehow, she still got half of Kenny Reid's vast estate. That seemed odd. Jube had met Kenny Reid and he didn't seem the kind to make a mistake with his last will and testament.

She has a huge property portfolio across Ireland, accounts in the Turks and Caicos Islands, and a bloody huge yacht, not to mention the Mainstay Barns in Millisle. Her sister Caragh Reid, Jube knew, was totally in control of the criminal assets Kenny left behind in Andersonstown. Protection rackets, drugs, rumours of people trafficking and, naturally, traditional links with terrorist networks that themselves require an innovative business model.

What if Saoirse and Caragh hadn't fallen out at all? What if Mainstay Holdings Ltd was still laundering the money coming in from the Andersonstown operation? Could the rift itself be another front? It all seemed possible and yet utterly insane in the same breath.

Whilst Jube was operating in vague possibilities and fairy stories, the thought occurred to him that Kenny Reid might not be dead at all. Perhaps Kenny was the murdering ghost? Maybe the Lower Belfast Brigade had shot the wrong man, or he'd survived? Could the body have been swapped? Stranger things had happened in Belfast.

Kenny was a man born and raised in Cork but then spent the rest of his life in West Belfast. He didn't have an Irish-American voice, but it would have been an unusual accent for the English kid to decipher, and Kenny Reid certainly matched the rest of the description. He was a large man, a sharpshooter and utterly heartless.

Jube shook his head again. Maybe these ideas were the ravings of an exhausted man and most of the hypotheses could be discounted as speedily as the thoughts had formed in his head.

But what use was Philip Bradley and why kill him? Perhaps Philip opened the gates to the loyalist communities for the Reid Empire? That might be a stretch, but it was just about possible. Or if Philip was aware of Kenny's survival and was privy to the business deal to launder the money, there's always the chance he'd gone rogue, got greedy or refused to sacrifice some of his loyalist beliefs for the benefit of the Reid's ambitions. Maybe Saoirse and Philip really did fall in love and Kenny Reid found a way of abusing that? The jigsaw was scattered.

Jube pulled another little bottle of Bushmills from the minibar and poured it into the water glass. These were theories, that's all. But no-one else had pulled any rabbits out of hats yet. Jube's

Bushmills' brainstorm was worth careful consideration. He wrote some more notes and thought on. For a few moments, he'd forgotten about the situation back in Surrey. The Jacobs family was missing an eight-year-old. A call from Eric Rogers brought him back to his senses.

"Spencer, I've just spoken to my opposite number at Surrey police," Rogers explained. Jube wondered if he'd found time for his supper, too. "I admit, he was surprised that we hadn't made contact before. But I've ensured Sergeant Bristow is now the link, and we'll help the Surrey team bring the parents fully up to speed."

"I can't help but think this is a bloody shambles, Eric. We should have linked up with Surrey long before now. Imagine how those parents are feeling? We need to help find that girl. This was on your watch."

"There are certainly lessons to be learned. I'll do all I can, this end. But please leave the police liaison to us now. Good police work will find the girl, believe me. I'll leave you to the rest of your evening. Goodnight Spencer."

McNally would want to send someone over to Surrey to interview the parents. But he resisted the temptation to ring McNally straightaway. Instead, he put his brown brogues back on, straightened up his yellow and red tie, and grabbed his tweed jacket from the back of his hotel door. If his various theories about the Reid family had any legs at all, he needed to speak to the only person who could give him the background to the Kenny Reid shooting, the officer who arrested the Lower Belfast Brigade lads who shot such a high-profile target.

Jube Spencer rang down to the reception of The Europa Hotel and arranged a taxi to City Hospital. He needed an audience with Orla Massey, if she was well enough.

The journey to City Hospital was brief, the taxi driver unusually quiet, and Jube made a point of stopping on the way at a newsagent to pick up a few magazines and some flowers. Having not eaten, he also bought himself a white corned beef and pickle sandwich, the last on the shelf, and a Twix. The taxi driver watched on in dismay as Jube left crumbs on his back seat.

It felt odd selecting magazines for a woman who kept her personal life so very private, so he settled on a home décor-themed title and an upmarket fashion glossy. That would cover all bases. Had Jube been at home, just ten miles from the hospital, he'd have bought her a book, one from his own collection. Maybe a John le Carré or Len Deighton title. But his house, a wonderful three bedroomed affair in the suburbs of Holywood, had been rented out during his secondment to Balfron Tower.

As the driver dropped him off, Jube weaved through the families leaving the hospital as visiting hours were ending. He made his way through the entrance concourse up to the bank of lifts. City Hospital, on Lisburn Road, was effectively a huge tower block and stuck out like a sore thumb on the local cityscape. He found his way to floor seven and spotted the two protection officers, both armed, flanking a side room opposite the critical care facility.

Jube showed both officers his ID, and they looked quizzically at each other.

"We haven't been told to expect any visitors," the officer on the left side, with an impressive moustache, explained. Jube, generally a very calm and dignified man, smiled and was primed to explain this was an urgent matter, when he heard Massey's voice projecting through the closed doors.

"For God's sake, let him through!" she shouted. "He's an old friend and goodness knows I need the company."

"She's making a recovery, then?" Jube laughed, and both protection officers half-smiled knowingly. Jube imagined that guarding Orla Massey wasn't the easiest of assignments. They pushed the double doors open for him and he assessed the scene. Massey was in a grey hospital gown, her hair pulled back into a ponytail and her injuries were obvious. She looked gaunt and pale and was attempting to move herself up on the bed. Jube offered his help, and she grabbed his arm to pull herself upwards.

Jube had seen his fair share of blast injuries in his time in Northern Ireland. High explosives cause skull fractures, fractured bones, head injuries, and a series of other nasty conditions prefixed by the word 'blast'. Blast lung (which was generally fatal), blast eyes, belly, ear and blast brain. The latter could last for years and sometimes only showed itself long after the actual explosion. This might lead to depression or anxiety and was linked to an injury to the brain parenchyma - even with no direct injury to the head. Where blast injuries aren't fatal, they cause such long-lasting damage that it's like a punishment that keeps giving, a constant reminder of what unfolded and how they miraculously survived.

"It's good to see you, Orla," Jube smiled, trying not to focus on the collection of clinical instruments around her bed.

"It's good to see anyone," she replied. "You'd think I had Ebola or something, and those two muppets are hardly chatty," she pointed outside to the two officers.

"What's the prognosis?"

"Well, where do I start? I keep being told I've been lucky. But with a broken pelvis, collapsed lung, three broken ribs and a large laceration down my left leg, I don't feel lucky. But it's my hearing that's the main thing. It's like living in an echo chamber."

"I'm so sorry, Orla. This is just awful for you, and we are all aware it should never have happened," Jube said, noticing that Massey was focusing hard on his face as he spoke. Her hearing must be badly affected, he thought.

"Well, it would never have happened if I'd have been more vigilant. If I'd checked under my car, like we're told every day. It's been ingrained in my very psyche and it's just part of my daily routine. I can't believe I got distracted."

"Don't be too harsh on yourself, Orla. We all get distracted in the moment." Jube could see she'd been thinking about that oversight.

"But, if you're talking about Rogers not assigning me fecking protection, obviously that's never far from my brain, either. It was all so avoidable," she added.

"Declan McNally has given Eric both barrels about that. Believe me," Jube explained. "He laid into him during that meeting with the Secretary of State and Clive Gentry. Eric knows he's screwed up, royally."

"Ah, bless McNally. But I'll get out of here. I'll make a recovery. And when I do, I'll make Eric's life a living hell and then, ideally, take his job." Massey mustered a laugh, gritting her teeth as she did so, as the pain from her pelvis took hold. But Jube knew she meant it and he was delighted to hear her so focused on recovery.

"What news on catching the bastards that did this to me? I'm guessing no-one has yet claimed responsibility?"

"No," Jube replied. "I don't think they will either. I don't think this is your regular targeted car bombing. That's part of the reason why I'm here. Do you remember Kenny Reid?"

"Wow. There's a name from the past. Yeah, he was very much on my radar. I must have arrested various extended members of that family twenty or thirty times. I was on the scene when he was shot. His wee daughter Caragh's pulling the strings these days, I believe. Although she's virtually a recluse now. No-one has seen her for years," Massey replied.

"What about Saoirse?"

"Met her once; nice woman. She's quite the looker, but both are very pretty. She went to Kenny's funeral with her husband, but they sat right at the back. They were shunned. There was certainly no sisterly love in evidence."

"You knew her husband was Philip Bradley? It appears we didn't have that detail in our initial briefing from Eric. Which I find a wee bit worrying." Jube was perplexed by this omission but knew he had to keep Massey sweet.

"Of course I knew!" she responded, again grimacing with pain as she spoke. "But I had almost zero to do with them. Eric Rogers led on all the anti-terrorism stuff. My role was limited to the donkey work. I was dealing with the actual body count, rather than the strategy behind it. That was all Rogers' bag. He wrote the briefs, updated the files. You'll find details about the Bradley's marriage in all my notes. Ask Marie for them, be my guest. Tell you what, I'll even make a few calls myself and get the full background."

"Thanks Orla, that's really helpful, but don't do too much. We need you back healthy and firing on all cylinders," Jube smiled, reassuringly. He needed her onside. "And do you buy the big family fall out? Between the sisters?"

"I never heard much about the schism. I'll find out more. But with Philip being a prod, I can't imagine they had cosy family meals out together. The whole thing was a fecking unusual arrangement." Massey struggled to pull herself forward again as she spoke.

"That's what I found really confusing, Orla. Eric's on the front line and yet no-one seems to be aware of Saoirse and Caragh's problems. The issues over the Will, Saoirse being targeted by the Andersonstown family and the hostilities. Saoirse's house is allegedly like Fort Knox." Orla Massey, tired from the sudden switch back into police mode, adjusted the drip on her left arm which had become hooked on the bed guard.

"So, what are you thinking?" Massey responded after a moment of contemplation.

"Firstly, I'm thinking Kenny Reid might be alive."

"Yeah, I guessed that might be your train of thought. But he's dead, Jube. One hundred per cent. I saw the body myself. He had half of his face blown off."

"It was definitely him? He was recognisable?"

"Well, kind of, but you're making me doubt myself now. There'll be photos of the body at the morgue. That can be checked out if you ask Bristow. But remember, Bradley's killer had some kind of Irish American accent. Kenny was as Irish as they come. Cork and Belfast twangs clearly evident, a bit of a bizarre mix, but not a yank."

"Okay. Let's strike that idea off, then. But I'm also thinking that Bradley was shot because he went rogue or against orders. I'm wondering whether the Reid family has been using Saoirse Bradley's apparently clean accounts to launder the money coming in from the Andersonstown operation. The schism would have to be a hoax then too."

"Yeah. It's plausible, especially the money laundering aspect. That's a clever thought, Jube. If I wasn't half dead, I'd be all over that like a rash."

"Sorry, Orla. Just a few more questions, I promise. I can see you're flagging. What about Eric Rogers? Why would he be surprised by the Reid split? They're one of the biggest crime families in the North. Surely Eric would have been aware of this? He'd have known the family dynamics?"

Massey frowned. "You're asking the wrong person. But I have severe doubts about Rogers. He's a wee English weasel, and there's more going on with him than meets the eye. He's a freemason, probably in the Orange Order. I mean, he could be in the Illuminati for all I know. Otherwise, I don't understand how he's risen through the ranks. It's a fecking mystery. Pass me that drink there."

Jube handed her a plastic beaker of water and she sipped whilst holding her finger up to explain she wasn't finished.

"However, let's be clear. Eric knew about the sisterly conflict, the schism and all of the other information about the Reid family business. He'd know every detail. I'd be more interested in why he didn't share it."

"So, you're thinking Rogers could be corrupt, Orla?"

"Absolutely, yeah," Massey instantly responded. "He's a smarmy wee bastard. But proving corruption is going to be challenging, even for the sneaky beakies at MI5." Orla gave a little whimper as she moved awkwardly and Jube stood up, offering to help.

"I'll ring Thames House. I'll get them to do some digging on Eric Rogers, behind the scenes. I have a few favours to pull at GCHQ too. Maybe something will come to the fore." Jube was writing in his notebook again. He'd neatly crossed out a few ideas and adapted others, as was his style.

"Good plan, Jube," she replied, stifling a yawn. "I'd love to help but..."

"I understand. You're tired. I should go," Jube said, feeling guilty. "I nearly forgot to give you these." He reached into his carrier bag and passed over the House & Home and Ulster Tatler magazines, as well as the bunch of marigolds.

"That's kind of you," Orla responded, picking up the House & Home magazine and flicking through. "Not sure I'll be decorating the flat for a while. God knows what Georgie's been up to in there."

"Georgie? Boyfriend? Girlfriend? Sorry, shouldn't ask, that's your business," he inquired, suddenly feeling awkward.

"He's a ginger cat, Jube, you dope. Bristow's feeding him for me. I think he accidentally saved my life. I jumped out of the car to look for him when the bomb went off."

"Wow. We have Georgie to thank for your continued existence? Praise be!" Jube laughed. Orla Massey chuckled and put her hand on Jube's forearm as he stood up.

"Promise me," she implored. "That you'll keep me in the loop. I love your theories. Don't just let me rot in here. My brain still works. Mostly."

"I'll be in touch," Jube replied. "You'll be the first to know if I dig up any dirt on Eric Rogers." Massey gave him a little grin and they said their goodbyes. Soon, Jube was heading back down into the lift and looking for a taxi back to The Europa.

In the meantime, the impressively moustachioed protection officer took to his radio.

"Spencer has gone, Sir. Just this second," he said into the small black police issue radio, before resuming his watch on the injured DCI.

Twenty

The morning sun was bursting through the blinds in the Thiepval Briefing Room, and Jenny, Isadora, and Jones were all up with the lark for the early morning briefing. Likewise, McNally and Virginia had been in conference with Mr Singh to discuss the technical needs at the Hunter's Arms operation in Ballyramsey. Now everyone was furiously taking notes on today's plans, whilst mainlining coffee. The time was just after 06.45am.

"Emma Jacobs is 8-years-old, and she enjoys swimming, badminton and is a member of the local Brownies. She is not what you might describe as streetwise," Bristow explained. "I've been on the telephone to Surrey off and on since 9pm last night and all they have so far is a report of a blonde-haired girl, matching Emma's description, walking through a local park towards the Guildford branch of Safeway at about 8.15pm. Since then, nothing." Bristow scanned the room.

"They are taking this extremely seriously, as you can imagine. It'll be all over regional television. They have helicopters on standby, and they're asking for volunteers to help with the search," Bristow continued.

"Are Surrey expecting us to send someone over to assist?" Jones asked, still surprised that he'd dodged a hangover bullet after last night's exploits.

"It's funny you should say that, Jones. Whilst Surrey can call in specialists from the Met, we really need to interview the parents. Not just to get an understanding of the motives behind Emma's disappearance, but also to look for any other obvious link," Bristow explained, looking tired. She'd clearly not slept and seemed to be leading a skeleton team at Knock Road. Living in Ballymacash, she was balancing her time driving between the RUC HQ and Thiepval.

"I think we need to do this ourselves," McNally replied. "Rogers keeps dropping the ball and sending one of the RUC over is just going to muddy the waters. Jones and Richmond, can you pack your bags for a trip over to England? Maybe an overnighter? Get some intel about the parents and see how the search is going?"

Jones swallowed hard and realised last night's excesses had been a very bad idea. The hangover tap on the shoulder was bound to arrive at some point. This could be inconvenient.

"Absolutely, we'll get over there," Jones responded, looking at Jenny, who nodded.

"Okay, grand. How much does Sam know about his wee sister's disappearance, Marie?" McNally asked.

"Your colleague, Wendy, is with him at the safe house and has been talking him through the missing person procedures. He's also been in communication with his parents. She's doing well for a first assignment," Bristow added.

"I must say, this is all very confusing," Mr Singh pitched in. "I was expecting Wendy here yesterday for an induction and suddenly she's working in witness protection. Wendy is quite brilliant, but she's got quite a short temper and doesn't suffer fools gladly. This kind of work really isn't in her sweet spot."

"He's right," Tom agreed. "Literally, any of us here would have been a more sensible choice. I feel for the lad. How long will she be away?"

"We're talking a matter of days," Bristow replied. "We are short-staffed, and, to her credit, she volunteered. She wanted to be thrown into the action. McNally agreed it." McNally looked at his feet, realising he probably should have mentioned this to the QD team.

"That I can believe," Carl said, smiling. "But we could really do with her at the Hunter's Arms if things get difficult out there. I mean, Tom and I can handle ourselves, but Wendy is on another level altogether."

"Okay," McNally intervened. "Let's move things on. We have a big day ahead of us. Jones and Richmond need to head to England and Marie needs to be back at base. Let's wind this up after a quick update from me."

"I raised Wee Joe McCartney at the Hunter's Arms last night and I'm meeting him at a service station café at 11am. Should Joe green-light the plan, Carl and Tom will be in place this evening. It's the Quiz League and meat raffle tonight, so it'll be busy there. Mr Singh, we'll need you there this afternoon to shape the covert surveillance, the microphones and receivers, around the pub and function room."

"I'm gathering equipment and the three of us will be ready to install when the pub closes after lunch," Mr Singh added. "I'm guessing the forensics team have swept the function room?"

"I've got their report here. It's an odd read. Wee Joe told us the function room hadn't been touched, but it's totally deep-cleaned and sanitised. There's the smell of bleach everywhere. There was not a single scrap of evidence." Bristow gave the report to McNally and Virginia peered over his shoulder.

"There's a mention of petrol," Virginia pointed out. "Does that not link back to the attempted torching of the body of George McCool?"

"Aye, it could do. But it tells us nothing. Forensically, we are nowhere," Bristow answered, still staring at the report. "But I'm going to have to love you and leave you now, folks. I have a meeting with Rogers in an hour."

With the meeting over, Jones felt an urgent need for sustenance. His head was stinging, and he knew he smelt like a brewery. A good fry-up would sort him out, he decided. And they were experts in the dark arts of fry-making in the barracks cafeteria.

He caught Jenny's eye and motioned out of the double doors, their agreed sign for feeding time. Isadora clearly had similar thoughts, and with Marie Bristow heading out of the doors; Virginia on the phone getting flights for England for Jones and Richmond, and the rest of the team devising plans for the Hunter's Arms surveillance operation, it was time for a pre-airport breakfast. Their flights would be much later, Jones convinced himself.

Jenny watched as Isadora manoeuvred out from the large briefing table and explained to McNally that they'd be in the cafeteria should their services be required. This led to three orders for breakfast baps from Tom (ketchup, double bacon), Carl (brown sauce, no egg) and McNally (brown sauce, double everything) as well as a round of buttered toast for Mr Singh.

The cafeteria was still half-full from the breakfast rush and uniformed squaddies were liberally scattered throughout the maze of white-MDF tables. The smell of frying bacon and cigarette smoke hit Jones as he found a seat near to the main exit doors. With the Irish late summer now in full swing, he noted an unnecessary amount of pasty alabaster legs on show from off-duty soldiers and a few shirtless bodies too. Jones couldn't think of anything worse.

Isadora ordered her normal muesli, with added red berries, Jenny an unusually carb-loaded Cookstown sausage sandwich and Jones an almighty breakfast bap, but without the awfulness of fried egg. He added his own personal touch by sprinkling grated mature cheddar cheese over the wonderful local sausages. Jenny, who had become friendly with one of the cashiers, paid for the food, including the batch of orders from the briefing room, and brought the hot drinks over. She had opted for an orange juice instead.

"Is it a legal requirement for soldiers to have those moustaches?" Isadora asked, as Jenny approached the table.

"I'm not sure. But they are quite the fashion statement here. I couldn't grow one, so I won't be joining in. But I see Carl is sprouting something underneath his nose," Jones said.

"Grow a moustache and I'd leave you instantly," Jenny chuckled. "Those things are bloody dreadful. I thought being stuck in a barracks with all these men would make for decent levels of eye candy. But their obsession with facial hair is very off-putting."

"I'm right with you, Jen. Yuk," Isadora agreed.

Jones spied one of the cafeteria staff plotting a route through the rows of tables. She had their breakfasts, plus the brown paper bags full of carbohydrate goodness for the rest of the team. "I'll take these bags back now, before they get cold," he announced, and whisked them off the tray and headed back in the YCU.

He passed the apprehensive-looking YCU recruits, who were ready for another intense programme of physical activity with the army, shaking the hand of Niall for good luck on the way past and giving the thumbs-up sign to the rest of the Echo team. Ailsa was doing her stretches away from Delta and looked fired up and eager.

"Right," Jones called over as he pushed through the double doors. "Breakfast is served." The team eagerly clamoured for their named bags.

"You're a legend," Carl said, unwrapped his bap and created a bite-mark in the bread roll which accounted for almost one-third of it. That, Jones thought, was an impossibly large mouth.

Virginia then stuck her head around the door from her small admin office. "We're in luck," she began. "Jones, you and Jenny are on the next flight to London Gatwick. You need to get up to Aldergrove urgently." Virginia threw the Land Rover keys at Jones, who was still aching to eat his breakfast, and thrust a large yellow briefing folder into his hand. "You'll need this too. Off you go, quick sticks!"

Virginia then darted back into the office. She was deep in preparation for the YCU training camp with the Royal Irish Regiment but was clearly enjoying the buzz.

Jones sprinted back to Isadora and Jenny, who were still chatting, and explained the schedule. He wrapped his own breakfast in a napkin and raced back to the accommodation block to grab some clothes and his Walkman. Jenny wasn't far behind. Isadora stayed behind and people-watched, knowing she'd be spending the rest of the day child-minding Carl and Tom.

It took less than five minutes for the pair to throw all their remaining clean clothes into a holdall, some toiletries and various case notes to accompany the briefing pack, and they headed to the airport. The traffic was light and with Jenny's foot predictably heavy on the accelerator, the twenty-minute journey was soon pared down to sixteen. Jones barely had time to eat.

With the time now 08.10am, Jenny swung the Land Rover into the private car park to the rear of the terminal building and they sprinted to the departure gate for the 08.30am flight, waving their official documentation at anyone who seemed minutely interested. As they sped through the gates, they were stopped by two armed military officials who checked their accreditation documents before pointing them towards the ticket desk. The queue was short and, once aboard, the plane half empty.

"Let's look at what we're dealing with here," Jenny said, as she leafed through the papers. Jones was seated right next to Jenny, with an empty aisle seat and a vacant set of seats behind them, providing some limited confidentiality. Jenny attentively wiped ketchup from Jones' top lip and waited patiently as this apparently highly intelligent man battled with the seatbelt as if it was part of a MENSA examination. He'd already frustratedly fiddled with the holdall for a few minutes trying to locate his Walkman.

"Emma's been missing less than 24-hours and was last seen in a park near a Safeway supermarket in Guildford. That's a train ride or bus journey away from their family home in Ash," she continued.

"She was due home earlier in the evening from swimming, also in Guildford. Do we know how she was supposed to be getting back afterwards?" Jones asked, now successfully strapped in.

"One of the other parents was taking her back to Ash. There's no name listed here for them. Surrey Constabulary believe Emma vanished from the car park outside the swimming pool, at the spot they're normally picked up from. The other girl had popped back inside to use the vending machine. Post-swimming crisps were always a winner for me," Jenny explained. "That was probably her plan, too."

"This all sounds very opportunistic." Jones was speed reading the details as Jenny turned each page. "Or she was being watched, and it was all planned," countered Jenny.

"Yeah. But we're not going over to assist with the disappearance. Are we? We need to ensure there's nothing we've missed in the broader operation. McNally seems to think Eric Rogers has totally lost the plot, so we need to gather as much intel as possible. We need to get to know the parents and Sam's background." Jones had settled back in his seat and was half watching the safety demonstration.

"What are you doing?" Jenny asked.

"Listening to my Walkman. Maybe grabbing forty winks," Jones replied, settling down further.

"Forty winks? You're only nineteen. You sound like my grandad. Read the notes, get your brain in gear! Are you hungover?"

"Hungover? Me?" he smiled. "I've read the notes. I've fully digested them. I'm totally on this," he replied and soon fell fast asleep. As the plane ascended into the cloudy County Antrim skies, Jones was already gently snoring. Jenny read on.

Nearly an hour and a quarter later and a perky, excited Jenny Richmond made her way through the British Airways arrival lounge in North Terminal, Gatwick, closely followed by a groggy Jones, with the large leather holdall dramatically slung over his shoulder like he was carrying a heavy bag of coal. He'd been half-listening to Bandwagonesque by Teenage Fanclub for the past twenty minutes, and even the jauntiness of their pop indie hadn't helped him emerge from his post-breakfast slump. The English weather was predictably miserable and as the clock was now close to 10am, the airport was busier than ever.

They sat in silence on a bench near the exit, awaiting some form of transport to arrive, knowing full well that Virginia would have had this detail in hand. It was no surprise when a man with a small white signboard with the names 'Jones and Richmound' written in block capitals appeared amongst the throng of taxi drivers.

"Richmound?" Jones laughed.

"Let's just go, shall we?" she replied, failing to see the funny side.

The black BMW coasted through the Sussex countryside, crossed the border into Surrey, and stopped at a Little Chef just off the A3. The driver, who had not said a word the entire trip so far, turned to Jones and beckoned towards the half empty restaurant.

"I've been told to drop you here. Someone from Guildford CID is going to update you. I'll stay put." Not waiting for a response, he opened the driver's door and lit a cigarette.

The pair wandered over to the Little Chef and scanned the room for a likely policeman. There were two families happily tucking into grills and Olympic breakfasts and, in the far corner, a large Asian man in a business suit slowly sipping a coffee. He paid absolutely no attention to Jones and Jenny as they walked in. This sealed the deal. He was the policeman.

"Hi, I'm Jenny Richmond and this is my colleague, Jones. We're from the Royal Ulster Constabulary, or we're working with them." The man stood up and shook hands with both before sitting down and unzipping a plastic document wallet.

"Nice to meet you both. I'm DC Amit Khan from Guildford CID. We are actually not currently involved in the mis-per operation with Emma Jacobs, but due to the nature of your enquiries, I'm your liaison."

"You've been chatting to Sergeant Marie Bristow?" Jenny asked.

"Yeah, she's filled me in a little with your investigation. It sounds complicated," he responded, suddenly smiling broadly and easing off the formal façade.

"You could say that. It's a double murder and a pretty murky backstory that could involve organised crime or paramilitaries," Jones explained.

"And Emma's brother, Samuel, he saw one of the killings?"

"Apparently so. He's now in a safe house. Tell us about the Jacobs family, Amit." Jenny was clock-watching and was trying to speed things up. She'd have preferred to meet the Jacobs and hear all this from them. Amit felt a little unnecessary, but it was his patch.

"Okay. Before we start, do you guys want a drink or something to eat? They do a decent breakfast in here."

"We had a 6.45am briefing and I was savagely ripped away from my breakfast," Jones answered. "I was still finishing it as we sped to the airport."

"Oh," Amit chuckled. "Well, maybe an early lunch, then? I'll stick it on Guildford CID expenses."

"You know, I could really murder a toasted ham and cheese sandwich," Jones replied without hesitation. Jenny immediately rolled her eyes in frustration.

"I'll have a sparkling mineral water," she said, half-smiling at Amit, but quickly grabbed her notebook and pen. "Whilst we're waiting, let's get the facts down," she added.

"Okay, I'll crack on. You two don't sound very Irish, if you don't mind me saying," Amit observed.

"Long story," Jones replied. "We were part of a kind-of YTS training scheme in Belfast. It's all very dull. It was a scheme set up in partnership with the Met Police to help with RUC numbers," he lied, probably unnecessarily. Jenny drummed her fingers on the table as a waitress appeared to take the order. Jones ordered his toastie, with crisps on the side, and a large tea.

"So, William and Rosie Jacobs, he's 45 and she's 38. They live on the border of Surrey and Hampshire, in a little village called Ash. They own a semi in a fairly large former council estate called Fogarty Road. They're clean as a whistle and, from what I understand from the Family Liaison Officer. Both are really lovely."

"She's a finance clerk in the local borough council, but until recently also worked as a barmaid in the Dover Arms, a charming little boozer in the centre of the village. They had a few money worries, I think. He's a former squaddie, saw active duty and became a fireman after leaving the army. Salt of the earth people," he added.

"Not being rude," Jenny interrupted. "But we could have established this all for ourselves, surely? Why the pep talk?"

"Good question," Amit smiled. "I'm here to pre-warn you that there's a bit of family history that the Jacobs might not immediately reveal. I think you'll find it interesting. Believe me, I'm not here to waste your time or mine."

"Please continue," Jenny smiled back, realising how she might be coming across. Maybe she'd spent too much time with Orla Massey, she thought.

"Sam and Emma are adopted. Both from the same mother, but as two separate adoptions and years apart. The Jacobs had been fostering other kids for years before deciding to formally adopt. But here's the interesting thing... they were both born at the Royal Victoria Hospital in Belfast."

"You're kidding?" Jenny responded.

"Nope. However, that's as far as we've gone. We haven't pushed it, as Rosie Jacobs is a little sensitive about it all and she's beside herself about Emma's disappearance, naturally."

"So, you're unaware of any contact between Sam and Emma with their birth mother? You don't have a name?" Jones asked, as some of the food and drinks arrived.

"No, no name currently, and I'm unaware of any contact. As I said, we've not pushed it," Amit continued. "Look, this could all be a red herring. Emma could stroll back home any second. But when I spoke to Marie, was debriefed by the FLO in Ash and read the detail, it was clear that this was a lead you'd want to follow up." Amit had been presented with a sizable chicken mayonnaise baguette mid-sentence and was now looking to set about enjoying it. But, with his mouth stuffed full, he continued.

"Marie gave me some names to check on Surrey's police database. Saoirse and Philip Bradley, Kenny and Caragh Reid and, er...," he stopped to check his notes, "George McCool." Crumbs rained down from Amit's mouth as he chewed. Jenny cringed.

"Philip Bradley, your first dead man, has a few parking tickets and a speeding offence issued by the City of London Police. Nothing else. However, Saoirse flashed up. How on earth do you pronounce that name?"

"Sur-sha," Jenny politely corrected him. "What did you dig up about her?"

"Nothing since the mid-1980s. She was a history student at Brunel University, and she was picked up graffitiing the Uxbridge branch of Freeman, Hardy and Willis with pro-IRA slogans. Very little detail on this, aside from the fact that she was expelled from the university as a result. However, she continued her university education back home. I understand."

"My word," Jones responded. "And she's supposed to be the quiet one. Anything on Kenny, Caragh, or George."

"Nada, zero. But, of course, the National Police Database

nearly blew a fuse when I typed in Kenny Reid's name, but nothing in England. All in your neck of the woods."

"That's really useful, Amit. It's great of you to meet us like this," Jenny said, still feeling that she'd slightly misjudged the Detective Constable.

"If I'm honest," Amit mumbled, as he almost demolished his baguette in record time, "the entire case intrigues me. We get nothing like this round here. Lots of drugs, knives, gangs, bit of fraud and street crime, but nothing that interesting. I'm a bit jealous, but I feel for the little girl, too." As he popped the last piece of bread in his mouth, he grabbed the pager from his belt.

"Christ alive. I've been called for a briefing. The plods believe they have two or three plausible sightings of Emma. A new sighting at London Victoria. Maybe she's getting the bus up to Belfast?" Amit looked up at the pair.

"You mean ferry? There's the Irish Sea to contend with first," Jenny reminded Amit.

"Ferry, of course. Look, I need to go, sorry. Here's my card, if you need me. The FLO will probably be on site when you get to Ash. She's a good egg." With that, Amit dashed out of the door.

"Blimey, another spanner in the works. Nice fella though. Looks like we are going to need your tact and diplomacy when we speak to Rosie Jacobs. It was sadly not so evident over the past hour. What is wrong with you?" Jones said, scraping the remains of the melted cheese from his plate.

"Yes, point taken. I was impatient with Amit. I'll find my soft and fluffy side. Right, finish that cappuccino, it's time to go." Jenny nearly dragged Jones from the Little Chef and found the driver sitting in the same position they left him, waiting in the car park.

"We need to go to Fogarty Road in Ash, please. As fast as you like," Jenny requested, and the car was soon back on the A3.

Twenty-One

Sam Jacobs had slept in. His brain had been working overtime, thinking about Emma and the horror of Philip Bradley's murder. He'd finally slept at 4am and was now looking at the clock with an air of guilt and regret. It would soon be lunchtime. He needed to do much more to help Emma, and he was stuck in a cottage in the middle of nowhere, surrounded by water, wildfowl, and high fencing.

He'd spent half of the night staring at the Fleur de Lys plaster coving around the edge of the ceiling. It was the cottage's only attempt at class. He counted the patterns repeatedly, trying to stop his brain from catastrophising and replacing those terrible thoughts with positive outcomes. But it was almost impossible.

He could hear Wendy downstairs on the mega drive. She hadn't let him beat her once on Super Mario Brothers or Outrun, but she had shown him a few tricks that made it a little more competitive. He had grown very fond of her. She was like no-one he'd ever met before. But he wouldn't be telling her that. That admission was totally out of the question.

As he walked over to the mirror to pick out a lump of pepperoni, still lodged between his back teeth from last night's pizza, he heard Wendy's mobile phone ring downstairs. It was more of a chirp than a ring, but it made his heart-rate redouble its efforts as he wondered whether this was news about Emma. He heard Wendy's voice and a little to-and-fro of conversation before the call ended. He didn't hear specifics.

"Sam?" Wendy called from downstairs. "Are you awake yet? You know, it's cracking on a bit now?"

Sam grabbed a t-shirt from his rucksack and threw it on before heading to the top of the stairs.

"Yeah. Sorry. I overslept a little," he replied.

"That's fine. You needed the rest. I have some news. Why don't you come downstairs, and we can chat it through? I'll make tea."

"Alright," Sam responded and went back in the room and pulled his jeans and socks on. Wendy didn't need to see his favourite Bananaman underpants.

"Right," she began, when he finally arrived downstairs. "Surrey police believe they have two or three possible sightings of Emma. They believe she boarded a coach at London Victoria Bus Station. The theory is that she's coming to find you. Maybe she misses her big brother?"

"Oh my god. Poor Emma. Perhaps she heard about the murder from my mum and dad? She's very sensitive," Sam said. "She's heading up to the ferry. She's only little, she looks much younger than she is. Surely someone would've spotted her and sent her home?"

"Apparently not. Maybe she's spun people a very good story. Now, there is some less good news, but I don't want you to worry," Wendy continued, using her best people skills. Skills she never knew she had. Sam looked back at her wide-eyed and nervous.

"She was seen at London Waterloo, getting off a train from Guildford, but she wasn't alone. Or rather, Surrey Police don't believe she was alone. Can you think of any friends that might have tagged along with her?"

"She has one good friend, Tanya. She's taller than Emma, with long brown hair. Does that match the description? But surely, with all this information, they must be on the verge of picking her up now? There can't be too many coaches up to Scotland," Sam asked.

"It doesn't match the vague description, no. They tried to pick up when the bus reached Oxford, one of the early stops, but she'd gone. Her friend too. But look, don't worry. There are good people working on bringing her home," Wendy reassured him.

Sam stared at Wendy. His brain was still running through possibilities. Emma was far too young to be out there alone, and he couldn't think of anyone who'd chaperone her up to Cairnryan port.

"Emma and I were like a little team at home. I have been worried about her since I left. But I didn't expect her to do this. This isn't like her at all."

"Try not to worry. Let's eat some breakfast. You can ring your parents soon. They're already aware of the update." Sam spied a box of Weetabix in the kitchen and guessed they'd been given fresh provisions, but he hated Weetabix. He thought they tasted like a damp milky mattress.

"Oh, and we have a visit from the RUC in a few hours to talk about the identity of the killer. Maybe piece together another identikit? Are you up for that?" Wendy added.

"Yeah, course," he replied, wanting to appear super helpful. But already panicking inside.

Out of the corner of his eye, Sam saw some movement outside. Someone was near the reedbed. Wendy saw the horror in his eyes.

"Sam, I'm sorry, I should have mentioned. You now have three protection officers, all armed and largely hidden. I think you've just seen one near the front window. They are there to keep you safe."

"But why? We just had Sandwich Man before. Wasn't he enough?" Sam questioned.

"Okay. You need to be brave. But last night a few people visited your student halls. They were looking for you. This means we have to take your protection up a notch. But you are in the very best of hands." Wendy knew this was going to be a tough sell for Sam.

"Dele, my neighbour? Is he alright? Did they get into my room?" Sam spluttered, now looking more nervous than ever before.

"Everyone's fine. You have nothing to worry about. We just now know what we're dealing with. Hence the lads with guns, hanging around in hedges, and Sandwich Man." Wendy smiled at Sam, hoping he would see the small glimmer of humour in this, no matter how dark it was.

"Anyway, no more talking. Let's eat. And then I'll thrash you at Super Mario again, before the police come."

"That sounds like a plan," Sam agreed, but his head pounded with worry. Wendy was pretty cool though, he thought. There were worse ways of spending time in a safe house. But little Emma was out there on her own, somewhere. That just didn't feel real. None of it did.

Twenty-Two

The driver had pulled into the car park of Ash railway station, and they got out just as a high-speed train careered past, en route to Guildford. The shock of the train's sudden appearance nearly knocked Jenny off her feet, as she was concentrating on reading her briefing notes for the umpteenth time.

They rounded the corner between the station and the small high street and soon identified Fogarty Road on the left, the entrance opposite the Dover Arms public house. The pair forgot themselves momentarily and walked hand-in-hand to the entrance of the estate, before Jones pulled away and started counting house numbers.

"It's number seventy-four, isn't it?" he asked.

"It's the one with the police car outside and a couple of TV crews opposite in the van. See it? The screamingly obvious one?" Jenny grinned.

"It's still number seventy-four. Smart arse. I'll let you do the talking."

Jones followed Jenny as she made her way up the street and

turned left down the garden path. They were immediately met by a young-looking uniformed officer.

"Jones and Richmond from the RUC," Jenny informed the female officer. "I think you've been expecting us?"

"Absolutely," the officer responded. "Go right in, but they've just been told the news about Emma being seen at Victoria Bus Station and Sam's been in touch via mobile phone. It's all a touch fraught."

"We'll tread carefully," Jenny calmly replied. "Feel free to join us. They'll be used to you by now, and we're just strangers."

Jones, Jenny, and the officer, who was acting as Family Liaison Officer, walked into the living room and the edginess and tension in the air was palpable.

"Rosie, Bill, this is Jones and Richmond from the Royal Ulster Constabulary. They've flown over this morning to see how they can help with the investigation." The officer announced. It was an introduction with elements of truth sprinkled in it.

Jones hastily acclimatised himself to the suburban semi. He had already seen the abundance of family photos that adorned the corridor leading to the living room, not just of Sam, Emma, and their adoptive parents, but also of other children that he guessed the Jacobs had fostered in the past. There were lots of smiling faces and evidence of adventures. To Jones, it felt like a house full of warmth, safety, and happiness.

In the living room itself, styled in modern white and silver wallpaper, with matching light grey curtains and an olive-green three-piece suite, made the room bright and cheerful. On the top of a dark wood sideboard was an array of trophies, one or two with ballerinas on the top and others with footballs and swimmers and blue-tacked behind them were swathes of children's certificates and merit awards. This was a family very proud of their children's achievements.

In the centre of the room was a large television on mute. The opening credits for 'Going for Gold' were in full swing, and Henry

Kelly was on the screen. Jones was a fan. However, he focused on the faces in the room instead. Rosie Jacobs was a young-looking late thirtysomething with mid length blonde hair, wearing jeans and a long baggy Benetton t-shirt. William, or Bill, was still wearing his uniform trousers and a short-sleeved white shirt. He had green faded tattoos on both arms and a large Omega wrist-watch. Jones guessed this was his gift when he was discharged from the army. Bill looked ready for work. It was as if he was expecting Emma to arrive home any second, and he'd then be able to get back to the station. Alternatively, Jones thought, Bill just wanted to feel normal, and his uniform would be exactly that comfort blanket. Both faces were etched with worry, and both fidgeted as they sat on the edge of the sofa. Waiting for something. Rosie spoke first.

"Goodness me, you've come such a long way. We really weren't expecting so many visitors today. But PC Holland has been very kind." The FLO, standing behind Rosie, smiled. "And we've just had a reported sighting of Emma. It all seems so wrong. So awful," Rosie then dissolved into tears and Bill rushed to comfort her.

"We won't be disturbing you for too long, Mrs Jacobs. We just have a few questions to help our enquiries and then we'll be on our way," Jenny began. As she did, the telephone rang in the background and PC Holland sprinted to pick it up.

"Hello, Jacobs' residence?" PC Holland looked over at Bill Jacobs and shook her head. "No, I'm sorry we will not be making any press statements at this time, and Mr and Mrs Jacobs will not be doing media interviews. Goodbye and kindly refrain from calling this number. Use the police press office in the future." The receiver was swiftly replaced.

"As I was saying," Jenny restarted. "We are working on the police investigation into the murder of Philip Bradley MP. You've probably heard about it on the news. Sadly, your son, Sam, was a prominent witness and is being held in a safe location. As I'm sure you're aware, he's in good spirits and is helping us a great deal."

"He would, bless him," Rosie responded. "That's so like Sam.

He wants to help wherever he can. We spoke to him a few minutes back. He's being a brave little soldier."

"What do you need from us?" Bill asked.

"Just some background first," Jenny began. "What made Sam chose the Ulster University?" Jones wanted to intervene instantly, as this seemed such a blunt entry point.

"Oh, he loved the prospectus, and we went to two open days. It's a lovely place. We made a real family trip of it, didn't we, Bill?" Rosie replied, still dabbing her eyes.

"We did, but I'm not sure that's why she's asking that, Rose." Bill said. "It's not, is it? You want to know about the adoptions?"

"We want to get a full picture, and the adoptions are one part of it. But only if you want to talk about it. We don't want to make a difficult situation worse by upsetting you both." Jenny, without being invited, seated herself on the closest armchair to Rosie and passed her another tissue.

"You two are from the police? In Northern Ireland?" Rosie queried, in between more dabbing.

"Actually, we're both English," Jones answered. "I'm from Suffolk. Jenny is from Bermondsey in London. We're both on detachment to the RUC."

"Fair enough," Bill responded. "Tell you what, Rose, could you and PC Holland fetch some tea and the good biscuits, and we'll have a little chat?"

Rosie and PC Holland, after grabbing the box of tissues from a footstool in the middle of the room, disappeared into the kitchen.

"Sit down, old son," Bill gestured to Jones, and he sat in the other armchair. Jones spotted copies of the Beano, Dandy, Topper, and Buster comics piled to the right of the chair and a 1994 World Cup Panini Sticker album. He'd had that himself. He never found the Republic of Ireland foil crest. That still upset him.

"Look, this whole adoption thing upsets my Rose, so let's get it over and done with before she's back." Bill looked over at them both and Jenny nodded sympathetically.

Bill cracked his knuckles loudly, which made Jenny wince, and paused slightly, as if to get his thoughts in order.

"I did some voluntary work on my leave days in Belfast when I was based out there. Sort of winning hearts and changing minds stuff. It had mixed results." He paused again. He had quite a thick West London accent, which surprised Jones.

"Anyway, I helped rebuild an outbuilding of a church that had been caught up in an explosion. I'd like to think it was an accidental hit, but I'm fairly sure the outbuilding was being used as an ammunition store. But, to cut a long story short, I got to know the priest over the course of a few years. One evening, after work, I explained that we wanted to be foster parents once I was back home and maybe even adopt." Bill looked over at Jenny. "You see, Rose and I can't have our own children, but she has so much love to give. She's an incredible woman."

"I'm so sorry to hear that, but do go on, please. Tell us about your conversations with the priest?" Jenny nudged.

"He put me in touch with an adoption service called the St Federico's Mission. They were based in Belfast but had other homes across Ireland. It seemed that I ticked the right boxes, even though I was a British soldier, but I had to wait until my tour of duty was at an end. I couldn't ask Rose to bring a child up on her own and with so much uncertainty."

"Of course," Jenny smiled. "You wanted things to be on an even keel."

"Absolutely. But when I left the army a few years later, I got in touch with Father Peter again, and he acted as an intermediary with Sam's mother. The mission just wanted him away from harm, I think, and we were happy to help." Bill quickly looked over his shoulder to see if his wife and the FLO were listening in.

"I honestly never knew the mother's name and only met her once, during Sam's adoption. I realised it was wrong, but everything was very hush-hush, and I had to give assurances around secrecy," Bill spoke quietly and nervously. Jones guessed Rosie wasn't aware of all this finer detail.

"Why?" Jenny asked.

"I think, whilst the adoptions were all formalised, there was a bit of corner cutting. Don't get me wrong, Father Peter was a fantastic man. But he was more focused on getting the children away from what he believed was an unfit mother urgently, rather than ensuring we were the right adoptive parents. Things have changed now, I'm sure."

"And the same process repeated for the second time? With Emma?" Jones asked.

"No, I travelled over to Belfast myself for Emma. I met Father Peter at Larne Port, and he simply put her in a baby seat in my car. No questions were asked. It was all astonishingly simple. But he made it clear it was the same mother and father. It just seemed very sad to me."

"It does," Jenny agreed. "But the process seems unconventional."

"Yeah. That's the word. Unconventional," Bill repeated. "But why are you even asking about the adoptions? Do you think the birth mother is involved? Are you thinking she kidnapped Emma?" He was looking for a pen and paper as he spoke. "Father Peter always told me she was very grateful."

"I'm sure she is. This is just one line of inquiry. That's all. But it would be quite a coincidence if your son witnessed a shooting of an MP, just at the very moment that their birth mother kidnapped Emma. We need to follow everything up, though," Jenny gently explained.

"Between you and me, I've certainly not told Sam this, but their mother was a very sick woman. She was an alcoholic, had developed an addiction to sleeping pills too and, Father Peter told me, she'd attempted suicide more than once. But this was all off the record from Father Peter. I just can't see how she'd be involved in all of this."

"I'm sure you're right, Mr Jacobs," Jenny smiled.

"Call me Bill, please."

"You really have no idea of her name? Can you remember what she looked like?" Jenny had been writing most of this down in her shorthand pad, whilst Jones listened intently.

"No, we never knew her name, and we met very briefly. She came here and we gave her a small amount of money for expenses. Less than £200. She dropped Sam off and was gone. She left a little note for Sam, which he still has. We never hid anything from him."

"Could you describe her?" Jenny asked.

"She was a very thin woman, jet black bobbed hair and very pale skin. The only thing that I remember vividly were her deep brown eyes. They were very powerful. Weirdly, neither Sam or Emma have those features. But please don't ask me about the father. I know nothing about him. He wasn't even mentioned."

"What about your own contacts in Ireland? Anything we need to know?" Jenny continued.

"Sam has a list of all my mates in Belfast and Lisburn. I gave him a contacts book with names, addresses, and contact numbers. He'll happily give it to you. There's absolutely no-one on that list I wouldn't trust with my life. They're either ex-army or civilian staffers. There was never any trouble." Bill looked nervously over his shoulder again to the kitchen as PC Holland and Rosie walked in with a tray of tea mugs and biscuits.

As Rosie Jacobs handed mugs of tea around the room and Jones snapped up a couple of pink wafer biscuits, Bill jotted down a name on a piece of paper and passed it to Jenny. It read:

Father Peter O'Callaghan, Church of the Blessed Resurrection, Mitre Road East. Belfast.

She folded it up and placed it in the back of her shorthand pad. She'd use the handheld when she was back in the car and ask Isadora to look into him, the church, and St Federico's Mission. But this all seemed like a stretch that a series of coincidences would line up in such a dramatic manner.

There was a brief moment of silence as the five people in the room either sipped their tea or, in Jenny's case, pretended to, as a non-tea drinker.

"What will happen to my poor Sam?" Rosie asked, handing the biscuits around. The good ones were a chocolate shortbread in a green wrapper and Jones grabbed three. Jenny shot him a withering look.

"There is no doubting that he is a key witness to the shooting. Therefore, we are sparing no expense in giving him the protection he needs." Jenny was plucking comforting words from the air and hoping they were true.

"The team back in Belfast is trying to track down the person or persons responsible and bring them to justice. But it's certainly a complicated case and I understand your concern. Jones and I have met Sam and he's doing brilliantly under really trying circumstances."

"He moved out there a few months early, just to get settled before term started. But he made a good friend in his student halls, almost straightaway," Bill chipped in. "An African lad called Dele. Huge bloke, by all accounts. They're pretty inseparable. Sam isn't always so good at making friends, so we were relieved when he mentioned Dele, weren't we, Rose?"

"We were. And he's so organised, is our Sam. The lawn mowing, making a few extra bob, his studies and watching his films. But friendship or trust has never come easy to him and the university lifestyle really isn't his thing either. He's not a laddish big drinker and he's hardly up with all the latest trends. He just plods along in his own time and space." Rosie smiled before the emotion hit her again. "They are both such special kids, the fact that anyone would want to hurt either of them..."

Rosie wept on PC Holland's shoulder and Bill peered over anxiously.

Jones looked over at Jenny, who was caught up in the emotion and had reached to grab more tissues. He nodded surreptitiously to suggest now was the right time to leave them. Jones felt uncomfortable being in the thick of all the raw emotion but also knew that this was what the job required.

"Mr and Mrs Jacobs, thank you for sparing us your time during such a distressing period. I'm so sorry if we've added to your worries. We'll be on our way now." Jones stood up and offered his hand to Bill Jacobs, who instantly shook it with a very firm handshake. In the background, Jenny smiled warmly at Rosie, who was still being comforted by PC Holland.

"Find my girl and keep Sam safe. That's all we can ask of you," Bill said to Jones, staring him in the eyes.

"We'll do our best," he replied. "We'll be in touch with any further updates."

PC Holland briefly left the Jacobs supporting each other and showed Jones and Richmond to the door. She passed Jenny her business card and rushed back to the living room. Jones was immediately impressed with the young PC.

As they headed back past all the smiling faces of the children adorning the walls of the passageway, they saw the rain. It was bucketing down and, with the car a good five-minutes' walk away, they sprinted back to the pub car park with Jones using the plastic wallet full of briefing notes as a makeshift umbrella. They were soon saturated.

The driver was ready for them, with both doors already open and the car air conditioning system on full, to begin the process of drying them out.

"Why didn't you drive around the corner and pick us up?" Jenny asked, with the rain now dripping from her ponytail.

"You didn't ask," the driver responded. "Anyway, I need to get you back to the airport. There's a flight at 4pm and the powers that be want you on it."

"What?" Jenny responded. "We have an overnight bag. We haven't met the team investigating the disappearance. That's insanity."

"Not my call, love. I've been told to get you on the next flight," the driver indicated left out of the pub car park and raced back towards the A3.

Jones, feeling Jenny's vibes, pulled out his handheld and attempted to reach Virginia on the open channel. There was no immediate response. Instead, McNally answered, there were no niceties.

"McNally? This is Jones, I was..."

"If you're going to ask why you're being dragged back," McNally interrupted. "Read the room, big lad. We have a double murder on our hands and an Acting Chief Superintendent who's acting like a prize dick. I can't have you two propping up some bar in Guildford until midnight and then getting back here at lunchtime, probably hanging like bats." McNally wasn't joking.

"He's got a point," Jenny whispered.

"We'll be on the next flight back, McNally. We'll be there before 6pm. We can debrief if it's useful," Jones responded, hating that McNally had second guessed him correctly.

"Aye, that'd be useful. Is there anything I need to know now?"

"There's another paper trail we need to look into around Sam and Emma's birth parents. They were born in Belfast, and the adoptive father seems to have done some kind of shady deal with a parish priest. Not once, but on two separate occasions. Almost ten years apart," Jones explained.

"What does your gut tell you, Jones?" McNally asked.

"I'm much more interested in who kidnapped Emma and why. That's the only gap in our knowledge. I can't believe that's the birth mother, but we need to rule that out. Problem is, we know nothing about her and the records will be sealed."

"Alright. We've some work to do, then. I'll warn Isadora. I'll also get on the telephone to Eric Rogers and explain that, yet again, we've done his fecking job for him. This is all police work." McNally signed off.

The driver, hearing most of the conversation, sped through the persistent English rain and even used the hard shoulder to swerve and slalom through the built-up traffic to get to the flight.

Suddenly Jenny's driving didn't seem quite so troublesome, as Jones gripped tightly to the 'Oh my God' handle above the door. They had an hour to get the flight and another trail of breadcrumbs to follow.

Twenty-Three

As the car sped to Gatwick, Jenny used the journey to explain the background and new intel to Isadora. Isadora had spent most of the day working with Carl, Tom, and Mr Singh on the gadgetry required for the Hunter's Arms surveillance exercise and whilst she liked tech, she yearned for action and was feeling frustrated with her back injury that kept her in the wheelchair. She could walk two or three steps unaided, but the strength required to do so was immense and her physiotherapy appeared to have plateaued at that three-step barrier.

Still, she thought, she had her own line of enquiry now. This would at least drag her away from the mundanity of QD. Jenny had given her the address of Father Peter O'Callaghan at the Church of the Blessed Resurrection and the sketchiest of details about St Federico's Mission. She would drive to Mitre Road East to track down Father Peter and, with luck, a lead to the birth mother.

After making her apologies to Mr Singh, she manoeuvred herself out of the Quartermaster's Department with relief. The two lads had been combining their efforts in setting up the tiny clandestine cameras while playing a series of Buck-a-Roo games.

Tom was winning 3-1. It was a Christmas present from Carl's sister and he was convinced there was a strategy that would prevent the buck from happening at all. This rather fruitless endeavour, along with mainlining animal biscuits, cola laces and Wham bars, had been the order of the day in QD and frankly Isadora was done with them.

Isadora's modified Land Rover featured a mechanism to open the doors, which in turn lowered a ramp, which she drove up with ease. There was a lock on the floor in the driver's pit, which engaged a bolt on the bottom of her chair, ensuring security and stability. There were basic hand controls, like pushing down on the lever to accelerate, and pushing forward to slow or brake. There was also a knob on the wheel to enable Isadora to turn the wheel with just one hand. Most of which had been designed by Mr Singh, but with the added flexibility of being hastily adapted back to enable a non-wheelchair user to drive. It was a feat of engineering genius.

She waved at the two soldiers manning the gates at the entrance to the Barracks and sped through the tight Lisburn roads. One in particular, nicknamed 'Noodle', a muscular tattooed Yorkshireman, had been the object of her affection for a while now. But they hadn't got past the smiling and waving stage yet.

It was only seven minutes into the journey, somewhere around Belsize Road, that she had that telltale niggle that she might be being followed. But, fearing this might be paranoia from being cooped up inside the YCU for too long and drinking too many coffees, she indicated left and pulled into the layby near a small supermarket. She fiddled with the radio, finding BBC Radio Ulster for company, and checked her mirrors repeatedly. There was nothing out of the ordinary. The green 4x4 she had suspected was taking too much interest continued past her and she set off again. It was a false alarm. She was overthinking things, she decided.

The rest of the journey was uneventful. She'd listened to the mid-afternoon news and had updated herself on the ongoing peace talks. There had been an interview with Fred Martinsen and the NI Secretary of State. She was so engrossed that she almost missed the turning for Green Lane that led down the suburban Mitre Road East. An urban part of Catholic West Belfast.

The Mitre pub, adorned with tricolours and surrounded by empty bench seating, was the first building of note. Her unmarked Land Rover caught the attention of three men standing near the entrance of the pub, all with autumnal coats and lighted cigarettes, but their interest was only a fleeting glance and she drove on, looking for any church-like structure. Nothing was obvious.

A row of shops, with at least two looking derelict and heavily graffitied, appeared on the left-hand side of the road with a Sinn Fein advice centre, a small off licence, a charity shop, and a new-looking convenience store. With Gerry Adams, the local MP, West Belfast was dominated by nationalist voters, and Sinn Fein representatives had a reputation of being the most conscientious of councillors. They were generally extremely successful in ensuring that their constituents' concerns were dealt with promptly and efficiently by council officials and civil representatives. The tide was turning. There was a feeling that the differing sectarian parties and political groups might work together to find a peaceful solution, and with six Sinn Fein councillors already in Belfast City Council, there was a power base emerging. Fred Martinsen would need to pull at those strings harder to bring Belfast, London, and Dublin together.

However, all this hope wasn't always reflected on the streets. Mitre Road East was a working-class area and looking like it had suffered from underinvestment for many years. As Isadora continued to drive along the road, there were no signs of a church. There was a church steeple in the distance, but by the look of her map, that could be the well-known St Bernadette's, just visible but not close.

At the next parade of shops, she spotted a small gathering of older women. They had congregated outside a launderette, and

Isadora pulled over and wound down the window. She parked up on the left-hand side of the road and had to crane to talk through the open window. After calling out 'excuse me' a few times in her painfully English accent, one lady wandered over.

"Are you lost, love?" the woman asked, resting her arm on the roof of the car.

"I'm looking for the Church of the Blessed Resurrection. I've driven up and down this street a few times..." Isadora started to reply but was interrupted.

"You'll have a job. It was knocked down about three years back. Keep driving up this road and you'll see a kiddies' playground. It was just to the left of that," the woman explained.

"Knocked down? Why?"

"Why do you want to know? You're a long way from home, aren't you?" the woman responded, with a couple of the other women walking over to join the conversation.

"I'm looking for the grave of an uncle," she lied. "He died in the 1950s and I'm doing some family history."

"I wouldn't spend too long around here, love. There are no graves at that church, you see. It was a modern building, like a prefabricated thing," she gesticulated to explain her point, somehow. "It just crumbled and was costing too much. The congregation moved on," the same woman replied and walked away. But another woman took her place leaning on the roof.

"What was your uncle's name? We might be able to help you," she began. "You're in a wheelchair, poor love. What happened to you?"

"Paralysed from birth," Isadora fibbed again. She decided a bullet in the spine might not be an ideal response. "His name was Odhran Kelly. He was my father's little brother. He died very young."

"Oh, that's a tragedy for you, so it is. But Kelly's a fairly common name, there's loads of them around here. But if you take my advice, you'll go to St Bernadette's and ask for Father Peter.

He'll be able to help, so he will. There are loads of graves up there and there'll be more information, too."

"I'll do that," Isadora said, before driving off and waving at the group of women. They were already back in their huddle and didn't see Isadora waving cheerily.

As she drove further up the road, she noticed the children's playground, with a couple of young mothers and their toddlers on a little see-saw. The equipment looked dated, and the area was entirely surrounded with a chest-high metal fence, with a small, gated entrance. Graffiti was everywhere. As she looked to the left, there were the remains of a building with two smaller outbuildings behind. These had survived the demolition and Isadora guessed these were now probably used for storage. But there was certainly nothing to see.

As she drove away, she noticed the red LED on her handheld flashing. She knew picking it up with eyes on her in West Belfast would be a bad idea, so she pulled into a cul-de-sac of houses and indicated right back up Mitre Road East towards the pub, to find a better spot to talk.

As she passed The Mitre at the top of the road, the pub was now busier. A few people were now sitting on the bench seats outside and, looking at her watch, she presumed these were probably the first batch of drinkers who had finished work for the day. They certainly looked happy enough, she thought.

Back on the main road, she spied a lay-by and grabbed the handheld and made an all- channels call.

"Hello, this is Isadora. Was anyone calling me?"

"Yes, we're back," Jenny responded, almost straightaway. "Just landed. Any news?"

"Well, the church Bill Jacobs visited has been demolished. There's just storage buildings on the site, that's all. I'm en route to St Bernadette's Church now. There is a Father Peter based there, whether it's the same bloke, I don't know yet."

"That's quick work. Keep us informed," Jenny replied. "By the way, Jones reckons we ought to speak to Sam Jacobs about his birth mother. Do you know where the safe house is?"

"Not a clue, and we'd best not talk about that on the open channel," Isadora said.

"Too right," came a third voice. It was McNally. "I can arrange for you to meet Sam later on tonight, if you're not too jaded from your wee trip abroad?"

"I'm guessing that's a mild dose of McNally sarcasm. But if tonight is on offer, we'll take it." Jenny responded.

"You know me too well. Let me see what I can get set up. I'll revert when I can. Good work all," and with that, McNally left the call.

"How hard do you want me to push Father Peter?" Isadora asked. "Do we genuinely believe there's something fishy going on?"

"I don't think it's out of the question. Find out what you can. Jones thinks it's a dead end. He's been in the airport gents for about a quarter of an hour, otherwise he'd tell you himself."

"Jesus, Jen. What is it about men and extended toilet breaks? Look, I'll get over to St Bernadette's and we can discuss it back at base. I'll see you there."

St Bernadette's Church, just a seven-minute drive from Mitre Road East, stood out as a gem of a historical building along Elgin Road in West Belfast. It wasn't far from the local Post Office and was clearly in the heart of the community. As Isadora pressed the ramp release button in the Land Rover and she swung the chair around to exit the vehicle, a few teenagers took an interest and one, in an Antrim GAA shirt, offered to help. She declined politely and made her way from the roadside down the long driveway leading to the church.

As she scanned around her, she noticed a green 4x4 parked up near the church car park but then decided this was simply more overthinking. There were plenty of green 4x4s around and there was no good reason to be tailing her. As she got closer to the church, she could hear organ music and the hum of activity from inside.

However, whilst she could get as far as the partially opened front door, she could go no further. There was a row of three steep steps preventing her. So, she rapped loudly on the front door and before too long steps were audible.

"Oh dear," was the first response from an older woman who opened the door wider. "Give me a wee minute and we'll get you inside. We should have a ramp but, I'm sure you understand, some things just get forgotten."

Isadora nodded, but in truth, she didn't sympathise at all. "It's fine," she replied. "If someone could help me down, though, I'm here to see Father Peter. Is he around?"

"He'd be delighted to speak to you. He's just over at the back dealing with the choir. Just give me a moment," the woman said, before scurrying off to the back of the building.

As Isadora teetered at the top of the steps, she watched a group of youngsters in the far corner of the church chatting with an older grey-haired man. They were sitting in a group and the youngsters had small cartons of Um Bongo in front of them. Before too long, a tall man dressed in a clerical suit emerged at the bottom of the stairs.

"I'm Father Peter. How can I help you? Would you like me to organise you some help down? I'm sorry you've been so inconvenienced."

"Are you Father Peter O'Callaghan? From the Church of the Blessed Resurrection?" Isadora asked.

"Yes, the very same. I moved here about three years ago. How can I help?" The clergyman smiled broadly. He had a soft and gentle way of speaking.

"Well, firstly, if you could get me down these steps, I'd be very grateful. Do you have five minutes for a chat?"

"Absolutely," he responded and summoned two of the choir

over, who grabbed either side of the chair and helped her down the steps. "Let's take a seat over near my office," he continued.

St Bernadette's was cold, but Isadora felt peace exuding from the calmness of the building. It was grey with slate walls but, at the same time, colour was everywhere from the windows to the drapes and the paintings, which were both modern and classic. She remembered family trips to Rome and Florence with people hushing the general public as they enjoyed the remarkable Italian religious architecture and artwork. She swiftly felt the need to be quiet and almost solemn. She felt herself breathe and the pace of life calm slightly.

"I'm Isadora. I'm working with the Royal Ulster Constabulary on a murder case. But please, don't be alarmed, I'm simply here to join some dots around one of the witnesses," she began. He didn't ask for her identification.

"One of the witnesses?" Father Peter repeated.

"Yes, I believe you helped with the adoption of two children to the same English family. A boy and a baby girl. About ten years apart. This was through St Federico's Mission, I understand?"

"Oh, that was all a long time ago. I have no role with that mission now. But I'll help if I can, of course." The Father now looked flustered. Isadora knew this was probably going to be a quick exchange unless she could keep him chatting.

"It was an English former soldier called Bill Jacobs. He adopted two children, one boy who would have been about five, in the mid-1970s, and a baby, maybe ten years later. The boy is the witness to the murder."

"I remember Bill," he volunteered. "He was a very nice man who came and helped rebuild the church buildings after an explosion. It was actually a really dangerous thing for him to do around there. But I can't say I remember anything about the children."

"I realise you're not able to tell me who the mother is," she began. "But, aside from the boy being a witness, his sister is now missing, presumed kidnapped, and I just need to know whether the mother is likely to be pursuing access to her children? I just need to discount this."

"I can't tell you anything. I realise this sounds obstructive, but I helped hundreds of children. I don't have access to the records; this is mired in legalities and bureaucracies." Isadora got the feeling this was a well-rehearsed line.

"You remember the man but don't remember a brother and baby sister being adopted to England? To the same family? That doesn't sound like a regular arrangement to me, especially in the 1970s, with the Troubles at fever pitch. Come on, Father Peter. I really need your help. This is serious." She knew she was pushing her luck.

There was a moment of silence as Father Peter, a prematurely grey-haired man who smelt strongly of Old Spice aftershave, inspected his hands and deliberated. Isadora put him in his late-50s and noticed the top of the collar of his white shirt was frayed heavily.

"Are you telling me that the girl, who was adopted as a baby, has been kidnapped? She's out there now?"

"Yes," Isadora said, looking into his eyes. "She was at a swimming lesson and didn't return. My two colleagues visited her parents today and they were distraught. She's a very young girl."

"How does this relate to the murder? Couldn't she have been kidnapped by someone trying to silence the boy?" Isadora was immediately impressed by his quick logic. He was correct, of course.

"You're right, Father. That is another line of enquiry. As I said, I'm just joining the dots. All I'm asking is whether the birth mother is likely to be pursuing her children? Especially the girl."

"Okay. There is a life at risk here. I would never normally get involved in this type of conversation. God knows I've been asked before. But I can confirm unequivocally that the mother would not be the kidnapper."

"How can you be so sure?" Isadora countered.

"Because I buried her about eighteen months ago." As he spoke, he deliberately broke with Isadora's gaze.

"I'm so sorry. But I have to ask, what was her name?" Isadora asked.

There was another brief uncomfortable silence. Father Peter was looking down at his hands again and slowly shaking his head.

"I want to help. But I just can't tell you anymore. She died, isn't that enough?"

It wasn't enough for Isadora. But she knew she'd pushed hard enough. She could come back again, maybe. Perhaps Father Peter needed time. Something nagged at her as she made the decision to stop the conversation.

It is often said that eyes are the window into the soul, especially when spotting a liar. But something about Father Peter's manner made Isadora immediately believe him. She had spent the past few years looking for deceit, deception, and liars. But intuition made her totally accept this as the truth.

As Father Peter looked back at Isadora, she saw his face had changed. There was emotion there. It was as if he needed to bite his bottom lip to stop this merest of flickers of emotion become a torrent. There was a bigger story here. There was much more to this.

But Father Peter was already standing up and dusting down his clerical suit in an attempt to resume his role, to put the mask back on and deflect from that sign of emotion.

"Thank you, Father," Isadora said and gave him one of Marie Bristow's cards. "Ring this number if you remember anything else. Marie will get a message to me."

"I have nothing more to say. I'll pray for both of the children, and I hope you find her safe and well. I'll ask two of my choristers to help lift you out of the doors. Sorry again for the inconvenience. Otherwise, I'll bid you goodbye and a safe journey home."

"I'll be in touch if we need more," she called back, as the two helpers hauled the chair up the steps. Father Peter didn't respond.

It took Isadora just over thirty minutes to get back to Thiepval. Flickers of green 4x4s punctuated her journey, but this was just her paranoia gnawing away at her. No-one would tail her. She was investigating a tiny aspect of the case. It would be a waste of their time.

As she rounded the corner to the briefing rooms, she spotted both Delta and Echo teams watching a presentation from Mr Singh. She'd enjoyed the same sessions less than three years previously. Before the Limehall and Lennoxville bombings that robbed her of her YCU colleagues, before she'd been shot by Armstrong and before the chair became part of her life. Despite that, she'd come so far and could smile and reminisce. She remembered Mr Singh would barely pause for breath and only five per cent would sink in around the room. But nobody would challenge his utter brilliance.

In the other briefing room, Jones and Jenny were joined by McNally and Virginia. She could smell fresh coffee. Jones instantly jumped up and held open the double door to assist her passage inside. She'd told him it was unnecessary hundreds of times, but she'd given up. McNally, with the stench of cigarillos still on his breath, began proceedings.

"Right so, I've arranged for Sam to meet you both at the City View Hotel, just outside Belfast, in a place called Eden Vale. He'll be in room 47 and he'll be accompanied by Wendy. She's been good with him."

"Makes sense," Isadora responded, feeling a little put out that once again, she was on the outside. "What am I doing?"

"I need you to write up your evidence log from your meeting with Father Peter," McNally responded. "Is there anything we need to know?"

"Well, Father Peter says the birth mother is dead. He said he buried her about eighteen months ago. I believe him."

"Yeah," Jones added. "I'm not getting any vibes from this. The parents are simply scared out of their wits. Bill Jacobs didn't hold back on any information and Rosie was so emotional that we could barely ask her anything without upsetting her. But I guess that's understandable."

"Surrey appear to be doing their utmost to find Emma. Their DC was pretty impressive. It puts our RUC effort to shame," Jenny remarked. "It feels like we've been doing their jobs for them."

"Let's be clear. We are doing their jobs. Because we don't believe Eric's head is in the game. They're low on staff and even Clive Gentry is relying on us to sort this mess out," McNally looked over at Virginia, who was looking anxiously towards the team.

"What exactly are you hoping to gain from the conversation with Sam, Jones?" Virginia was looking over the top of her half-moon glasses. The look immediately unsettled Jones.

"It just completes the circle, doesn't it?" Jones replied defensively.

"I see," Virginia replied, continuing to stare over at Jones. "I've been thinking about this a great deal. He is an extremely vulnerable young man. He's been held away from his family. He knows there's a price tag on his head and his sister is missing. He's also in a new environment for him. This is all virgin territory. We need to tread carefully." Jones sat back in his chair briefly, realising that Virginia was right. She had always been the pastoral lead, the carer and almost a mother figure for the YCU.

"You're totally right," he began. "So, how do I play this?"

"You don't play anything. You put yourself in his shoes. Remember that night you arrived here, after hiking from the airport? How you felt? The scenes you saw from the Limehall explosion. The utter terror on your face. He's in that same ball-park." Virginia tapped her pencil on the table, as if to make her point.

Jones nodded. He felt Jenny move her chair a little closer to him.

"You had each other. He has no-one that really understands his predicament. But you do," Virginia continued.

"Maybe you should see him alone?" Jenny asked. "The two of us going will feel like another interview."

"I'll drive you over," Isadora suggested. "I'll wait outside, and you can chat properly. Let him open up. We can ask Wendy to step outside."

"I think sounds like a marvellous idea," Virginia smiled.

"I agree," McNally said. "This kind of soft soap stuff isn't my bag. But I can see he's a wee lad lost in all this trauma. Are we all happy with the plan?"

"Yes, I think we are. But can I suggest you avoid any mention of the alleged death of his birth mother? I think we carefully swerve any discussion about that. Let's not add to his plate." Virginia looked over at Jones, waiting for his agreement.

"Absolutely, but I've got to touch on the two adoptions and his rationale for being in Northern Ireland. That's the point, surely?" Jones responded.

"Aye," McNally agreed. "But don't throw him under any buses. Listen to him, get the facts and get out. If you can do that and leave him feeling that we care about his situation, you've done your job."

Jones nodded again. He suddenly felt a great weight of expectation on his shoulders and as they stood up to go their separate ways, Jenny gazed over and smiled.

"I'll be here when you get back. We'll have a drink, and you can debrief. You can do this," she said, quietly. He smiled back.

Within five minutes, Jones and Isadora were back on the road, heading towards the City View Hotel. Jones played 'Fuzzy' by Grant Lee Buffalo on the stereo, a rare foray into American music. But it calmed him. He got lost in the wistful sounds of Grant Lee Phillips until Isadora interrupted his train of thought.

"It doesn't really get going, does it?" she said. "Have you got any Kylie?" And that killed his mojo.

Twenty-Four

Sam Jacobs had been watching a video of The Young Ones, a personal favourite, for the past hour when Wendy appeared. He'd heard her on the phone and wondered what was happening.

She was in her Minnie the Minx-style long-sleeved jumper with red and black hoops. Sam liked her fashion choices. She had already donned her platformed Doc Martens and he'd guessed they were going somewhere, but the thought of leaving the cottage filled him with dread.

"We're going out?" Sam enquired.

"Yeah. Not far, though. You'll be perfectly safe," Wendy replied, passing Sam his green Hi-Tec trainers. "We'll have a protection officer with us at all times, and there'll be other officers patrolling the perimeter."

"Alright. But what's happening? Am I being moved?"

"Nope. You're meeting a friend of mine. He just wants a chat. Nothing to worry about. I'll be close by too." Wendy watched as Sam tied his laces in a double knot and picked up his wallet from the table.

As the door of the cottage opened, Sam saw that Sandwich Man was still in his car, and he waved over to Wendy. She gave the A-OK sign back. It looked like he had a Tunnocks Wafer Bar in his hand. The man was constantly hungry, Sam thought.

Seconds later, a rather portly protection officer strolled over the now opened lock-gates and beckoned Sam and Wendy to follow. The light was fading, but he could still see the swans and Canada Geese enjoying the clear evening. It was almost silent in Eden Vale, aside from the occasional bird call and the breeze rustling the leaves in the tall trees. There was a chill, and Sam had left his jacket in the cottage. He thought about mentioning this to Wendy, but she appeared deep in thought.

As the noises in the trees grew louder Sam felt his heart rate jump and he could feel sweat running down his spine. He made his hands into fists, curling his fingers tight into his palms and tried to focus all of his mind on Wendy. She strode in front of him behind the protection officer, who was wearing an earpiece and was scrutinising the scene with every step. Sam then heard the mechanical whirr of the lock-gates opening again, leaving the safe house cut off from possible intruders.

In the distance, he heard a car engine start. Maybe that was his lift? But soon that noise abated, and they paced quickly to a slightly muddy track. It seemed to follow the curve of the Lagan Navigation. They then came to a break in the trees and a shingle footpath with a metal gate blocking vehicle access. The officer, Wendy and Sam ducked underneath the gate and Wendy looked back at Sam and winked at him.

"Not far now. See those lights in the distance?" Wendy called back.

Sam looked up and saw a long row of floodlights.

"Yeah, what's that?" he asked.

"It's a hotel car park. Literally a five-minute walk from the cottage. But don't worry, when the lock-gates are open, there's absolutely no way anyone can get across to our cottage without swimming. That's one hell of a safe house."

"But they've not been closed properly since we've been there? Only just now to let us across," he replied.

"Sandwich Man can open and close them. He has a kind of remote control. You see, when a boat enters the lock, the gates close behind it. The motor then winds the paddles open, and water then fills or empties from the lock through small sluice gates. But these gates are rarely used now. So, it's an ideal base. People can only get across to the cottage when the gates are down or closed."

"How do you know this stuff?" Sam asked.

"There's a pamphlet in the cottage. I read it last night. Believe me, I wouldn't normally know that level of detail. Anyway, has that stopped you worrying? And look ahead, we're just coming into the car park now, just through this little track."

Although it hadn't stopped him worrying one jot, he didn't have the heart to tell Wendy. Instead, he paused for breath and watched as the protection officer spoke, barely audibly, into his police radio. They were now within a few feet of the hotel car park.

"We're clear," the officer called over and motioned for them to head onto the concrete path. Wendy then moved behind Sam and let the officer lead them onto the perimeter of the hotel grounds. Sam felt this short walk was taking forever. He hunched his shoulders forward and was almost willing himself to follow, whilst doubting every movement around him. The closer the hotel came; the more movement became evident. Guests, cars, white-shirted staff fetching and carrying drinks or food to the clientele in the hotel's garden bar. Sam could now see it all. Surely, they can't expect him to stroll through a crowded area? He'd be in clear view of everyone and anyone. His heart rate raised another notch.

With the hotel reception looming, the officer suddenly took a sharp left on the path towards an outside area marked 'staff only' and then mounted a set of metal fire exit steps. As he did so, another officer appeared two storeys up, holding the doors open.

"Not far now, we're just in one of the rooms at the top of this staircase," Wendy calmly explained.

Sam looked up and edgily made his way up the steps and soon entered a carpeted area with a row of hotel bedrooms. His fingernails, previously digging into his palms, relaxed slightly as a feeling of normality resumed. Get into one of these rooms, he thought, and I'll be alright.

As he scampered behind the protection officer, one of the bedroom doors opened. Sam's heart nearly burst through his chest. A middle-aged woman in a cream towelling robe quickly placed the remains of a room service lasagne on a wooden tray on the ground outside her room. She'd left all the salad, too. She should know better, Sam thought. She looked around quizzically at the stunned faces around her and darted back into her room.

The protection officer banged on the door of room 47 and a youngish man in a brown long-sleeved t-shirt and black jeans opened it. Sam recognised him. It was the same chap who interviewed him in Coleraine station. They were similar ages, and he had seemed okay back then. Sam stepped inside, with Wendy following him, and the man shook his hand.

"Sam, this is Jones," Wendy said. "He's going to have a chat with you. I'm going to wait outside, unless you need me, and the two officers will be on the front and back doors. Take your time and try to be calm. You're safe."

Jones ushered Sam onto a small leather sofa facing the basic hotel double bed and settled himself in a wooden chair opposite. Wendy gave Sam a comforting grin and gently closed the door behind her. The television was on in the background. It looked like the highlights of an international football match, but the sound was muted.

Sam looked around the room. It was an anonymous, magnolia-painted hotel room. He'd seen so many hotel rooms like this in movies he'd studied. You'd only visit places like this if you were a frustrated salesman, perhaps attending a regional conference or having some kind of disappointing low-level affair with your boss.

He scanned the tea bags and coffee sachets next to the budget-style kettle and little pots of UHT milk. There was no hot chocolate on offer. That was the clincher. Either this was a two-star hotel for travelling salesman and people with fidelity issues, or the RUC had just booked a shitty room. It was then that he noticed Jones was staring at him and he remembered why he was there.

"Are you okay, Sam?" Jones asked. "Can I get you anything?"

"Like what?" he responded, noticing a carrier bag on the floor. "I've been introduced to Harp Lager by Wendy. I'm not sure it's my thing and I don't fancy Guinness either. It looks like black soup and tastes like rust. What have you got?"

"Well, all I've stolen from my colleagues is a Twix, two cans of Club Lemon, a few bags of cheese and onion Taytos and a box of Cadbury's Animal Biscuits. No booze," Jones explained.

"I'll have a Twix and a can of the lemon stuff. What's it like?" Sam was wondering about the obsession with Animal Biscuits, although they were admittedly very tasty.

"Lemony. With bits in." Jones was picking up the yellow can and reading from the description.

"Sounds perfect. Why am I here?" Sam asked, looking over at Jones, who'd removed the ring pull from his own Club.

"I saw your parents today," he began. "You've got a lovely house in Ash and they're both really nice people."

"You saw them?" Sam adjusted his position on the sofa and stopped fiddling with the Twix wrapper. "How's mum? She was so upset on the telephone earlier. I hate what I've put them through."

Jones took a long swig from his drink and pulled open the box of biscuits.

"Your mum is a little fragile. She's anxious about you both. But you've not put them through anything. They think you're behaving courageously and so do I. You might be the person who locks up a murderer."

"I know. But I wish I hadn't said anything. Then Emma wouldn't have been taken, and I'd be in my halls getting on with my course. My parents wouldn't have all this upset. They don't deserve it."

"You did the right thing, Sam. One hundred per cent. Your parents are so proud of you and remember Philip Bradley had children and a wife, too. You're helping them find out who killed their father and husband. This is real bravery," Jones explained.

"Don't mention bravery, please. I don't deserve that. That's not right. You've met my father, haven't you? That's bravery." Sam bit the end of his Twix and looked over at Jones. He was easy to talk to. He could see why he and Wendy were friends.

"Your father was in the army and is now a firefighter. I agree, that's real bravery. But it's a different kind. You didn't ask for any of this. You've witnessed something horrific and you're making a difference."

"I guess so," he said, unconvincingly. "Why did you visit my parents? Is this about Emma?" Sam diverted the conversation, preventing further talk of bravery. It made him feel awkward and even more stressed about his predicament.

"Kind of. I went to understand whether there's more to this case. To get a complete picture. A bit like when you're writing a complex thesis for college, I need to look at every angle and understand how it affects the decisions we make and our assumptions."

"I haven't written a thesis yet," Sam said. "But I think I understand. So, what are the missing parts of the picture?"

"Well, for a start, you didn't come to Ireland by accident, did you, Sam?"

"Oh, I see. No, it was my first choice. Second choice was Nottingham Trent, and I didn't really fancy that. Everything was too modern. But when we came to Coleraine on two of the open days, I really loved the area. I felt right at home there."

"Why do you think that was?" Jones nudged. Sam had already worked out where the conversation was going, but it wasn't an avenue he was keen on. After all, what the hell has his adoption got to do with a murder and a kidnapping?

"The people, my dad's contacts from his time here. Just a general feeling of belonging. I'm not much of a social animal, so a campus in a relatively small town worked for me. Coleraine isn't even as big as Guildford or Aldershot. I'm a small-town person." Sam looked at Jones and realised that this avoidance tactic wasn't going to work. He was probably a skilled interrogator. He just didn't want a cul-de-sac conversation.

"I think those are all perfectly fair answers," Jones started. "But I think you know what I'm driving at. You and your sister were born in Belfast and adopted separately by the same family. How long did you live here for? Before moving over to Surrey?"

"I don't know. Maybe four or five years? I think I was with a foster family prior to my adoption, but I can't remember that. Emma wouldn't have been older than six months when she left. Why do you need to know this?"

"I'm sorry, Sam. I wouldn't be asking any of these questions if it wasn't important. Do you want one of these biscuits? My friend bites the heads off the animals and thinks it's hilarious." Jones passed him the box.

"I understand. I think this is supposed to be a tiger," Sam concluded, after pulling a small biscuit from the box. "They're okay, actually. What else is in there?" he emptied the box onto the small table between the sofa and chair and they identified the creatures. Sam watched as Jones tried to work out whether it was a tiger or a lion, before finding another large cat-shaped biscuit, which confused them both.

"So, did you try to find your birth mother?" Jones asked, with Sam still focused on animal identification and consuming them.

"I wouldn't know where to start. I have this little letter, which she wrote before I was adopted. It's here in my wallet. Do you want to hear it? I'm not sure it explains much." Sam hadn't shown the letter to anyone else outside his family before. It was a treasured possession, albeit a copy – the original was still safely in the family bureaux at home. But it was so special to him that he hadn't even let Emma hold it. He didn't want Jones to touch it either, but he didn't mind reading it aloud. He wiped his hands, fearing they'd still be covered in chocolate.

"Are you sure you don't mind?" Jones asked as he watched Sam jump up and take the folded paper from a section in the back of his near-empty wallet. He carefully unfolded it. Although it was a copy, it was clearly well-loved. The paper was now wafer thin and the indented squares from the constant folding were showing signs of damage. He read it slowly and purposefully.

"*To my boy,*

I have let you down. I've relied far too much on the people around me. But I am tired, ill, and incapable of giving you the life you need. Sending you to England will keep you out of harm's way and give you a proper future.

These are kind people. Be kind to them too and don't forget where you came from and the love that remains. Never let the goodness inside you ever get away."

There was a pause for a few moments whilst Sam worked out what to say. He wasn't emotional, as he'd read the letter so many times that only the mystery behind his mother's identity ever really saddened him anymore. Jones broke the silence.

"She sounds like a wonderful woman. The letter must mean so much to you."

"It does, but she's right, too. It got me out of harm's way, and she gave me a proper future. I guess that's a sign of real love, that she felt able to let me go to ensure my safety and a new beginning. I'm just sad Emma didn't get a letter and that's why I hide it from her. One day Mum and Dad will explain her story too." Sam pondered that thought for a second and moved on.

"Going back to your question, I know nothing whatsoever about her current location. All I know is that this letter was written in the Posthouse Hotel in London a day before my adoption and that she was an alcoholic. That's it."

"Would you trust Wendy enough to get a couple of photocopies of this letter? One for you, as that copy looks very frayed, and one for us for our investigation? Otherwise it might break up over time," Jones knew this would be a tall order. But Sam surprised him by quickly agreeing. Jones knocked on the door and Wendy emerged to gently take the letter from Sam. She gave him a little hug and disappeared down to the hotel lobby to find the business centre and the photocopier.

"What does all this mean?" Sam asked. "Why are you so interested in this stuff? If my birth mum hasn't been interested for all these years, why would she suddenly turn up? I don't get it." Sam was beginning to feel a little hemmed in. He liked Jones and knew this was all background information, but this was a subject area he'd been trying to park for many years. Bringing it to the surface, amongst all the other issues, was becoming painful and felt unnecessary.

"Yeah," Jones started. "I feel like I'm pressing a bruise here. I'm sorry. It's just we need to look at all possibilities. One of them, although it's really going out on a limb, is that your birth mother has taken Emma. We just need to rule that out."

"Bloody hell," Sam replied. "I get it now, but I still can't help. I mean, I know nothing about her. I've not even tried to look. Coming here is the closest I've been to taking that step," he stopped, picked up another biscuit, and then a thought hit him. "Hold on, you're going to find her, aren't you? That's where all this is leading. You've got to rule her out. That's why I'm here."

"Not entirely," Jones responded. "You were brilliant when we chatted through what you saw from the wardrobe. Absolutely top class. Normally, these conversations simply wouldn't happen. But I think we have some mutual trust, don't we?"

"You mean, you believe me, and you think you can trust me to help with this aspect of the investigation, too?" Sam liked that idea. He sat further back on the sofa. He wanted to be helpful.

"I think, if our roles were reversed, you'd think the same of me. I want to help you. You're a good lad. You'd want to help me. It's that simple. There are no games, no hidden agendas. I want to catch the killers, and you want to me to find Emma. We're completely on the same page. You've even got one of my friends looking after you, haven't you? She's fantastic, isn't she?" Jones smiled at Sam, and he blushed a bit.

"She's brilliant. Scary though, I'm pleased she's on our side."

"Me too," Jones grinned.

Sam grabbed his can of Club Lemon and held it up.

"Okay. Let's cheers this. We have a deal. You can investigate my birth mum, dig into my past a bit, as long as you keep me posted and help find Emma. I hate that she's out there alone. I really do."

"And chase murderers? With your help too?" Jones clinked cans with Sam. He was impressed with his bravado. God knows what was going on in his head, Jones thought. Although Jones never had the onslaught of family pressures, he could see a lot of himself in Sam. Only twelve months ago. Jones was a raw, confused, and questioning recruit. Now, he felt able to cope. This conversation, without Jenny and without a camera or handheld in sight, was his first solo interview.

"Yes..." Sam replied. After a moment's thought. "Chasing murderers or, in my case, hiding from them. That's like a constant nightmare. It's wedged in my head and I'm not entirely sure how to deal with it. I've been waking up and, well, crying a bit. I feel so alone."

"I know, Sam. But we're all here for you. Wendy's a star and I'm only a few years older than you. My sleep is punctuated with thoughts and dreams that I never want to think about. But my dad used to give me some advice," Jones explained.

"Before you joined the police?" Sam asked.

"Kind of, Sam. Yeah. He said that life is full of moments that don't need to be stitched together. If we can accept that this is just one such moment and move on from it, then there'll be plenty of better ones to come in the future. You're going to have a fabulous life."

"I think I see what you mean," Sam replied.

"I've met your parents and they're amazing. You're at an epic university here in Northern Ireland and the craic will be ninety," Jones added, smiling.

"The craic will be ninety? What does that mean?"

"They say it a lot here. Craic is good fun, yeah?" Sam nodded in response. "Well, some Irish people say 'the craic is ninety' because it could never reach the full capacity craic of one hundred. If you say the craic is a hundred, that means it can't possibly get any better. When we all know things can always get better. Agreed?"

"Oh, I like that. There's always room for improvement. The fun can always get better. But it sounds weird not being Irish and saying Irish phrases, doesn't it?"

"I've only been here a little while and I'll never get away with using the local lingo. It just sounds wrong. But Sam, my friend, you were born and raised here. You're an Irishman!"

"You're right! Thanks for this," Sam said. "You've really given me stuff to think about. But look, I can't stay here all night. I have another round of Sonic the Hedgehog to play with Wendy later. Is it alright if she comes in now?"

"Absolutely," Jones replied, swigging the bottom of the can of Club. "I'll find her and you can head back to the safe house. But if you need me, Wendy knows where I am."

"Cheers mate," Sam shook hands with Jones and watched as he headed out of the room. Jones left all the remaining goodies from his bag on the table.

As Jones walked past the protection officer, he spied Wendy sitting at the top of the stairs waiting for him.

"How did it go, Jones?" she asked.

"I have two things to report. One, he's a bloody brilliant kid and thinks the world of you. Two, I think I might have learnt how to handle sensitive interviews. I think I did okay."

"Well done, Jones," Wendy grinned. "I'm learning sensitive stuff too. But it's so bloody draining. Anyway, I'd best get him back in the safe house. Give Mr Singh my best."

Wendy disappeared back into the hotel room and Jones strolled back down the stairs to look for Isadora.

This was progress, he thought.

Twenty-Five

Jones and Jenny sat up until close to midnight, running through the details of the chat. Jenny was madly proud of him for being so warm and fuzzy with Sam Jacobs. Jones wanted to 'let the emotion sink in' and therefore he limited himself to just two large glasses of red wine. A mature drink for a wise head, he decided.

However, with another early start planned, the two did something rare. They sat in bed, reading their respective books. Jenny was enjoying The Body Farm by Patricia Cornwell and Jones started The Russia House by John le Carré. An hour later, Jones switched the light off and they slept. Jenny wrapped herself around Jones and she awoke in the same position at 9.30am. They then showered together and made their first steps into the day. They'd overslept, but this felt the closest to normality they'd come for some time.

Jones dashed out of the door exactly ten minutes after they stepped out of the shower, and Jenny wasn't far behind. But she knew exactly where to find him. In the middle of the queue at the barracks refectory, Sadly, so did Virginia Curry, who rushed through the breakfast throng and clapped eyes on them both straightaway.

"Where have you been, Jones? You've just missed a call from McIlhinney at Knock Road," Virginia began. "Saoirse Bradley has reported a break-in on their yacht, The Mainstay, at Bangor Harbour. She was with her kids, so said very little. Can you two head up there?"

"Is there honestly no-one else?" Jenny responded. "Can't we eat first? This keeps happening."

"You can eat on route. She asked for you both personally." Virginia was in no mood for a discussion. She had YCU waiting for a bleep test in the parade grounds and a call from her husband, Sir Charles, to return.

"Isn't this more police work?" Jones replied hungrily.

"You two made the connection. She trusts you. Get yourselves over there. That was an order from McNally, by the way," she added.

Jones left the queue and wandered back to the briefing rooms to find Isadora, whilst Jenny grabbed her vitamin fix, an enormous glass of orange juice. Isadora was sorting through a large box of circuit boards that Mr Singh had ordered for the QD. She looked less than enamoured by the task.

"Isadora, Jenny and I have to get back to Saoirse Bradley. Their yacht has been broken into. Can our debrief wait?"

"What about me?" Isadora jumped in.

"I think McNally wants you working on the surveillance operation. Sorry. Moan at him," Jones explained. "I'm just the messenger."

Isadora rolled her eyes. This was becoming a trend. Her action girl image was being tarnished by all this mundanity.

"I really hope there's no action over at Saoirse's. Assembling this recording equipment and dealing with Tom and Carl is hardly a life affirming experience. There'll be trouble if you two have any fun or get involved in anything dangerous," she smiled sarcastically.

She then took a mouthful of coffee and threw the Land Rover keys to Jenny, who had just appeared behind Jones. The pair then sprinted to the car.

The trip to Millisle was relatively quick. The roads were clearer than normal during the morning commute, and Jenny soon got the hang of resetting Isadora's adapted controls. Jones was busy fiddling with the stereo and settled on the *'I Should Co-Co'* cassette by Supergrass for the journey.

As soon as they hit the coast road again, the air seemed to change, with only wispy clouds in the sky and the heat of the day taking hold. A few holiday-makers were already on the sandy beaches and there were people braving the sea, and it wasn't even 11am yet. It was expected to hit 25 degrees Celsius later. This was hot for Ireland and Jones was in jeans and one of Jenny's brown long-sleeved t-shirts, again.

Mainstay Barns were instantly recognisable, and as Jenny pulled into the long driveway, Saoirse was obviously waiting for their arrival. The gates opened instantly, before they'd had a chance to push the entry control panel.

As the Land Rover arrived outside the front of the green-themed barn, Saoirse stepped outside in a short white tennis dress and white flat trainers. Jenny wound down the window and greeted Mrs Bradley. There was no small talk in return.

"You've been told about the break in?" she asked, without waiting for a reply. "Well, yous two need to get to the marina urgently. The yacht is unlocked and it's a wee way from other boats. It's an expensive model and I know someone has been on board. This is absolutely the last thing we need now."

"I'm sure. We'll head there straightaway. How do we get to it?" Jones called across. Jenny scowled at him, as she knew Saoirse looked good today and Jones would notice that. She was often over protective and this was a trait that needed some attention.

"You're looking for a wooden walkway. There are two. You want the one on the left. The Mainstay has a grey hull and is the only large yacht on that walkway. It's by far the biggest there and it's quite isolated. That was done deliberately."

"I understand, Mrs Bradley. Somebody will probably come back here afterwards and report in," Jenny explained.

Saoirse walked back into the barn, calling her dogs in at the same time. The entry gates opened again. Jenny turned left onto Donaghadee Road and took the coast road past Orlock Point and Groomsport. It was rare for Jones and Jenny to have this time together, and she wanted to make the best of it. If the boat had been ransacked, there was no rush. Their last trip to Bangor was to visit Stephen Finch, who during the Topaz mission had turned out to be a Russian sleeper agent, and that was a memory that needed erasing quickly.

"Saoirse looked good today. She's stunning. Don't you think?" Jenny said, keeping half an eye on Jones' body language as she swung the car towards the town centre.

"Jenny, for God's sake, she's a young widow and in the centre of our case. I couldn't care less what she looks like," he responded, realising she was looking for a reaction. "We showered together less than an hour ago and I've told you repeatedly that I owe you my life. Do you need any more hints that I'm totally committed?"

"Yeah. Okay. But are you not complimented that I wanted to keep you all to myself?" she smiled.

"I'm complimented every day we wake up together. But you need to rein in that other nonsense. Please."

"Noted," Jenny replied. "I'll get my head back into professional mode."

After a few minutes of awkward silence, the Land Rover soon arrived into Bangor town centre. They passed the bus station before heading towards the bustling shopping centre, with shops of all kinds on both sides of the street. Families were everywhere with ice creams, drinks, and full shopping bags. Bangor looked like a town in the midst of a boom, despite the ongoing unpredictable nature of Ulster. Jones stared out of the passenger window with growing interest. He would bite his tongue on Jenny's over protective wobble.

He focused instead on the townscape as they weaved past the shops and turned left into the marina. It was packed with tall ships, yachts, and sailing boats of a variety of sizes and descriptions. Further along the coast, shipping boats were bobbing on the calm sea, having already returned with their catches earlier. It was an idyllic scene. Jones saw the silhouette of a gigantic container ship far in the distance, and he turned away. That was a memory that needed locking away for now.

Jenny found a parking space, Jones grabbed an equipment rucksack out of the boot and walked along the high sea wall. They took the steps downwards and strolled onto the long wooden walkways which sat on top of the water, dividing the different yachts and ships like veins of a leaf. The ebbing and flowing of the boats against the gentle sea breeze made a barely audible knocking noise.

"Okay, the two walkways part here. According to Saoirse, we stick to the left-hand route," Jones said, reading the names of the smaller boats out loud. "Look, there's a tiny sailing boat called Who's Shore Daddy, that's amazing! Oh, and a fishing boat called Test Tackles!" And they both burst out laughing, which reset the atmosphere. As they reached the end of the walkway, there were only two large yachts left, and neither looked to be quite expensive enough to be The Mainstay.

"Ballerina II, nope, and the last one is Irish Coffee, with a brown hull. Where the hell is The Mainstay?" Jones started running up and down the walkways.

"Right, let's split up." Jenny suggested. "I'll search down the other route and see if Saoirse got her left and right mixed up. It's not beyond the realms of possibility. Isadora struggles sometimes." Jones smiled and nodded, and he carried on checking the names of the yachts down the furthest walkway.

Jones soon realised that the Bradley's yacht wasn't there. So, he sat on the end of the walkway and looked out to sea. All he needed was a can of Vimto and a kiss-me-quick hat and this would be like his family holidays in Clacton. But this moment of sentimentality was short-lived. Two teenage lads, one in a light blue Adidas shell-suit and the other in a red Liverpool football shirt, pitched up behind him. The shell-suited youth spoke first.

"Have you lost your boat, big fella?"

"That isn't funny," Jones responded. Feeling strangely old, suddenly.

"He wasn't being funny," the lad in the Liverpool shirt chimed in. "There's a fecking massive boat floating down the coastline. You can just make it out if you look to your left."

Jones followed the lad's gaze. Sure enough, an enormous yacht was visible just off the coast, past all the expensive houses on the foreshore.

"Bugger," Jones exclaimed.

"It's not moored. It's just floating, like. Someone's taken the anchor up and untethered it. It's mad and pretty dangerous. If it's yours, we can scoot you out there on our wee dinghy. But it'll cost you," The first teenager offered.

"Tell you what, lend me your boat and I'll give you £25. I'll bring it back in an hour."

"Fifty quid," he replied. "Then you can have it for the rest of the afternoon. Can you use an outboard motor?"

"Of course," Jones lied, having never skippered any floating object in his life. "I'll give you £35. I can't go any further, as that's all I've got. Deal?" The lad in the tracksuit shook hands with Jones.

As the lads brought the dinghy round to the end of the walk-way, Jenny arrived back from her search, shaking her head. Exchanging no words, Jones pointed at the yacht in the distance and Jenny rolled her eyes.

"Classic Jones. Bloody typical," she said. "Let me guess, you're proposing to get in that thing to check it out? Can you handle it?"

"Yeah, naturally. Unless you can? I wouldn't stand in your way if you wanted to ... er ... skipper?"

The lads, hearing the conversation, winked at each other and grinned.

"Tell you what. Show me your skills. Get on board. Crank it up and you can pick me up at the end of the jetty. I'll be your passenger. We can then investigate the yacht together," Jenny said.

"Yous two are pretty laid back if that's your boat. It'll get damaged if you don't get it back soon," the shell-suited lad explained. "Here, I'll hold the dinghy for you. Step on board, big lad."

Jones gingerly stepped onto the dinghy from the walkaway. He'd never been the steadiest of people, even on dry land, but with only one foot in the dinghy he was particularly uneasy. With the eyes of the two lads and Jenny on him, he carefully slid the other foot from the walkway into the middle of the little boat. He wobbled and had to stabilise hastily. He knew he was making a hash of things.

To underline this further, the dinghy then started to rock wildly, and Jones had to rebalance himself. For a moment it looked like it might tip over, but just in time, with Jenny looking on exasperatedly, he corrected himself for the second time. He then waved over to Jenny proudly, like a toddler on the swings waving to his mum.

"Piece of piss," Jones called up, grabbing hold of the tiller on the motor and immediately putting the dinghy into a spin. The boat span in two complete circles before he gained full control, and the two teenagers laughed loudly.

"Class," the lad in the Liverpool shirt said. "The English fella is an absolute dort."

"What on earth are you doing? You bloody idiot!" Jenny screamed. Jones veered away from the walkway and into the sea, struggling to gain any kind of control.

"Lads!" Jones shouted over the engine. "How do I switch this thing off?"

"There's a key and a switch on the left-hand side. I thought you knew how to use this?" The lad in the shell-suit called over. By now, Jones had manoeuvred the dinghy further away from Jenny and the lads. To save any face, he thought, he was going to have to head to the yacht alone and make this all look deliberate.

"I've just not used this model before. That's all. Right, Jennifer Richmond, I'm going to head over to the yacht, because I'm not sure I can stop this now. I'll be right back. Hang around here, yeah?" Jones shouted.

"Jennifer? What are you on, Jones? Are you okay? Jesus Christ!" But he didn't hear, Jones was too far away, and he had somehow stabilised the tiller towards The Mainstay in the distance.

'Bastard thing,' Jones said to himself. 'Stupid bravado, idiot Jones. Idiot!'

As the dinghy headed into open water with Jones trying to repel a panic attack, his attention was drawn to the yacht in the distance. And the fact that, knowing it was unmoored and heading in the wrong direction, he'd never skippered a yacht either. God alone knew how he was going to sort out this mess.

Twenty-Six

Jones had propelled the dinghy to within about 750 yards of the yacht when he noticed what looked like two bright red lights flashing on the deck. It was difficult to make out against the sunshine and the reflections from the waves. He had a cheap pair of sunglasses deep in his equipment bag, but he didn't want to take his hand off the tiller. He thought he could also make out a large brown suitcase near the stern of the boat. The yacht was now listing badly towards the coastline and the tide was pulling it closer to the rocks.

He knew, from some of the long-drawn-out chats with Jim Shiels in the sick bay on the General Eduardo, that two round red lights flashing didn't signal distress, but indicated an inability to manoeuvre. Someone had activated those lights. Was someone on board?

Jones was regretting single-handedly taking the small boat out to sea. This was well out of his comfort zone, and he had one of those awful feelings that made his brain ache with edginess and fear.

Jenny was now in the distance. He could see her standing with the two lads. Jones could imagine her desperately trying to defend her idiot boyfriend and shuddered with horror at the memory of the dinghy circling in front of them all. However, there were more pressing issues now. He needed to get on board.

As it loomed closer, he could see The Mainstay was shiny and expensive looking. It had a silver-grey hull and gold handrails along the perimeter. The white steps leading onto the deck shone in the sun and the mainsail and jib-sheet were so perfectly white that it made Jones question whether it had ever been out in the sea. The whole craft, from afar, looked untouched and polished.

As he got closer, the sea calmed. The journey in the dinghy became easier and Jones' use of the tiller became more confident. But his sixth sense, that awful cold tap on the shoulder, was still there. A reminder that his brain sensed something terrible. But he cast that aside and focused on the job in front of him. When he was within a few metres of The Mainstay, he noticed a large reel of rope and thought through how to secure the dinghy to the yacht.

He grabbed the length of rope, which had eyes spliced at each end, and threaded through a hole that had been pre-drilled in the transom. Jones then ran it back around a beam under the dock on The Mainstay. He pulled it tight and held his balance and nerve as he was doing so. He remembered how to tie a cleat hitch from his brief stint as a sea scout, and for a few brief moments stared in wonderment at the brilliance of the knot and how he'd secured the dinghy. That, he thought, wasn't going anywhere. To finish the job, he paced to the stern of the yacht and found the anchor. He released it into the sea and felt a wave of relief that The Mainstay would not plough into coastal rocks or ground on the beach.

He looked around. From his position on deck, he could see a beach speckled with large stones and seaweed. Further away, a row of expensive-looking Victorian houses was visible. He could just make out their windows shining in the summer sun. He could smell the saltiness of the air and the small of his back was caked with sweat from the heat of the day and the stress of the situation.

He considered calling out to warn anyone on board that he was there. But something stopped him. Instead, he slowly walked around the deck and held onto the handrails as the listing continued. He felt unsteady and there were the first signs of sea-sickness, something he'd never succumbed to on board the General Eduardo. Then again, that beast was like a floating village. This was a much smaller vessel.

The air was cooling, and he had to remind himself that despite the unusually warm weather, this was the Irish Sea, and this stretch of water was unpredictable. As he completed the full circuit of the deck, with nothing to report and no signs of a break-in, he decided he needed to go below deck and into the cabin.

The area leading to the cabin's white double doors was dominated by two large sun-loungers with long, cream-coloured padded cushions. Each sun-lounger had a little novelty pillow at the head end with pictures of Italian renaissance art displayed on the cushion cover. There were little zones to rest a wine glass, and he spotted a tiny fridge underneath one of the loungers. There were signs of children's play equipment, a bucket and spade, a little fishing net and some plastic beach shapes. Sandy moulds of a starfish, a crab and a jellyfish in bright cheerful colours. His brain wanted to look inside the beer fridge. God knows he needed something to take the edge off, but he couldn't. He needed to focus.

The double doors of the cabin were already unlocked. He pulled them outwards and stepped inside the living quarters. He was greeted by a lounge area, with an immense sofa and a sizable built-in television. There were large prints of famous Italian works of art on the walls, including The Birth of Venus, The Last Judgement, The Creation of Adam, and Venus of Urbino. Jones loved this type of art and paused briefly to ground himself in the beauty of them all. However, whilst he realised this was a luxurious status symbol, there was something about the pine clad walls and the beige material of the furnishings that took him back to a caravan, perhaps a family holiday in Hayling Island in Kent. Maybe it was the smell, too.

On the left was a well-appointed galley kitchen and a small dining area. There were enough seats for maybe six people to sit comfortably. Adorning the table were placemats showing photos of Tuscan landmarks in sepia, and in the middle of the table were two fluted wine glasses and a half-finished bottle of rose. Everything else in the galley was pristine and seemed untouched. He noticed a kettle and a toaster that were unplugged and the digital LED clock on the oven was flashing midnight. The power had been tripped, or perhaps the oven had never been used.

But importantly, there were no outwards signs of a break-in. If anything, it looked more likely like someone might have broken in and cleaned it thoroughly.

The next room, bedroom one, had bunk beds with duvets emblazoned with the sun, stars and moon in a deep blue. It was tiny. Jones would have felt claustrophobic in this little room but could only imagine the fun the kids would have had in there. There were a few scattered kids' books on the bed, Meg and Mog, Mr Daydream and Charlotte's Web, for the older child.

One pace further and there was a single room. But this seemed to have been utilised as a storage space. Although the single bed, with a grey duvet and sheets, was made up in the corner of the room, the rest of the space was filled with two large wardrobes filled with male and female clothing. On the left-hand side, there was a small table cluttered with an electric razor, a hair drier and various luxury-brand cosmetics. These must have been Saoirse and Philip's. Remnants from their unusual marriage.

There were provisions, like tins, oil, beer, even fruit juice, piled up on top of the wardrobes and ready for the next adventure. There was even a selection of board games poking out under the bed. This was the closest The Mainstay had got to untidy and even so; it seemed as if it had been organised with purpose. He could feel Saoirse's touch in this room, ensuring things were just right for the family.

There were two more doors. He imagined one was a bathroom, that would be his last room to explore. But the largest bedroom, he guessed, was the room that sat back from the lounge area. There were two framed photos of the Rome Colosseum on either side of the doorway, and the door itself appeared bigger than the others, with pine slats running vertically down the door.

He pushed hard at the door and turned the handle. It wasn't locked, but the door appeared to be blocked or caught on the frame. The door simply wouldn't give way. He used his shoulder and the weight of his body to create a small gap between the door and the frame and peered in. He could just about make out a king-sized bed. There was something furry on the bed, maybe a faux fur bed runner or throw and a few scattered brown cushions. But he was still feeling unnerved and felt the need to get through that door. Something was blocking his entrance and whilst he knew he soon had to turn his attention to getting the yacht back to the harbour, there was something very wrong here.

He knew this boat was the Bradley family's pride and joy, so he was loath to break into the bedroom. It would feel like vandalism. But after pushing and heaving at the main bedroom door, he gave up and resorted to charging at full pelt, to gain entry. He could imagine Jenny laughing at his efforts to use his average male frame to smash through the door. But when he finally succeeded and created a big enough opening to squeeze through, he wished he hadn't. Every core of his body recoiled at the awfulness in front of him.

There, hanging from the coat hook on the back of the door by a leather belt, was the body of a woman. It was the weight of the body suspended from the door that had prevented him from entering. Jones staggered back away in disbelief and covered his mouth.

Her widened eyes bulged in bewilderment and her mouth gaped open, stuck in the throes of the torture that beset her final moments of life. The horror of the situation was compounded by her tongue hanging out and the bright red lipstick smeared around her mouth. The belt was so tightly fastened around her neck that her face was contorted.

It was a face of fear fixed with pain, anguish, and hopelessness. Her right hand was still in a defensive pose, forming a fist and there were scratches on her arms. This was an evil death. A murder so callous that the woman had stood no chance. As once she'd been hoisted up by the belt, she would have been totally unable to get down. Jones could imagine her helpless flailing of arms and legs as her last breaths left her body.

Jones felt his stomach turn and his heart-rate increase rapidly. He was so shocked by the scene that he needed to look away from it. Instead, he briefly focused out of the porthole and far away into the distance to reset and ground himself. Almost to assure himself that the macabre vision in front of him was real.

This was what he had been dreading. This was all of his fractured senses wound up into a nightmare and presented in front of him, like some savage proof of proficiency that his mind could predict such viciousness. He hated the gift that he'd been given.

The dead woman was in her late twenties or early thirties. She was pale and petite, with bobbed auburn hair. She was slight in build and her features were almost doll-like. She was wearing an unseasonal black hooded top, with the sleeves rolled up, and grey joggers. On her left arm was a rose gold Citizen watch and a pearl ring was on the little finger of her left hand. Contrasting this casual look was her perfectly applied make-up, aside from the lipstick smudge.

It was as if she was readying herself for a big night out or an event. Jones stared her up and down, reminding himself to be respectful and to memorise key features. But something was nagging at him. The victim looked vaguely familiar. There was also a perfume, a sweet smell, that he recognised. It could have been a well-known brand, but something pulled at his memory.

There was a small purple clutch bag on the floor. It was open. He kicked the contents onto the floor, ensuring he didn't leave his fingerprints on them. The first item he saw was a brand-new Blockbuster video card in the name of Martha Maddison. There were a few other knick-knacks, like a BT Phonecard and a Northern Bank ATM card, but anything else was typical handbag fodder. A lipstick, some sanitary towels, a biro, loose change, and a roll of fruit pastilles. There was a green leather pound coin holder with all five coins still in place. Jones found this discovery particularly tragic, somehow feeling sad that she'd never had time to spend them.

Knowing her name felt odd, too. She didn't look like a Martha. But he knew that this would be her final introduction and that the name Martha Maddison, the woman hanging from a door on The Mainstay, would before too long be 'the body'. The body found on the yacht, the body in the morgue and the woman's body found murdered off the coast of Bangor. The hanged body.

She would now forever be a victim. No more Martha. Jones struggled with that notion.

The woman couldn't have been dead long, he decided. Her freckled skin was still warm to the touch and there was none of the smell that comes with death. It was a smell Jones knew far too well.

His brain now kicked into gear, scanning the scene and looking for anything out of place. But, as he'd already evidenced, the yacht was almost perfectly clean. The carpet in the bedroom, a light marl colour, looked freshly hoovered. The duvet and pillows were carefully positioned, as if ready for another night on the seas. The faux fur throw, across the final third of the king-sized bed, was equally perfect and ordered. Nothing seemed amiss.

In fact, aside from the dead woman on the back of the door, this was a yacht in tip-top condition. Jones, still thinking on his feet, squeezed past the body of Martha and stuck his head around the door of the bathroom. Everything shone. The walk-in shower, the taps, the white plastic sink, and the chrome towel-rail. Even the three chocolate-coloured towels lined-up on the rail were symmetrical. The green and white bar of Shield soap on a silver soap holder, and the Imperial Leather shower gel all sat there, waiting for their next guest. Everything was suspended in time, just like poor Martha.

Jones walked over to the large sofa and shook his head hard, to repel the awfulness and to concentrate on his next tasks. He located his equipment bag, unzipped it, and found his handheld. He would make two calls. He pressed transmit and attempted to reach McNally.

"McNally, are you reading me? This is Jones. I'm on The Mainstay just off Bangor Harbour." Jones heard his voice quiver slightly as he spoke.

"Aye, go ahead Jones." McNally responded. He sounded irritated.

"There's the body of a young woman hanging from the bedroom door on board the yacht. It seems very recent. The rest of the boat is spotless."

"Jesus, that's awful. Can you describe her?"

"Late twenties, perhaps, maybe slightly older. Dark red hair, quite short and pale-skinned. I have a name too, from her handbag. She's Martha Maddison."

"Okay. Could this be Wonder Woman? Your description fits Sam Jacob's recollections. She had red hair, pale and he thought around that age."

"Yeah, that was my thought, too, McNally. Maybe somebody knew she'd called the police?"

"Maybe," McNally replied, Jones could hear his cogs turning. "What a fecking nightmare, though. What a way to die. Anything else amiss on the yacht?"

"No, everything is perfect otherwise. Saoirse Bradley told us there had been a break-in. The yacht had certainly been cast adrift and was heading towards the rocks, but there was no sign of any burglary. How did she know?"

"Alright, big fella." McNally responded. "I'll speak to the

RUC, and we'll get the scenes of crime team down there. I'll ring Bristow now. Sit tight."

"Okay, McNally. I'll wait on board. Keep her company."

McNally killed the call, and Jones contacted Jenny. She was a matter of half a mile away, probably sitting on the walkway, wondering what the hell was going on.

"Jenny, it's me. Can you hear me?"

"Yeah, what's going on? You've been ages. The lads here are getting restless about their dinghy."

"Are they within earshot?" Jones replied.

"No, they're over getting a few tinnies from the off licence near the harbour. Hold on. Oh god, you've broken their bloody boat, haven't you? What have you done?"

"No, I've not broken their boat! There's a body on board. A female called Martha Maddison; we think it might be Wonder Woman. She's been hanged. I've never seen anything so tragic in my life." Jones heard his voice crack a little, with emotion. But he held firm and explained what he'd seen. He explained the lack of a break-in, the normality of the initial scene.

"I'm so sorry. That sounds horrifying," Jenny replied.

"It is. She's young, she's been strung up with a leather belt. It's truly savage. I've told McNally. The scenes of crime team are on route, McNally is speaking to Bristow. Stay there and I'll come back once they arrive."

"Stay here? No. I can't do that," Jenny responded. "I need to get back to Saoirse Bradley. I'll radio Bristow myself and talk through an approach. Oh, and are you okay? That must've been quite a shock."

"I'm alright. I knew something was up. I just hate that my instinct was right. Makes me sick to my stomach."

"Okay. I can't believe you've had that to contend with," Jenny said, hearing the change in his voice. "Let's try to focus on the job and talk about it all later. Contact me again once the RUC is on the scene. I'll get more from Saoirse. I'm sending you a hug, you poor thing."

"Oh, shit," Jones exclaimed. "I forgot to tell McNally. There's a huge brown suitcase on the deck here. I've not been into that yet. Hold on, stay with me and I'll open it up with you on the handheld."

"Righto," Jenny responded, noticing the two lads were wandering back. They had a can of Red Stripe each and were swaggering up the walkway as if they were gangsters from the Bronx.

Jones walked from the cabin, through onto the deck, and then walked to the stern. The suitcase, propped against a gold handrail, was very old-fashioned and had two large leather clasps pulling it together, with a zip finally securing the contents. Jones carefully unfastened and unzipped the case. He opened the lid and was astonished by the contents.

"Oh, my good lord!" Jones exclaimed. "I don't believe it."

"What is it?" she replied, the handheld reception crackling slightly.

"It's full of money. Tonnes of it. I think they're all Northern Bank £50 notes. There's got to be a million pounds in here."

Twenty-Seven

The Hunter's Arms was having a small refurb courtesy of the brewery. It hadn't been updated in years and needed some new carpet, an electrical rewire and a modernised kitchen. Wee Joe hadn't had a holiday in almost a decade and had taken his son out of school for a week in the sun. Or that was the story. The only grains of truth were that Joe and family were in Pontins in Pakefield, a holiday camp in Norfolk, and there would certainly be a few changes in the pub.

Carl, Tom, Mr Singh and Isadora had made themselves quickly at home in the early 17th century coaching inn, and a few of the locals had popped their heads in to see what was going on. There were electrical wires and coils littering the bar and a new cooker was delivered midway through the lunchtime session. The pub would now close for a few days, with the locals believing the three outsiders working in the weather-beaten pub were from the London & Newcastle Brewery. There would be a grand reopening night on the Saturday.

The only added complexity was Reginald, a small brown and white hamster that Wee Joe's son doted on. The team was asked to feed the little furry thing and keep an eye on it.

Carl was well-used to serving Guinness and he grinned patiently when a few of the locals gave him tips on the perfect pour. In the meantime, Mr Singh and Isadora were having to get used to a few awkward glares from the lunchtime clientele. Strabane wasn't an ethnically diverse community and, with Mr Singh wearing a turban and Isadora of mixed race and in a wheelchair, the locals stared unhelpfully. Isadora simply stared back indignantly, knowing she could probably take most of them down if her presence was offending them, wheelchair or not. But she'd play nice in the short term.

Once the lunchtime doors were bolted and the team was happy that the village jungle drums were, at least, modified to fit their agenda, they began their work in earnest. Beforehand, Tom went upstairs and looked in on Reginald and he put some food down in his cage. There was no sign of him but there was also a cosy-looking straw-filled home in the middle of the cage. He was probably asleep inside.

The bar was around twelve feet long and Mr Singh had planned to add a long piece of coving with strip lights along the ceiling above the main bar area. This would be home to a series of covert cameras and some listening devices. The strip lights would look rather smart too.

The largest of the four metal fonts on the bar, selling Satzenbrau Lager, would be prized open and a further receiver would be hidden inside. A large air conditioning unit that hadn't worked since the mid-1980s would be repaired and would also house three cameras in the rear of the seating area of the lounge bar. Mr Singh and Isadora would complete this work, whilst Carl and Tom would lay some new carpet, which had been sitting disused in the stores at Thiepval for years. They'd also repaint the internal doors. Mr Singh was reluctant to give his two apprentices anything too technical to undertake with Isadora around, who was very skilled in clandestine communication methods.

"Right," Mr Singh began. "We have two days to give our

Ballyramsey friends the illusion of a modernised pub and ensure the whole place is wired up. We need to act swiftly and monitor the nosey villagers."

"Agreed," Isadora replied. "But my concern is that this is going to stink. People aren't stupid. We are four strangers fiddling with their local. Wee Joe has vanished, and you can bet that everyone in this village is trying to second guess our motives."

"Free beer is the solution," Carl chimed in.

"Oh, for God's sake, Carl. Let's take this seriously, shall we? I know you're excited about being in a pub, but..." Isadora started.

"No, no," he interrupted. "I'm being serious. On Friday night, we'll re-open with a two-hour free bar for locals. We win them over with generosity, good humour, and free alcohol."

"He's right." Tom said. "I don't want to be stereotypical, but the Irish love their beer. We could try to break down some cultural barriers that way."

"Well, if the beer flowed, it might also loosen some tongues," Isadora agreed. "But that's only if we actually get the right people in the room. We need links to George McCool, Andrew and the big man, whoever that might be. McNally wants quick results."

"Okay, as long as McNally green lights this, we'll offer a free bar on the opening night. Although, I'm a little conflicted by this as a tee-totaller." Mr Singh was screwing one of the receivers into the ceiling above the bar and was clearly trying not to smile.

"Isadora, please ignore Mr Singh. He's the equivalent of the secret lemonade drinker, but with Scotch," Tom added. Mr Singh laughed in the background.

"That may be true," he called over. "But we all need to stay off the beer on Friday. Eyes and ears need to be on the regulars, and I'll run the surveillance operation from the function room. You two can serve behind the bar." Tom and Carl nodded at Mr Singh, with Isadora wondering when she would see any real action again.

As Tom and Carl began pulling the carpet up in the rear of the lounge bar, releasing a dust cloud comparable to the Great London

Smog, Isadora took a call on the handheld from Jenny Richmond. The conversation looked deep and complex, and the lads left her to it. They had their own issues to deal with.

Carl pulled a bag of animal biscuits from his trouser pocket, with only a handful left in the bottom, and popped them on the floor in the centre of a bare piece of concreted floor whilst he worked around them. He occasionally dipped into the bag and bit the heads off the chocolate animals, chuckling to himself. It was a joke that kept on giving.

Tom had worked hard and had pulled up most of the old beige carpet, patterned with typical pub debris, mainly chewing gum and old fag ends, and revealed partial floorboards (in the lounge bar) and concrete (in the public bar). Carl started sweeping dust and detritus from the floor, ready for the new sea grass floor covering, and watched on as Tom removed the polythene wrapping from the new flooring. Neither of them had laid carpet before, but how difficult could it be? Carl remembered his dad undertaking the job in just a few hours with a metre ruler, a Stanley knife, and some good old-fashioned brute strength.

In the background, Mr Singh stopped briefly to knock out his pipe and refill with Old Holborn tobacco. It was a habit he had given up for a while, but the pressure of getting the Quartermaster's Department up and running in Thiepval had led him back to the pipe, like an old flame in desperate times. Carl, waiting for Tom to single-handedly pull the heavy roll of sea grass into the public bar, watched as Mr Singh sparked up and assessed his work above the bar. It was all coming together.

As Isadora carried on enthusiastically chatting in the background, Tom and Carl pulled the sea grass carpet along the full length of the bare concrete. It was a near perfect fit. Tom had done well with his calculations. There was just some light trimming underneath the skirting boards, and Tom and Carl worked together to precisely slice off a long strip of the sea grass and then carefully pulled it underneath the boards. They tacked the carpet to the floor and stepped back. It was a job done well. Mr Singh looked over and pointed his pipe at the floor.

"That looks good, lads. Top work."

"We have the rest of the bar to do yet. Let's not count our chickens too soon," Tom replied as Carl seemed to be gazing around the room aimlessly.

It was then that Carl realised that there was a small mound in the centre of the room. He'd left his animal biscuits on the floor and was immediately mortified. He knew that to retrieve them now would mean unpinning a large section of the seagrass and starting again. Carl had been responsible for his fair share of cock-ups in his time and, earlier in the day, had narrowly avoided super-gluing his hand to the floor. This new mistake needed to be hushed-up or dealt with. He would think about solutions when the bar was quieter.

Tom gathered up the rest of the sea grass and measured it to fit the floor-boarded area. Carl smiled as his friend stuck his tongue out in concentration and used a pencil to draw cut-lines on the flooring. Mr Singh, with his pipe now lit and happily puffing away, disappeared to the electrical supply box to check whether the listening devices in the ceiling were live. This was Carl's moment.

He grabbed a claw hammer from Mr Singh's toolbox and quietly smashed the mound on the floor to ensure no-one would notice the biscuit bag under the newly laid carpet, stamped on it for good measure to ensure maximum flatness. It was a success. The deviation in the carpet was no longer noticeable.

Isadora then returned with an anxious look on her face. She carefully briefed everyone on the key points of the dead body on The Mainstay and explained that Marie Bristow was on her way to Bangor to support Jones and Jenny. Mr Singh, Tom, and Carl looked shocked. There were a few moments of contemplation as the team realised the terrible lengths to which the killer would go to silence witnesses.

"It's an absolute tragedy," Mr Singh said. "Another life lost needlessly."

"I feel really sorry for Jones, seeing that poor woman on the back of the door. That must've been horrific," Tom said. "Is there anything we can do?"

"I think we just need to do our jobs. We crack on here. Putting names to the many faces in this case is becoming more and more important. We just need a bit of luck with all these covert devices," Isadora replied. "This is how we make a difference."

Carl and Tom nodded. Mr Singh, puffing energetically on his pipe, was looking shell-shocked in the background.

"Oh, but you two also need to look out for that hamster. I swear I saw it on the stairs a while ago. Wee Joe's son would be devastated if it were lost." Isadora pointed over to the stairs near the bar.

"Absolutely, but some of us aren't very observant, are we, Carl? I found these on the floor earlier." Tom handed Carl his half-eaten packet of animal biscuits. "I can't believe you mislaid them. I think you have developed an addiction to these things."

Mr Singh, now resembling a speeding locomotive with his pipe wedged between his teeth, paced to the centre of the floor in the public bar, onto the new sea grass flooring.

"That's a shame. There's a nasty red stain on the floor over here. No wonder Thiepval didn't use the carpet," he said, looking down. "I'll look in the kitchen for some stain remover."

Carl looked at the red patch and swallowed hard. Reginald must have scampered under the carpet. Carl closed his eyes and realised this was probably his darkest hour yet.

"Everyone," Carl began, feeling his cheeks redden with shame. "I have an announcement to make."

"Not now, Carl." Isadora replied, looking at her watch. "We really have to put our noses to the grindstone. I'm sure it can wait."

"Whatever it is," Tom chimed in, expecting Carl to announce a new armpit farting technique or a record-breaking toilet break. "We can deal with it later, mate. We're in a bar. The world is our oyster!"

"Yeah," Carl agreed resignedly, as Mr Singh arrived back on the scene with stain remover. The pink stain was growing. Somehow, in the midst of a rare success, Carl had accidentally beaten a hamster to death with a claw hammer.

With Carl quietly returning to help Tom in the lounge bar and Mr Singh scrubbing the stain with a hard brush, Isadora carried on setting up the small cameras that would sit above the bar. She was thinking hard about her next moves.

Isadora had driven the team to Ballyramsey in an innocent-looking Ford Mondeo but suddenly felt an urgent need to get to Bangor. The crime scene investigators would take a good while to get to Jones, and Jenny wanted to re-interview Saoirse. She made a quick decision to leave the Quartermaster's team rigging up the pub and head to back to her Topaz colleagues. The problem was, with Ballyramsey at least two hours from Bangor, she'd need a good reason to change teams' mid-operation.

That reason came soon enough, as she noticed the transmit light was flashing on her handheld. It was Virginia, who was sounding more flustered than normal.

"Isadora? I'm guessing you're up to speed with the situation at Bangor Marina? You've been briefed? The murdered woman, the million pounds..."

"Hi Virginia, yes, Jenny rang me. I'm stunned."

"Quite. Well, whilst that's the absolute priority, we have another delicate issue. I wonder if I could ask you to get over to Belfast City Hospital. It appears our friend Orla Massey has had a visit from Caragh Reid, Kenny Reid's other daughter. She was there in the morning." Virginia sounded unusually fraught.

"Really? What did she want?" Isadora asked.

"We think it could be a scare tactic. But we need detail from the horse's mouth, so to speak. McNally and Jube Spencer are at

Hillsborough with the Secretary of State, updating him on the investigation. They are particularly vexed about the money in the suitcase. That's set all kinds of hares running. So, we need your help."

"It's fine. I'll go right away, Virginia. But aren't the police at the hospital already?"

Isadora glossed over the mention of the million-pound discovery, knowing that McNally and Spencer would crawl all over this detail. Isadora was subconsciously joining the dots to organised crime and paramilitaries.

"They sent the young officer, McIlhinney. But I'm not sure he's got the experience or tact to deal with Orla Massey," Virginia explained.

"I know him. He's very green. She'll eat him for breakfast," Isadora agreed. Massey's reputation wasn't diminished by her incarceration and Isadora could imagine her giving young McIlhinney very short shrift.

"You've heard that the body on The Mainstay matches Sam Jacobs' description of Wonder Woman?" Virginia continued.

"Yeah. This is all getting quite messy, isn't it? Have you heard from Wendy? Any news on the little girl?"

"I've heard nothing new whatsoever," Virginia explained. "Wendy is reporting into McNally. They had a confirmed sighting of Sam's sister in Oxford, but nothing since. The police now think she went walkies on her own accord, desperate to get to her brother. The family still want to go to the press. But they're in check for now. Jones and Jenny's trip to England helped there, I think."

"Alright. I'll head over to Massey. Can you keep me updated on The Mainstay?" Isadora asked.

"I'll explain all that to McNally when he's back. He'll be in touch. I've an appointment with an army assault course in Palace Barracks with the YCU. We have some anxious faces in here."

"Bless them," Isadora replied, remembering she still held the

YCU record for the assault course training. Although she knew Ailsa, who was astonishingly fit, would be after that accolade. But that was a thought for another day. Maybe she'd throw herself over those obstacles again once the wheelchair was consigned to history.

"I'd better get on the road. I'll speak to you later. Good luck at Palace Barracks."

Isadora turned off the handheld, looked at her watch and then over at Carl and Mr Singh as they battled to get the odd pinkish stain out of the carpet. They would be fine without her, she decided.

"Lads," she called over. "I'm needed elsewhere. I've rigged up all the receivers, but I've been asked to check in on Massey in Belfast." There were a few nods and waves. The QD Team seemed to be in their own little world. But she'd be back for the excitement of opening night.

She manoeuvred herself out of the pub and the chair juddered as she eased it down a step onto the shingle pathway leading to the car park. Outside, she caught the glances of two older women carrying shopping bags. They averted their eyes as she smiled over.

The blue Mondeo was Virginia's car when she was in Northern Ireland and was already an automatic vehicle. Mr Singh had recently added some modified hand controls to enable Isadora to brake and accelerate. These were fairly inconspicuous and gave Isadora the option of using an unmarked car when the job demanded it. She preferred the Land Rover, mainly because of its speed and comfort, but was impressed by Mr Singh's modifications.

As she indicated out of the car park and towards the main road, she ran through the latest developments and tried to assimilate a plan in her head. What made Caragh Reid head to Massey? Who killed Wonder Woman on The Mainstay? And how did this all link to the Philip Bradley murder?

After assessing Virginia's tape collection, which was a

ramshackle mix of Bette Midler, The Carpenters, and Elaine Page, she switched the radio on. There was a slight fuzz in the background but, as she headed towards Sion Mills, the sound improved.

"Its 6pm and now we head to the BBC Radio Ulster news with Rebecca Mallon."

"We are receiving reports that the body of a young woman has been discovered on a yacht off the coast at Bangor Marina. There is a significant police presence on site and local sources have witnessed a scenes of crime team arriving in a police dinghy."

"Shit," Isadora said, louder than she expected.

"An unconfirmed report has also alleged that police found a suitcase containing a significant amount of cash on the yacht, said to be owned by the late Unionist MP, Philip Bradley. We will bring you more on this story as it develops."

Isadora pulled the Mondeo over to the service station near Sion Mills and grabbed her handheld. She pushed transmit and communicated on the all-frequencies channel, hoping she would alert as many of her colleagues as possible.

"This is Isadora. I'm en route back to Belfast. Is anyone receiving me?"

"Yeah, loud and clear," Jones replied. There was a great of noise around him, but Isadora recognised his voice instantly.

"I'm here too. Is everything alright?" Jenny added.

"Aye. I'm just leaving the meeting at Hillsborough. What's the problem, Isadora?" McNally chimed in.

"The media know about the yacht, the body of the woman and the million pounds in the suitcase. Someone is feeding this information directly to the press and unless we get on top of this, we're going to be carrying out this entire investigation in the public eye."

"A leak? Blimey," Jones said. "Could things be any more complicated?"

"Aye. That's a massive problem," McNally responded. "Being a leak cost George McCool his life. Someone has a death wish. But I reckon this was a rather more planned briefing. Maybe someone in the RUC is on the take?"

"Any ideas?" Jenny asked.

"None we can talk about now. But I have some news too. Martha Maddison doesn't really exist. Jube organised a rush-job with GCHQ. They can find no record of her existence until December 1993. So, she's either changed her name or..."

"She's a field agent for another agency. She's a spy? A Russian?" Jones interrupted.

"Catch yourself on, Jones. You're getting way ahead of yourself. She's been living some kind of double life though and she definitely had something to hide. But this is an important piece of the jigsaw. I can feel that in my bones," McNally added.

Twenty-Eight

The City View Hotel bar was busy for a week-day afternoon. The long-curved bar, littered with menus highlighting a decent selection of snacks and meals, was popular with tourists and day trippers because of the reasonable prices and the local amenities. It was close to the Lagan Navigation and just a gentle walk into the countryside. Belfast didn't have many operational hotels, but this one was far enough away from any perceived threat of trouble that it had become a bit of a haven.

Standing at the bar were two men carrying briefcases. To the casual observer, they looked like salesmen. They were perhaps debriefing after a long day in the field. But the casual observer would be wrong.

"Are you sure your intel is bulletproof?" The first man said, straightening his tie and brushing some stray lint off his suit. He had a silver tie pin, with a shamrock embossed in the centre, which looked as if it had been polished to within an inch of its life.

"Absolutely, Mac, he's not let us down yet. And why would he? This is a huge win-win for him. I hear the big man pays a decent whack for this level of information," the second man said, casually eyeing a tall blonde woman standing next to one of the hotel's large windows. The sunlight from the window was making her dress slightly see-through, and the man was struggling to focus.

The first man, Mac, following his gaze, snapped his fingers in front of his companion.

"Wake up, for God's sake, Ethan! This is important shite. She's not going to pay your wages. She's also about half your age! Focus on the job, man!"

Ethan adjusted his stool and faced his colleague.

"Aye, dead on. I'm ready," he said, slightly embarrassed.

"Right, let's get these down our necks and get over there. It'll be dark at about nine. That gives us three hours to stake the place out. We can't afford a smash and grab."

Mac, wearing a dark business suit with a white shirt and black tie, gulped down his Guinness and put the empty glass on the hotel bar. His descent from the bar stool was a slow one. Mac's days of doing odd jobs for the big man were nearly at an end. But being a contract killer or henchman was not a pensionable job.

Ethan, perhaps in his late thirties, was dressed similarly. He gulped back his cold lager and belched loudly. The barman momentarily looked over, but the rest of the clientele were chucking back the late afternoon beers happily, too. Long gone were the days of decorum in lounge bars.

"We know there's one other person in the cottage. She's a young officer, an unknown. They'll be at least one protection officer on site, but I predict more. We just need to take them out, ideally together, before we get into the cottage." Mac, breathing heavily but speaking insistently, stared at Ethan. Almost as if he was looking for a weakness in the younger man.

"The big man knows this is going to stoke the fires. That was his last transmission. But we do not show the wee lad any sympathy. He saw everything, or that's what our man on the inside says. So, we need to stop him from talking. It puts everything at risk."

"I know the plan, Mac. I've got this. I'm not about to drop the ball here. Stop with the hyper-analysing. You're beginning to sound like the big man's messages." The younger man reached over to the back of his stool and grabbed his suit jacket.

"You haven't actually met him, then?" Mac asked.

"The big man? I know enough about him. I've heard him on all the transmissions, and I get the messages. He's only got a few on the inside that he meets regularly. The inner circle, so, I hear." Ethan was staring aimlessly around the room but with half an eye still on the attractive woman near the window.

"Don't you ever wonder?" Mac continued. "Why the secrecy? Who he is? I mean, I was higher up the chain at one point and I never met them."

"Nah. That's well above my pay grade. I just take the money and keep my mouth shut. It keeps things nice and deniable. If I don't know who the big man is, I can't tell anyone if the Peelers come knocking." Ethan stared at Mac and nodded, as if bringing the conversation to a close, and stood up.

"We better skedaddle. It'll be dark before we know it," he added.

The pair nodded politely at the barman and exited the hotel through the main doors and past reception. A couple of taxis were waiting in the courtyard and there was a smell of rain in the air. It had been a hot day so far and a small shower would be a welcome relief from the heat.

As they walked with their briefcases along the towpath, they saw a couple of kids running with their parents and doing loud impressions of the ducks in the middle of the canal. Mac smiled. He had grandchildren at home, and they loved the countryside. The pair grinned at the passing family and carried on their stroll, heading towards the lock-gates in the distance. The sun was beginning to set and there was a little breeze coming from the east. Ethan did his jacket up and checked his back pocket for the van keys.

About fifty yards from the lock-gates, the pair stopped. Earlier in the day, Ethan had parked the van in a disabled parking space which overlooked the navigation and the Lock Keeper's Cottage. It was away from prying eyes and was overrun with weeds and bramble. The van's back windows were fully tinted and from there they could see all the entry points to the cottage (except the rear) and the two cars in the Lock Keeper's Cottage car park were in plain sight. One was a canary yellow Ford Capri, looking smart, and the other was a cheap unmarked police car. They could even just about make out the officer slumped in the front seat. Probably asleep.

The dusk of the day was casting a stream of sunlight across the navigation. Ethan nudged Mac and pointed towards a patch of grassland next to the water. There was one, maybe two, security officers sitting in the long grass. But they were facing in the opposite direction.

"Do you think they've seen us?" Ethan asked.

"Doubt it. Nobody can stay vigilant for twelve hours straight, and the next shift is due in forty-five minutes. If we trust our informant."

"He's not been wrong yet, Mac," Ethan replied, looking at his watch.

Mac watched as his partner opened the sliding door of the Rascal van and clambered into the back. There were two fishing stools facing outwards and they took one each. Mac reached into his jacket pocket and pulled out his hipflask.

"Want some?" He asked Ethan.

"What is it?"

"It's Jameson's. The good stuff."

"I'll leave it for now. I'm not much of a whiskey drinker." Ethan pulled a face of disgust.

"Ah, but you will be. Mark my words," Mac responded. "It's a mature gentleman's drink."

"If you say so," Ethan replied. "Let's get this done."

As Mac took a swig from his hipflask, he watched as Ethan pulled out a long gun case.

"What the hell is that?" Mac asked as the rifle revealed itself.

"It's a manually operated De Lisle carbine .22 LR rifle. We're using CCI Quiet ammunition." Ethan responded as he opened the back door of the van.

"It's actually made from a modified Enfield rifle to fire .45 ACP ammo out of ancient magazines. The barrel only extends to the end of the front sight. The rest of this large tube is a suppressor," Ethan continued.

"Holy shite! That's an impressive piece of kit. Is it not a museum piece?" Mac said, looking on in admiration.

"Well, they reckon an observer 15 feet away can't hear it being fired. So, it's bloody handy, if we want to get out of here alive," Ethan added.

"But it looks like a relic," Mac said.

"It is. It was used by British Commandos in World War Two. The big man's team stole it. That's the legend. But he thought the RUC would have fun trying to trace the ammunition from a gun which is almost a myth," Ethan smiled.

"You've got to admire his balls," Mac replied.

"I'm not sure I'd go that far!" Ethan responded. They both roared with laughter.

When the laughter ended, Ethan pointed his gun at the RUC officer asleep in the car and, after a few moments of silence, calmly despatched a bullet that ripped through the front windscreen and into the face of the policeman. The sound of the smashing windscreen must have alerted the other protection officers as two quickly came running from their cover with their guns raised. This was a mistake.

Ethan shot the first of the running officers in the neck and he went down heavily, holding the wound as he hit the ground. There was little or no chance he would survive that horrific injury. The second officer quickly found a hiding place.

"I'm going to get a closer look. Keep an eye on the front door of that cottage. If your woman, the young officer, shows herself, take her down." Ethan said. "I reckon the lad won't be far behind."

Mac turned around from his stool, past some large black bin bags stored in the back and buried his hand in a small grey haversack. He pulled out a Glock pistol with a silencer.

As the second protection officer hid in the grass, Ethan quietly opened the back door of the van and stood behind it, using the door as cover. His gun was rested on the top of the hinge.

"They'll shoot at us in a moment, mark my words. But this is toughened glass. It won't penetrate. We're okay." Ethan motioned to Mac to pass the haversack, and he then found the second Glock in the bag. He tucked it into his waist-band. As he did so the second officer moved slightly, attempting to find a better hiding place.

Ethan fired twice. Once into the arm of the officer, leading to a violent cry from the injured man, and he then fired again into the side of the officer's face. This led to a horrific explosion of blood, visible from the other side of the navigation. Two protection officers were either dead or dying and the RUC man in the car clearly hadn't survived. The pair could see him slumped forward in the vehicle.

"There's bound to be another one," Ethan muttered. "They always operate in wee units. But we best get over there now. We need to get closer to the lock-gates," he added.

"There's a decent view of the cottage behind these trees. Follow me," Mac explained. Before he'd finished the sentence, the first of two shots hit the side of the van. One clipped the nearside tyre, and the van slumped slightly as the tyre deflated. The pair were a few feet away.

"Feck!" Mac shouted. "You were right. Another one! But they won't shoot onto the path behind the trees. There's a risk of passers-by. But let's shift our arses. We need to get to the cottage."

They sprinted through the trees onto a small bridleway which skirted the navigation. One more shot rang out, again hitting the rim of the wheel, before ten seconds of quiet. But Mac and Ethan were now further away in a small patch of undergrowth, just ducking down to view the scene.

In the cottage, Wendy crouched at eye-level and had seen the attack take place. Her hands were in the pockets of her long black denim skirt and her heart was racing. She knew she had to hide her emotions and stay strong for Sam, who was behind the sofa. Wendy was a willing volunteer but hadn't been properly trained for this. She knew nothing about firearms but had been promised that the protection officers and security detail would see them right. She now had a decision to make.

She guessed Sandwich Man was dead. She'd also seen one of the protection officers hit the deck immediately in front of her and was tempted to run outside and help him but knew it would be too late and too dangerous. The other was out of sight. Instead, she ran to the kitchen and found her mobile.

"Sam," she called out. "Keep an eye on the path in front of the house and shout if you see anyone."

Sam didn't answer straightaway, but she heard him scamper to a position near the window.

"I can't see anything," he called over. "What are you doing?"

"I'm calling the police and a few friends. Try to stay calm. We'll get through this," she replied.

"They're going to kill me, aren't they?" Sam said, quietly.

"They will do nothing of the sort. They don't know who they're dealing with here," she called back, knowing this was mainly bravado but hoping it sounded convincing.

Wendy telephoned the front desk at Knock Road and explained her circumstances to McIlhinney. He promised immediate support. She also pushed the panic button installed next to the front door and waited for reinforcements to arrive. She hoped the remaining protection officers were unhurt. She knew there were two posted to the front of the property. She guessed two were at the back. She hadn't counted the shots. But If they had all been gunned down, they were alone. She knew she had to hide her utter panic from Sam, she had to stay strong.

She pushed the transmit button on the handheld and spoke on the open frequency.

"This is Wendy. I'm under fire. There are at least three men down, maybe more, and I have no location for the gunman. I need urgent assistance." She waited breathlessly for a reply.

"Jesus Christ, Wendy!" McNally shouted. "Have you called Knock Road? Is there a firearms unit on their way? Where is Sam?"

"Sam's okay. I'm okay too," she replied. "I've called for reinforcements. I'm waiting for an ETA."

"Sit tight. Stay out of sight. Both of you. Wait for the firearms team," McNally ordered.

"I'm not too far away, Wendy," Jones added. "I've just finished giving a statement at Knock Road. I'll get to you as soon as possible."

"Whereabouts are you now, exactly?" Isadora chimed in.

"I'm near St Columba's Church. Are you close?" Jones answered.

"I'll be two minutes. Massey can wait," Isadora said. "We'll get over to the safe house."

"Wendy!" Mr Singh shouted, who was clearly panicking. "Keep out of harm's way. Listen to McNally."

Wendy killed the call. She had a decision to make. Did she take McNally's advice and sit tight? Or make a move? She carefully peered out of the window, surveying the scene. Looking for any sign of life.

"Can you see anything?" Mac asked, trying to get a good vantage point out of the undergrowth.

"Stop moving around! You'll get us shot!" Ethan snapped back. "There are no signs of life in or around the cottage. I think it's time we closed that lock-gate. We need to get over there."

He rummaged around in the grey bag and pulled out a small

rectangular device, with a long LCD screen across the front. The screen immediately came to life when he pushed a button on the side.

"What's that thing?" Mac asked, watching on.

"It's an old pager. Watch this." Ethan then typed out the word 'NOW' and sat back in the undergrowth. "You see, old timer, this is why you're retiring and I'm on my way up. I understand technology."

"Shut the feck up, you patronising wee..." Mac started, but was then interrupted as the mechanics of the lock-gates whirred into operation.

"We'll soon be over there. No bother, Granda." Ethan winked at Mac.

On the other side of the navigation, Wendy ran back to the window before peering through the tiniest of cracks in the front door. She squinted out into the countryside in front of the cottage. For a few moments, there was nothing, not a murmur from her surroundings. But somehow, she knew she was being watched. Someone was out there. She knew their job wasn't finished. Sam was alive and he knew too much.

Suddenly she became aware of the lock-gates closing and put her hand over her mouth. She wanted to scream. But instead, stared over at Sam who was near the sofa.

"Why are the gates closing?" Sam shouted. "What's happening. Wendy? Who's closing the gates?"

"Take a breath, Sam. Go and hide behind the sofa. Stay there until I get back. Say nothing. Just breathe. In and out. Nothing else."

Wendy ran over to the front door of the cottage and, despite her lack of training, she cleverly used the commotion of the sluice gate motors to silently slip out of the door and sprint over to the car park and Sandwich Man's car, ducking behind a small wall for cover.

She opened his passenger door, still constantly checking

around her, and then paused briefly. She scanned the scene, listening for anything. But aside from the motors, the nothingness and the gentle breeze were becoming almost eerie now. At least three dead bodies were nearby and the fate of others unknown. Wendy could hear Mr Singh's calm voice back in Milton College, telling her to focus on what was immediately in front of her, and deal with the rest later. That was sound advice.

The sight that greeted her was the most horrific thing she'd ever seen. Sandwich Man lay dead in the front seat, a flask of tea still in his left hand. The light blue upholstery of the car was splattered with blood and with glass fragments everywhere. She threw open his bag on the passenger seat, itself caked in blood, and discovered a small gun. Aside from her gaming exploits, she'd not used a gun in many years. She remembered successfully shooting tin cans with an air pistol on her family farm in Somerset, but this was different. This was real life, and she knew she had little choice but to arm herself. Wendy braved the debris and gore and found spare ammunition in the bottom of the bag and pocketed that, too. She tucked the gun in the top of her long denim skirt and hid it under her long striped jumper.

As she turned, she saw the yellow Capri. She rapidly added that to her list of options. Maybe she could grab Sam and put him in the boot and get the hell out of there? But that looked unlikely, as the Sandwich Man's car was blocking the entrance out. She couldn't see any way of easily getting the Capri out of the space and out onto the road. There was just no room.

Just then, her decision-making skills vanished as she heard another shot. It seemed further away this time. Was this the other security officer or the gunman taking aim? For a few seconds, she hid behind the Capri and silently prayed that Sam was safe, regretting leaving him alone.

The gates were slowly closing and she had no time to overthink. As the seconds turned to minutes and the gloom of the early evening was beginning to take hold, the ducks started to sound again. It was an incessant quacking that almost seemed bizarre against the backdrop of the gates closing and the gunman hiding somewhere in the woods. That and the scenes of death around her.

Just then the gates stopped. She risked a look over to check. They were still three-quarters open and there was no safe passage between them. Maybe, someone had intervened? Had the armed response unit arrived? Were the reinforcements there.

She looked over at the Lock-Gates, rusted and archaic, probably there for years. But with small wires protruding from the rusted ends. She wondered how they opened and closed remotely. Was there an automatic mechanism? She decided to call Mr Singh when she was back in safety. He'd help her with a plan. This was the only access to the cottage. Could she cut this off permanently by simply pulling out the wires and keeping them open? As long as there was no rear access to the cottage, they'd be safe. Or this would buy her time, if nothing else.

With the silence and stillness taking hold once again, Wendy raced back from the car park and threw herself over the small wall, slowly crawling behind it on her hands and knees back to the front door of the cottage. Another shot rang out. She saw concrete dust hit the ground only inches away from her, as the bullet glanced the wall. The only open ground was the gap between the wall and the door. When she reached that point, she dived unceremoniously through the entrance, landing awkwardly on the back heel of her platformed Dr Marten boots, and shut the door behind her.

Sam was back hiding behind the sofa and popped his head around the arm of the chair when he heard her arrive back.

"Did you stop the gate?" Sam asked, his face white with fear.

"No, that wasn't me. But I'm thinking that's the only way in. We're okay, Sam. As long as that stays open."

"Is he dead? Sandwich man?" he quietly added.

"Afraid so. But the police are on their way, and I think my friends will be here soon too. This will be all over before you know it," Wendy smiled, whilst taking off her thick boots to inspect any damage.

"Sam, be a love and go and stick the kettle on," she added, desperately trying to normalise the situation and take his mind off things.

"Really?" Sam replied. "Tea? At this time?"

"A cup of tea sorts everything out," she explained. "Plus, I have some calls to make."

Sam rushed off and Wendy continued to stare at the partially open Lock-Gates, praying they would remain stuck, whilst looking for any movement outside. She picked up the handheld and radioed Mr Singh.

"Mr Singh, can you hear me? This is Wendy."

"Goodness, Wendy. We're all so worried. What's going on?" Mr Singh responded almost instantly.

"I think it's a stand-off. It's very quiet. I can't see the gunmen. But Sam is safe and we're waiting for police firearms. They're taking their time. But I have a question."

"Anything. How can I help?" he replied.

"There are lock-gates in front of me. They are open, which means no-one can walk over them to gain access to the cottage. But someone has remote access. A few minutes ago, they started closing. I think the mechanism has seized up or something."

"Describe them, Wendy. Quickly."

"They look rather old, but there are wires, maybe electrics, at each end. Does that mean they're likely to be automatic? Electrical rather than mechanical?" She asked.

"It's possible. I'm no expert on Lock-Gates. How would that help?"

"I've already explained that! They have to remain open to prevent access. It's that simple. If they closed, the gunmen could just sprint over them and storm the cottage. Is that not clear?"

"Sorry, of course. I'm panicking!" he stammered.

"You're panicking?" Wendy fired back.

"Sorry, sorry. That was insensitive. I understand. What about other access points?"

"The back of the house is thick with very tall conifers and a wire fence. I can't see any access from the back. I guess that would be sensible, as it's a safe house. But I think the gunshots are coming from the other side of the navigation, the canal. It's much too far to jump. We need to cut off their options."

"Roger. I see," Mr Singh shakily replied. Wendy could imagine his pose now. Pipe in one hand and with his thinking face on. She could also hear Tom and Carl milling around in the background.

"Wendy, my guess is that you'll need to break the circuit. It'll be the circuit that's keeping the gates in one position or other. There'll probably be a mechanism that automatically opens all the gates, but there'll be something that overrides that. I think they'll be mechanical but with an electric starter motor. Or something similar."

"For god's sake! How do I override that? I'm stuck in the house. It's too dangerous to open the door again. The gunmen could be anywhere!"

"I was going to say cut the wire to the main electrics. But..."

"What if I shot at the electric box?" she interrupted. "I think I can see a black box to the right of the mechanism."

"You have a gun?" Mr Singh sounded surprised.

"It's a long story. It's not mine, but yes, I have a gun."

"Point the gun at the entry point to the electrical supply and hope that breaks the circuit. Do that. But, for God's sake, stay safe. I'm sure you'll have support soon. I'll keep this line clear for you."

"Okay. I'll do my best." Wendy ended the call and looked along the length of the Lock-Gates. There was a thick plastic-coated box on the right-hand side. That had to be the supply. Wendy inspected the gun. She had never used a gun with real bullets. But she was a gamer. How hard could this be?

It was then that she heard the mechanics kick in again. But it was a higher pitch sound than before. There was movement from the gates, but they were juddering rather than closing. Perhaps someone was trying to reset the system?

The large bush at the front of the house was obscuring Wendy's view. So, she ran upstairs into the bedroom facing the lock-gates and aimed downwards at the plastic-looking box, using a paisley-patterned curtain for cover. She knew the sound of the bullets would alert the gunmen to her location and the fact that she was armed, but she felt she had little choice.

She fired once and was immediately surprised at the recoil. Sam came running up the stairs, spilling tea as he did so. The bullet missed the box and there was a loud 'ping' as it ricocheted off the metal gate. But she was closer than she thought was possible with her first attempt. Sam immediately saw the gun and was wide-eyed. He had no idea she was armed.

She shot again. This time, the bullet missed and flew into the trees. She put her head down for the briefest of moments to gather herself.

'I'm a gamer,' she told herself. 'This is a game. Four more shots left. I can do this.'

"Tea?" Sam asked, in a whisper.

"Not for the moment, mate. Rest it down over there on the bedside table. I'm just shooting at an electric supply box. I'll explain why in a second."

She gathered herself again, preparing to squeeze the trigger. But with her mind in a hundred different places, she squeezed too hard as she tried to fix on her target. The gun went off unexpectedly. God knows where the bullet had gone.

She cursed loudly. A bullet wasted. She put her head down and closed her eyes momentarily.

"Look, Wendy," Sam shouted. "The gates are opening again. Did you do that?"

Wendy watched with a mixture of delight and surprise as the gates slowly opened again and anchored themselves into their new position. A loud mechanical clang broke the silence and ducks started quacking again, as if annoyed by the further interruption. Somehow, accidentally, Wendy had hit a target no bigger than a school lunch-box and bought herself more time.

"Yeah," Wendy responded, grinning. "That was me. Whoever's shooting at us will need to bloody swim over here now."

She walked over to the table and sipped her tea in quiet celebration. Sam looked down in genuine awe as the gates had completed their final opening procedure. This was a little victory in the face of the real danger.

Twenty-Nine

Jones had walked to St Columba's Church and was standing next to a bus stop. The road was busy, and he stared out into the traffic. He found a chocolate chip Tracker bar in his pocket and munched on it, telling himself this would provide a little energy for what lay ahead. The juxtaposition of the scene wasn't lost on him. The longer he waited for Isadora, the more significant the danger was for Sam and Wendy. He needed to get there urgently.

It was then that he spotted the dark green motorbike propped up against the church. It was, without a doubt, a Simson MZ.

Jones had often regaled his knowledge about Simson's in pub chats and had also over-exaggerated his proficiency in riding one. Simson was a German company which produced firearms, automobiles, bicycles, motorcycles, and mopeds. Under the Third Reich, the factory was taken from the Jewish Simson family, and was renamed several times under Nazi, and later communist, control. This was fascinating stuff for a pub quiz connoisseur, but Jones thought the MZ itself was a horrible and rather clunky 50cc motorcycle. However, he'd learned to ride one when he worked for the newspaper office back at home, and Jones had passed his motorcycle test on the first attempt. Successfully gaining his actual driving licence was another story altogether.

Jones ran up the steps to the church and checked out the bike, with half an eye on the road for Isadora. The keys were still in the ignition. He sprinted over and opened the small side door to the church and peered inside. He didn't want to shout. But he did want to borrow the bike, fairly urgently. Lives were at stake. Politeness would have to wait. He called out three or four times, as loudly as he could muster. But there was no response.

He jumped onto the bike and desperately tried to remember the starting routine. He turned the choke on (leaving the ignition turned off), kicked the bike over a few times and then turned the choke off again. He then waited for a few precious seconds. He was slowly recalling the starting process, but was also aware that someone could angrily accost him at any moment. He turned the ignition on and firmly kicked the bike over. It fired into life. Jones was mobile.

He hastily looked around the ground near the bike for a helmet. With the bike spluttering and complaining, he saw a glimmer of fluorescent yellow in the long grass. It was a 1960s-style moped helmet with a picture of Muttley, the cartoon dog, stencilled on the side. Without thinking, he thrust it onto his head and slowly headed down the verge, next to the steps leading to the main road.

The Lock Keeper's Cottage was about twelve minutes from St Columba's Church, but with any luck, he'd be able to skirt round the traffic and make up some time. As he careered down the main road heading towards Castlereagh, he found the handheld in his pocket and pushed the all-frequencies button.

"I don't know if anyone can hear me, but I've found transport to the cottage. It's an MZ motorbike. I'm making progress. I'll be there as soon as I can. Isadora, you can head straight there." The wind and the helmet made communication almost impossible, but he made out one response.

"You've done what?" Jenny shouted back.

"Roger," Isadora called back. But Jones didn't hear that. He was too busy bursting onto the pavement to avoid two sets of red traffic lights and narrowly missing a pensioner on a mobility scooter.

Remembering a cross-country running route that Joseph Armstrong had led them on prior to becoming a mass-murderer, Jones nipped down a narrow path that led to a golf course. He gamefully rode the Simson, now at full pelt, along the side of the deserted fairways and then found himself back on the main road.

He received a torrent of abuse from motorists as he zoomed on and off the road, using gaps in a hedgerow to advance further up the slow line of traffic. There were further horns and howls of derision as he emerged again and nearly caused an accident on the nearside carriageway. But Jones didn't care. The bike may have been struggling and spluttering, but he was entirely focused. He had his head down and wrung every ounce of speed out of the cumbersome motorcycle. That said, the bike was still hovering at about 38mph, but it felt a great deal faster.

As the bike hit the A55, Jones closed his mind to anything other than getting to the location as soon as possible and prayed there was fuel in the tank. There was still no sign of Isadora in the Mondeo, who he guessed would be coming from the same direction. But he was wrong.

Isadora was just pulling into the car park of the City View Hotel and was contemplating doing a recce of the paths leading to the navigation and the lock. She had broken every speed limit and was also very low on petrol herself. She grabbed her handheld and made a call to McNally.

"Do we have an updated ETA for the firearms team, McNally? I'm solo and there's no-one here, no police presence at all. What the hell is going on?"

"Nothing at all? No-one?" he said in disbelief. "I'll find out. Where are you now?"

"It's bloody quiet. I'm at the hotel car park which backs onto the towpath. But I can't see anything from here and this damned chair is going to cause major issues on the shingle path."

"Ok, Isadora. I know exactly where you are. You're within spitting distance of the safe house. Take the first left out of the hotel car park and you'll see a white metal gate. That's the emergency entrance point to the lock and the towpath, managed by the local council. I'll get the code to open it. Hold fire."

Isadora swung the car out of the car park and waited patiently in line as a queue of cars flowed out of the hotel and onto the main road. She shook her head in disbelief that no-one was aware of the horror unfolding by the towpath. Were Sam and Wendy even alive?

When she finally made the left turn, the only car to do so, she had to slowly manoeuvre the Mondeo onto an overgrown and bramble-filled driveway. Shingle spat from her tyres as she edged closer to the entrance. But the white gate, which McNally was seeking a code to unlock, was already wide open. Someone already had the code.

She drove slowly through the gates and past a small timber storage shed. A clearing was then visible where a Rascal van had been parked. It looked tatty, and Isadora initially wondered whether it had been dumped there. As she made her way past the shed, its windows were the same height as the car window, and she peered in. Nothing was amiss. The door was still secured with an enormous solid-looking combination padlock.

As she pulled up behind the Rascal, she could see the driver's door of the red-coloured van was ajar. Her legs hadn't recovered enough to enable her to walk unaided over to the van, but if she clung onto the driver's door and then onto the door of the Rascal, she'd probably be stable enough, she decided. She gently pushed open her driver's door and listened for movement. With the silence almost overwhelming, she hoisted herself up onto the door frame and then, with an almighty heave, clung onto the door of the Rascal. She used the seat as leverage and then pulled the weight of her body into the rear of the van, where she saw two small fishing stools, a small grey haversack and three or four large bin bags. Two stools, maybe two gunmen. That would be a fair assumption, she thought.

She manoeuvred herself further forward to look inside the haversack and was astonished to see two grenades, a large quantity of ammunition and, what looked like, the top half of a silencer mechanism. From her position, she could now see the gunmen's view through the two blacked-out windows of the van. She could see the cottage dead ahead with the front door open. Was she too late? She grabbed the handheld and radioed McNally.

"Don't worry about the entrance gates. I'm through them and I'm in a red Rascal van. Registration RGH 575B. It's the gunman's vehicle. There's no doubt. But I'm fairly sure there are two of them," she whispered.

"Aye, understood. Is there still no sign of the firearms team?"

"Still nothing. All quiet here. Hold on," Isadora squinted towards the reed bank in front of the cottage. "I think I can see one of the bodies of the protection officers. But I can't see Wendy or Sam."

"Jesus. Poor bastard. Where the feck is the firearms team? What is Rogers doing?" McNally said. Isadora was wondering who he was talking to until she heard Jube's voice in the background. Jube loved a drama, she thought.

"Isadora. Something has gone badly wrong here. I'm going to phone Acting Chief Superintendent Eric Rogers. Stay where you are and keep McNally updated," Jube explained in his most formal tones.

With the handheld quiet, Isadora propped herself up on the fishing stool, using what tiny power she had left in her legs to keep her upright. From here, she could see everything. The only risk she faced was the gunmen returning and she had no firearm of her own. That, rather stupidly, she'd left in the boot of the Mondeo in an equipment bag. But the mere fact that she was in situ and had found an observation point was miraculous enough.

As she began thinking about her next move, the handheld buzzed again.

"It's me, Jones," he shouted above the noise of the MZ. "I'm close. Where are you?"

"Head for the hotel. Don't turn right into the car park. Keep going towards a white metal gate. But, for God's sake, leave that machine somewhere out of the way. It's almost silent here. That sounds like a bloody pneumatic drill."

"Roger," Jones replied. He'd heard most of the conversation above the engine.

Jones could see the City View Hotel straight ahead and had indicated towards the car park. He then carried on past the main entrance and saw the gates. He pulled over, parked the bike near a large hedge, and left the yellow helmet next to it. He jogged through the brambles and saw Virginia's old Mondeo and the red Rascal van. The quiet and stillness struck him. It all felt very strange.

"You took your time," Isadora began.

"Am I too late?" Jones countered, wiping the sweat from his forehead. "What's happening?"

"Nothing's happening. I think the gunmen are out there, waiting for something. God knows what. There's a dead body on the other side. So, something's gone down already."

"Blimey. Did you say gun*men*?" Jones replied, emphasising the plural.

"Two stools. Look. Brain for thinking, feet for dancing, Jones. Logic suggests that this is the vehicle belonging to the gunmen." Isadora then stopped as she heard a little rustling as they both stared through the blacked-out windows of the Rascal.

"What was that?" Jones asked, looking outside the vehicle and seeing nothing.

"Maybe the breeze," Isadora suggested. "Let's not get jumpy.

One of us needs to get over to the cottage and see what's going on with Wendy and Sam."

"Sam?" said a hushed voice. The pair stopped and stared over towards the mound of bin bags. Jones rushed over and pulled the bags away until he found a green and black rug hidden at the bottom. At the end of the rug was the head of a young girl. Jones carefully unwrapped the rug to find she had her hands and feet cable-tied together and her mouth partially taped, although somehow this had slipped down. She looked in a terrible state but was alive, at least.

"My goodness, you poor little thing. Let's get you out of there. You're going to be okay," Jones gently explained and pulled his Swiss Army Knife from his pocket and started hacking away at the cable ties. Both Isadora and Jones tried to hide their shock and focus on the girl and keeping her calm.

As she was carefully freed, the girl immediately burst into tears.

"I'm Emma Jacobs," the little girl said, between bursts of emotion. "Where am I? Did you just say Sam? Is he here? Can I see him?"

Emma's face was painfully white. Her hands shook as Jones released them from the ties and her hair was matted. The ties had cut into her wrists a little and she appeared very confused. Jones felt towards the back of her head with the palm of his hand and, after inspection, he saw traces of blood.

"What did they do to you, Emma? How did you get here?" Isadora asked, gently.

"I don't remember anything," she sobbed. "I went to find Sam. There was a lady. I don't know anything else." Emma broke down again and Isadora offered her a hand. The little girl crawled next to Isadora, and they hugged.

"I feel really sleepy," she said, gripping tight to Isadora.

Isadora looked up at Jones as the girl continued to cling to her.

"We work with the police in Northern Ireland. I'm Isadora. This is Jones," she explained.

"Northern Ireland?" Emma said, confused. "Is that where I am?"

"Yes. Everything is going to feel a little odd. I think you've been given some pills to make you sleepy. We need to get you checked over. But you're safe now," Jones explained.

"Well, you *will* be safe," Isadora corrected him, still holding the hand of the youngster. "Sam is nearby, but he's in danger. My friend Jones is going to head over and see if he's okay."

"I am? I'm doing that?" Jones replied. "We're not waiting for the police?"

"The police were due twenty minutes ago. Something really odd is happening. Jube's on it. You're going to have to get over there. There's a gun in my equipment pack in the boot of the Mondeo. I'll get someone to pick up Emma and take her to safety."

"I want to see my brother," Emma said in a quiet voice.

"I know. My friend is going to make sure he's safe, too," Isadora squeezed Emma tightly to reassure her.

"We need to get an update from Wendy. I need an understanding of what and who is out there. I'll buzz her," Jones said, pulling out the handheld from his jeans.

"Wendy, are you reading me? This is Jones."

"Loud and clear," Wendy replied, sounding surprisingly calm.

"Isadora and I are here, and we have Emma too. She's safe. We can see the Lock Keeper's Cottage dead ahead."

"Emma's with you? How the bloody hell did that happen?" she responded.

"Let's not worry about that now. Give me a situation update, please," Jones responded.

"That's easy enough. We have three dead, I reckon. A fourth protection officer missing, maybe a fifth too, and a gunman out there somewhere," she explained matter-of-factly.

"We think two gunmen, Wendy," Jones clarified.

"Oh, great. Double the fun. There have been no shots fired for maybe ten minutes now, though. So, your guess is as good as mine as to their whereabouts." Wendy sounded irritated. Jones had heard talk of her incredible resilience and intelligence, but her self-belief seemed to be winning through as well.

"Okay," Jones said. "I'll get over there now. I'll turn my hand-held off until I get into the cottage. Keep McNally informed."

"Hold on," Wendy interrupted. "I'm not sure you can get over here. I've shot out the mechanics for the Lock-Gates and opened them. There's no way across."

"You shot out the mechanism? You're firearms trained?" he replied.

"Nah, I'm just good on the Sega Mega Drive. Anyway. I can't see any access points behind the cottage. We're effectively cut off. I'm not even sure where the next nearest bridge or lock gate is. Could be miles away."

"Okay, I'll have a scout around. I'll see if I can work out what's happening and locate the gunman or gunmen."

"Great. But urgency is the key word," Wendy replied, a little sarcastically. "Perhaps someone could hurry the police, too. But be bloody careful, Jones." Wendy hung up.

Jones calmly stood up and quietly opened the driver's door of the Rascal, grabbing the gunman's haversack full of ammunition and other party tricks. With the late afternoon turning to evening, the air was cooler. The shadows from the trees were getting longer. Soon there would be the cover of darkness. Jones silently opened the boot of the Mondeo and found Isadora's equipment pack. He unzipped it and located the gun, before slotting it into the top of his leather belt. He emptied the gunmen's bag into hers and swung it onto his back.

Sitting in the boot, still looking pristine, was Isadora's purple Everything book, the almanac gifted to every YCU recruit on their first day. He looked for the maps section at the back and located the map of Belfast. It showed the city and the River Lagan's course and the Lock-Gates. A few miles away, the crossing at Shaw's Bridge would be the nearest means of getting to the other side.

With Eden Vale the most secluded of the locks along the route, Sam and Wendy might be slightly safer, but they were also isolated in that safe house. Reaching them was incredibly challenging, with the gates open. The gap was over ten feet; it wasn't jumpable, and the water was bound to be deep.

As Jones walked carefully along the towpath and got closer to the lock gate itself, his mind became less jumbled. He knew that somewhere out there were two gunmen and that he needed to end this. His brain whirred as he tried to fathom out a plan. He wondered what Jenny would do. What was she doing now? Should he call her?

Jones examined the scene in front of him and thought about what presumptions he could make. Are the gunmen too lazy to run to the bridge a few miles away? Or get back in the Rascal? Are they waiting for Wendy and Sam to show themselves and simply take pot shots? Are these amateurs? Jones was trying to coordinate his thoughts whilst keeping himself calm.

He pulled out a pair of small binoculars from Isadora's equipment pack and surveyed the scene. Everything appeared serene. He then focused on a large patch of foliage near the towpath. Initially, he saw nothing in the gloom. But, unusually for Jones, he remained patient and soon he spotted the telltale sign of a flame. Someone up ahead was lighting a cigarette. Their cover was deep, the bushes and foliage thick, and he couldn't make out much. But their location was dangerously close to the gates. He couldn't take a pot-shot at them, as all hell would break loose, and he certainly didn't want to break cover. But these must be the gunmen. They were still there, waiting for something.

After he assessed what was in his bag, he quietly slipped back to the clearing where the Mondeo and Rascal were parked. He then scoured around the floor. He had a plan. He just needed a brick and some luck.

Thirty

"Look, I've been doing this job for nearly twenty years. I have never once seen that lock gate open and close like that," Mac explained in a whisper. "I've staked out this safe house many, many times. Believe me. That was a heck of a shot to take out the electrics. She must be a specialist."

"Yeah, you're right," Ethan replied, taking a drag from his cigarette. "We can't get over there, so we need to wait for them to show themselves. That's fine."

"Fine?" Mac parroted. "It's nearly fecking dark. Time is ticking."

"Patience is a virtue, Mac. Our wee friend in the RUC has clearly held off any police attendance at the scene. We can deal with minor complications. Let's just bide our time."

"Don't be soft. He's only delaying the inevitable. They'll be here. We need to end this!" Mac urged.

"If we didn't have the Peeler on side, the whole place would be swarming with them by now. He's cut off the connection to the panic button in the house and promised he would take his time a little before he rings the firearms team. But, as you're getting edgy, we can speed things up a wee bit." Ethan looked at his watch.

"Edgy? I'm just keen, sunshine. I say we use the grenades. Chuck them as close to the house as possible and wait for the kid and the other officer to make a break for it before taking them both down."

"Well, yes. But the minute we do that, everyone for about two miles will know there's shite going down here," Ethan replied. "But I don't have any better suggestions and I'm not telling the big man that we've messed up."

Mac nodded his head. "Right, let's not upset the big man. I'll head back to the van and get the grenades."

"You don't need to do that," Ethan said. "I've got two in my bag here." He took off his backpack and pulled out the two grenades and put them on the floor in front of him.

"What about the wee girl in the van?" Ethan said as he stared down at the two grenades. "This will all be over in a few moments, and we still have no plan for her."

"She's drugged up to the eyeballs," Mac responded. "She was only ever going to be a lure for her brother. To get him to come out. But that ship has sailed, I reckon. Leave her in the van. She won't remember a thing. She'll be easy breezy."

"You think? I just hope this doesn't bite us on the arse. The big man's messages said to leave no trace." Ethan was now rifling through his bag, looking for something.

"What's the problem?" Mac asked.

"I can't find the thermal sight for my pistol." Ethan explained, now emptying everything out of his bag. "The bastard light is going. I reckon we have about half an hour before this dusk turns to pitch black."

It was then that they both stopped in their tracks and listened as they heard the noise of an engine. Something had started up nearby. They looked at each other, trying to rationalise what was happening.

"That's not a car," Mac whispered. "What the hell is it?"

"I'm not sure. But I suggest we ready ourselves. This could be the cavalry." Ethan stood up and pointed his pistol towards the noise. Mac followed suit and stood in the middle of the bridleway with guns raised.

"Jesus," Mac said, quietly. "We had a plan. This was all shaped. We had strict orders. I was close to retirement. Why do I suddenly feel a sense of foreboding?"

"Shut up!" Ethan whispered. "This isn't over. Man up!"

As the two gunmen stood waiting for whatever the noise was, another engine started. But in the other direction. This time, it was clearly a car, and it was revving its engine loudly and erratically. Mac and Ethan changed direction and faced the car engine noise. Pistols still pointed.

"What's happening? Are we surrounded?" Ethan asked loudly, above the noise.

"No, you silly bastard, someone is playing games. This is an old school distraction technique," Mac replied.

From the same direction as the engine noise. Another sound started to fill the air.

"Music?" Ethan said. "What the hell?"

"Distraction! Remember that," Mac shouted. "Stand your ground! Stay ready!"

"Feck me. It's The Carpenters. I know this one," Ethan replied. "My Ma loves this. Calling Occupants of Interplanetary Craft..." As the sound of the power ballad hit the air, the two gunmen continued to point towards the revving of the car engine and the loud music.

As the car revs screamed at their loudest and most violently, the high-pitched noise from the other direction matched its intensity. It was a wall of deafening noise. Karen Carpenter's dulcet tones provided the backdrop as the normal serenity of Eden Vale was obliterated by angry sounds from different directions.

Ethan was now absent-mindedly tapping his foot as the drums rolled in for the chorus.

From nowhere, Jones, in his yellow Muttley helmet and riding the Simson MZ at full pelt, screeched down the bridleway towards the Lock-Gates. The bike was at maximum throttle, and Jones had his head down. The bike turned the corner of the path and sent a volley of shingle towards the gunmen.

As they turned to face him, guns aloft, Jones unleashed one of the grenades from the haversack in the Rascal. It landed a few metres in front of the pair and rolled into the water. As the grenade detonated, the pressure from the explosion created a blast so high that the two gunmen were immediately blown off their feet and deep into the bushes next to the trees. They were accompanied by a few of the ducks and a torrent of dirty green water and sludge from the top of the navigation. It was total carnage.

What happened next almost took place in slow-motion. Jones hadn't appreciated that such an underwater explosion would transmit pressure with greater intensity over a longer distance. So, as he rounded the path leading to the open lock gate and sped the MZ as fast as possible over the gap in the gates, he grit his teeth. This was shit or bust, he knew that. He'd either fail and fall head first into the navigation or triumphantly make the leap and land on the other side. Greeting Wendy and Sam like some heroic modern-day Evel Knievel.

Instead, a last minute third option arrived, he was hit by the undercurrent of the grenade explosion and was blown off his bike headfirst into the large hedge at the front of the building. He'd made the leap over the navigation, but only thanks to a little help from a watery detonation.

It was over in seconds, but Jones was alive and had made it, albeit landing in a less than helpful position. He was upside down, with the motorbike ten feet away and somehow stuck in the wire fence beyond the house. This was less Evel Knievel and more Benny Hill. But his gamble had paid off.

He checked himself and the situation around him. Jones was wedged in a large green bush at the front of the house, and he was desperately trying to free himself. As he did so, Wendy came running out with her gun pointing towards the two gunmen.

Mac was the first to move. His previously pristine business suit was now caked in algae and his hair was full of weeds and the muddy water. He now resembled a swamp creature, and as he jogged awkwardly towards the Rascal, Wendy caught his left leg with a bullet. Mac went down quickly.

Ethan was clearly hurt too and lay face down on the floor. A few dead fish were on the ground in front of him and stunned ducks waddled around. Wendy watched his eyes as he scanned the ground, looking for his bag. He was looking for his own weapon, which had been blown from his hand during the blast. She sent a warning shot in his direction, which fizzed off the path in front of him. Ethan put his hands flat to the ground and opted to stay put.

"You're both bloody lucky I can't get over there. You sad cretins!" Wendy screamed over. Neither responded. Mac whimpered with the pain from his leg.

With an air of predictability, a cacophony of police sirens now sounded in the car park towards the City View Hotel.

Sam appeared at the front door and registered the scene around him with horror. He helped Jones down from the top of the bush and retrieved the Muttley helmet from a huge puddle that the water explosion had created near the front of the cottage. This wasn't quite the moment of victory he planned. He'd got his angles all wrong and the bike was heavier than he remembered. He briefly wondered whether he'd have made the jump without the help of the explosion.

"I think you're safe now, Sam," Jones said as he straightened himself out. He took a moment to gaze over sympathetically at the state of the MZ stuck in the wire fence.

"I really hope so," the young man said quietly. Amidst the blaring police sirens, Wendy embraced Sam in disbelief at the events unfolding around them.

"You were bloody brave, Jones," she began. "I'll admit that.

But bloody stupid too. I'm guessing you hadn't thought about the effect of a grenade on water? You could have killed yourself and us all. As it is, I think even most of the ducks survived. That's a win."

"I'll take that," Jones responded, a little sheepishly. "We got the job done, didn't we?"

Wendy didn't have time to respond. Sam was still needing her attention and ambulance sirens were now adding to the mix of noises. As The Carpenters had now moved onto 'Only Yesterday', a few RUC officers made their presence known on the towpath. Jones walked over to the side of the navigation and shouted over.

"What the hell took you so long? The call was made about forty minutes ago."

"That's not possible," a young PC called back, as she handcuffed Ethan and another colleague was tending to Mac. "The Police Control Room Operator only got the emergency call about seven minutes ago."

"Seven minutes? From who?" Jones shouted over.

"Front desk at Knock Road Station. Anyway, we need to sort these two out. Is there just the two?"

"Yeah, just those. My colleague and the young girl are in the Rascal van," Jones called back.

"Right you are," she replied. "Another team is on their way round to your side and will deal with the bodies." The PC added. "The scenes of crime team too. Are you lot security services?"

"Yeah," Jones shouted back. "My colleague in the Rascal will show you her identification."

Just then, Jones saw Sergeant Marie Bristow head up on the path on the other side, holding Emma's hand and with Isadora back in her chair, following close behind. Somebody then stopped the music, thankfully.

When Sam clapped eyes on Emma, Jones saw him smile for the first time.

"We'll get you over there, somehow. Don't worry. We need to get her checked over, but I think she's fine," Jones said to Sam. The

Jacobs siblings waved at each other, and the little girl beamed. Amongst the carnage and trauma, she had her big brother back.

"What did you do over there?" Wendy asked. "I have to say, whatever it was, it was quite ingenuous."

"Oh, I asked Isadora to sit in the Mondeo and rev the engine hard to create the noise, and we placed a brick on the accelerator of the Rascal. We used Isadora's unheralded hot-wiring skills to get it started. I fired up the MZ and we created the illusion of many people on the scene. We did all that in a matter of minutes."

"Clever..." Wendy responded.

"Virginia will be delighted that her Carpenter's tape has been so useful. It was quite the soundtrack to the operation. Not my choice, obviously. But there was no Smiths or Cure handy," Jones smiled, still picking pond weed from his hair.

"Yeah, The Carpenter's aren't really my bag either," Wendy shrugged.

"She'll be less pleased that I pulled out one of the Mondeo's speakers to direct the sound over the trees. She'll not like the damage to her car," he continued.

"I'll get it fixed for her," Wendy smiled. "That'll be an easy enough job. I'll just need some Gaffa tape and superglue."

"Hold on," he interrupted. He felt for the handheld amongst the sludge in his pocket. The red LED light was flashing. He answered it straightaway.

"What's going on over there?" Jenny asked. "I'm only getting updates from McNally. I had the briefest of chats with Saoirse. I'm guessing you'd been having fun with that bike you stole?"

"Borrowed," he corrected her. "And fun would be an exaggeration. Let's just say the Simson MZ is just as aerodynamic as I remember. But when you give it some welly, it really flies!"

"Anyway," he continued. "It's all over now. I'm going to suggest Sam stays with us in the Barracks. Emma's here too. I think our leak revealed the location of the safe house. Oh, and I think I know who the leak is."

"Do you..? My word. Emma's there?" Jenny said. "Let's reconvene at base. It sounds like you've had a day of it. I need all the details."

"Yeah, I'll ask Wendy to drop me back at Thiepval in the Capri. I need a pint or two. I'll explain everything. I'll speak to you soon, Jen."

As he looked over the now peaceful Lagan Navigation, he saw Isadora back in the Mondeo and reversing out. She'd been quite brilliant, he considered. He'd have to heap some praise on her later. Then, in a rare moment of spontaneous masculinity, Jones removed his brown long-sleeved t-shirt and wrung it out over the large puddle. His pale stomach was bruised and there were still thorns from the bush that needed pulling out. His arm and wrist also hurt badly. But all that could wait.

He stood and focused on catching his breath, whilst trying to reconcile what had just happened. He knew he must smell incredibly badly too, but after his eventful day, he really wasn't that bothered.

Thirty-One

Isadora found driving the Mondeo more complicated. The driving controls and clutch adapted by Mr Singh were fantastic, but she didn't have the same mechanism to lock her chair in position to drive. Therefore, instead, she had to collapse her wheelchair and store it on the back seats whilst using what little power she had in her legs to get into the front seat. It was a chore, but coping was one of her key strengths. She was fiercely independent, and the chair would not curb her ambitions.

Once she'd painstakingly manoeuvred herself into position, she reversed the Mondeo back down the path, looking to turn the car around in a lay-by near the hotel car park. As she did so, Marie Bristow appeared, walking back down the path. Isadora wound down her window.

"What's happening? Where's Emma?" she called out from the car.

"One of my officers is taking her to the hospital in a minute to be checked over. I think her brother and your colleague are heading back to the barracks at Thiepval, now that this safe house cover is well and truly blown," Bristow called back.

"That makes sense. Do you need a lift? It'll be dark soon."

"Oh, you're a lifesaver, Isadora," she responded. "I was going to get the control room to send a car to the hotel, as I need to get back to Knock Road. I can't be sitting at the hospital for hours." Bristow got in the passenger seat and Isadora drove towards the car park exit.

It was then, out of the corner of her eye, that she saw the green 4x4 she suspected had been following her for some time. The car in question was a few rows back in the hotel car park with its light on and she'd picked up the faintest of glints from the driver's binoculars. But there were still enough questions in her mind to not want to actively engage. Instead, she sat near the car park exit and waited.

"What's going on?" Bristow asked.

"Third row back, green 4x4. Lights on. I think he's wearing a blue baseball cap and holding binoculars. I have a feeling he's been tracking me for a day or so."

"What are you thinking, Isadora?"

"I'm going to wait here and see if he leaves and then play him at his own game. Are you happy enough to be part of this?" Isadora was now watching the vehicle through her rear-view mirror, and Bristow had pulled down her vanity mirror on the passenger side.

"Yeah, I've got him," Bristow then snapped the mirror back in position. "As long as I get back to Knock Road in one piece, I can happily follow this through. You've got remarkable observation skills. I can barely see him in this gloom. Have you done a PNC check on the plate?"

"Yeah, the plate belongs to a Paul Michael Chambers, who lives in Oswestry Street in Fermanagh. He's absolutely clean and there are no reports of the car being stolen. But something feels wrong. I swear I saw him yesterday parked at a church, when I was getting some intel. He was also a few cars behind me when I was driving down Belsize Road in Lisburn, not far from Thiepval. I thought I was being paranoid, but three times can't be coincidental."

"Nothing's ever coincidental. Let's give him five minutes. Turn your lights off, park up for a bit. See what he does."

"Yes, Sarge," Isadora replied, smiling. "I've always wanted to say that."

"Hold up," Bristow said. "Look, the RUC car is leaving. That's the one with Emma in." The unmarked car, an old silver Ford Granada, passed Bristow and Isadora and headed out of the exit.

"This'll be interesting." Isadora muttered. She was still staring at the 4x4 through her review view mirror.

"Right, it's moving, Isadora. Let's get behind it," Bristow was now fully invested and on board.

The pair watched as the green vehicle slowly drove out of its parking space and through the gates. The gloom of the evening was descending, but there was still enough light to see the car clear enough.

"Were you driving this yesterday?" Bristow asked.

"I had the Land Rover yesterday. I get the feeling he's not following me, per se. I think he's keeping tabs on what we're doing generally. This Mondeo may not even have been on his radar. Maybe he was waiting for Sam and Emma to leave."

"That was my fear," Bristow responded.

Isadora waited to see which way the 4x4 was going and then pulled out onto the main road three or four cars behind it, with the Granada another few cars ahead. They were crawling slowly in a line of traffic.

"I'm going to have to contact the two officers in that car. We'll need to divert them. I know them both. It's Lizzie and Briony. It's too dangerous for Emma to go to the hospital now. Not without an armed car. It's quite late, we'd better find her somewhere to rest." Bristow picked up her police radio.

"Bravo Delta 19. This is Romeo Uniform 7- 4. Are you receiving?"

"Receiving you, yeah, go ahead Sarge."

"I'm a few cars behind you. You're being trailed by a green 4x4. Abort and head for Lisburn Road Station. Confirm abort."

"Roger, Sarge. We'll abort. See you later. Bravo Delta 19, out." The radio crackled and the young female officer was gone.

As the cars moved further up the main road, Isadora glimpsed both cars ahead. But the Granada had now picked up speed a little.

"Lisburn Road Station is just six minutes away from here. She'll be safe in there until we get something sorted. I'm guessing, if your hunch is right, that this fella has been employed to monitor your operation." Bristow was craning her head to see past the three cars in front, one of them a black taxi, to check on its position.

"Let's just follow him. I don't reckon he's seen us. Who knows what we'll learn from this?" Isadora replied. "This is better than wiring up security cameras, anyway. I've been doing that on and off for days now."

"Cameras? For what?" Bristow asked.

"Ah, just prep. Mr Singh's been inventing things. We're trialling them in the office," Isadora casually responded, remembering that the RUC was purposely out of the loop on the Hunter's Arms operation.

Ahead, the cars had pulled up along Malone Road and both the Granada and the 4x4 were visible, but the unmarked police car was now indicating left and the 4x4 hadn't followed suit. They slowly pulled forward and watched as the Granada turned left down Balmoral Avenue. The 4x4 carried on past the turning and further up Malone Road.

"Our unmarked car has taken another route to the Lisburn Road station. Our stalker will either double-back on himself and follow them in a wee bit, or we've got this all wrong." Bristow picked up her police radio and looked tempted to call the team transporting Emma again but seemed to think better of it and sat back in her chair.

A few hundred yards up the road, the 4x4 turned right into Deramore Park. They pulled over into a convenient bus stop and watched as the green vehicle headed into an affluent area of Malone Road, a suburb of Belfast known for vast houses and similarly large prices.

"Do you know where you are, Isadora?"

"Yeah, I know this area. I've visited the Malone Road Barracks a few times. I've got an odd feeling about this, though."

"What do you mean?" Bristow turned and faced her.

"I don't know, Marie. But the right thing to do is to follow that car and see where he's off to, isn't it?"

"Oh, dead on, Isadora, you go on ahead. You need to follow your gut. But there are no through roads past Deramore Park. So, this is either a wild goose chase and your sense that you were being followed was wrong or he's up to no good. Let's take a wee look."

Isadora turned right and they drove slowly down the road, looking for the vehicle. Behind them, the main road was quiet as it was well past rush hour, and this was a largely residential area. The only consistent traffic was a few buses, taxis and the stream of cars heading into the city centre. But Deramore Park itself was virtually silent.

As they rounded the first corner, and parked up behind a grey Volkswagen, they saw the green 4x4 ahead.

"There's two in there now," Isadora whispered. "There's someone in the passenger seat. Shall we do a drive past?"

"Stay put, let's see what they do," Bristow advised.

The answer came quickly. After less than thirty seconds, the car pulled off and headed further down the road. The pair waited again and then slowly followed behind. Isadora was counting streetlights to keep herself calm and focused.

"Where the hell are they going? What's down there?" she asked. Bristow shrugged her shoulders in response.

"There's the back entrance to the cricket pitch for Collegians. I think it belongs to the Methody, or the Methodist College. I've only ever been down there once, for some event, with my brother. Other than that, there's just more expensive houses."

The Mondeo crawled slowly up the road and occasionally ducked into parking spaces to avoid being detected. But the green 4x4 kept going, following the road round and heading towards the sports pitches. Once again, the pair stopped as they saw the green vehicle drive onto a small piece of open grassland near the perimeter of the cricket pitch.

"Just carry on up to the gate on the right and leave the car there. I'm going to get out and have a look-see at what they're doing on that wee field. It's really fecking strange. You alright with that, Isadora?"

"I can't do much else, but I don't have my firearm. I gave it to Jones earlier," Isadora responded.

"It'll be fine. I have mine and I'll just take a dander around the corner here and come back. It's all very quiet around here. We'll just put all this to bed, shall we?"

"I'll wait here, Marie. No dramas."

But this was a drama for Isadora. She hated waiting and watching other people do her job. She now wanted this to be over and to be back sharing a few bevvies with Jones and Jenny in the mess bar. Instead, she watched as Bristow picked up her firearm and got out of the car. Isadora folded her arms in frustration and put the fan on. The speaker was still hanging out from the earlier distraction technique, and even that untidiness was annoying Isadora.

To divert herself from all that frustration, Isadora trawled through Virginia's glove compartment and found a small round tin of honey flavoured boiled sweets. They were covered in icing sugar and the lid was tricky to remove. But it was a welcome distraction.

Marie Bristow was beginning to wonder whether Isadora's

training had failed her and whether the green 4x4 wasn't simply a member of the public going about their business. However, as she approached the rather overgrown path leading to the grassland, she immediately spotted the car and crouched behind a small wooden fence. There were a few tall trees and saplings in evidence on this apparently disused piece of grassland, but the centre of the field was open and anyone walking through it would be seen easily. The car had driven over a shingle driveway, and she noticed another gated exit leading to the residential area.

The sergeant thought about this for a second. There were many parking spaces up and down Deramore Park, so there was no need to randomly park the car in the only piece of grassland left in the area. To the right was a small industrial estate and that was about 750 yards away behind a tall steel fence. To the left was the Methodist College sports ground and cricket pitch, with a club-house further on. There were building works taking place even further to the left and signs of scaffolding.

Orla Massey had taught her to consider every conceivable option before acting. She could almost hear her blunt tones telling her to wise up and go back to the car. But she was curious now and she'd come this far. She could see a route that would get her to within a few metres of the car, which was now in darkness. She'd be able to have a 'wee hoke about' inside and see whether she could pick up any clues to its ownership or their motives.

As she used the cover of the trees circling the grassland, she moved from hiding place to hiding place until she was within reach of the car. It looked completely empty and as she scanned the field, she opted to break cover and simply investigate the car. As a police officer, she had every reason to do so, and if anyone queried her presence, she'd simply show them her warrant card.

She reached for the torch in her bag and shone it around the car and across the back seats. The large boot space of the 4x4 was clear. The whole car was bereft of life and property.

She directed the torch under the car to check for explosives before she tried the handle. Irish paramilitary groups often used random parked vehicles in urban areas to detonate bombs. She knew any vehicle could carry a large amount of commercial or homemade explosive with no telltale signs at all. However, her training told her this was clean. She was right.

She shrugged her shoulders, even though no-one was watching, and walked back towards the car. She briefly thought about what she had to do before she arrived back home. She had a report to file about the Eden Vale incident, but that could wait until tomorrow. She had the rest of the paperwork to finish relating to a nasty GBH on a pensioner in Library Street, near the Art College, and that had been pressing for a few days now. Maybe she'd finish that and head home.

There was a frozen pizza in the freezer, and she had a few nice bottles of Sauvignon Blanc in the fridge. She'd be able to enjoy most of that in relative peace, unless her mother called. Her only hesitation is that Isadora might want a pint and chat before she headed back to Thiepval. She'd probably be feeling foolish after the rather pointless trailing exercise. There was a decent bar up near Stranmillis. Perhaps they could pop there for a quick one?

The grassland was beginning to feel a little wet, so she opted to head back onto the path and then over the shingle driveway. Isadora would be gutted by this waste of time, but she'd do more digging, no doubt. There must be more to this 4x4, Bristow told herself.

As she approached the rear of the Mondeo, Bristow saw Isadora had switched the lights off and was probably sitting and listening to the radio. She opened the passenger back door and threw her bag on the seat, noticing her shoes and the base of her black suit trousers were a little damp.

"I'm sorry, Isadora. The car is absolutely empty, no-one inside and no property. It's locked too. There's nothing more we can do. Can I suggest..." Bristow then stopped and looked over at Isadora from behind, preparing to get back into the front seat. But she was motionless and hadn't uttered a word.

"Isadora?" Bristow said, chirpily. "Have you fallen asleep?"

But as it became painfully clear, Isadora hadn't fallen asleep at all. Bristow screamed for the first time since her teenage years when she saw the bullet-hole in Isadora's head, with her eyes still wide open and her mouth gaping. Blood was dripping down the back of the Mondeo's navy headrest and Marie, more on instinct than hope, grabbed Isadora's wrist to check for a pulse. There was nothing.

Isadora Brown, the shining star of the Young Communicators Unit and the last survivor of the Limehall bomb, was dead. She and Bristow had been lured into a trap, which had cost poor Isadora her life. But Bristow didn't want to think about that. She didn't want to think about anything. Her instinct told her to run away, as the assailants had to be close by, but she couldn't leave Isadora. Not like this. She felt her eyes well up and a lump in her throat, was this her fault? Should she have left Isadora alone?

Bristow had seen the cruelty of the remnants of human beings strewn across the road after a bomb blast. Horrific murders, tragic car crashes and had witnessed more dead bodies than anyone should ever see in a lifetime. But this was different. This was someone she was talking to barely ten minutes ago. Someone in the prime of her life, with plans and ambitions in the security services. Someone who was becoming a friend.

With the tears now flowing down the face of Marie Bristow and the hideousness of the situation now clearer than ever, she noticed there was a small piece of yellow paper in the dead officer's other hand. Marie pulled an evidence bag out of her pocket and wrestled the note free from her grip. It was a bright yellow post-it note. On it, in block capital letters, were two words.

STOP NOW.

In the pocket of the driver's door was a small black box, which she recognised as a YCU handheld. She picked it up, her hands shaking desperately, and pressed the transmit button.

"This is Marie Bristow. Can anyone hear me?" The raw emotion in her voice was obvious. She didn't care whether there were protocols she was breaking by using this piece of equipment. People needed to know.

"Marie? What on earth is the matter? Where are you?" It was Virginia. Somehow, she had wanted it to be Virginia.

"Virginia. Isadora's dead. She's been shot at close range. I don't know what to say. I left her alone for five minutes. It was a trap," she blurted out, emotion rising from the pit of her stomach again.

"Oh, my poor girl," Virginia said. "My poor, poor girl," she repeated. "She's dead? You're sure?"

"There is no question. I'm so very sorry. There's nothing more I can do for her." Bristow took another look at Isadora, her face contorted, and head slumped back in the driver's seat. She didn't want this to be real.

"Give me your exact position, Marie. Make sure you're away from any risk and call it into your team. I want you safe. Do you understand?" She was holding herself together well, but Bristow could hear the torrent of emotion about to be released behind Virginia's caring and organised persona.

The notion of safety, when one of the pair was already dead, made total sense in Bristow's mind. Virginia wanted her body away from the scene. She had seen Isadora blossom and achieve, despite everything. But sadly, Isadora would be poured over by scenes of crime within the hour and photographed from every angle in the mortuary. This was not a dignified matter. Isadora would have hated that. She didn't deserve this ending.

"I understand. I'm at the far end of Deramore Park, on the south side. We're parked up near the back entrance to the cricket pitch. Come as soon as you can and I'll call it in."

"Take care, Marie. We'll be there soon," Virginia added, and the line was dead.

Marie Bristow took two deep breaths and picked up her police radio. Once she called this in, it would open all manner of investigations and probes into exactly what they were doing in Deramore Park in the darkness. But for now, she just wanted to let people grieve and for the investigation to find who murdered Isadora in this barbaric manner. It was now personal.

Stopping wasn't an option now.

Thirty-Two

With the hour heading close to 11pm, Knock Road HQ was still abuzz with life. The night shift was out patrolling Belfast, and the custody suite was rammed with drunks, shop lifters and one henchman looking particularly sorry for himself.

Ethan Smyth sat upright as the Custody Sergeant opened the door of his cell and led him to one of the interview rooms. There, sitting with a batch of notes and a large coffee in a polystyrene cup, was Declan McNally. Leading the questioning solo when he knew this broke every police and MI5 protocol in the book.

"I've got absolutely nothing to say to you," Ethan began. "You haven't offered me a solicitor or my telephone call. I'm saying nothing."

McNally took a long swig of his coffee and adjusted his round glasses.

"Saying nothing isn't going to help you though, is it? You'll notice that there is no tape recorder in this room, and you may be interested to learn that I'm not a police officer." McNally explained.

"You could be St Francis of Assisi, and I'd still not talk to you,"

Ethan smiled sarcastically. "What are you then? MI5? You're not a traffic warden, I know that much."

McNally ignored him.

"Your friend, Eamonn MacMillan, he's doing well in hospital you'll be pleased to hear. The bullet has been removed from his leg," McNally explained, whilst absent-mindedly twiddling a pencil between his fingers. "He's been very helpful."

"If he's been helpful, then you won't need anything from me," Ethan said, staring up at the bearded Derry man.

"Can I ask you something? If I sanctioned your release now. Literally, just opened the door and let you walk out of here. What do you think would happen?" McNally asked.

"What do you mean?" Ethan responded.

"Well, you've been here for, let's say, four hours now. Normal police interviews and follow-ups, they're at least ten hours. I'm sure you know the routine. They might even take longer, if further investigations are required. But the RUC only releases people this fast if they've given them everything. If they've spilled their guts, so to speak."

"Right?" Ethan offered in response, shrugging.

McNally continued. "Well, I think if you decide to stay completely schtum and give me absolutely nothing, I'll let you go straightaway. I reckon, even if you can get to the airport or ferry rapidly, your life expectancy is less than six hours. Do you agree, Ethan?"

"Oh, I see. They won't kill me," he smirked. "They might kill Mac. He's old bones, close to retirement age and pretty useless. But not me. I've got far too much to offer. Nice try though."

"You're prepared to take that chance?" McNally added.

"Oh absolutely. I'm dead on. Thank you. I could give the big man's daughter a wee slap and he still wouldn't kill me. I have a cast-iron guarantee."

"The big man's daughter? That was a slip, wasn't it? This is crucial intelligence, thanks Ethan," McNally smiled.

"You already knew about the big man. Your woman told me when she put me in the car, the mixed-race girl. So, it's yous that are slipping. The daughter could be a red herring. I'm clever like that. Now, can I have some water?"

"Just to remind you again, Mr Smyth. There's no tape. No solicitor and no Code C of the Police and Criminal Evidence Order. You're on your own here. I'm not a police officer and I can happily deny this meeting ever took place."

"Suits me, Spook," Ethan replied. "I still have nothing to say to you."

"What if I told you, or warned you, that we have a plan that would disgrace you in front of everyone? Your peers, friends, the big man, even fellow criminals would hate you? You'd be tagged forever as the worst kind of human?" McNally said, between more sips of coffee.

"You see, that wee girl, she made quite an allegation against you. An allegation that would raise all kinds of eyebrows." McNally didn't look at Ethan as he delivered that line.

He knew it was a ghastly tactic. And he knew, if Massey had been in the room, she'd have kicked him under the table as he spoke. But McNally had his own style guide. He didn't give a single damn.

"No, she didn't. I didn't touch her. I have my own kids. What are you? Some kind of arsehole? Nobody is going to believe I touched that girl," Ethan smarted. McNally knew straightaway he'd landed a useful blow.

"Just imagine the kind of prison you'd be in. Your fellow inmates. What reception you'd get when we finally realised our mistake and moved you to a regular prison? Perhaps Maghaberry, you've been in there before, haven't you? The lifers in there would know you."

"Wise up, nobody would believe you," Ethan said, but the look on his face suggested otherwise. He was cracking. McNally could feel it.

"Now, Ethan. I really don't want to do that. But not being a police officer means I can suggest such an approach to my friends at the Royal Ulster Constabulary. They may opt against it. But it's an option that I'm prepared to consider."

There was silence for a few minutes. McNally left the room and asked the duty Custody Sergeant to fetch Ethan a glass of water and a couple of biscuits. Digestives were the standard fare at Knock Road. He returned to the interview room and waited for the refreshments.

"What's Mac told you?" Ethan asked straightaway.

"Now, now, Ethan. Wait for the Sergeant to return with some water. We can't be interrupted. This is a crucial conversation for both of us."

"I'm not a nonce. I didn't touch that kid, as well you know."

"Wait. Ethan. Hold those wee horses." McNally held his hand up, making Ethan wait.

The Sergeant entered the room a few moments later with water and digestives for the prisoner and more coffee for McNally. The door was swiftly closed again.

"We can avoid the nonce wing, with a few helpful steps. Let's begin with this. Tell me who the big man is, Ethan. That's a good starting place."

"You're not being serious?" he replied. "There's absolutely no way I'm giving away any identities. You can put me in a paedo wing. I'd still not sing for you on that one. Not that I know anyway."

"You don't know who the big man is?" McNally responded with a look of surprise.

"Jesus Christ!" Ethan replied, realising he'd slipped up. "Alright, you got me there. Nah. I don't know him. I've never seen him face to face, like. But he communicates with us all, so he does."

"Like some kind of omnipresent being?" McNally shot back, smirking.

"I'm pleased I've never laid eyes on him. Then bastards like you can't interrogate his identity out of me. Then I'm safe, aren't I?"

"Fair enough. Let's pretend I believe you. So, tell us something else. Why was Philip Bradley killed? Who was Martha Maddison?" McNally responded.

"Nah. Aim lower. Those are not amongst the questions I can answer. I can tell you why George McCool was killed. Does that help?"

"George McCool was killed because he stole photos of Philip Bradley's murder and sold them to the newspaper. We know that one, you dope!" McNally grinned.

"Who's the lad with the teardrop tattoo? The one that was on the scene when the big man killed George McCool? Do you know him?" McNally asked.

"Will that keep me off the nonce's wing? If I tell you?"

"Maybe," McNally answered. "How old are your kids, by the way? How would your family feel about your little perversions hitting the headlines?" McNally knew that was well below the belt.

"You evil bastard," Ethan countered and stared at McNally. "The man you're describing is Andrew. Andrew McIlhinney. I think you might know his younger brother. RUC Officer Stewart McIlhinney. One of yours, I believe?"

"Sweet Jesus," McNally muttered.

"Yeah, that is a very useful piece of information. I'll leave you with that. Yeah? Can I go back to my cell now?" Ethan said, looking a little nervous.

"Is he the only officer the big man has paid off in Knock Road?"

"I'll not be telling you any more names. But the big man pays off officers across the RUC, British Police, the Garda, even customs officers. The big man is very well connected. That's what we're told anyway. I've no reason to doubt it."

"Why did you have orders to kill Sam Jacobs?" McNally was making notes as he spoke.

"That's an easy one. Your man, Officer McIlhinney, told us Sam Jacobs had witnessed the killing of Philip Bradley. He was hiding in a wardrobe or something. But, to be clear, I'd never have killed his wee sister. I don't hurt kids."

"That's very moral of you. But murdering the protection officers at Eden Vale, that was fair game?"

"That's my job. But killing police officers is hardly a chore, I'll admit. You might argue my career is also my hobby," Ethan laughed, some of his bravado was returning.

"But you're less of the billy big-balls, the paid assassin, when we talk about the murders of Philip Bradley and Martha Maddison. You seem very jumpy indeed. The big man killed three people in short succession. What's he so keen to cover up?"

"I'm not nervous. It's just above my pay grade. I can't even tell you who killed Bradley, McCool or your woman, Maddison. You've assumed it was the big man. I can't help you there."

"What?" McNally replied. "The big man was seen killing Bradley. You know we have a witness. What are you talking about, fella?"

"I've said enough. I want to get back to my cell," Ethan responded, picking up a digestive biscuit and taking a bite.

"I'm guessing the mention of the £1 million found with Martha's body will fill you with dread, too?" McNally added.

"You're having a laugh. £1 million? Nah, that's nothing to do with the big man. The big man's empire doesn't touch cash. Ever. It's too traceable. That's a big no. Where was it found?"

"On Philip Bradley's boat, The Mainstay. It was moored off Bangor Marina. Know it?"

"You've got me there. I knew about the yacht. But I know nothing about the money. I think you're way off target thinking the big man was involved in that. That's crazy." Ethan's confidence was rising again, and McNally seemed to believe his lack of knowledge.

"Did you ever meet Martha Maddison? Was she on your radar?" McNally went back to sipping his coffee.

"Look, I'm not saying anything else. If I've given you enough to avoid being banged up with the nonces, then it's happy days. But if I tell you much more, I'm putting my family at risk."

"Did you meet Martha Maddison?" McNally pushed.

"Oh, for God's sake. Did you not hear me? I can't talk about that." Ethan looked indignant for a moment, as if he was determined to hold onto some tiny victory, before looking up at McNally and seeming to reassess slightly.

"Look, why don't you ask your colleague, Massey? She's probably met her a few times. I dare say a few more of your Peeler friends have too. Now, I've been generous with my time. But I want to go back to my cell. I have nothing more to say now." Ethan crossed his arms like a petulant child and drew an invisible zip across his mouth. He was done.

McNally pushed a small red button on the right of the desk and within a few minutes the duty Custody Sergeant arrived back in the room. Ethan waved goodbye sarcastically as he was led towards the door and picked up the other digestive biscuit as he was finally ushered out.

McNally listened for the loud clang as the cell door was slammed behind Ethan Smyth and walked with the Custody Sergeant back to front of the building.

"Thanks for letting me have a crack at him, Sergeant. I realise that's a big favour," McNally could feel a wave of tiredness hit him as he spoke.

"I'm not sure what Superintendent Rogers would think of it," the officer replied. "But we're all on the same side aren't we? Did Smyth give you anything?"

"He did, yeah. But I'm not sure what to make of it," McNally and duty Custody Sergeant had now walked as far as the lobby of the station. McNally rubbed his eyes again and yawned, almost theatrically.

The balding officer, who also looked haggard after a long shift, tapped McNally on the shoulder, but the spook already had his handheld ready.

"Can I have a minute before you leave, Mr McNally?" the policeman politely asked. "I have a wee message for you."

"Sure, sure," McNally responded. "Let me just speak to a colleague. I'll come and find you afterwards."

He quickly raised Jube on the handheld to talk through Ethan's interview. He knew Jube would be on the ball, even at this hour, and respected his opinion.

"I've just finished a quick interview with Ethan Smyth. It wasn't as enlightening as I'd hoped. But I do think he's telling the truth," McNally explained.

"What do you mean?" Jube asked, immediately interested.

"Well, I think there are a few conclusions we can draw from this interview. Philip Bradley and Martha Maddison knew something significant about the big man, his operation or an impending plan. I think George McCool was just natural wastage due to him selling the photos. But I'm unclear what Sam Jacobs knows or what he saw that makes him such a target."

"He saw the big man kill Philip Bradley. That would be enough, surely?" Jube said.

"He saw Philip Bradley being killed. But it says all over his interview notes that he couldn't identify the killer. There was also this other conversation involving a woman's name and a business transaction. I reckon they believe he heard all of that, too. That must be damaging stuff."

"Right enough," Jube replied. "I've been thinking the same."

"Ethan Smyth also said something cryptic about whether the big man really killed Bradley, McCool, or Maddison. And Sam said he never saw his face. But that could all be bluster." McNally was using Jube as an information dump. Massey had left quite a hole, but at least he knew Jube would fast-track any assistance.

"He's going to prison for a long time, Declan. Ethan Smyth hasn't really got a great deal to gain by giving you anything. Unless you promised to protect his family. Was that the approach you took?"

"Kind of," McNally muttered. "Well, I suggested I could make it worse for him and his family."

"That was another option, I guess," Jube responded. "Anything else?"

"The other massive headline is the mole. We have a name," McNally began. "It's Stewart McIlhinney, a young RUC Officer based here at Knock Road."

"Good God! Now that *is* a sizeable pain in the arse. He would have passed every shred of useful information onto the big man's team. Information is power," Jube exclaimed. McNally knew he'd be writing this all down in his notebook.

"But let's not be hasty. Don't interrogate Stewart McIlhinney yet. Let him think he's in the clear. I think we can both conjure up ways of how he might lead us back to the big man."

"Understood, Jube, my lips are sealed. I'm way ahead of you there." His brain had already logged that opportunity, but he was pleased the two of them were on the same page.

"By the by, McNally, do you really think Sam Jacobs saw or heard something else? More than just the identity of the killer? You think this is more than just the big man keeping his identity quiet?" Jube asked.

"That's entirely possible, but what? That's a big question mark. But I'm also struggling with the Martha Maddison murder. Who the hell is she?"

"That sounds like a morning question, McNally. I've got notes to prepare for the mother of all meetings tomorrow," Jube replied. "Bloody politics. If proper peace talks ever happen here, it'll be at the expense of my sanity."

"True enough. Okay, I'm reading the room. You want me to disappear. But one last thing, Jube."

"Go on, McNally,"

"Ethan Smyth said in his interview that he believes the big man won't kill him but would kill Eamonn MacMillan, the other gunman who's now in hospital with a bullet wound. But they both screwed up. How has Ethan got a get out of jail free card?" McNally continued, as Jube made more notes in the background.

"Well, let's think about that. Maybe Ethan has a familial connection with the big man. He's a nephew or something. You rarely kill your own family. Not unless the proverbial shite really hits the fan."

"And this doesn't merit it?" McNally responded. "I take your point, but plenty of mafioso, drug barons, and big men have murdered family members to protect themselves."

"You're right," Jube conceded. "I'll sleep on that one once I've done these blasted notes. Oh, by the way, did Isadora Brown see Massey in the end? I think we need to know more about her morning visit from Caragh Reid."

"No, she was waylaid by the carnage at Eden Vale. I dare say she, Jones, Jenny and half of Thiepval Barracks are half-cut by now. I'll see if one of them is likely to pop into Massey tomorrow. I agree, we need that intel."

"Okay, I'm heading back to my writing desk. Let's chat on the morning once I've completed my meetings with the Minister. Goodnight McNally and good work."

"That'll do, cheers, Jube," McNally killed the call.

McNally waved over at the Custody Sergeant as he prepared to leave the station. He knew he had to put his notes and theories in order before another team briefing in the morning. He was beginning to enjoy this police/espionage hybrid arrangement.

He then remembered the Sergeant wanted a word.

"Before you go," the Custody Sergeant called over. "Yes?"

McNally called back, poking his head back around the custody suite door.

"There was a fatal shooting just off Malone Road earlier. I was asked to bring it to your attention." The uniformed man looked nervous, and McNally felt the vibes.

"Do I know the victim?" McNally quietly asked.

"I'm afraid you do," the Sergeant put his hand on McNally's shoulder. "I'm really sorry. It's a young woman called Isadora Brown. I believe she's part of your investigation team."

"No. Jesus wept. She's dead? Not Isadora," McNally swallowed hard and had to lean on the wall for a couple of seconds. The Sergeant, well versed at delivering bad news, put a small glass of water in front of McNally and led him to one of the chairs in reception.

"Take your time, my friend. I can imagine this is an awful shock to you."

"I just... I just can't believe it. She's such a wonderful officer," McNally was struggling to compute this horrific news against the backdrop of his interview. "Do you know what happened to her? What was she doing in Malone Road?"

"Aye. She was following up a suspected tail. Someone who'd she suspected had been following her for a few days. One of my team, Sergeant Marie Bristow, she was with her at the time of the incident.

"She saw it all?" McNally asked, taking a small sip of water and trying to compose himself.

"I don't know. We have a team out there now supporting Marie. I believe one of your colleagues is there too. Would you like me to arrange some transport for you, Mr McNally?"

McNally didn't know what to say. He'd lost colleagues before, many times. But this was a young officer that he'd taught himself. He knew her better than members of his own family. In fact, she had reminded him a little of his younger sister, Gloria, on occasion. He would have happily described her as a friend, and that was unusual for a man whose Christmas card list stopped at low single figures. He felt himself well up but battled against it and coughed loudly to ground himself and refocus. He'd need to do any grieving away from the world.

McNally kept on staring at the Sergeant's name badge. Sergeant Geoff Robinson. He'd remember this name for all the wrong reasons.

"If you wouldn't mind getting me to the scene, I'd be very grateful, Sergeant Robinson." McNally stood up and fished out his cigarillos from his trench coat pocket. "I'll just be outside, taking the air. I just need a moment."

"Take all the time you need; I'll radio a car for you."

The Custody Sergeant picked up his desk phone and watched as McNally, with a haunted expression, headed out of the main doors. As McNally did so, he tried to digest the news, but his head was full of questions, and he urgently needed to get to the scene. Another wave of tiredness hit him and he felt the weight of emotion hanging like a millstone around his neck. He pulled his handheld from his coat pocket and stared at it. Why hadn't anyone been in touch? Who knew? He thought about Virginia and her undisguised affection for Isadora. This was going to hurt like hell.

He lit a cigarillo and stood with one foot on the wall of the station entrance. He needed to calculate his next steps. As he thought, he watched a middle-aged man walk slowly towards the gates of the police station. For some reason, McNally couldn't help but stare out at the man amongst the headlights of the passing cars and the brightness of the floodlit entrance area. He continued to watch as the man approached the buzzer and intercom at the front gate. He was almost engulfed by shadows.

The Custody Sergeant appeared at the doors and motioned towards McNally.

"Two minutes, Mr McNally. They'll pick you up from outside the main entrance."

"Thanks," he quietly responded and stubbed out his cigarillo on the path outside. As he did so, the phone started ringing behind the Sergeant's desk. It was answered immediately and McNally watched as information was exchanged. Presuming it was none of his business, he walked back to a row of green plastic chairs and felt the handheld in his pocket again. He knew he had to call Thiepval.

"Mr McNally," the Sergeant called over. "There's a gentleman at the entrance who is asking to speak to Marie Bristow."

"Okay. I don't want to tell you how to do your job, but can't you contact her at the scene?" he replied.

"Oh, you're right. Normally I would. But after my colleague on the front desk explained she was unavailable; he asked for Isadora Brown."

"Did he?" McNally nodded, swallowed hard again and stood gazing at the Sergeant for a second. Who would ask for Isadora? Why would she give her name? He thought.

"We'd better let him in, Sergeant," he called back.

Thirty-Three

Less than four miles away, the stone-cold sober Topaz team arrived at City Hospital. They'd opted against a few drinks at the mess bar and decided to focus on the investigation. News of Isadora's shooting hadn't reached them yet, and there was a general feeling of bonhomie after Jones' accidental heroics.

Jones was sporting a bandaged right arm and had a few cuts and bruises on his face. Otherwise, he was miraculously unhurt from his leap over the navigation and tussle with the large hedge outside the cottage.

"You probably should have got yourself checked out properly," Jenny said, as they reached the automatic doors leading to the main reception.

"I'm fine," Jones assured her. "Virginia is a dab-hand with the medical kit and the witch-hazel on these little cuts will do the business. I'm absolutely chipper. Although, I'll admit, I'm parched. I could have done with a few pints."

"Focus on the case," Jenny responded. "I know you think you're action man now, but there's plenty of time for a drink later. We need to speak to Orla."

Jones nodded. He knew, in reality, he was far from chipper. His shoulder ached from the crash into the bush, he still had plenty of new injuries to discover, and he needed some alcohol to self-medicate. A few pints of lager, maybe a nip of whiskey, practically anything to take the edge off. He'd dislocated his shoulder a few times in the past and wondered whether it had popped out and back in again as he performed his ill-judged stunt.

However, he also jumped at the chance to join Jenny at the Massey interview, as he had that nagging feeling that something important was about to happen. But he knew he wasn't entirely right and as Jenny chatted to him as they strolled towards the lifts, he realised he'd stopped listening and it was all basically white noise. As the lift pinged, Jones decided he needed a re-brief.

"Right, so we know Caragh Reid was here earlier today. What else do we know?" he asked.

"Haven't you been listening at all? Are you sure you're alright? We discussed all this on the way here." Jenny looked concerned.

"It's the codeine that Virginia gave me, I think. It's making me feel a little odd. But I'll be fine. I'll battle on. Please recap for me."

"If you're sure," Jenny replied. "So, Caragh arrived in the morning and spent about 15 minutes with Massey. McIlhinney was the only police officer who's been able to get a debrief from her. He tells us that Caragh simply checked on Massey's health and made some observations about how there's been an uptick in sectarian violence, asked a few questions about the Bradley case and generally chewed the fat. This seems a bit bizarre, if you ask me."

"Agreed," Jones responded. "McNally says Caragh and Massey have met once or twice, maximum. It's hardly like they were ladies that lunched."

As the lift arrived on the floor leading to Massey's private room, Jones noticed that the ward was still very busy for such a late hour. Medical staff and visitors were still to-ing and fro-ing around the corridors. The two heavily armed protection officers were standing on either side of her door and keeping an eye on proceedings. The pair made themselves known to the officers.

"We're here to see DCI Orla Massey," Jenny explained.

"Do you have any identification? We have no further visits planned today and she's very tired," one of the armed officers replied.

"We're part of the Bradley investigation, led by McNally and Marie Bristow," she added.

"Okay, give me your surnames, please." The officer grabbed a notebook from his inside pocket and was poised to scribble some details when Massey's voice boomed out from behind the double doors.

"Let them in, they're Box," she shouted. "Jube Spencer's mob. He'll provide clearance. You can get us some coffees, too."

Jones mouthed the word 'Box' at Jenny with a quizzical expression, who responded with a shrug.

The policeman rolled his eyes and reluctantly replaced his notebook back in his pocket. He pushed the doors open, and Jones and Jenny walked into the small hospital room.

"You must have heard of Box?" Massey began, having seen Jones' gesture. She grabbed hold of a plastic pulley above her bed and pulled herself up on her pillows.

"It's a slang term for MI5 and quite common over here, especially amongst the RUC. Jube tells me it comes from 'Box 500', the old wartime postal address in London. I doubt this'll be the last time you'll hear it. You're either Box or sneaky beakies here."

"Every day's a school day," Jones commented, moving the subject on. "So, how are you?"

"I'd love to say that I'm resting, recuperating and enjoying the hospital cuisine. But I can't. The food is dire. I'm bored and haven't touched a cigarette in ages. It's like accidental cold turkey. What did you bring me?" Massey looked around for signs of a carrier bag.

"Nothing, sorry," Jenny said, following her gaze. "But we'd love to hear about the visit of Caragh Reid earlier."

"Right. Of course. Straight to business. Tell you what, I'll give you chapter and verse on Caragh's visit, but I need a favour," Massey responded.

"Of course," Jenny smiled, feeling slightly awkward about the lack of grapes or chocolate.

"Check on Georgie for me, my cat. I've asked Marie to feed him, but I've heard nothing from her, and I need someone ultra-reliable to check on the wee man." Massey, in a rare moment, allowed her caring side to shine through.

"Absolutely," Jenny said. "We'll pop in on the way back to Thiepval. I love cat cuddles. Now, Caragh Reid? Why did she visit?"

"Your guess is as good as mine. She arrived before ten, brought me a very expensive bouquet, certainly not from a garage fore-court, and chatted about everything and nothing for about twenty minutes. It was all very surreal." As she spoke, she pointed out an enormous bunch of flowers in the corner of the room, filled with sunset yellow roses, calla lilies and cream-coloured carnations. Jones' mother had trained as a florist, and he knew an expensive arrangement when he saw one. This looked like a statement gift.

"Why surreal?" Jones asked, still admiring the vibrant colours of the bouquet.

"I've met her twice and seen her in the wild too, but rarely. She's a solitary, almost reclusive, woman. She wasn't much involved in the family firm before her Da, Kenny, died. My intelli-gence suggested she was the financier. She kept the books and knew where the financial bodies were buried. But she was hardly public facing."

"Go on," Jones nudged, taking the cups of coffee from a sullen-looking protection officer, who had emerged in the background.

"That's just it. She talked to me like we were old friends. Like we had loads of history and there was a common bond. But, as far as I'm concerned, she's a total stranger and certainly had no reason to bring me an expensive bouquet, let alone have a civil conversation."

"What did you talk about?" Jenny probed, grabbing her own shorthand book to write some details down.

"Ah, you don't need that. It's all here." Massey reached behind and grabbed a copy of Ulster Tatler, passing it over to Jenny. She pointed out the detailed notes and scribbles in the margins. "I didn't have any notepaper," she added. "It's not really my kind of publication but bless Jube for the thought."

Jenny scrutinised the notes and realised they were as good as verbatim before passing the magazine over to Jones. He scanned the pages and memorised as much detail as possible. He took a swig of coffee, realising it tasted like Bisto mixed with gravel and hastily put it down.

"What are the tally marks at the top of the page? There are seven lines?" Jones queried.

"Mentions of her sister, Saoirse. Someone she allegedly considers dead to her since she took half of her father's estate. But there was none of that hatred on show. She mentioned her casually, as if they'd just had a family picnic. It was fecking strange." Massey hoisted herself up from her bed again, almost as if to get closer to her visitors. She then lowered her voice.

"The main thrust was that since Philip had been killed, Caragh had suggested a truce and wanted to reconnect with her sister. She explained this offer had been happily accepted and they were back on speaking terms. She also talked to her nephews and how delighted she was to be one family group again. But I don't buy any of it." Massey kept looking over towards the double doors to ensure the protection officers were not listening and then continued.

"Saoirse and Caragh, they're chalk and cheese, you see? Caragh was the closest Kenny had to a prodigy and was always by his side as a youngster. Saoirse was always closer to her mother. She was into history, art and architecture. She took her education seriously. Even eventually went to Queen's University in Belfast and studied for a combined history and business degree. Caragh stayed at home and supported her Da. They didn't do sisterly drinking and clubbing together, double dates or anything. They were almost estranged by their teenage years."

"How do you know all that background, Orla? The investigation log suggests you were mainly out of the loop with the Reid family and this was Eric Rogers' domain," Jones asked.

"You're a bright button, aren't you, Jones? Yeah, I got a wee briefing about the Reid family from one of my team back in Knock Road earlier today to fill in the blanks. I've been sitting here bored beyond belief. Can you blame me?"

"Of course, Orla. Just following the notes," Jones responded.

"I want to help. Jube knows I've been making calls from my bedside too. He encouraged me. He's been here trying to get my thoughts on the whole investigation too."

"Absolutely, Orla. And we appreciate it," Jenny shot Jones a questioning look. "But is there no way Caragh could mean it? She really wants to end the feud? Could she have had some Road to Damascus moment that has changed her entire mindset? Is that out of the question?"

"Look at it this way, Jenny. According to the intel I heard today, less than two years ago, the Reid Family took Saoirse to court. They threatened to kill her, ex-communicated her, and wanted her out of their lives permanently. There have been petrol bombs thrown through her windows, credible threats on her life, and Philip Bradley even paid for security for the children when they were at their private school. This wouldn't be a Road to Damascus moment, this would be a spectacular miracle."

There was silence as Jones and Jenny tried to digest the information. But it was clear no-one understood the logic behind Caragh's visit. Massey continued.

"The thing weirder than Caragh's apparent brain transplant is the fact that she also apologised for her family's drain on RUC resources over the years and wants to draw a line. I kid you not."

"Apologised? That's astonishing. But there has to be a reason for this," Jones replied. "Especially as we were told earlier in the investigation, that Knock Road didn't really get involved with the Reid Family."

"Not Knock Road. It was my team that were excluded," Massey interrupted. "Rogers anti-terrorism squad would have had chapter and verse. Any scant background I had was purely on the basis of their low-level arrests. It was all arm's length."

"Righto. But it seems he gave Kenny Reid free rein around West Belfast. Was he purposely keeping his eyes closed to their dramas?" Jenny asked.

"Hmmm," Massey pondered. "I had the same conversation with Jube a few days back. He's looking into this, on the quiet, so to speak. You'd best keep that to yourself."

"Jube's looking into what? Eric Rogers' background with the Reids?" Jones asked.

"Something like that, yes," Massey said, attempting to move the conversation on.

"Most of the Reid family's biggest misdemeanours in this city happened when I was still working in Derry," she continued, on a safer line of narrative. "But their reputation spread quite a distance and I was aware of them. Everyone was. Kenny was an arsehole. Forget what side of the fence he was on, he was just a nasty piece of work, full stop."

"Right, this is useful. But you haven't really answered my question about Eric Rogers," Jones reminded her.

"Come on, Jones. Don't speak to me like I'm a muppet. I know what you're asking. Is Rogers bent? I think there are two answers to that question. He's certainly a career policeman and he'd basically do anything to rise to the top. I think that includes nods and winks to his pals in the Lodge and wearing his Stevie

Wonder glasses when one of his mates gets pulled for speeding, maybe drink driving and even low-level financial crimes. But I'm struggling to see him covering for a crime family."

"You said there were two answers?" Jenny prompted.

"Yeah, the second point is that Eric Rogers is a lazy bastard. If he can avoid doing something or kick it into the long grass, he'll do it. Maybe he saw the Reid Family as an avoidable task? He led the anti-terrorism squad for donkey's years around here and he'd be very focused on the big picture. Whilst Kenny was in league with the Republicans and a hardliner, he was always more interested in drugs, maybe protection rackets and occasional gun running."

"He was too lazy to investigate Kenny Reid? Really?" Jones said, sounding disbelieving.

"Possibly. But you also need to check with Jube to ensure that nothing was going on behind the scenes that I'd be unaware of. I'm not a fan of Eric Rogers. I've never hidden that. But it's quite a leap to suggest that he's been bought off by a crime family. Is that what we're saying?"

"I think it's a possibility. It's certainly something we need to consider," Jones responded.

"Understood. All options on the table, I get that. That makes sense. What on earth happened to you, anyway?" Massey asked, looking at Jones' injuries.

"Jones jumped the Lagan navigation on an old East German motorbike, up at Eden Vale. In doing so, he saved the lives of Sam Jacobs, his little sister, and Wendy Watson. The RUC has detained two of the big man's heavies who shot and killed three protection officers. Those are the headlines," Jenny explained.

"Three dead?" she began, looking distraught. "That's tragic news. I'll need to find out who they were. We're quite a tight-knit lot at Knock Road. I'm bound to know them. The losses are mounting up."

"And you jumped the Lagan at Eden Vale?" Massey looked over at Jones. "That's quite a feat."

"Yeah, but I'm a bit battered from it. The two goons are currently in custody, or in hospital, chatting to McNally. Isadora has gone AWOL with Marie Bristow, but the smart money is that they're chasing up a lead of some kind." Jones felt his batteries draining as the conversation went on.

"Yeah, and there was a fresh line of enquiry about Sam and Emma Jacobs' adoptions. It was always a bit of a long shot, but Isadora is leading on that now. We were just checking the birth mother, from Belfast, hadn't taken the child. But as she's safe now. It seems like a red herring. But I'm absolutely knackered and I think the codeine is getting to me." Jones was desperately trying to look nonchalant as Jenny had already sung his praises and he just wanted to blend back into the background.

However, he soon realised this approach wasn't going to work. Massey and Jenny were both smiling at him and after finishing the detail about the adoptions, he opted to stare down at his battered brown Gola trainers to avoid their unnerving glances. They still had the remnants of the reed bed plastered around the soles. Jenny briefly touched his arm. Jones wasn't sure whether Jenny saw his exploits as heroic or imbecilic, but he'd find out later.

"The adoption stuff was just box ticking, I get that," Massey nodded. "But I'm genuinely impressed with you, Jones. You're a real dark horse!"

Jones looked up momentarily and Massey shot him a beaming smile, which he realised was a collector's item. Massey wasn't a smiler. She had a face that suggested she was scrutinising those around her, looking for mistakes or weaknesses. Hospital bed or not, Jones would log that little grin for posterity. He then went back to staring at the floor.

"Confusingly, the two heavies that killed the protection officers guarding the safe house used some rather odd equipment. Ballistics suggest they used a gun firing antique bullets. They're trying to investigate what gun might have fired them."

Jenny added further detail from her notes. "Oh, and the fourth and fifth protection officers only avoided being gunned down because they'd popped to the City View Hotel for a piss. They were the next shift on and were late," she continued.

"I need to get out of here. This is utterly frustrating. I just need to be in the thick of this. This is my patch." Jones could see Massey meant it. The fire was still there.

"Tell me about the wee girl," Massey continued. "Emma, isn't it?"

"Emma Jacobs. She's at the hospital for a check-up. She'd been drugged. Then she'll join up with Wendy and Sam at Thiepval. They're planning for her parents to fly over and join her at an interview tomorrow. Poor thing has really been through it,"

"You're not joking, Jenny. Poor wee dote. Who kidnapped her?"

"At present, we have absolutely no idea who brought her over the Irish Sea. The two lads in custody claim they picked her up from an anonymous source at Larne Port two days ago." Jenny continued reading directly from her notebook. As she did so, Jones was still trying to put the jigsaw pieces together and was feeling more addled than normal. The codeine was making him feel hungover and a little nauseous, but he needed to power through this.

"Hold on," Jones said, summoning some extra strength from somewhere. "Let's just get back to Caragh and Saoirse for a second. Before we totally lose our train of thought on this. Massey, can you think of any reasonable rationale for her visit whatsoever?"

"I'm going to need to think about this," Massey said, after a thoughtful pause. "Because, on the face of it, there is no explanation. But, I'm not busy, my social diary is empty. I'll think it over. I'll get back to you."

"If you could," Jenny said, looking over at Jones, aware he was still in processing mode. No-one stares at their trainers for that long, she thought.

"Did she look any different to your previous encounters?" Jones questioned.

"They're visually pretty similar, the sisters. But I'd say she's had some work done. She'd certainly been to the beautician. Saoirse is white-blonde, petite and alabaster pale skin. Caragh is similar, but younger. Thinner face and dark strawberry blonde hair, some people might call it auburn. Darker than yours, Jenny. In the past, it was always shoulder length and wild. She'd had it cut into a neat bob."

"Alright, you say she'd been to the beautician. What was she wearing?" Jenny, now intrigued, asked.

"Well, she wasn't dressed lavishly but was heavily made-up, as if she was on her way out somewhere nice. I'd never seen her like it. But I think she was wearing a black hooded jumper and some fairly frumpy grey joggers. But she had a really lovely wee pink or peachy bag. I'm not a handbag person, but it was certainly cute."

"Oh my God," Jones replied instantly. "Oh my good God," he repeated.

"What?" Jenny shot back.

The sinews in Jones' brain started popping and the nausea momentarily giving way as the realisation hit him. "What time was your meeting, Orla?"

"Maybe 9.45am? She was supposed to arrive later. She'd even booked an appointment through the protection team."

"What time did we arrive in Bangor, Jenny?" Jones was now furiously flicking through his shorthand book.

"We got there just after midday. But I don't think you were on the boat before 1pm," she responded. "You had to learn how to drive that dinghy."

"Yeah. But that would be bloody tight time-wise," he said, rather mysteriously.

"For what?" Jenny was trying to tune into his wavelength but was failing. She and Massey just looked at each other, perplexed.

"Unless this is an incredible coincidence, I think Caragh Reid is Martha Maddison. The description matches," Jones announced confidently. "Or, Martha Maddison was pretending to be Caragh when she came to you today. That's also a possibility."

"Oh no," Jenny responded. The penny was dropping.

"Right?" Massey interrupted. "The woman I met was definitely Caragh Reid. I'd bet my life savings on it. But who the hell is Martha Maddison? You haven't mentioned her at all."

"Martha Maddison is a dead woman. A body I found hanging from a coat hook on board The Mainstay, Philip Bradley's yacht, at Bangor Marina. At about 1pm today. Everything you said tallies. Her clothing, hair, and handbag. It's her."

"Sweet Jesus," Massey, again uncharacteristically, put her head in her hands. "I was the last person to speak to this woman? Before she was found dead on the yacht? That's horrific."

"That's one word for it," Jones replied. "Especially as we think the dead woman also matches the description of Wonder Woman. The woman, we believe, was having sex with Philip Bradley just before his death."

"You're saying Philip Bradley was having an affair with his sister-in-law? That's momentous. I can't imagine that would have gone down well with Saoirse," Massey said. "Are you absolutely sure about this?"

"Yeah, I think so. One woman, three personas. It's also making me wonder about Sam Jacobs and his 'unheard conversation'. Do you remember? The business transaction, the woman's name and the money? I reckon there's a good chance that woman's name might be Martha or Caragh." Jones, who had diverted his attention away from the floor, now stared at a rather dusty looking NHS ceiling fan behind Massey as he organised his thoughts.

"This just makes things even more complicated," he continued. "I'd better get hold of McNally." Jones walked out of the hospital room with his handheld poised and with the dead face of Martha, Caragh, or Wonder Woman etched indelibly into his thoughts.

"One woman, three personas," he repeated.

Thirty-Four

The visitor squinted and raised his hand to shield his eyes from the intensity of the floodlights outside the police station. There was a loud metallic noise as the reinforced gates, the only entry point that punctuated the cage that surrounded the building, shut behind him. The Duty Sergeant slowly trudged back to his post after showing him through. It was late and the temperature was dropping.

Being in the RUC was a dangerous profession and the stations themselves were often targets of indiscriminate attacks. There was a constant tangible feeling of nervousness inside, as if something was about to happen at any minute. Identities were often hidden, families waited nervously for shifts to end and vehicles were constantly checked for car bombs, or vehicle-borne improvised explosive devices (VBIEDs), often the terrorists' deadly weapon of choice. The next round of talks, year after year of discussion and false hope, were the only real signs of progress.

But as the man walked closer, McNally could see the visitor was in the midst of his own personal crises. He was in his early fifties, maybe older, wearing a dark grey suit and an unseasonal thick black coat. But his face was ashen. Something triggered

McNally as the visitor greeted him at the reception desk. He needed to talk to Virginia urgently.

"Hello, you asked to see Sergeant Bristow?" McNally asked, as the man pitched up at the reception desk.

"Or Isadora Brown, yes. It's quite urgent." There was the noise of the front door gently closing and the Duty Sergeant pressed a button behind the counter that secured the building. McNally nodded at the policeman. He'd take it from here.

The man had a gentle Belfast accent, and his eyes were intense. Many years had passed since McNally had been taught about body language, almost a quarter of a century. But here was a man desperate for something, McNally knew. But he had to put this on hold, as his brain screamed that he needed to tell the team about Isadora's murder.

"Please, take a seat. I have a quick call to make, and then I'm all yours." McNally showed him to the small row of green plastic chairs and, with a half-smile from the visitor, he excused himself to an interview room to the right of reception. He grabbed his hand-held and selected Virginia's channel.

"Virginia, this is McNally. Are you receiving me?"

"Go ahead McNally. I'm guessing you know where I am?" Virginia was initially blunt, almost cold. But McNally knew that was her response to disaster. He remembered it well from Limehall and Lennoxville.

"I've heard. I was told by the Duty Sergeant here at Knock Road after my interview."

"I rang there myself. I told him to make you aware after your interview with Ethan Smyth. I knew you'd want the headspace to focus on that. Should I have interrupted?"

"No, no. You did the right thing, as always. Tell me what's happening, Virginia."

"Marie Bristow is still here, talking to scenes of crime. They know the protocol for the death of an officer from the security services. It's all in hand. I've spoken to Jube Spencer and we are already working on a narrative for her parents. I'll make the call later." She spoke professionally and calmly.

"I need to tell the rest of the team. I'm going to say that Isadora was shot and killed instantly when she drove into a trap. What more can you tell me?" McNally asked.

"Isadora thought she had been followed for a day or so. It seems she was right. It was a green 4x4 with stolen plates. It had tracked her for days, just going about her intelligence gathering. She was chasing up a lead relating to the Sam Jacobs adoption." Virginia was softening. McNally was registering the emotion in her voice.

"The worst thing is," Virginia added. "The killer left a post-it note in her hand. It reads 'stop now'. Marie had to prize it out of her palm."

There it was. Virginia's emotion was now clear. But McNally couldn't ask her how she was. He couldn't even say he was sorry. He couldn't break through that barrier yet. Instead, he had to tell the team. He had to build the right narrative.

"I'm going onto the open channel now and I'll break the news. Who's at Thiepval that can deal with this? Now that..." McNally broke off.

"You mean who's going to play the Virginia role? Now that I'm here? Mr Singh will, I guess. But this is going to hit them all very hard. They're such a tight-knit unit. So, please be careful Declan. Are you sure you can't wait until I'm back there?"

"Rumours and misinformation will already be circulating. The barracks will be abuzz soon enough. They need to hear it from us. I'd prefer one of us to be there, but..."

"I get it. Make the call," she interrupted. "Be gentle. This is their friend, and this is going to feel painfully familiar for some of them. Let's talk after. Are you okay doing this, Declan?"

"It has to be me," he responded. McNally didn't say goodbye. He switched to the open channel and felt the sweat drip down his back.

"This is McNally. Virginia's also on the line. I need all the team on this call. Mr Singh, can you assemble them? Is everyone receiving me?"

"I'm with Tom and Carl. Wendy's here too, fresh from her heroics. We're in the QD assembling equipment for the Hunter's Arms operation," he replied.

"Very good, Mr Singh. Jones and Jenny?"

"On our way back from visiting Orla Massey in the hospital," Jones responded. The sound of the engine was clear in the background. "But Isadora seems to have gone AWOL with Bristow." McNally ignored the reference.

Instead, he inhaled deeply and tried to make himself believe this was about being an absolute professional. He'd dealt with loss and death before. That had always been his approach.

"Look, I'm really sorry to say that I have something terrible to share," McNally closed his eyes for a fraction of a second and the professionalism vanished. He saw Isadora's face in his mind's eye. He saw the look she gave him when she was rescued from roof of The Europa. That look of utter defiance and the self-belief she radiated.

"I'm afraid we've lost one of our own," he began again. He didn't want to say her name and make it real but he knew they needed to hear it from him.

"There's no easy way of telling you, but Isadora has been killed. She was shot at close range earlier this evening whilst following up a lead. It appears to have been a trap. Marie Bristow was with her, but wasn't harmed. I'm so sorry to be the bearer of such tragic news."

McNally felt the emotion rise up inside him as the words were transmitted to the team, But he fought against the tears and anger that were desperate for release.

There was silence.

"Isadora will be remembered as an incredibly brave and ambitious officer who fought hard for fairness. Marie tells me she was desperate to clear up the Jacobs adoption issue. She was absolutely focused to the end," Virginia added, needing to fill the void the silence had created.

"That appears to be the lead she was chasing." McNally said. He was grateful that Virginia intervened. He could interrogate, but commiserating wasn't in his skill set.

More silence followed. It was as if the team had to collectively believe what they were hearing. Like a communal heartbreak that prevented words from being communicated. McNally waited for someone to break the silence again.

"Oh my God," a tearful Jenny half-whispered. "I don't believe it."

"There must be some kind of mistake. Our Isadora? I just don't understand. I just can't..." Mr Singh stammered in disbelief. McNally could hear Wendy in the background already comforting him. People were struggling to find words.

"It was a trap? Connected to the investigation? Do we know who killed her?" Jenny spoke hurriedly, as if the words were being propelled out of her mouth to allay the onslaught of emotion.

"It's all too early to say. The RUC is on the scene. I'm here too," Virginia responded.

"Are you okay, Virginia? Are you with her?" The engine noise in the background had paused. McNally knew he should have asked Jenny to pull over. It was too late now. Jenny was already trying to unpick the tragedy.

"Yes, I'm with her and I'm doing okay. I won't leave her until all this has all been processed," Virginia's voice was cracking now, but continued. "I know you'll all need to digest this. This is just such a tremendous shock. Everyone, please be kind to yourselves. Take your time." Virginia was good at this, McNally thought. The pastoral stuff. But it was all so soon. Even the thought of Isadora lying somewhere felt wrong, almost impossible.

"Thank you for letting us know," Wendy summoned up.

"We need to get back to the barracks. Shall we meet up when we get there? I know I'll need the company," Jenny added. She and Isadora were the closest, but Jenny was also the most stoic. McNally had always been impressed with that. But Jones was silent.

"We'll be at the mess bar," Tom replied. "All of us. I just can't believe it. I only spoke to her earlier today. We were building the cameras."

"This will take time, Tom," McNally found himself saying. "Get back safely, Jenny. Virginia and myself will be back there as soon as we can. I know how much this will hit you all."

"We will get through this together," Virginia added. "Honestly, we have each other to lean on."

There was a loud sobbing noise in the background. It was indistinguishable initially, but it became clear that Mr Singh had taken the news particularly badly. McNally knew that Wendy, Carl, and Tom would help him, but he'd forgotten that Mr Singh was such an emotional man.

McNally cut the call. He'd let people deal with this in their own way. He knew this was a major emotional bomb that he'd dropped on the team, and he'd never had to deliver this kind of news before. And yet he didn't know how to deal with it himself yet. This was all new, and his own fortitude was being tested. He could feel a lump growing in his throat again. Maybe Virginia would stay on the line and answer anything else. For now, he'd get back to the visitor.

McNally walked out of the interview room and saw that the man was now sitting forward in his chair with his head in his hands. This would need careful attention, whatever it was. He would have to summon up his last remaining supplies of energy.

"Hello, I'm sorry I've kept you waiting. My name is Declan McNally and I'm working with Sergeant Bristow and Isadora Brown as part of a multi-agency investigation. How can I help?"

"Help? Well, I'm not sure that you can," the man replied

somewhat forlornly. "But I wonder if you might give me ten minutes of your time?"

McNally led the man through to the interview room. The sergeant paid little attention but was clearly getting used to the security services adapting to the police environment. Box, or MI5, were viewed suspiciously at all times in the RUC, but there had been a cooling of tensions during the Bradley investigation.

"My name is Father Peter O'Callaghan. Isadora Brown visited me yesterday to talk about two children. I believe the young boy was witness to a murder and the girl had been kidnapped."

"That's correct, Father," McNally confirmed, realising this was his first interaction with a Catholic priest since his own faith had lapsed some years previously. "But I'm unable to speak to either Sergeant Bristow or Isadora currently. Perhaps you could give me a little background to your meeting yesterday?"

"Of course, Mr McNally. Your young officer knew that I facilitated the adoptions of the two children with Bill Jacobs. One in the mid-1970s and the second about ten years later. I briefly worked as part of the St Federico's Mission, and I was the conduit. Those were different times back then. Violence was all around us."

McNally had seen the very worst of that violence. He knew how the people on all sides had suffered.

"Do go on, Father," McNally gently urged. "I'm fully aware of the case."

"I've not slept since our conversation. The whole Jacobs adoption, it's not left my mind since I met Isadora Brown yesterday. I can't believe that, as a man of God, I didn't help your young officer clear things up. As I am now the only person who can. I was actually an obstruction and I'm so sorry."

"I'm not sure I understand, Father. In what way were you obstructive?"

"Isadora explained they were investigating whether the birth mother would have been involved in the wee girl's kidnapping.

That maybe she'd suddenly wanted her back and regretted the adoption. Do you follow me?"

"Of course, do continue." McNally wanted to grab his notebook from the inside pocket of his trench coat but couldn't look away from the man.

"Well, I know their birth mother regretted the decision to have them adopted every day. There was not a day that passed without reference to her children. She came to see me almost daily, right until her last days."

"So, what you told Isadora was correct? Their birth mother is now dead?"

"Sadly, that is the case. She passed away around eighteen months ago. She died of something called alcoholic ketoacidosis. You see, she had been a heavy drinker for many years and then ran so short of money that she prioritised her drinking above eating or nutrition. It was a terribly sad case and ultimately the adoption of the children was right for them. But the mother never forgave herself. She saw it as two of the most shameful moments in her life, two adoptions and ten years apart."

"Thank you for this, Father. This really helps. But you'd already explained about the death of the mother. Why was this playing on your mind so much? What made you come here?"

"I'm afraid that I also lied about the father. He is alive and well but cannot have any contact with his children. It is a complicated matter and I must ask for your complete discretion before I go any further. I wouldn't want this forming any part of your investigation." Father O'Callaghan looked pleadingly at McNally. All the colour appeared to drain from his face and his hands, now flat on the table, seemed to shake slightly.

"I'll do what I can, Father Peter. You have my word."

"I don't want you wasting any time looking for their mother and father with all this turmoil in their lives. The mother is dead, I can prove that."

"You've explained that, usefully. I appreciate your candour," McNally repeated.

"That's not quite it. You see... I'm their father." And with that, Father O'Callaghan began to cry. The tears rolled down his face uncontrollably. "Those poor wee children. And me with my ridiculous notion of devotion. I'm so sorry. I've let everyone down."

McNally sat and watched as the priest dissolved into sobs in front of him. His tears punctuated with more explanations and confessions.

"I know I abused my position. But being told I'm not allowed to love anyone, or be loved by anyone, in the physical sense, just felt wrong when I was with her. She was my world. I loved her with every core of my being. It was a mutual loving relationship." The flood of emotion was almost too much for McNally to bear, with his own so brittle, but he held firm.

"You don't need to justify your love, your relationship, to me, Father. I can assure you of that," McNally gently intervened. He'd never seen someone fall to pieces quite so catastrophically before.

"We both felt we could bring two children into the world as a loving family. Both times, I was ready to leave my profession. Both times, she forbade it and we knew her mental state and her illness wouldn't allow her to be a single mother. Do you understand me, Mr McNally?"

"I believe I do, Father Peter."

"We loved each other. I cared for her every day, often in ways no man should ever have to do as her alcoholism worsened. But she begged me not to give up my faith. So, everything was a secret. Our entire existence was a lie until now."

"No-one else knows?" McNally asked.

"No-one. Not a soul." The Father stood up, as if to leave. Before having second thoughts. "I'm not wearing my collar because I knew I'd be admitting a sin that would challenge the very foundation of my faith. But tomorrow, I need to put it back on."

"Take your time, Father. I'm in no position to advise you." McNally felt numb and brittle. But this collision of emotions made him feel empathy for Father Peter. He stared at the broken clergyman and knew he had to throw away the rulebook.

"Father, I can tell you I would give up everything for the love of a woman," McNally whispered. "Just for that feeling of being loved. To be in love with someone who felt the same and wanted my affection. Instead, I have a vocation that dominates every second of my day. I'd say that, despite everything, you were a very lucky man."

"You really believe that, Mr McNally? Even though I've lied in the face of God. Absolved people of their sins when I'd never confessed my own?"

"Only you and your God can be the judge of that. But I'd rather have you out there doing your job and spreading the good word than sitting as a lonely man with regrets as I do all too often." McNally couldn't believe these words were spilling out of his mouth.

"Your children, for what it's worth, are both okay. Emma, the young girl, she is now with her brother in a very safe place. Her brother may have some more challenges to come, but I think he'll deal with it all. You have every reason to walk away from this conversation with confidence about their futures."

Father Peter was attempting to calm himself by breathing deeply. His eyes were bloodshot and his face a vivid shade of red. McNally knew his emotional battles wouldn't end after their meeting, no matter what he said.

"Thank you, Mr McNally," Father Peter said, after a few minutes. "I have some thinking to do," he added. McNally gave him a sympathetic smile and offered him his hand, which Father Peter shook gratefully.

"Take your time," McNally said. "Don't be too hard on yourself."

After another few minutes, Father Peter, his confession

complete, left the building and started the walk back up to the heavily fortified barrier. McNally felt sorry for him. No-one should deprive themselves of a real life, even though he'd been doing just that for over twenty-five years himself.

But, as McNally walked back to the car park and lit another cigarillo, somehow, completing this side of the investigation felt right. Knowing that the Jacobs' adoptions had nothing to do with the Bradley or McCool deaths was oddly cathartic in the face of everything that had happened during the day.

This was the knowledge Isadora had died for. This tiny fragment of the investigation had led to her being gunned down in cold blood, all to stop her understanding any more. It was all so unnecessary. McNally knew now the Jacobs story was a red herring, but Isadora always wanted the truth. She never cut corners. He had ensured that her final investigation was followed through.

As he looked over towards the parking bay, a young RUC officer flashed the lights of a Land Rover Saracen towards him.

McNally put his hand up. "Are you waiting for me?" he called over.

"I've been waiting for well over an hour. You still want to go to Deramore Park?" the officer called back.

"Thanks for the offer, but I think we have that covered now. Can you take me to Thiepval Barracks instead?"

"Alright," the officer called back and McNally, with the cigarillo hanging from his bottom lip, ran across to the parking bay and jumped up into the front seat of the Saracen.

"You're sure you want to go to Thiepval?" the driver confirmed.

"Yeah. If that's no bother?" And for the first time in his professional career, McNally closed his eyes and fell asleep in the front seat of the car as the officer drove him back to the barracks.

The man that was always on, finally switched off. It was a blessed relief.

Thirty-Five

In The Europa Hotel, Jube Spencer had finished packing his bags for his flight back to London the following day. He was planning to pop to the garage of his rented-out house in Holywood to pick up a few ancient de-classified files he'd been storing there.

Jube prided himself on being an archivist and a historian, as well as a spy. He needed to keep his brain ticking and was convinced that key moments in history were also learning points that pay dividends in the future. He hoped that Fred Martinson, the US Peace Envoy, would use the same methodology in his approach at the upcoming summit meeting with Conor Steele, the Northern Ireland Secretary of State. Preparatory peace talks were looming and there was plenty going on behind the scenes. Jube had been working on that meeting for a good percentage of his time back home and ferrying notes and briefs back for Steele, who was safely ensconced in Hillsborough Castle.

The rest of his trip had been focused on the Philip Bradley murder. He'd been trying to stay aligned with Declan McNally's thinking and also keeping his own boss happy. That was difficult when the man in question was MI5's Clive Gentry, based at Palace Barracks.

Still, with all those plates spinning and a hotline to McNally that was regularly ringing, Jube was feeling on remarkably good form. As he hung the last of his blazers in his in-flight carry bag, with their matching ties and pocket squares, he nipped over to the mini-bar and poured himself a whiskey. He stole a quick look at his wristwatch and settled down on the large leather Chesterfield sofa in his bedroom.

It was then that the phone in his bedroom rang. With the time at almost 01.30am, this could only be McNally or Clive, and the smart money was on the former.

"Hello Jube. Sorry for the late-night disturbance, but I have an update which I thought you'd want to hear."

"Go ahead, McNally. I was only winding down for the evening. You're not interrupting anything. My body clock has been screwed for years."

"Thanks, Jube. I know you're aware of the news surrounding Isadora Brown. The team has taken it badly. There is much sadness, but they are prepared to wait for a proper send off. I'm hoping you'll join us?"

"Absolutely," Jube responded. "I've already confirmed with Virginia Curry. Isadora was an excellent prospect. Such a tragic waste. Have you spoken to Sir Charles? She was his pride and joy."

"Not yet, Jube. He would have hit the hay hours ago," McNally reminded him. "Virginia will be in touch first thing, I'm sure."

"True, true. How else can I help?"

"Well, before all the carnage of the past twenty-four hours, we gathered intelligence that suggests the body found on the yacht at Bangor Marina was that of Caragh Reid, Philip Bradley's estranged sister-in-law. But she was carrying false identity papers."

"Yes, I heard about that bombshell. Martha Maddison. No

wonder GCHQ drew a blank on that name. We're absolutely sure this is Caragh Reid?"

"We will have definite confirmation by lunchtime tomorrow. But it's a racing certainty. This could be quite explosive from a media perspective. If word got out that Bradley was caught having sex with his own sister-in-law and that led to his death, this could destabilise talks and embarrass one of the key parties in the forthcoming summit."

"The NUC? Yes. You're right, McNally," Jube agreed. "That's quite a big picture conclusion you've drawn there. That's not normally your game. Why do I get the feeling you want something from me?"

"I need the identity of The Mainstay body to be withheld. I need time to put the pieces of the jigsaw together without the glare of the media, the Northern Unionist Coalition Party interference, and the nightmare of the Westminster bubble. Is that possible?"

"You know it is. The peace summit needs to be the priority at the moment, not the discovery of the body of Caragh Reid, a well-known republican crime boss's daughter. As long as there are no leaks, I can give you a press blackout for a week."

"Until then, we'll maintain the line that the body is Martha Maddison. Happy enough? Can we also keep quiet news of the £1m sterling found on The Mainstay too?"

"The media already know about the suitcase full of money, but I can certainly take any further heat off it for 'reasons of national security'. Who's in the know already?"

"Jones, Jenny, and Orla Massey. Tomorrow morning, after a motivating early morning meeting, I'll brief Sergeant Bristow," McNally continued. "But you'll remember from the Ethan Smyth interview, we also identified a mole. The young RUC Officer called Stewart McIlhinney?"

"Yes, we discussed this earlier. This must all seem like a haze to you. You've had a challenging twenty-four hours," Jube responded.

"I'm grand. But I've been thinking. If Stewart McIlhinney is being paid off by the big man and his own brother, Andrew McIlhinney, is the lad with the teardrop tattoo, then surely we need to turn up the pressure a bit?"

"I'm on the same page. He could be a useful communications link. Does he know about the operation at the Hunter's Arms in Ballyramsey?" Jube asked.

"I'll need to double check that. Knock Road is a small station, but we have tried to keep that operation to a small group. What are you thinking?"

"Well, I think we need to draw the big man's team out into the open. We need to understand their motives and why all these people had to die. We may need some bait to do that." Jube took a long pull of his whiskey and adjusted his position on the Chesterfield sofa. "This is going to need thought."

"Wee Joe is one of our most useful assets. We don't want to do anything that might suggest the Hunter's Arms is under surveillance, or suggest Wee Joe is anything other than a loyal contact for the big man's local network," McNally explained, thinking out loud.

"I'm aware, Declan. However, the Hunter's Arms is a safe zone, right? A pub that the local republican lads can have their command meetings in the function room. Somewhere that actively raises money for their cause?" Jube said.

"Yeah, Jube, agreed. It's a staunchly nationalistic area and this is like a wee social club."

"So, if say, Sam and Emma Jacobs were seen strolling to the ice cream parlour in the village centre, or maybe getting a cowboy supper from the local chippie, where would the big man's local network, almost certainly connected to the paramilitaries, go to discuss this?"

"Jesus, Mary and Joseph, Jube. You're not really suggesting using the young Jacobs as bait?"

"Give me a better option?" Jube replied instantly. "I realise it's unpalatable."

"I don't have one. But rigging up the local pub was supposed to be a medium-term fishing expedition. Mr Singh and the lads would simply run it for a few weeks and see what the microphones captured."

"We really don't have time for that, McNally. We need quick results. Isadora's death has changed the rules. We've had four deaths in six days now. We nearly lost Massey too. God knows what's around the corner."

"But I'm guessing speed is also important to ensure your summit with Fred Martinson and Conor Steele progresses seamlessly?" McNally probed.

"Naturally. Anything that enables us to grease the wheels of diplomacy is useful. But that's not my sole concern. You know me better than that. I'm not a machine. Losing one of our own has punched me in the guts."

"Aye, I know the feeling, Jube. I'm struggling myself. But can we ethically parade that wee family around Ballyramsey just to entice her murderer to the pub for a drink to chat about it," McNally admitted. "It just feels wrong."

"It is wrong, Declan. But we can mitigate risk here. We brief the Knock Road team that Sam and Emma are being moved to a safe house in the Ballyramsey neighbourhood. McIlhinney will relay that information to the big man. He'll have eyes and ears on that village. We take the Jacobs on a little trip for a nice lunch and an ice cream, and we put non-uniformed bodies on the streets nearby to ensure their safety. Once they've eaten, we carefully despatch them back to Thiepval."

"It's damn risky, but it could work," McNally replied, but feeling no more comfortable with the plan.

"And with Mr Singh's Quartermaster's Team in play at the pub, we'll get as much useful intelligence on the re-opening night.

That's Friday, isn't it? Forty-eight hours." Jube scribbled a few notes in his leather notebook and took another swig.

"That's do-able. Aye. You'll be back at Balfron Tower by then?" McNally asked.

"I'll delay my flight until Saturday. In the meantime, we need to get as much useful intel about Caragh Reid as possible. Work out why she was killed and why she appeared to be carrying £1m in a suitcase." Jube was itching to get more involved, but knew he had to balance his time carefully with the vital talks looming closer.

"It's something troubling me, too. But you have bigger fish to fry. Leave this with me, Jube. We have a good team. I'll keep you updated." With that McNally wished Jube Spencer a good night and the conversation ended.

Something was nagging Jube though. There was something that felt horribly wrong about this entire investigation. He walked over to the small hi-fi in the hotel room and selected Classic FM, a familiar choice. Vaughan Williams' *The Lark Ascending* filled the air and Jube sat back on the sofa, loosened his tie, and rested his head on the arm of the chair.

Kenny Reid was dead, Caragh Reid had been found hanged. Saoirse had married against family wishes and was estranged from the Reid Empire, even receiving death threats to stay away and get her hands off her father's ill-gotten legacy.

So why did Caragh embark on an affair with her own brother-in-law? Why was she carrying fake papers in the name of Martha Maddison when she was found? Perhaps more importantly, what the hell has this got to do with the big man, whoever he is? Was Jube really putting the Jacobs at risk to protect the talks?

With those thoughts percolating, Jube turned Classic FM up a notch and closed his eyes.

Thirty-Six

It was a cool, almost chilly, 08.00 hours at Thiepval when the entire team was summoned back to Briefing Room Alpha for a swiftly coordinated breakfast meeting. No-one had forgotten about Isadora, but it almost felt as though she was in the room, to Jones at least.

The Barracks were eerily quiet and, aside from the soldiers on gate duty and the ebb and flow of visiting vehicles, the clatter of the breakfasting British Army in the canteen was the only obvious sound.

Jones had been up with the lark and had walked around the barracks to clear his head. It was becoming almost a daily routine. He kept dreaming of their night in the bar with Massey, before heading to the gruesome discovery of George McCool. That was their last big night. Isadora had loved it. She had been on such good form. Jenny had the same vivid memories, but first they had to focus on the bigger picture. The killings of McCool and Bradley were the priority.

The perfect late summer weather had been momentarily interrupted by a rainstorm in the early hours, and this had also disturbed his sleep pattern. All of this was unusual, as Jones had now been sober for a few days and hadn't benefitted from the sedative properties of his normal heady mix of lager and late-night whiskey.

Wendy had fetched the team from Ballyramsey for the conference last night and they'd remained in situ for the morning meeting. Later last night, she'd regaled the story of both Carl and Tom sleeping through most of the near two-hour trek before waking to play 'spot the yellow car' and Mr Singh chatting almost non-stop about the configuration of the devices in the pub. This was before the bombshell of Isadora's death had hit, but Wendy was exhausted from nurse-maiding the QD already.

She had also been entertaining Sam and Emma for the previous ten hours and was grateful to be amongst adults. Sam definitely had the hots for her, and Emma was, understandably, like a limpet attached to her beloved big brother. Emma had been given the all-clear from the hospital but would take time to recover from the nightmare experience she'd endured.

Wendy had left the Jacobs sleeping before disappearing to Ballyramsey the previous evening. She'd arranged an early game of pool for them, with one of the security officers tasked with guarding them onsite. They'd be woken at 10am. Virginia had promised to take a turn with them, too.

Elsewhere, the new intake of YCU was down on numbers, as some had failed the signs and ciphers test that had been set by McNally and invigilated by Virginia. They'd return to Milton College to rebuild their careers. Those remaining were on an early PT session with the 39 Infantry Brigade to prepare themselves for an exercise in the Yorkshire Moors in the coming weeks. So, the YCU buildings were as good as empty aside from the briefing rooms.

With everyone now seated around the long rectangular table and fresh coffee available alongside a large Family Circle tin of biscuits, the normal hubbub from the briefing room was limited. The team were busy waking, dunking biscuits and awaiting

McNally and Virginia, who were still in deep conversation inside one of the side offices. There was a feeling of apprehension in the air, alongside the raw devastation of losing one of their own.

Jones, still bruised and slightly dishevelled from the incident at the Lagan Navigation, was the first to notice a complete lack of Knock Road representation. There was no sign of Eric Rogers or Marie Bristow, who was probably still recovering from her own exploits, let alone any of the more junior RUC officers who had been almost ever-present during the investigation. Clearly, what came next was limited to YCU or those drawn into this unique mission.

Jones sat people-watching as Wendy was chatting quietly with Mr Singh about gadgetry and Tom and Carl were smirking about something, Jones guessed this was unlikely to be anything rigorously academic. Feeling detached for a moment, he wandered over and helped himself to more coffee and poured a glass of water for Jenny. As he did so, and purely accidentally, he caught the end of Virginia and McNally's private discussion.

They appeared to be talking about the RUC mole and if his elementary lip-reading skills were correct, the suggestion was that the mole was the young officer, Stewart McIlhinney, which seemed to make sense in Jones' head. He'd hung around the investigation team like an unpleasant smell. But Jones was more quizzical about why this might be kept from the rest of the team. Before this thought process was fully shaped, McNally strode into the room and picked up a whiteboard marker and proceeded to write bullet-pointed headings in his familiar handwriting.

McNally mumbled quietly under his breath, and he wrote the headlines on the board and the team watched impatiently as the list was drawn.

'Nine Key Questions' was written in block capitals at the top and then underneath in a series of numbered questions.

1. Who is the Big Man?
2. What does he have to hide?

3. Why did he kill Philip Bradley?
4. Who killed Caragh Reid / Martha Maddison and why?
5. Who kidnapped Emma Jacobs and why?
6. The Philip / Caragh Affair – rationale?
7. ONE MILLION POUNDS
8. Caragh's Road to Damascus Meeting with Orla Massey.
9. Who killed Isadora Brown?

"Okay, can we all quieten down a little, please?" Virginia called out, in her most prim headteacher voice. "McNally is going to take you through the next stage of our plans for this operation and we will then discuss the bullet-points he's illustrated on the board. Is everyone happy with that?"

Those assembled nodded, in between swigs of coffee and mouths full of biscuit.

"If that's the case, I'll hand over to McNally," Virginia then walked away from the board and seated herself next to Jenny. The smell of Yardley seemed to follow her around.

"Good morning everyone, apologies for getting you out of your pits so early today and for delaying the grieving process. I know you'll all be feeling it. There will be time to grieve, I promise." McNally scanned the room. There was no movement, just eager eyes and determination.

"We have to make progress on this and, with the murder of Isadora and Caragh Reid so fresh in our minds, I need to explain our next steps." McNally carefully looked around the room to gain an understanding of who was up for this. Everyone appeared focused, even Tom and Carl, who were assessing the list on the board.

"Firstly, Isadora's tragic death is to be treated squarely as part of this investigation. My gut tells me she was assassinated by the big man as a warning to us all to stay away," McNally saw Jones nod.

"This makes sense," Virginia added, somewhat forlornly.

"I also have some distressing news to tell you about this too," McNally continued. "Someone, most likely the killer, placed a post-it note with the words 'stop now' written in block capitals in Isadora's hand. This probably happened after the shot was fired. After her death." There were a few shaking heads in disbelief and Jenny grabbed Jones' hand under the table.

"We'll get this bastard, believe me. But we have to stick together and focus. Isadora's death is one aspect of an appalling set of crimes and we need to solve this as one investigation. Do I make myself clear?"

Everyone swiftly nodded.

"Secondly, outside this room, Caragh Reid's name is not to be mentioned. As far as the media, Knock Road RUC and anyone else is concerned, the body that was found was that of Martha Maddison. No-one is to mention Caragh. Does everyone understand this approach and the rationale behind it?"

Again, there was nodding.

"Talk us through the rationale, though, if you don't mind. Even as an aide-mémoire," Jones piped up.

"Absolutely, Mr Jones. You've clearly been at that thesaurus again," McNally forced a smiled at Jones, adjusted his round glasses and pushed on. Strangely, McNally wasn't being sarcastic. He seemed to be genuinely trying to keep the atmosphere light.

"Okay, this ties in neatly with another fact. There is a mole in the Knock Road RUC station. We know who it is, but I am not yet going to share that information with you. The reason being, is that I want everyone to act normally and shape their conduct as if the mole didn't exist. However, we are going to create the illusion of normality to ensure the mole passes on either duff or tainted information to the big man."

"In effect, McNally, you don't want us to trust anyone in Knock Road and that's why none of them are here?" Jones confirmed.

"Absolutely, except for Orla Massey, who is rather confined at the moment, no-one in Knock Road is to have knowledge of our plans. That starts with this operation and is also the reason we will not be sharing our knowledge that Caragh Reid was Martha Maddison and was Wonder Woman, the other witness who saw Philip Bradley's final moments. This needs to remain one hundred per cent confidential."

"Are you completely sure that the mole and other members of the RUC aren't already aware of her identity?" Jenny interrupted.

"Jones, you made the link yesterday at Belfast Hospital. That's right, isn't it? You've not mentioned it outside this group?" McNally asked.

"Nope. And I don't think her two protection officers heard either. Only Massey was aware of my assessment," Jones explained.

"Grand. That's keep it that way." McNally moved back to the board.

"Aside from our guess that the big man is responsible for the murder of our colleague, I think we can only have a stab at one of these questions currently. But I believe that if the Hunter's Arms operation goes well, we'll fill in more blanks. Does anyone want to tell me which of the bullet-points is answerable?"

"I can have a go," Jones answered, feeling the eyes of the room on him. "If I may, I might speculate on a few other things, too?"

"Fire away," McNally replied and took a seat next to Mr Singh.

"I don't think we can answer the first two points. But I don't believe this has anything to do with paramilitary issues. I think that's a red herring. We are looking at a criminal network of some kind and Philip Bradley paid the price for something." Jones then pointed at the fourth note on the board.

"I think Caragh or Martha was killed because she was at the Philip Bradley murder scene. But I'm convinced she was off to a new life with the million pounds, plus the Martha identity. I think this was someone's way of helping with that new life. But I don't know who. I reckon Caragh's sudden epiphany was designed to draw a line before she vanished. Maybe to leave some kind of positive legacy."

"Finally," he announced, with the group growing more and

more interested in his theories. "What if the big man didn't know that Wonder Woman was Caragh Reid? Everyone tells me she was a bit of a loner or recluse. She had no kids, no dependents, and was only seen a few times at her father's funeral and tending to his wounds when he was shot. Maybe whoever was in the room when Philip Bradley was shot assumed Wonder Woman was a sex worker?"

"You've read my mind, Jones," McNally said, standing up again. "But I hadn't thought that Caragh might be off to a new life with the money. That's clever but also annoyingly obvious. Good work, fella."

"Anyone else?" McNally asked the group.

"Is it possible that Caragh stole the million pounds from the family firm to get away from the drama? I mean, it was the Bradley's yacht, and we haven't accounted for Caragh being on The Mainstay, anyway," Jenny added. "Why was she on board?"

"Good question. And why kidnap Emma?" Jones asked.

"I had a little chat with her last night," Virginia said. "In a sort of grandmotherly kind of way, I bought her a doughnut and we talked. The RUC's child protection unit are waiting for her parents to arrive later today to chat properly, but it was just an off-the-cuff thing."

"Go on," McNally replied.

"She told me it was a woman who picked her up from the bus station in Oxford and she was with her right until they reached Scotland for the ferry. She said she was really nice and caring. I guess she was building trust."

"What did she look like?" Jones butted in.

"Well, Emma was pretty vague. She just used the word 'pretty' and kept banging on about her nice hair. So, that's no help. Until the RUC gets involved and a photo-fit is available, we're still on the ground floor," Virginia concluded.

"There is no CCTV at the bus station, and we don't know what car she was in, so we can't even run checks on the registration plate going up to Scotland," Mr Singh said thoughtfully. "I haven't checked the port cameras, though. Do you want me to? Or are we leaving this to GCHQ?"

"Mr Singh, you have my blessing to use any means open to you. As long as we keep it within this wee group," McNally smiled at Mr Singh, who immediately looked excited by the challenge. Two smiles in one day, thought Jones; McNally was a changed man. He'll be hugging and cracking jokes soon.

"But I can confirm that the adoptions have nothing whatsoever to do with the kidnapping or the case, more broadly. Isadora's fantastic work tracked down Father Peter O'Callaghan and, after another meeting last night, that now becomes a closed investigation." McNally didn't seem likely to enlarge on that explanation further, so Jones ventured another theory.

"I'm pleased the adoptions were a red herring. I knew Isadora would crack that. But we still haven't assessed why Emma was kidnapped," he piped up. "Can I suggest it's all to do with the conversation Sam didn't quite hear?"

"You mean the woman's name? The words, agreement, and money? That could be anything, couldn't it?" Jenny replied.

"It could also be the reason Sam is such a target," McNally announced. "Maybe the big man thinks Sam knows much more than he does? Perhaps the woman's name or the business agreement is why all these killings have taken place. This is something Jube and I have discussed at length."

"Yeah. I'm with you on that, McNally." Jones folded his arms and looked around the room. There seemed an acknowledgement that this was a vital theory.

"Okay, moving on. Let's get back to the operation at Ballyramsey. I've given you all briefing packs for the Friday lunchtime operation. But, in a nutshell, we are going to make the big man's network aware that Sam and Emma Jacobs are in the area. We want them to be seen. With any luck, some of the key players will then descend on the Hunter's Arms later in the evening for the opening and give us some intel. Do you understand?" McNally scanned the room again.

"It's a hell of a risk. Are they safe?" Jenny asked. "I mean, we all know this breaks every protocol in the book. We have a duty of care over those two."

Virginia, whose half-moon glasses were now wedged at the end of her nose, raised her head from reading the hastily created briefs and cleared her throat. "I've babysat more young people than I can count, including some of you. I think this is an excellent plan and, if I'm reading this correctly, you'll have one person on top of the church tower watching their every move, a couple of you chaperoning Wendy and the Jacobs to the ice cream parlour and the cafe, and two more in one of our vans in the centre of the village. They'll be fine."

"Hold on," Wendy stood up. "I'm being chaperoned? By Carl and Tom? Why? That's like giving a lioness two hamsters as bodyguards." The group laughed loudly.

"I note you've picked the person scared of heights to stand on top of the church tower," Jenny added, looking over at Jones. "Looks like I've drawn the comfy van. Bingo!"

"Blimey, eighty feet tall. That's going to be bastard high. Can't someone else go up the tower?" Jones piped up.

"You have the best memory; the best recall and you've proved you can deal with heights. You jumped that gap on The Europa Hotel and the Lagan Navigation on a motorbike. This should be child's play," McNally explained, in his most reassuring voice. Jenny momentarily put her hand on Jones' knee, in a show of solidarity.

"Did someone say ice cream parlour?" Carl suddenly exclaimed. "Tell me they have rum and raisin?" Ignoring him, Tom raised his hand.

"Shouldn't we be back at the pub, gearing up the microphones? Prepping? Will we be back in time?"

"Good point," McNally replied. "But Mr Singh will remain at

the pub at all times, in the function room. By the time it comes to open the pub, the Jacobs should be safely back in Thiepval. It'll be grand."

"And you're sure I need these two? Did you not see my exploits in the Lock Keeper's Cottage?" Wendy looked dismayed.

"Carl and Tom's cover is as Sam's university friends. They are taking Emma on a nice wee dander around Ballyramsey. Let's stick to the plan. But if it helps, Wendy, imagine you're *their* chaperone."

"Oh, yes. I think I can work with that," she responded, grinning.

"Jenny, without Isadora, we are down a marksman. Can you take that on? How are the sessions going at Palace Barracks?" McNally queried.

"Fantastic," Jenny replied. "I'm ready. Isadora was an excellent teacher."

"Right. On that positive note, I think we'll call the meeting to a halt there," Virginia intervened. "Just to reinforce McNally's point about Caragh Reid and the RUC mole. Keep things normal, keep schtum about Caragh, and make sure we have closed communications at all times from now on." Virginia walked to the whiteboard and used some kitchen roll to wipe off McNally's scribblings.

As the meeting broke up and the team either grabbed more coffee or headed to the canteen, Jenny made a bee-line for McNally. Jones followed her.

"McNally, we really need to get over to Mainstay Barns and talk to Saoirse. It feels like she's the missing link. Can we approach her?" Jenny quietly asked. McNally nodded enthusiastically.

"Absolutely. But be careful. We need to see if she's aware of Caragh's death and work out if there's more to her than meets the eye. So, don't make an appointment, head up there and surprise her. She's aware The Mainstay is a crime scene and the media has reported on the million pounds found on board. Otherwise, say little and listen lots."

"Understood," she confirmed. "Let's get the Land Rover keys. We can head down there now." Jones nodded and downed his coffee in one. His head was buzzing with ideas, but there seemed to be too many loose ends.

As Jones and Jenny walked towards the double doors leading from the briefing room to the car park, Mr Singh called out. He held the receiver of the briefing room phone away from his mouth and shouted.

"Hold on everyone. I think you're going to want to hear this."

Everyone edged back around the table and McNally said, "Go ahead, Mr Singh. Enlighten us."

"Right, my friend in ballistics has just called me. The gun that was used in the Eden Vale shooting was possibly a museum piece or antique. The bullets had been adapted to fit a chamber that acted as a silencer. There are also two sets of fingerprints on the bullet. One is Ethan Smyth's. The other isn't Eamonn MacMillan's. We have no match for that second fingerprint."

"But we never found the actual gun, did we?" Jones asked.

"We interrogated both of the gunmen about it. Ethan suggested they threw it into the lock. Police divers are dredging that part of the Lagan Navigation looking for it now," McNally confirmed.

"But wait," Mr Singh continued. "You've not heard the best of it. There is a strong possibility that this unique gun could have been stolen from The Royal Military Museum in London, next to Chelsea Barracks, back in 1989. We need access to the Metropolitan Police reports about the theft, and maybe this will link directly to the big man. We might even get an identity."

"Surely the RUC will be all over this information by now?" Jenny asked.

"My friend will give us 24 hours before they release this to the RUC. But we need to get our skates on." Mr Singh took out his pipe and started knocking it nonchalantly against the briefing room table. Noticing Virginia's look of horror, he promptly placed it back in his top pocket.

"Leave the Met to me, I'll deal with that too. I might be able to get into their files," Mr Singh said. "I smell a possible game changer. I'll report back later."

"Agreed," McNally said. "That has a wee bit of potential."

Thirty-Seven

The journey between Thiepval and Mainstay Barns was peaceful. Jones had been lost in his thoughts and once he'd organised them into a more regimented order, he put *Modern Life is Rubbish* by Blur into the car stereo and sang heartily to *Chemical World* and *For Tomorrow*.

Jenny opened the windows and as she drove, she let Jones enjoy his moment. He hadn't recovered from the loss of Isadora and neither had she, but the sticking plaster of work was helping. She was growing used to the idea that Jones was at his best when his brain stopped whirring. That was generally when the music was loud and he was singing along to the lyrics he'd memorised. His thought process wouldn't disturb those moments.

The electronic entrance gates into the cul-de-sac of barns were already open when they arrived, and Jenny drove the Land Rover into one of the parking spaces. Jones switched off the stereo and stepped out of the vehicle into the seemingly deserted courtyard. They looked around for signs of life.

"This is a bit eerie, isn't it?" Jenny said, quietly.

"Hold on, can't you hear that?" Jones replied. "It's like a ticking noise."

They both stood still for a few seconds until Jones, head cocked in the air like a dalmatian hearing the food tin being opened, headed towards a colourful pathway leading between the Bradley's Mainstay Barn and the second unfinished property. Jenny followed him, noticing the sound herself moments later.

"You have ears like a radar," she called over. "What the hell is it?"

"Sounds like someone trimming a hedge to me," he answered. "I'm good at this."

"Yes, you are. So unusual for you to have extra sensory skills. What's next? X-ray vision? The gift of flight?"

"Stop it," Jones said, trying to focus on the source of the noise.

There were no signs of life down the alleyway between the two properties, aside from some newly planted box trees with their price tags flapping in the gentle breeze and a small white cat who welcomed the pair of visitors by urinating against the new trees.

Jones peered over an equally fresh-looking willow fence panel and soon spotted the source of the noise. It was a man in a set of blue bib-and-brace navy overalls and a green baseball hat trimming the edges of the lawn. He was using a set of ancient-looking long handled lawn shears and Jones could hear him humming.

"Hello?" Jones called over, with no immediate response. He looked at Jenny, who shrugged her shoulders. He then bellowed significantly louder.

"HELLO! CAN YOU HEAR US?"

"Christ alive! Of course, I can bloody hear you! You just scared the living shite out of me. What are you doing creeping around here like this? How did you get in?" The man responded, startled.

"The entrance was open. I called over," Jones said.

"Did you? Well, I guess my hearing isn't what it used to be. I used to work with loud machinery. It takes its toll. Anyway, no harm done. How can I help you?"

Jones couldn't place the accent but noticed his weather-beaten hands.

"We're looking for Saoirse," Jenny chirped, feeling a touch embarrassed by the loudness of Jones' outburst.

"She's out. Are you friends of hers?"

"No, we're working with the RUC on her husband's death. We just wanted a chat." Jenny was smiling and looking to put the man at his ease. She guessed he was mid-60s and she spotted a few military-themed tattoos on his bare forearms. He reminded her a little of Malcolm, who permanently wore a green baseball cap. He was one of the *last hurrah* crew who was shot and killed during the Wild Flowers Project.

"She's gone down to SuperValu to lift some sausages for one of her wee lads. He's in bed poorly and had a hankering for a cowboy supper. Sure, she'll be back soon. I'll let you in to the living room next door and you can wait for her there."

"That's really kind of you," Jones replied. His mind drifting momentarily to the thought of sausage, beans, and chips.

"Are you employed here?" Jenny asked, as the man led the two of them back through the alleyway, the white cat keeping a close eye on them both perched on top of the willow fencing.

"Yes, I'm proud to say I led the team who built these barns. Kind of project managed the whole thing from start to finish. My fellas have finished the hard landscaping now and I'm just tidying up the garden before we start the viewings to sell it. We have an estate agent coming tomorrow morning."

"The barns are stunning," Jenny responded.

"It's the biggest job I've ever undertaken, and it's been a real labour of love, so it has." The man paused for a moment as he reached the front of the two barns and looked up at the two properties. Jones could see the satisfaction in his face.

"This feels more than just a regular contract for you, if you don't mind me saying? You seem to have a personal connection to this project," Jones queried.

"Is it that obvious? I guess you're right. I specialise in buildings that use locally sourced materials and reclaimed wood. Some of the beams in Mainstay Barn, the Bradley's house, are from an old Irish tall ship. Saoirse and Philip really loved that idea. It's so sad he'll never see them completed."

"Did you know him well?" Jones continued.

"I've known them both for about seven years. When Philip was an architectural draftsman, he often recommended me for jobs. He was a fine man, with real passion and belief in the north of Ireland."

"I'm sorry," Jenny interrupted. "We haven't even introduced ourselves. I'm Jenny Richmond, and this is my colleague, Jones."

"I'm Mickey, Mickey Reilly. I live over on the Runnymede Estate, if you need to get hold of me. You're Brits, aren't you? What do you make of it here?"

"We're both English. It's beautiful here. The people are incredible. We both love it," Jenny replied. The man instantly smiled.

"Couldn't agree with you more." Mickey shook both their hands and gestured for them to sit down in the living room. Jenny was taken by the man's gentle manner.

"Grand, you know who I am. I know who you are. If the family silver vanishes, we know who to blame!" And Mickey let out a loud laugh. "I'm teasing," he added. "Make yourselves at home and I'll get back to my gardening. She won't be long."

The door to the living room was closed and Jones sat and took in the opulence of Saoirse's living room. Jenny went to investigate.

"Nice chap," he called over to Jenny. She was looking through books displayed behind glass in a mahogany sideboard.

"Should we have asked him if he knew Caragh? Or had any connection to the boat?" she called back.

"Probably. But there's time. I think playing it nice was the right approach. He could have told us to piss off, couldn't he? I wouldn't have argued with him," Jones said, stretching out his legs and stifling a yawn.

"Remember, there's one of her son's upstairs. We need to keep it quiet. We have no idea what the poor lamb can hear."

"True, Richmond. But these walls are made of bloody stone. You could probably have AC/DC play in here and the lad wouldn't hear," Jones smiled.

"Hold on, I think we have a car pulling in," he continued, and raced to the front window. "Ah, scratch that, it's Mickey. He's just pulled out. He's got a green Land Rover Defender. Looks like it's seen better days."

"She's got a bizarre interest in the Roman Empire," Jenny called over, ignoring Mickey's departure. "Book after book about different Emperors and the like. Roman artefacts, you name it. Do you think that means anything?"

"I think it means she has a fairly intellectual brain. It certainly beats collecting beer mats or joining the Women's Institute."

"Don't be so bloody rude about the WI. My mum and granny were members. It welcomes all types," Jenny retorted. "Wait a second. These books all seem to have library stamps in them. Date stamps."

"They're old library books?" Jones walked over and helped Jenny to slide back the rest of the glass door to reveal the rest of the books.

"It's a bit of a bizarre order. She's catalogued the emperors in alphabetical order and not chronologically. That's not very scholarly, and there are loads missing." Jones pulled out a random book from the shelf.

"Here's one. Titus Aelius Hadrianus Antoninus Pius," he read aloud and then turned to Jenny. "Did you know, he was Roman emperor from 138 to 161. The fourth of the Five Good Emperors from the Nerva–Antonine dynasty. He was the adopted son of Hadrian. Of wall fame. You know, Hadrian's Wall."

"Of course, I've heard of Hadrian's Wall. But where do you store these facts? I'm becoming a little worried that I'm having a relationship with a nerd," Jenny grinned. "Tell me you're not a nerd, please."

"I'm not ruling anything out. I had a bit of a thing about Romans when I was growing up. Romans, flags of the world, the Olympics and old episodes of M*A*S*H." Jones continued to read the book. Jenny looked back at him and just shook her head in mock disgust. She already knew what she was dealing with.

"Flags of the World? Really? Who are you?" she laughed.

"But you're right about the library stamps, Jenny. There's one here from three weeks ago. Is she casually stealing books from libraries? Or just forgetting to take them back?"

"Well, you'll be able to ask her in a second. There's a car coming up the driveway. I'm surprised you didn't hear that? I guess that means you're not infallible?"

"Who said I didn't hear it? Anyway, let's close this up and sit on the sofa. I don't want her to think we've been snooping."

Jones watched as Saoirse, in a similar short white tennis dress to before, but this time donning a pair of off-white women's boat shoes, swung her legs out of the door of a silver sports car. A small boy hurried behind her, with a carrier bag in his hand.

"Stop staring, Jones. Isadora was right, wasn't she? You have quite a thing for our Saoirse, and her perfect little legs, don't you?"

"Stop going on, Richmond. We've had this conversation. I'm trying to work her out. Nothing else. Stay in professional mode. Remember what we are here to do. We need to suss out what she knows about Caragh, if anything. The money, the yacht, and see if she lets anything else slip."

"Okay, okay. I'll cool my jets. I'm sorry."

"It's fine. Let's just focus on the job in hand. You're key to this."

"I'd better put my game face on," Jenny responded before hearing the little boy's feet scamper up the path.

The boy pushed the front door open wide, and Jenny rushed

over to greet them both as they entered the house. Jones followed behind.

"Saoirse, I'm so sorry that we've invaded your house whilst you've been away. We just have a few more questions." Saoirse didn't bat an eyelid as the pair emerged from her home.

"Hello, Jenny isn't it? It's grand, make yourself at home. Mickey let me know. I saw him on the way out. I have some questions for you too. But I need to check on my child first. I'm sure you won't have any problems with that?"

"We're in your hands," Jenny responded. "Take your time."

"I'll be five minutes. Do me a favour though, stick these frozen sausages in the microwave for me. I can get dinner ready whilst we chat." Without waiting for a response, the boy gave Jenny the SuperValu bag and chased after his mother as she headed up the stairs to tend to her other son.

"The kitchen's down the corridor. Second door to the left," Saoirse shouted down the stairs.

Jenny waited for the door to shut before turning to Jones and shrugging her shoulders theatrically. "Does her maid have the day off, I wonder?"

As the pair headed into the kitchen, Jones felt a vibration is his jeans pocket. The handheld had sprung to life. He walked through the length of the vast kitchen facility, which was littered with high-end white goods, stainless steel preparation areas and complemented by black marble worktops and found a side door leading to the rear garden.

"Hello, this is Jones,"

"Afternoon Jones. How are things progressing with Saoirse?" Mr Singh chirped back.

"Well, I won't say too much, as we're supposed to be keeping comms to the bare minimum. But it's all a touch surreal. I can update later. How can I help?"

"Please stop being paranoid. I invented these handhelds. This line is 100% secure. Has Mrs Bradley given you any fresh leads?"

"Too early to say. She's only just arrived back, and she has a sickly child. But we met the chap who designed and project-managed the build at Mainstay Barns. A fellow called Mickey Reilly. Lives on the Runnymede Estate. Can you check him out? He has a Land Rover Defender, the reg is HZ12 149."

"Absolutely, I'll get on that." Jones heard Mr Singh scribbling notes down. He continued, "The reason for my call is that we have a lead on the big man. My pals at GCHQ have spoken to the Garda and they've matched the other set of fingerprints on the bullets to a Michael Doyle."

"Does he have form?"

"My god, yes. It reads like an A-Z of crimes. Extortion, obtaining money with menaces, armed robbery, assault, GBH and most recently a speeding ticket obtained on the trunk road in Swords, in the Republic. I'm very pleased with this information, Jones." Mr Singh sounded genuinely chipper.

"This is a real breakthrough. I'll brief Jenny."

"One second, please. There is a curious thing, though. Aside from the speeding ticket, which was in 1987, all of his crimes seemed to stop in 1983. There is no record of him whatsoever from that moment on."

"Okay, you're right - that is weird, Mr Singh."

"We've also pulled up some files from GCHQ and found that Michael Doyle fought for the British in World War Two. He was a member of the 38th Brigade. That unit was composed of North Irish infantry regiments. According to the records, he served with distinction in the Tunisian and Italian campaigns. That would put Michael in his early sixties. That matches the big man's description." Mr Singh sounded breathless with excitement.

"This is wonderful intel. Thanks for your diligence on this. Top stuff. But where is Michael now?"

"That's the million-dollar question, Jones. Mr McNally is off to speak to Jube Spencer and see what else we can find out. But this is the first lead we have on the big man."

"True. I hate to pour cold water on any of this. But going from a journeyman criminal to the top man in a huge organised crime network seems quite a leap."

"McNally seems pretty convinced he's our man," Mr Singh replied. "But I'll pass on your concerns."

"Does this change the plans at the pub or the Jacobs' visit to the ice cream parlour?"

"Not a jot. The team will be back at Ballyramsey by tea-time. That's all being planned as we speak. Keep in touch if you get anything from Mrs Bradley."

"Of course, over and out." Jones put the handheld back in his pocket and walked back to the kitchen.

Jenny was prising apart partially frozen sausages, fresh from the microwave, and was laying them out on a plate.

"News?" she urged. "I love how I've somehow been relegated to sidekick whilst you play spy games."

"Oh, don't talk rot. If anyone's getting anything out of Saoirse, it's you, Jenny Richmond. Stop overthinking stuff." Jenny put her hand up in a gesture of apology. Jones tried to refocus the conversation.

"Anyway, the headlines from Mr Singh are that an ex-British Army infantry man, Michael Doyle, is the now the lead suspect for the big man. His fingerprints were found on the bullet. But he's been off the radar for years. He's from the south."

"That's quite a development," Jenny replied. "Anything else?"

The door to the kitchen opened slowly and stopped the conversation in its tracks. Saoirse Bradley walked in with purpose. She had changed from her tennis dress into a pair of denim shorts and an oversized white t-shirt. Her short blonde elfin-styled hair was hidden under a baseball cap with a Boston Celtics motif.

"Everything okay?" Jenny asked.

"He's got a bit of a temperature, poor thing. But I think he'll live. It's just a stomach bug. Both of them have had such torment in their wee lives recently. It's no wonder he's unwell." Saoirse pulled up a tall bar-style stool and sat down.

"We have about twenty minutes. The lads are playing quietly together, and I'll give them some time before I make dinner. But thanks for defrosting these."

"No problem. Did you say you had some questions?" Jenny responded, moving the plate of sausages to one side before settling down on a stool and encouraging Jones to join her.

"Yeah, I have a couple of questions. Did I hear there was a suitcase full of cash on The Mainstay? How on earth did that get there?"

"I'm not sure how the media got hold of that detail, but yes, there was a suitcase containing one million pounds in used notes. But I can tell you no more than that. What was the second question?" Jenny was trying to push through Saoirse's queries hurriedly, and Jones was purposely taking a back seat.

"The obvious one. Who was the dead body on my yacht, and how did she get there? That yacht was our pride and joy. It's just so upsetting."

"I'm sorry that it's upset you, Saoirse. With everything going on, I can imagine it's added to the awfulness." Jenny smiled sympathetically.

"However, we were going to ask you the very same question," Jenny continued, "as you reported a disturbance on your yacht earlier and yet there were no signs of a break-in. It was virtually untouched when we arrived. We wondered if you knew more?"

Saoirse's face went bright red. She stared at Jenny as if amazed by the line of questioning.

"Listen, Jenny, if that's your real name. I don't know what you're insinuating. But I'm the victim here. My husband has been murdered and now someone has been found dead on our pride and joy. The Mainstay was our tenth anniversary gift to each other." Saoirse was clearly riled and seemed to be trying to balance her emotions between bursting into tears and tearing

Jenny to bits. Jones felt edgy and the room was suddenly full of emotion.

"Have you heard of someone called Martha Maddison?" Jenny asked, trying to move on from Saoirse's outburst.

"No. Who is she? Is that the name of the body on The Mainstay?"

"That was the name on her documents, found in her handbag," Jenny replied.

"Never heard of her. What did she look like?"

"Your height, your build, your complexion. The only difference was age and hair colour. She was probably a couple of years younger than you and she had auburn hair," Jones squeezed Jenny's knee under the table to remind her that telling her the body was Caragh's was off limits. But she'd already painted the picture.

Saoirse fell silent for a few moments. Jones was desperately trying to read her body language. Was she already aware that Caragh was the victim? Or had the penny just dropped? He decided to drop the pretence slightly.

"Does that description remind you of anyone? Anyone you know?" Jones probed.

"No," she countered, firmly. "I don't know Martha Maddison. I know no-one that fits that description. But I can correct you on one thing. It wasn't me that saw the problem on the yacht earlier. It was the Project Manager of the build here, Mickey Reilly. He told me he was down there picking up some local crabs and thought he saw someone on board."

"Oh, for God's sake," Jones said, frustrated. "Why didn't you tell us this? We've just spent half hour with him. How well do you know Mickey?"

"He's an old family friend. We trust him unquestionably."

"Of the Bradley or the Reid family?" Jenny asked.

"What have the Reids got to do with this? I've had no relationship with the Reid family since the death of my father. How many more times do I need to tell you that? They have had no time for me or my husband. End of story. Philip knew Mickey, from old."

"There has been no contact with Caragh or your family in Andersonstown since Philip's death?" Jenny continued.

"I have not been in the same room as Caragh since our last court date. She has not sent me a fecking sympathy card and I am not expecting one. What on earth made you ask that?"

"There's been no truce?" Jones was becoming concerned that in her desperation for a lead, Jenny might reveal too much detail and stood up to leave. Jenny followed suit.

"Truce? Reconciliation is not on the cards here. Wise up, Jenny! You're seriously deluded." Saoirse's voice was now loud and angry. Emotion was flooding from every pore. She stared furiously at Jenny. Jones made his move.

"I think we've got enough here," Jones said. "We've taken up enough of your time."

"Right enough," Saoirse agreed. "I have a sickly child and a dead husband. I don't know what planet yous are on."

"Hang about, I have another question," Jenny interrupted. "Just for the sake of clarity, what do you know about Mickey?"

"Oh, Jesus Christ, you're not honestly suggesting Mickey had something to do with the death on The Mainstay, are you? You've met him. He's one of the nicest and kindest people you could hope to meet. This is becoming surreal."

"If you could answer the question, Saoirse, we can leave you in peace," Jenny replied.

"If you must know, he was Philip's contact. He put some work Mickey's way in the past. I know he's a single man, but he's mentioned a son living in Ballyramsey. He dotes on him. Mickey lives up on the large estate and comes from an agricultural background. He often talked to us about his father, who owned land in County Cork."

"That's really useful. Anything else?" Jenny asked.

"He's been in the construction industry for maybe twenty

years, if I remember rightly. Moved up north because he got some really shitty treatment when he returned home from the war. They treated him like scum, so they did. He was a hero."

"Thanks Saoirse, that's all been very helpful. We'll be in touch. We hope the lad makes a decent recovery." Jones smiled amiably at Saoirse.

"I think you ought to think hard before you make accusations you regret. I'm the victim here, remember? I'd be grateful if you made an appointment to interview me in the future."

"There was a body found on your boat. We had no time for niceties. But we'll do our best," Jones replied, still smiling but felt a growing sense of awkwardness.

Jones escorted Jenny from Mainstay Barns as Saoirse turned her back on them both. She fetched a large pan down from one of the cupboards and started to prepare dinner. Jones could see she was angry and upset.

It took Jenny the time to manoeuvre the Land Rover through the electronic gates before she banged her fist on the steering wheel.

"We bloody had her. Mickey Reilly is Michael Doyle. Michael Doyle is the big man. I'd bet my life on it. Saoirse is as guilty as hell. She knew it was her sister. We've just let her off the hook!" she shouted. "Why didn't you let me get that out of her?"

"Because we still need her on our side at the moment," he replied. "We have no powers of arrest. We can't do anything without the RUC. We are simply listening. We need to remember that. Until McNally brings Bristow back on board, we are just gathering intel."

"It's bollocks!" Jenny spat back.

She turned the stereo up and Jones simply stared out of the window. He knew something wasn't right, but he just couldn't put his finger on it.

THIRTY-EIGHT

Jube Spencer sat in the Lobby Bar at The Europa Hotel and watched as a gentle trickle of late afternoon hotel clientele headed joyously towards the bar.

He had ordered and despatched a Cork Dry Gin with ginger ale, with a single ice cube and a slice of lime. It had refreshed him immensely, and he was considering another. As was Jube's way, he'd dressed as if he was going to a school reunion rather than for a meeting regarding an important matter of national security.

The Belfast temperature had hit twenty-three degrees earlier and yet Jube couldn't be without his thick and hard-wearing brown Harris Tweed blazer and orange and yellow school tie. His impressive Loake brogues were worth over two hundred pounds and even his brown tailored trousers were handmade in Jermyn Street, London. If necessary, he alone would keep espionage formal and esteemed. That had long been his mantra.

As he took a pull from the remains of his first gin, he watched as McNally came through the front reception doors. He looked awkward and uncomfortable. McNally's body language was all wrong, from Jube's perspective. He was hunched over and was almost race-walking through the lobby. Jube could feel his stress from the other side of the room. McNally had his own issues with attire, with a trench coat that seemed to be surgically attached, but now with new improved glasses that had taken possibly ten years off his age. But his stress still permeated every sinew. That was clear to see, even from Jube's secluded table at the back of the bar.

This meeting wasn't going to make McNally's life any better. In fact, the key headline was going to create a cluster bomb of problems that would probably take years to fully appreciate. However, it would certainly progress McNally's investigation.

"Jube," McNally announced as he finally orientated himself through the bar tables. Jube Spencer stood up and shook his hand. "Good to see you," he replied.

"You too. But why do I get the feeling that this isn't going to be a pleasant meeting?" McNally asked.

"I can't help with that, my friend. You're clearly getting the right vibes, though. But can I suggest we at least imbibe a little to take the edge off it?"

"Aye," McNally agreed. "I'll have a Bushmills. I'm guessing a very stiff one is in order?"

An impeccably dressed hotel waiter took the order from the pair and disappeared to speak to a bartender. Jube waited until a few stray guests moved away from their table before getting out his leather notebook.

"Before we kick off," Jube began. "But did you manage to raise Sir Charles? For Isadora's memorial? Have you found a venue?"

"I spoke to Charles. He's confirmed he can fly over with 24 hours' notice. I think he's trying to combine it with a round of golf at Royal Portrush. But he's naturally devastated about young Isadora," McNally settled himself in and looked suspiciously at Jube.

"So, what news?" he prodded.

"There's no easy way of saying this. But I think our friends in GCHQ may have found a financial link between Acting Superintendent Eric Rogers and Kenny Reid. If this is correct, then the notion of the Reid family literally getting away with murder may have some legs to it."

"Mary mother of God!" McNally replied. "The sly wee bastard!"

"Indeed, McNally. But let's keep our voices down." Jube put his finger to his lips.

"I'm in shock. Orla has always thought he was a corrupt shite-hawk, and I've given him the benefit of the doubt. That's incredible! Does this have any bearing on the case? Philip Bradley's death?"

"Hold on, McNally. Let's not get ahead of ourselves. We are still trying to ensure this is watertight. But, as things stand, there are a series of questionable payments going into an offshore bank account in his wife's maiden name, Heinz, held in the Cayman Islands."

"From Kenny Reid?" McNally queried.

"No, through an intermediary, but GCHQ believe they've traced the payment back to the Reids. Of course, there is nothing illegal about offshore accounts, it's how the owner conducts business that counts. This could be Rogers being paid to look the other way in the mid to late 1980s whilst the Reid family ran riot in West Belfast and across Northern Ireland generally. There are other questionable payments, too."

McNally tried to compose himself. He began to think operationally, looking at what boxes needed to be ticked by adding this new strand of information.

"Our friend, the mole, Stewart McIlhinney. Is there some potential that he was bought and paid for by Rogers rather than the big man?" McNally asked.

"Hmmm. That might be a bit of a leap. His brother worked for the big man, so I'm guessing the brothers were recruited together. That said, the big man could have scuppered Eric's little money-making empire with the Reids. Couldn't he? Perhaps without even knowing it. But that's another matter."

"So, what are you saying, Jube?"

"It's all conjecture. But I don't think the big man, or whoever he is, had anything whatsoever to do with the car bomb that nearly killed Orla."

"What? Who did then?"

"I think once Eric Rogers got his promotion, he wanted Orla out of the way pronto. She was getting too close to the truth. It wouldn't surprise me at all if Rogers has links to organised crime across this wee country and maybe further afield. I'm suggesting Rogers called in a favour and planned the car bomb in Sailortown himself."

"That's off the scale corruption. You really think Rogers is capable, Jube?"

"With the way the GCHQ intel is shaping, I think he's capable of anything. Remember, the crime rate in London sky-rocketed when he was in charge of counterterrorism. Maybe he simply looks the other way and, ker-ching, more money hits his bank account in the Cayman Islands."

"But can you prove he tried to kill Orla Massey, Jube? How much of this can we prove?"

"It's a tangled web, Declan. It's taken our friends in Cheltenham almost two weeks to trace back all the transactions. I'm not sure we can take this through proper law enforcement channels. I've spoken to the Home Secretary and a very nervous Conor Steele. We are of one mind."

"I see," McNally responded, quietly.

"The only positive spin I can put on this is that the payments into this offshore account stopped around this time Kenny Reid was shot. Or just before."

"But we never found who killed Kenny Reid. Orla was fully aware of that investigation. She's spoken about it often. They drew blank after blank. Do you think there's a possibility that Kenny had had enough of paying Rogers? Threatened to 'out' him?"

Jube pondered that thought for a moment, whilst the drinks

were placed on the table in front of the pair. Jube put down his notebook and took a quick swig of his drink.

"I very much doubt Rogers would get his hands dirty. But I think he had links to people that would kill Kenny Reid, for a price, and then Rogers would turn a blind eye. But I need to ask you to keep this information to yourself. I am telling you, in the strictest confidence, to enable you to factor this into your current operation and investigation. In the next twenty-four hours, you'll understand why. Any questions?"

"I see. So, I need to keep excluding Rogers from everything but give our wee snout, Stewart McIlhinney, a careful heads up that leads back to the big man. That's going to be damned tricky. What about Orla Massey and Marie Bristow? Are GCHQ saying they're clean?"

"As a whistle," Jube responded. "Exemplary service and utterly trustworthy. Marie has rather proven her mettle with the killing at Deramore Park, too."

"Agreed. Is there anything else I need to know?" McNally asked as he picked up his glass and drained at least fifty per cent of its contents before sighing loudly, as if dispelling some kind of demon.

"Two things. Use this as a signal of my complete trust in you. I have faith that you and your team will solve the Bradley case, even with all that's happened in mind. Clive is also impressed by the way your team have rolled their sleeves up."

"Thank you. Secondly?" McNally prompted.

"You have some incredible brains in that team of yours. They are going to put the pieces of the jigsaw together regarding Eric Rogers, I have no doubt. When they do, be ready to give an explanation that does not involve a single word said in this meeting. Understand?"

"Aye, you have my word," McNally nodded.

"You're a good man, Declan McNally."

"I wouldn't be starting that rumour, but I know which side

my bread is buttered." McNally picked up the last remains of his Bushmills and sank it in one.

As Jube and McNally pondered the conversation in silence, the hotel waiter appeared next to the table.

"Can I get you gents another drink?" he asked.

"You can indeed, fella," McNally replied. "In fact, bring me a bottle of Bushmills Black Bush and charge it to this gentleman's room. We have a great deal of thinking to do."

"Two glasses," Jube added.

Thirty-Nine

Jones had spent almost all the previous evening reading the briefing notes for the Ballyramsey operation. His brain was somersaulting as he went through the carefully choreographed plans and even the offer of an evening game of pool in the mess with Wendy had been spurned. He just wanted time to think.

Jenny had opted for an early night after spending time discussing the plans with Virginia. They'd also chatted about the YCU, about how her team were progressing, as Jenny knew that eventually she'd need to refocus her mind back on that. She hated that Ailsa would be learning the ropes without her support, although with Virginia around, the cream always rose to the top.

Jones, on the other hand, was totally absorbed in the investigation.

The minibus had left Thiepval at 10.00am and had Jones, Jenny, Wendy, Emma and Sam Jacobs on board. Jenny volunteered to drive.

It was an almost two-hour trek to Ballyramsey from Thiepval, with the QD team already in situ at the Hunter's Arms. McNally would take one of the Land Rovers and follow on once he'd taken part in a short RUC briefing back at Knock Road. He hoped that the mole, Stewart McIlhinney, had been given just enough information to alert the big man and his team.

Plans for the operation had gone seamlessly. The pub regulars seemed to have taken well to Tom and Carl. Their naivety and inexperience had totally thrown the villagers off the scent and there was a buzz about the reopening, especially the two-hour free bar. People seemed genuinely concerned about Wee Joe and were grateful that the brewery had spent money on modernising a pub that desperately needed it. Even the lads' Englishness had been accepted, if a little grudgingly in some quarters.

The minibus, with tinted windows, would be parked up in the main street in Ballyramsey to allow Jenny to keep a watching brief over the Jacobs' visit. She would act as communications lead and be on hand to step in should anything go awry.

Jones was going to be positioned at the top of the church overlooking the village centre. The church of St. Jude the Apostle's tower was around 120ft high, and he could see all movement in the surrounding area. He'd been given a pair of Soviet 7x40 Roof Prism Binoculars by Mr Singh, who was tight-lipped about where he'd found them. However, as with many other Eastern Bloc military binoculars, the view had a strong yellow hue intended to increase contrast under low light and low contrast conditions, and this would take some getting used to.

The only other slight issue was the dual roles of Tom and Carl. They'd been at the pub, on and off, for three days now, renovating and making local links. They would now need to be seen as Sam's university friends from Coleraine as they escorted the pair around the village.

Aware of the issue, McNally had advised Tom and Carl to explain to any confused onlookers they were doing degrees in hospitality and their work with the brewery at the Hunter's Arms was part of their vocational experience. That would end any awkwardness, but the sudden movement of goalposts had confused Carl massively.

The minibus pulled into a lay-by and Jones jumped out to make his way up the tower. It would be a steep climb up rotting wooden steps, but with the church barely used during the week, he could be assured that he'd be alone with his binoculars and handheld. Once he was in position, Tom and Carl would start the walk from the pub and take the Jacobs, with Wendy, to the small parade of shops, where they'd indulge in a meal from The Rumbling Tum café and then ice cream from The Poke, the local ice cream parlour.

With Jenny getting the okay from Jones on high, she carefully slid back the minibus door and let out the Jacobs and Wendy.

The door of the minibus was then slid shut and the Jacobs were in the hands of Wendy, who was holding Emma's hand, and the QD duo. Sam was immediately offered a Wham bar by Carl. He refused, not wanting to spoil his lunch. But the thought was there.

Wendy allowed Emma and Sam to take the lead over to the shops and hung back slightly to deliver a quick word of warning to Tom and Carl. "Lads," she said. "These two have been through enough. Let's not screw this up." Both nodded eagerly.

Back in the van, Jenny contacted Jones' handheld on the same radio channel as McNally, ensuring that when he arrived, he'd be immediately up to speed. Everyone was a little non-plussed by his lateness for such an important operation. McNally was normally a stickler for being punctual.

"We are all in place, Jones. What can you see? Is there any interest at all?"

"Okay, there is a bright yellow Austin Metro, which is sitting in the car park of the café. That would have direct eyeball on the Jacobs. Odd car to choose for surveillance, though," Jones replied.

"Can you see who's inside?" she asked.

"There's one man. I think the engine is still running. There's a

Spar convenience shop on the corner. Maybe he's waiting for someone to return with the shopping? It could all be innocent."

"OK. Let's monitor that, Jones. Nothing else?" Jenny was sitting in the front and was trying to manoeuvre her seat to see the Metro, with no luck.

"All quiet. Aside from the Metro, there's a little social club opposite the café, that opens at 12.30pm. Let's see what happens then. Hold on a sec, there's a tall black bloke with a green rucksack. He's walking up towards the shops. Can you see him?"

"Yeah," Jenny responded. "I've got him, I'll radio Wendy."

"Wendy, can you hear me? This is Jenny."

"Carl, will you just shut up a second? Someone's trying to reach me." Wendy was clearly busy. "Yeah, I'm here. Just dealing with the kids. What's happening?"

"Look out of the window. There's a large man coming towards the café."

"I see him," Wendy replied. "He's heading straight for the café. I'll cut him off..."

But before she could do so, Sam stood up and stared out into the road.

"Dele!" Sam shouted in delight. "He came!"

"Oh, I think Sam knows him," Wendy explained to Jenny. "I get the feeling he's been invited."

"Jeepers. This was supposed to be an absolutely hush-hush operation. How the hell did Sam invite a friend?" Jenny was bemused.

"I don't know. Sam's talking to him outside now. I'll find out. I'll be two ticks."

"Wendy. Don't let Sam stay outside. Bring him in and keep him with you. Emma too. This is really important," Jenny calmly instructed Wendy.

"Roger, understood. I'll deal with it. Carl, for god's sake, please stop playing with the ketchup bottle! Can we get Sam back inside, lads?"

Tom sprinted out through the main doors of the Rumbling Tum, avoiding an older man seated nearby who had been slowly demolishing an Ulster fry that could cheerfully have fed a family of four. Just as he did, the yellow Metro drove from the car park behind the parade of shops to the pavement outside the café.

"There's a yellow car. It's pulled up immediately outside. What do you want me to do?" Wendy asked on the handheld.

"Do you have a clear sight of the driver?"

"No, it's partially obscured. But Tom, Sam and his friend are now coming back into the café. We'll order and enjoy our lunch. We don't want to appear jumpy."

"Good plan. Sit tight. I have a decent view of the car now. Jones can see things from up high. We're on top of things." Jenny sounded confident. She wanted Wendy and the Jacobs to relax.

The Rumbling Tum was straight out of the 1970s. The table-cloths were red and white gingham; the walls were adorned with photographs of local landscapes in a romantic style; the ketchup was in a red plastic tomato-shaped dispenser; and the owner was happily sitting next to a tea urn smoking a cigarette. Even the metal napkin holder looked like it was a relic from a bygone-era.

Wendy was already a fish out of water. She was dressed in her goth-punk chic, black Ramones t-shirt, black leggings, a short black leather skirt and her platformed Doctor Martins. Her hair was dyed jet black, shoulder length, with a few purple streaks for good measure. Her ears were full of earrings and studs. She sat in-between the Jacobs and was trying to ignore the old man, eating the massive fry, who had been glancing at her in disbelief since she walked in.

However, when Dele joined the party, an extremely tall and muscular Nigerian, the man's eyes grew even wider. These were not the regular clientele of the Rumbling Tum. If the operation was aimed to gain the attention of villagers, it was going to be successful. It was more a question of whether the big man had sent his troops out to scrutinise proceedings.

Once Dele had introduced himself and Sam explained that he'd contacted him via the payphone at Thiepval, the group relaxed a little. They all ordered a fry or a sausage lunch, and Emma opted for the chicken nuggets. Carl ordered a butterscotch milkshake with extra cream and marshmallows. Emma followed suit, whilst everyone else enjoyed an enormous pot of tea which had been positioned in the centre of the large circular table. Even to the casual observer, this was an odd collection of people.

However, the yellow car hadn't moved, and the team was no closer to understanding who the driver was. Jenny made a quick decision to ring Mr Singh, who would use his contacts to check out the vehicle registration. This would avoid bringing the RUC back into the loop, or more than they needed to be.

The bell on the doorframe of the café sounded as another man walked in and selected a table. He too was smoking and was dressed casually. He sat on a table for four, immediately opposite the Jacobs' group. Wendy wouldn't be able to use her handheld, so opted to pop to the toilets to make the call to give an update.

Dele, who was clearly enjoying the local ambience, was happily talking through the menu with Sam and discussing which of the options he'd want to experience. Dele had his own scoring system, 'Deles', marked out of ten. The university café *fifteens* had been awarded eight Deles and he was already eyeing up a similarly impressive selection of traybakes for his post-fry delectation. He was already a sucker for Irish food and wanted to try everything.

"Sam, I have really missed you," Dele explained. "The university hasn't been the same."

"I'm sorry. But you wouldn't believe the kerfuffle I've been involved in the last few weeks. I meant to call," Sam replied, considerably understating his nightmare.

"What happened? Why is your beautiful little sister here?" Dele smiled at Emma as he asked the question.

"Sadly, we can't get into that," Tom answered. "All will be

explained in good time. But we have to keep the conversation light. Can we do light?"

"What bands and football teams are you into?" Carl asked, dumbing down the conversation instantly.

"I love En Vogue," Emma said, chirpily. "I know pretty much all the words."

"She does," Sam laughed. "I can hear her singing through the bathroom walls at home!"

"Can you? Oh my gosh, that's so embarrassing!" Emma hid her face behind her hair.

"I'm not a big music fan," Dele admitted. "But I love listening to a song called One Love by Onyeka Onwenu. My family love it too. It's a call for all of us to forget about our differences and come together. This song preached unity among Nigerians."

"I like Status Quo," Carl interrupted unsubtly. "And Dire Straits. Tom does too, don't you, mate?"

"Yeah. I'm also a fan of Gary Moore. He's an incredible guitarist and comes from Northern Ireland. I'm getting into the culture." Tom smiled, with Carl looking slightly offended that their music tastes had diverged.

The new customer, seated opposite, walked up to the counter and ordered some food whilst the conversation continued. He was carefully examining his change as he walked back to his seat.

"Right, I'm calling you from the ladies' loo," Wendy explained. "So, I'm going to have to be quiet. But there's a chap that's just walked in. He's early to mid-twenties, has brown hair and he's got some kind of tattoo near his neckline. I reckon he's the bloke from the yellow car."

"He's definitely the Metro driver. I watched him walk from the car," Jones responded. "That sounds an awful lot like Andrew McIlhinney. When you go back, check if that's a teardrop tattoo. Otherwise, just move onto the ice cream parlour and then we'll get the Jacobs back to Thiepval. It sounds like this has created the stir we were hoping for."

"But are they safe?" Wendy asked. "I'm with Carl, Tom, and a stranger. Is anyone even carrying a firearm?"

"Yeah, I am," Jenny said. "I've also got a few emergency packs in the boot of the minibus. I'm more concerned about where McNally is. He's supposed to be all over this. But you're doing a fine job, as always, Wendy. Stick with it."

When Wendy returned to the table, the food had arrived and was being quickly demolished by the group. She slid back into the gap between Emma and Sam and silently ate her lunch, whilst keeping one eye on the new man opposite and his round of buttered toast and marmalade. The teardrop tattoo was just above the collar line of his green t-shirt. Jones' instinct was correct.

Jones, still standing over 100ft high on the tower of the local church, then spotted one of the YCU Land Rovers heading into the village centre. He observed through his binoculars as McNally parked up and walked to the minibus where Jenny was keeping a watching brief.

"Welcome to Ballyramsey, Declan McNally," Jones announced dryly. "I hope this operation isn't too much of an inconvenience?"

"Don't start," McNally replied. "It's been a god-awful day already. I'm ready for the rope. But let's focus on the job at hand. I have some of the local briefing notes from Rogers' old anti-terrorism squad. They should help with some names and faces."

"Yeah. Useful stuff, but what are the headlines from Knock Road, McNally? Anything we need to know?" Jenny asked.

"There's plenty to discuss. They are one hundred per cent aware of our operation with some of the key details changed. I've made it clear they are to remain hands off and urged Bristow to keep Rogers at arm's length. But I gave PC Stewart McIlhinney enough detail to start some hares running, the wee dickhead. Hopefully, he's discussed this with his big brother?"

"The hares are running. Andrew's here," Jenny said. "He's sitting in the café immediately opposite the group. Wendy's description matches him."

"That's pretty ballsy. I wonder what his game is? We just need to ensure we go about our business as normal. Don't spook him, and then the minute they've exited the parlour, we move them back to Thiepval." McNally looked oddly tired, Jenny thought. The meeting at Knock Road must have knocked the stuffing out of him.

"Hello, Jenny, this is Mr Singh. Are you reading me?" The handheld buzzed into life.

"Go ahead, I'm here," she answered.

"The yellow Metro was stolen from a Mrs Miriam Clark on Sunday evening. She's a 96-year-old widow from Lisburn. What do you want me to do?" Mr Singh asked.

"Nothing," McNally intervened. "That makes sense. Thanks for the intel. Any news from the pub? Are we all systems go?"

"We are indeed. Everything is working and ready for the opening night," Mr Singh sounded extremely chuffed.

"There's one other thing, I spoke to the cleaner here, she's a bit of a gossip. She tells me that the social club in Ballyramsey is a bit of a flashpoint for the provos."

"Noted, Mr Singh," McNally replied. "It's useful local knowledge, but I'm wondering why we didn't know this. This should've been in Eric Rogers' briefing notes. There's nothing about the social club. He's very lax. Anyway, not much we can do now. We'll see you at the pub later."

Meanwhile, back in the Rumbling Tum, the lunches had been finished and Dele was ready to try the traybakes when something caught his eye.

"I don't want to speak out of turn. But I am most concerned about the gentleman sitting opposite us. Not only has the jollity, the bonhomie of the atmosphere changed markedly since his arrival, but I'm also very concerned that he's staring at little Emma. In my country this would be seen as disgraceful behaviour," he announced.

"It's disgraceful anywhere, Dele," Sam agreed.

"But we need to play it cool. He'll be gone soon, and we have ice creams to eat. Let's focus on that," Wendy added, in an almost maternal tone that surprised herself.

"I'm prepared to let it drop for the good of our wonderful lunch," Dele said. "But I will not tolerate his behaviour if this escalates in some manner."

"It won't," Wendy assured him. "Now, are we all sure we want a traybake? Or shall we head to the ice cream parlour? I hear they do a magnificent Knickerbocker Glory."

"That sounds epic," Carl excitedly added. "I vote we pay and leave. That seems the best approach." Wendy agreed with Carl. She was silently impressed that he'd helped diffuse the situation but was also aware he was also boyishly keen on the ice cream sundae. So, his help may have been entirely accidental.

Wendy walked over to the to the counter to pay, observing Andrew McIlhinney as she did so. She pulled her small dark purple purse from her skirt pocket and wrestled out two crisp £5 notes from inside. As she turned her back to chat to the café owner and hand over the cash, he stood up quietly. He dusted the toast crumbs down from his t-shirt and stood behind her in the queue to pay.

He carefully stood inches away from her and edged closer, purposely sniffing loudly to alert Wendy to his presence.

"I smell English," McIlhinney whispered, quietly.

"What did you say?" Wendy spat back at him, turning instantly to meet him face to face.

"I said, I smell English. You're not welcome here. None of you," he sneered back.

The café owner stood up behind the counter and stared at McIlhinney.

"I'll decide who's welcome in here. Thank you very much, Andrew. You'd do well to remember that," she said.

McIlhinney sniffed loudly again. "You know, I think I can

smell something else. I can't tell if it's pig or whether you've just shat yourself."

"Andrew..." the café owner shouted. "This is not the time or place for your petty hatred. Get out! You can have the toast and tea on the house!"

The sound of chairs being pulled out from the large circular table momentarily broke the tense atmosphere as the group readied themselves to leave. Wendy caught Dele's eyes and could see he'd been listening to the conversation.

As the group walked closer to the counter, McIlhinney stared at Sam.

"Wow! Look what we have here. Not just the piggies, we have the squealer too. Do you know what happens to squealers, Sam Jacobs?"

"Please stop with your impoliteness," Dele calmly intervened. "There is no call for this. I have no idea how you know my friend's name, but please step away and allow us to leave, if you don't mind."

"If I don't mind?" McIlhinney laughed. "Who are you? The bodyguard? Surely the RUC can do better than you!" He laughed again, as Wendy furtively pressed the transmit button on the handheld, hoping that Jones and the team would hear the rising tension in the café.

"Wendy, would you be so kind as to take Sam and Emma to the ice cream parlour?" Dele asked. "I just need to have a quick chat with our friend here."

"I'll take them," Carl offered, still wiping butterscotch milkshake from his top lip.

"We have nothing to talk about, big fella. Just get out of Ballyramsey. You're not welcome. Don't think we don't know who yous all are."

Carl, followed by Sam, Emma and Tom, made their way out of the Rumbling Tum, with the café owner giving Emma a small lollipop as she walked past. She mouthed apologies and stroked the little girl's hair.

Dele picked up the menu and feigned interest as he watched the rest of the party leave out of the corner of his eye. Wendy stood by the door and held her breath. She wasn't immune to an argument and would happily roll up her sleeves if she needed to, but this wasn't the plan. She wanted a quick escape. As she turned to close the door, she spotted McNally standing near a parked red Talbot Solara, a few hundred yards away from the Metro. McNally had a cigarillo on the go.

"Listen, my friend. I am not a violent man, but I warn you, I will not have this level of disrespect overlooked. Do I make myself clear?" Dele's whole demeanour changed. Suddenly, the polite and interested Dele became six feet of anger and muscle.

"Is this your girlfriend?" McIlhinney responded. "Is that the problem? Have I offended your girl? Or is Sam Jacobs more your type? Either way, you have no idea what you're dealing with here. You are way out of your depth. Step away from me," he smirked.

Quick as a flash, Dele punched McIlhinney hard in the face. The shock nearly knocked the Irishman off his feet, but he stayed upright and attempted to throw a punch back, missing.

Dele threw another punch, this time appearing to instantly shatter his nose, with blood flying from his face and splattering across his dark green t-shirt. McIlhinney responded by reaching for a gun. A small Ruger P90 that he'd tucked in his trouser belt. He pointed the gun directly at Dele and laughed again, the blood streaming from his nose and the café behind urgently emptying, including the café owner herself.

"I warned you that you didn't know who you were dealing with. Around here, we don't end disagreements with playground punches. We end people." McIlhinney wiped his arm across his face and looked at the blood as he held the gun inches from Dele's face. Dele appeared unmoved.

The Irishman, who was now extremely fired up and more

angered by the sight of his own blood, then took the pistol and smashed it hard across Dele's face. Even after that, he remained unmoved. He just stared at McIlhinney.

"You seem to be under some illusion that I've not dealt with snakes like you before. I'm afraid it is you that is out of their depth. Your little toy gun doesn't scare me," Dele responded.

Wendy, still standing by the door and with her finger on the transmit button, weighed up her options. Dele may not need her help, but he's an unarmed innocent. A bystander who got himself involved in protecting his friend's honour, or something like that. She considered using her Jiu Jitsu skills to kick McIlhinney in the testicles. With luck, the shock of that might see him drop the gun. But that was a risk. Maybe, she thought, Jenny would be close by and already had a gun trained on his head? She'd been up at the Palace Barracks range recently, honing her skills. But that was merely a possibility.

"Big fella, you've made a colossal error of judgement here. I would have been happy to let yous leave this shitty café and disappear back to whatever hole you come from. But look at my nose? I can't let that pass now." McIlhinney was now dripping blood from his nose onto the café's faded lino, but his bravado was still there. He continued to point the gun at Dele, only pausing to wipe more debris from his nose.

Wendy seized her moment and aimed a direct kick at his groin. She summoned up every sinew of strength and gusto in directing her foot towards his weakest area. As McIlhinney felt the awful effects and dropped to the floor, Dele jumped on him and punched him repeatedly in the stomach and kidneys. The Irishman called out loudly and let out a terrible whimper that suggested Dele had injured him badly. As the two men writhed on the floor of the café, blood still pouring from McIlhinney's nose, Wendy bent down and snatched the pistol from his hand.

She also then spotted that he'd dropped his car keys on the

floor, and she pocketed them too. But Dele wasn't done. He picked up the stricken Irishman, almost like cradling a baby, and threw him onto the pavement outside.

Wendy was now pointing the Ruger at McIlhinney, and McNally was now within spitting distance of the scene. Close enough to get involved, should the need arise and far enough away to appear like an inconsequential passer-by. Wendy wondered where Jenny was. She'd been off the radar for just a few minutes. But it felt much longer.

"Alright, alright. You've made your point," McIlhinney cried out. "Leave me be. But you'll regret this. There are people round here who have my back."

Dele marched over to the yellow Metro and opened the driver's door, beckoning him to get inside. Wendy felt for the car keys and watched as the now bedraggled and beaten Irishman made his way to the car.

She looked down and noticed that the car keys had a black central locking fob and as McIlhinney awkwardly climbed into the driver's seat, Wendy was poised to lock him in. This would be, perhaps, the crowning moment of ignominy as she and Dele would simply walk away to the ice cream parlour.

However, as she pushed the button, nothing appeared to happen. Assuming the battery was dead, she walked over towards the Metro and was poised to throw the keys near the driver's door.

"Stop!" McNally shouted from the other side of the road, before running over to help. His trench coat flapping behind him as he sprinted to the back of the Metro and began trying to open the boot.

"What are you doing?" Wendy called over. McIlhinney, who had shut his eyes briefly, was now slumped over the steering wheel and was oblivious to it all.

"Just a hunch," McNally replied. "We need to get this open now. Can anyone help?"

Dele rushed over and began furiously trying to help McNally force the boot open. Wendy stood next to the driver's door and watched McIlhinney. Jenny was also poised to run from the van and join the throng when she felt her handheld activate.

"What?" she responded.

"This is Jones. Jenny, in the top left window of the social club, I see movement. I could be wrong, but I think there's a sniper up there. Is there any way we can get the Jacobs away from the action?"

"Top left? With the net curtains?" Jenny replied. "I need to get on top of this minibus. I'll get a better view from there. Give me two minutes and I'll ring Tom first. Keep watching the window, Jones."

In The Poke, the QD lads and the Jacobs were midway through some of the largest ice cream sundaes they'd ever seen. Tom, who had been entrusted with the QD handheld, half-choked on peanut butter sauce as he noticed the call.

"Tom, don't say a word," Jenny explained. "Walk over to the shop owner and ask them to shut and bolt the doors. Tell them there's a security incident outside and you're concerned about the little girl's safety. Got it?"

Tom was silent.

"You can talk now, numpty," Jenny sighed.

"I'm on it," he quickly replied. "Where are you, Jenny?"

"I'm about to get on the roof of the minibus. We think there's a sniper in the window."

"Blimey. Do you want us to plan to get back to the pub? With the Jacobs?" he responded, nervously.

"No, refer to my previous instruction. Lock yourself in and keep the Jacobs safe. I'm leaving you in charge, Tom Marsh." Jenny signed off. Tom took a deep breath and walked to the shop's counter.

With Dele and McNally making slow progress on accessing the

boot, Jones watched in awe as Jenny clambered on top of the minibus. She had been training hard with Isadora on her target practice, and Jones was genuinely impressed at her progress. Jones watched as she positioned herself in the centre of the roof and pulled the gun from the pocket of her black combat trousers. Jones watched as she lay motionless, ready to fire into the social club.

He then cursed himself as he'd momentarily taken his eyes off the window. But, sure enough, there was the unmistakable glint of a firearm. The low contrast function of the binoculars had paid dividends, but who was the target? From his view on top of the church tower he could almost lip-read Wendy explaining about the shooter in the social club to McNally, but neither turned to look towards the window, cleverly.

Wendy, who had grown convinced that McIlhinney was unconscious, then walked around to the boot of the Metro and tried to use the keys to unlock it. She'd guessed that the central locking had jammed. But although the boot lock was now fully released, it still wasn't opening. It was stuck from the inside and immovable. Something inside was holding it down.

Finally, after some significant pulling, Dele's strength finally dislodged it. Staring back at them were four gas cylinders and three green petrol cans. The cylinders were strapped together with thick black gaffa tape and two long red wires connected the petrol cans to the gas. This didn't look good. McNally slammed the boot shut again.

"What the hell is that?" Dele asked at the top of his voice. "Who are you people? Police?"

"Kind of," Wendy answered. "Much more importantly, that's a bomb, isn't it McNally?"

McNally didn't answer. Instead, he ran around to the front of the car and pulled at the driver's door. It wouldn't open. The car had clearly been rigged.

"Let's get this open. Let's get him out. Bloody quickly. Wendy, try those keys." McNally was desperately trying to stay calm but clearly was two steps ahead of the game and there was no time to help people catch up.

As Wendy focused on attempting to open the driver's door, the sound of gunfire broke the silence.

"Shots fired," Jones shouted. "Yes, yes! I can hear!" Jenny quietly responded. "I just can't see who it is. This is all very new to me, but tradition suggests I need a target."

"Sarcasm?" Jones responded. "Now? Really?"

McNally, Wendy and Dele ducked down behind the Metro and watched as the second bullet thudded into the boot of the car.

"Is someone trying to kill us?" Dele stammered. "Is this my fault? Did I cause this?"

"No, no," McNally answered. "I don't think they're firing at us. They're trying to trigger the explosive in the boot. This is insanity," McNally said, as he tried in vain to get a view of the shooter.

"Why?" Wendy asked.

"I think our friend Andrew McIlhinney was asked to grab Sam Jacobs from the Rumbling Tum earlier. I think Sam was supposed to be in that car with him. Clearly, Andrew was going to be collateral damage."

"What? Why on earth did we drag the Jacobs out here then?" Wendy's face was red with anger.

"This one's on Jube," McNally replied. "It was his plan. But he must have miscalculated the risk. He didn't consider the big man might want Andrew McIlhinney dead too. I think that's what the bomb in the boot is all about. Killing two birds with one stone, so to speak."

"This probably isn't the time for pinning the blame," Wendy said, frantically staring up into the window. "I think that's one for later. No?"

"I'm not following," Dele interjected. "I don't understand any of this. But how can I help?"

"You can't," McNally shouted back, as another shot hit the

boot. It was an almighty thud and certainly too loud for a pistol round. "Just stay out of harm's way, sunshine, and we'll soon be out of here. Wendy, go and stand in the shop's porch. There's no need for all of us to be here. This car could go up any second."

"I will do nothing of the sort. I'm better here," she responded as Dele went back to trying to open the driver's door. He was using every fibre of his strength, so much so that the corner of the door was now slightly bent. As Dele moved to grapple with the door handle, McIlhinney was still slumped over the steering wheel. He was now in grave danger and McNally gave Wendy a questioning look. He wasn't used to his team disobeying orders.

"Do you have a shot, Jenny?" Jones asked from the tower. "Negative," was the reply from Jenny. "The sash windows are wide open at the bottom, but the bloody net curtains are obscuring the view. What can you see?"

"It's a male. His face is obscured by a balaclava, and he's ducking in and out of the window. That looks like a sawn-off shotgun he's using." Jones was getting a clear view from the binoculars.

"What's he firing at?" Jenny couldn't see from her position.

"I saw some gas cylinders and petrol cans in the back. There was wiring of some type, too," Jones replied. "I'm just unclear why he's not firing at people."

"Hold on. I don't reckon that sawn-off shotgun will penetrate the cylinders, unless he's lucky. Maybe he's aiming for something else in the boot? Perhaps there's a trigger of some kind in there. Tell me when he's in sight and I'll fire a warning shot towards the window," Jenny quietly explained.

"Wendy, leave the door to me and Dele. Go and tell all the shops to shut and lock their doors. Get the bystanders inside. That's an order." Wendy grudgingly nodded at McNally and ran towards the parade of shops, using the other cars as cover, before starting to usher people indoors. Most were ignoring her.

"NOW!" Jones shouted, as the gunman showed himself. Jenny

aimed at the open window and there was a metallic noise as her bullet ricocheted off something near the sash window. A few more onlookers disappeared inside as news of a second shooter spread around the parade of shops.

With Dele and McNally forcefully pulling at the door and McIlhinney remaining unconscious, Wendy had temporarily vanished. She had been speaking to some of the locals and when she returned, she was carrying two red house bricks. She chucked one to Dele, who instantly aimed blows at the glass of the driver's door. At this point, McIlhinney woke up and began to angrily lower the window.

"What is your game?" He shouted groggily, utterly unaware of his predicament.

"Is that *your* bomb in the boot?" McNally responded, almost matter-of-factly.

"Wise up, there's no bomb in the boot. There's no bomb in this car. Full stop."

"As God is my witness, there are four gas cylinders attached to petrol containers in your car. We believe there is someone firing from the social club in order to detonate them."

"Firing?" McIlhinney said, in disbelief. "No-one would dare fire at me."

As if answering him, another two bullets hit the boot. The car shuddered with the impact.

"Shit! Get me the feck out of this car!" McIlhinney panicked.

"Have you worked out what's going on, Andrew?" McNally replied. "Because I think I have. Why don't you tell me what you were asked to do today? As quick as you like."

"Tell you? I don't know..." McIlhinney paused until another shot hit the roof of the Metro. "Jesus. Feck! You'll get me out of here?"

"Scouts honour," McNally grinned.

"I was supposed to leave with the kid, Sam. I was given an

address in Derry, where he'd be held, but no-one mentioned a fecking bomb..."

"Yeah, I believe that. But you know the big man wants you dead too now, don't you? That's why they're firing at the boot. You know too much," McNally explained, trying to remain calm. "Perhaps the shooter thinks Sam's in the car with you? Can you contact someone and call the shooter off?"

"I can't!! I don't know who the shooter is! I didn't know any of this was happening. But for Christ's sake, I'll tell you anything you want, just get me out, please!" McIlhinney pleaded.

Incomprehensibly, the boot door then suddenly flew open again, and McNally ran round to shut it. But the catch simply wouldn't hold. With the driver's door still jammed shut, all the locks on the Metro had now failed - either by accident or by design.

McIlhinney then tried to clamber through the driver's window, he desperately manoeuvred himself around in his seat and stuck his head through the partially open window. Dele grabbed hold of his shoulders and t-shirt in an attempt to pull him out. But the Irishman was still dazed from his earlier battering and was struggling.

Suddenly, the sound of smashing glass penetrated the atmosphere. The attack had changed and from the open sash window. Molotov cocktails began raining down close to the Metro. With the boot open, the car was a sitting target, those petrol cannisters would create the mother of explosions. Time was ticking. McNally swore loudly as he realised the potential catastrophe.

"What is this now?" Dele shouted. "Flaming bottles? In God's name why?"

"Get me out, get me the hell out of here... Please... Hurry..." McIlhinney screamed as the first bottles smashed only inches from the car. He was grappling with the door handle and the window, trying to use anything as a lever to free himself.

Seconds later, as Dele continued to help McIlhinney, one of

the bottles struck the open boot and one of the petrol containers instantly burst into flames. The fire raged furiously and the terrible smell of burning petrol hit the air. Thick black smoke was immediately evident as far up as Jones on the church tower. He watched it all from afar, feeling powerless.

The car was ablaze and the efforts to get McIlhinney out were looking doomed.

"NOW!" Jones cried again. Jenny fired off another round, this time hitting one of the lit bottles, which dropped harmlessly on the floor below the window, and forced the man in the balaclava to temporarily halt the torrent of Molotov cocktails aimed at the Metro.

"So, why isn't the gunman simply shooting at human targets?" Jones asked as Jenny fired again. "Why create an explosion, when you can take them out one by one?"

"No idea. Maybe there's no clear view. Maybe they have a plan?" Jenny responded.

But Jenny's bullets were too late. The back end of the car was now thick with flames and at any second the car's petrol tank, plus the gas cylinders, would turn the small yellow car into a fireball.

"Walk away, big fella! Don't get yourself killed," McNally called out.

"Leave him, Dele, it's not worth it!" Wendy added as McIlhinney was still stuck fast in the window and now screaming despairingly as the flames got closer.

"I cannot. This is my fault. I put him in the car. I need to see this through." Dele was now frantically pulling the Irishman's green t-shirt to gain leverage. It was over his head and with the flames now in the back seat, there were fractions of seconds left.

If only to exacerbate the issue, the lit bottles continued to rain down and more hit the target. McNally was now walking backwards away from the scene and was grabbing hold of Wendy's red and black t-shirt, to pull her to safety, expecting the worst. Wendy shrugged him off indignantly.

In the space of seconds, Dele finally seemed to get some purchase on McIlhinney's shirt and pulled him, head first, out of the window. He landed on the pavement in a heap, and Dele tried to drag him away.

Just as he did so, the car violently erupted. It was all over. It was such an almighty explosion that the blast echoed around the centre of the village and the flames rose high into the afternoon sky.

It was a sickening blast of colour and flames which saw parts of the vehicle shoot skywards. At the epicentre of the blast, one of the gas cylinders shot out of the boot and across the road, with fire raging from the dispenser. There were a few muted cheers from the locals, who probably assumed this was a paramilitary skirmish. The fire had engulfed the entire vehicle and the car behind it, a vintage cream Allegro. Every inch of the car was ravaged by the inferno and black smoke. This had to be a scene of death now.

Wendy, who had now taken to kneeling just outside the Rumbling Tum, looked towards the social club window and saw the man in the balaclava brazenly looking down. Her fury almost burst inside her.

She grabbed McIlhinney's pistol that she'd tucked in the back of her mini-skirt and furiously fired three times towards the net curtain. Swearing loudly as the anger flowed from her. There was an immediate scream of anguish as she hit her target. She then ran over towards the last sighting of Dele and McIlhinney. But the flames were too much. McNally warned her to stay back. She watched hopelessly and waited for signs of life to emerge from the haze of black smoke and the fire.

"What can you see, Jones?" Jenny called up from her hand-held. "I'm going to get down and see if I can help."

"It's carnage, Jen. There's too much smoke for me to see anything clearly. Yeah, get over there."

As the smoke and the fire began dampening down, there was

finally a view to the area where the two stricken men had been laying.

But there was a more pressing concern, as the social club emptied and ten to fifteen local men stood outside the club. One or two holding pool cues or other implements.

"For feck's sake. They think this is a sectarian thing. Whoever you've injured up in that window wants them to create a diversion to get him out and treated," McNally grabbed the handheld. "Jones, get your arse down from there and get to the minibus. Jenny, you stay put," Jenny, hearing the plan on the handheld, immediately doubled backed on herself and sprinted back to the vehicle, banging on the window of The Poke en route, mouthing 'get ready' to the QD lads and the Jacobs, who were already huddled by the front door.

As Wendy and McNally waited for the minibus to arrive, Wendy saw something out of the corner of her eye. There was a flicker of movement from under a blue Volvo parked a few metres from the scene of the explosion.

Miraculously, it was McIlhinney and Dele.

"My God!" Wendy exclaimed. "How on earth did they survive that?"

McNally joined Wendy as they ran over to the Volvo to find Dele wrapped around McIlhinney, underneath a gap created by the car parking untidily with its passenger-side wheels on the pavement. The Nigerian's frame had all but enveloped the injured man, and the protection of the car had almost certainly saved their lives. The danger wasn't yet over though, as not all the gas cylinders had been set off, and the men from the club were now hurling stones at McNally and Wendy as they tried to pull the two men out from under the car.

"Why are they throwing stones at us?" Dele asked, showing obvious signs of injury on his face and hands.

"They think we're the enemy," McNally called back. "But I'm not sure they can see you under there anyway."

"And are we the enemy?" Dele responded, now huddled with Wendy and Andrew McIlhinney waiting for the minibus.

"I'm not entirely sure, Dele. That's probably a question for another time. But they've been told we are. So, just keep low and out of the way."

McIlhinney was still nursing what looked like a broken nose, and he had some significant bruising around his right eye and right cheekbone. Dele had all but broken him and then risked himself to save his life.

"I've had enough of this," Wendy shouted and in a break between stones being thrown over, she stood up and shouted over to the group of men. Before firing a few shots into the air as a warning.

"For god's sake, grow up! This is not what you think it is. We are not the police!" she screamed.

"Sit down, for God's sake, woman," McIlhinney called up at Wendy. "They don't care. They'll kill you without a second's thought."

Stones and empty bottles flew over towards the stranded group – with Dele and McIlhinney out of sight near the Volvo.

The minibus then arrived at The Poke, which was a good hundred yards up the road. They watched as the Jacobs, Tom and Carl slipped into the back of the vehicle. Jenny then manoeuvred it between the social club and the Volvo they were hiding behind, and Carl flung the sliding door open.

Several flying objects struck the minibus and Wendy, who was now sitting with Emma, cradled her head to distract her from the nightmare of the situation around her. Jones jumped down from the vehicle and assisted Dele, whilst McNally helped McIlhinney aboard. The angry mob was totally unsighted by the blacked-out windows.

One of the side windows of the bus then smashed suddenly and the glass splinters exploded onto the seats and passengers, with Sam Jacobs appearing to take the worst of it. The door wasn't even shut when the minibus turned the corner of the parade of shops and headed out into rural roads of Ballyramsey.

They had escaped. But the lack of briefing from Eric Rogers on the social club, and Jube's gung-ho attitude, could have cost many lives. McNally put that to the back of his mind and focused on the here and now. He was running the show and needed to get everyone to safety.

"Right. How is everyone?" He called from the front seat as Jenny drove onto the main road.

"I'm okay, only a few tiny cuts," Sam shouted back. "I've brushed the glass off. I'll live. I'm more worried about Dele."

"We'll get to the pub, make a base in the Function Room, and I'll sort some medical support," McNally explained.

"What are we doing with him?" Jones asked, pointing at McIlhinney, who was staring out of the window.

"We certainly can't keep him in the Hunter's Arms. There is only one safe place for him, I'm afraid. I'll need to get hold of Jube, and we'll get him taken to Palace Barracks. We can't trust the RUC. And he's now got a huge price tag on his head."

"Jesus, Palace Barracks?" McIlhinney whimpered. "Don't they torture people in there? Get me to an RUC station and I'll tell you everything."

McNally didn't respond. The bus fell silent for a while as the enormity of the past hour took hold. Emma was snuggled up to Wendy and Jones was helping remove more shards of glass from Sam, whilst keeping half an eye on Dele. Oddly, after all his earlier bravado, McIlhinney was mostly ignored.

"I don't get it," Dele said quietly. "It all seemed so lovely there. Everyone was so polite." There was no response. No-one quite knew how to explain it or where to start.

But what was clear was Andrew McIlhinney's role had now changed. He was now a prized asset. He was one of only two witnesses to the Philip Bradley murder and the only person who could probably name the big man. He had just avoided his own assassination with the help of a university student who wasn't even supposed to be engaged in the operation and his own target, Sam Jacobs, was sitting in the seat immediately in front of him in a YCU minibus. How the tide had turned.

This probably wasn't how McIlhinney had seen his day going, Jones thought, as the minibus sped to the Hunters' Arms and away from danger.

Forty

Orla Massey was already sick to death with physio. A young lad, with too many tattoos and the faint whiff of Blue Stratos aftershave, had already spent an hour with Massey yesterday. They'd lifted a few small weights, lifted her bottom off the bed thirty times and then spread her legs in a very unladylike manner. He'd then congratulated her like she'd won the Nobel Prize for Physics. She felt like fashioning a voodoo doll of him and stabbing it repeatedly. She ached all over afterwards and he was due again at 4pm. She needed a reason to call him off.

That reason arrived at 3.45pm and was carrying this month's edition of Take A Break magazine and a family pack of Double Decker chocolate bars, Massey's favourite.

"Orla, you're looking much better, there's more colour in those cheeks," Jube Spencer smiled.

"You're a bloody liar, Jube, but you're also very kind. The only cheeks that have more colour aren't visible from where you're standing. Bloody physio, I used muscles I haven't used since my teenage years."

"He put you through it?"

"Yeah, and he's a bucking Celtic fan. Bastard." Massey laughed.

"Anyway, you wanted to say goodbye to me before I leave for sunny East London. Here I am, like a good boy, and I brought you another magazine. I see the last one is now in the evidence log."

"Quite right, my notes from the Caragh Reid chat. That was a very strange meeting. Any update? Keep my brain ticking, Jube, tell me the latest." Massey pulled herself forward in the bed.

"Well, as ever, it looks like you were right about Eric Rogers."

"He's bent?" Massey replied, failing badly to hide a massive smug grin.

"It's early days, but our friends at GCHQ seem to have linked a series of transactions to an offshore bank account in his wife's name. Do you know her?"

"Aye. She's a right miserable cow, far too many teeth and a bit horsey. Right up her own hole too. It doesn't surprise me that she's part of the shitshow."

"Goodness, don't hold back, Orla, Jesus Christ!" Jube chuckled.

"So, what kind of money are we talking about here, Jube? From whom?"

"We're talking millions, over a series of years and perhaps dating back to his time in the Met. Before you ask, yes, this includes the Reid family."

"Does Knock Road know yet? Is he facing a disciplinary?"

"Disciplinary? He's facing prison, if this is all correct and evidenced."

"Good. Serves the bastard right," Orla smiled and folded her arms.

"But it's far too early for any of that and, to be honest, what they've found will need hundreds of staff-hours and resources that the RUC and MI5 simply don't have. I'm chatting with a good friend at Internal Affairs tomorrow. I'll sketch out a plan."

"And in the meantime, he carries on as Acting Superintendent?"

Jube put his hand up to stop Orla Massey in her tracks. He felt his handheld vibrate in his leather briefcase. "Hold on, I have a call. Bear with me... *McNally, good to hear from you. How can I help?*"

Jube then listened intently for five minutes as McNally explained the drama at Ballyramsey and Andrew McIlhinney's resulting injuries. Most alarmingly, that McIlhinney was now locked in the back of the minibus, whilst the rest of the team were in the pub's Function Room preparing for opening time and the free bar.

"Jeepers, McNally. That's a pickle," Jube summarised. "But you can't take him to Knock Road. His own brother is based there and we have to avoid Eric Rogers at all costs, too. I'll speak to Clive; the team can interview him at Palace Barracks, but I realise that's not ideal."

Massey was trying to listen in and was joining the dots. "How injured is he?" she asked.

Jube put the handheld between himself and Massey and turned up the volume. "Ask him yourself, Orla."

"McNally, this is Orla. How badly injured is Andrew McIlhinney?"

"He's got a broken nose, maybe a broken cheekbone. Possibly concussion," McNally explained.

"Bingo. Concussion. Bring him here, Belfast City Hospital. He needs to be seen. I'll interview him in the common room. Jube can assist. It'll be like old times." Massey looked up at Jube hopefully. Jube shook his head.

"You're signed off sick," Jube said sympathetically. "It's a non-starter."

"I tend to agree," McNally added. "But I'd prefer Orla did it than trying to brief a busy spook at Palace Barracks or getting anyone from Knock Road involved."

"What about Marie Bristow? Do you trust her?" Jube asked.

"She's my best sergeant. And she's feeding my Georgie, of course, I trust her. Have your GCHQ bods checked her out?"

"She's clean," Jube confirmed. "As you predicted."

"Then bring your wee tape recorder to Belfast City Hospital, Jube. You and Bristow can interview Andrew McIlhinney, and I'll merely observe from my wheelchair. Deal?"

"Works for me," McNally chimed in. "Can I get back to this pub reopening?"

"Agreed. Is he going to comply, McNally? How do we get him here?" Jube was thinking logistics, whilst Massey was rediscovering her mojo.

"I have a young technician, a lass called Wendy Watson, I can detail her to walk into Ballyramsey and pick up my Land Rover, swing past the pub and retrieve Andrew McIlhinney from the back of the minibus or wherever they've stowed him."

"Not Isadora Brown?" Massey asked. "This is very much her bag."

"Oh, my goodness, have you not heard? Isadora's dead. She was shot at point blank range. She effectively drove into a trap," McNally explained. "She died instantly. I can't believe no-one told you. It was a day or so back."

Massey stared at Jube for a second, in stunned disbelief.

"*Dead*? The poor dote." she repeated, shaking her head. "What a tragic waste. She was such a talented wee girl. Please send the team my condolences too." Massey was absolutely choked, Jube could see that.

"There'll be a memorial service. I'm working on it. Let's get you out for that," McNally added.

"Okay, carry on, McNally. I'll process those emotions later." Massey waved her hand as if this was all in a day's work. But she knew she'd feel it later. She rated Isadora. "Anyway, I agree. Wendy is an excellent candidate as she'll scare the living shite out of McIlhinney, so this is a win-win."

"Let's make this happen. Over and out." Jube said, before switching off the handheld.

He was so deep in thought that he promptly dashed off to brief Marie Bristow without saying his goodbyes to Orla. He'd need to get away from Knock Road to chat to Bristow and he'd have a variety of plans to get organised before the interview. He was now in his element.

The minute the door had swung shut, Massey picked up the Take A Break magazine and threw it unceremoniously into the metal bin in the corner of her room.

Forty-One

As Jones and Jenny made their way into the Function Room of the Hunter's Arms, there was an audible gasp. Mr Singh had transformed the once dingy room into a surveillance centre which wouldn't have looked out of place in the Doughnut, GCHQ's base in Cheltenham.

There were ten screens, all focused on different external and internal views of the pub, and a series of numbered sound mixing boards underneath. There were a further two computer monitors, with a keyboard and CPU, sitting on the former servery of the room, with one tracking a GPS signal. On the right-hand side of the room, away from the blacked-out windows, was a map of the pub divided into sections. This corresponded with the numbers on both the mixing boards and the screens.

"This is phenomenal," Jenny exclaimed. "I'd even go as far as miraculous. Top marks, Mr Singh!"

Mr Singh was sitting cross-legged on the floor amongst a maze of leads and wires, with his pipe in his mouth and his brown warehouse coat pockets fuller than ever with tools and titbits.

"We have forty-five minutes until opening and I'm trying to work out why screen number six won't fire up. I've changed the fuse, and nothing appears to be working. Once I've sorted that, I'll give you the grand tour." Mr Singh sucked frustratedly at his pipe whilst beckoning Tom over to help.

Jones peered down behind the bank of screens and immediately noticed that screen six hadn't actually been plugged in. Rather than embarrass Mr Singh, Jones corrected the error, and the screen sprang into life. Mr Singh was too busy tracing leads to notice Jones' helping hand, but Jenny did.

"Oh splendid! It's working now. Maybe it was a loose connection?" Mr Singh exclaimed.

"Most likely," Jones grinned.

"Well, that's the last piece of the jigsaw. So, the grand tour begins. Carl and Tom, please follow too. This will be a useful aide-memoire for you."

All five of the team made their way across the gravel driveway towards the pub. The early afternoon heat had now given way to more traditionally Irish overcast conditions. A nasty black cloud was visible in the distance and Jones wondered if rain would put off thirsty locals. He guessed not, as he'd have walked over hot coals for a free bar.

"The entrance and lobby area are marked on the map as zone 1 and the room is then divided into square metres of visible space with camera and microphones hidden therein." Mr Singh silently pointed to all the cameras in obscure locations. Jones was particularly impressed by the camera placed in the ear of a Toby Jug shaped like Oscar Wilde.

"Therefore," Mr Singh continued, "these are zones 2-7 and they each have their own screen back in the function room. Zones 8-9 are behind the bar, which should be safe areas because of the lack of customers on that side. Zone 10 is the ladies' and gents' conveniences. This can only see at head height, as it would be inappropriate to film in there otherwise." Everyone nodded.

"The private quarters upstairs and the kitchen are totally unmonitored, as we don't expect anyone in there. But I have a plan for a roving camera should the need arise. Do you want to explain, Tom?"

"Absolutely," Tom confidently took over. "Mr Singh has developed a pair of glasses that have two small cameras on either arm to capture movement outside our pre-planned areas. But there is no microphone."

"Exactly, questions?" Mr Singh added.

"I have a few," Jenny began. "Do we have predetermined roles here? What am I doing, for example?"

"Good question, Miss Richmond. I have subdivided the banks of screens into sections, and you'll take four each. Jones has 1 to 5 and you'll be watching 6-9. I'll be monitoring the GPS screens and number 10. I hope that all makes sense?" There was more nodding.

"Tom and Carl will be the only members of customer-facing staff unless Wendy returns later. You are all banned from the pub, and you need to remain in the Function Room. The locals will be told there is an electrical fault in the Function Room. Do I make myself clear?" Mr Singh looked across the team's faces for confirmation, and everyone agreed.

McNally, fresh from his call with Jube and Massey, then joined the group with trays of sandwiches and other snacks.

"Where do you want these, Mr Singh?" He asked.

"Just on the bar, if you don't mind, and scatter a few around the larger tables near the snug and lounge bar. Be sure to leave the samosas on the bar."

Carl and Tom, at the mention of the samosas, winked at each other.

"I saw that, lads," McNally smiled. "What's the craic with the samosas, Mr Singh?"

"All will be revealed. But let's just say that they're my sister's secret recipe and I'm eager to see the reaction of the locals."

"Intriguing," McNally replied, with Jones and Jenny looking equally mystified.

"One more thing," Mr Singh continued, with a slight Columbo-vibe. "Carl and Tom are also miked up and have hidden earpieces. We'll be able to communicate with them."

Just then there was a bang on the front door, and Tom rushed over to let Wendy in.

"Hello everyone. I'm on a deadline, so where's Andrew McIlhinney?" she asked, hurriedly.

"Locked in the cellar," Carl replied. "It's chilly down there, but I found him something upstairs to keep him a little warmer."

"Good work, Carl. I have a little piece of intel for you all that might make tonight a touch more interesting." Wendy seemed to aim the news at McNally, but everyone was instantly interested.

"The Ballyramsey locals seem to believe Andrew McIlhinney was killed by the explosion. There are a few wreaths of flowers and candles near The Rumbling Tum."

"Bloody hell," Jones responded. "That might be handy. Is it not possible that the chap you shot with McIlhinney's Ruger died at the scene?"

"I guess, but wouldn't they leave flowers outside the social club then? Anyway, I'll get McIlhinney. I'm guessing the Jacobs and Dele have gone back to Thiepval?"

"Yeah, the taxi arrived about ten minutes ago. The Thiepval medics are going to give Dele the once over. They've found him overnight accommodation on-site and Virginia will monitor things. I've suggested she buys Sam and Dele a few drinks," McNally explained.

Wendy then disappeared to escort McIlhinney to the Land Rover and back to Belfast for his interview with Bristow and Jube. Seconds later she re-emerged with the rather down-trodden and bruised looking McIlhinney, who was now rather sheepishly wearing a dressing gown, or house coat, that Carl had found upstairs.

"Carl, you found a kid's pink Bagpuss dressing gown for him to wear?" Wendy laughed.

"Well, yeah. There wasn't anything else that fitted," Carl responded. The group chuckled as McIlhinney was led to the Land Rover and Wendy vanished.

With Wendy only gone a matter of minutes, there was a heavy knock on the door and McNally went with the rest of the surveillance team back to the Function Room. The first of the regulars had arrived.

Tom ran to the door and three older men, all sporting grey beards and wearing dark cardigans, entered the pub. All three paid little attention to the changes in the pub's décor and simply strolled straight to the bar.

"Three free pints of Beamish, please. These are definitely free, aren't they?" a man in a dark brown cardigan asked.

"Yes," Carl confirmed. "The first two hours, all pints are free, and spirits and wines are half price."

"In that case, we'll have three Jameson chasers too, young man. There's never been a free bar in this pub since Wee Joe took over. We'd better make use of it before he's back." This time, it was the turn of the man in a grey cardigan to speak, with the last man, in a dark maroon version, remaining silent.

They ignored the free snacks on offer and sat in a window seat overlooking the front of the pub. This was directly below screen 4, Jones' zone. He picked up his headphones and was ready to listen in, but the resulting silence as they slowly sipped their free stout gave him little to do.

A trickle of other locals arrived, and Carl and Tom busied themselves serving Beamish, Harp Lager, and Kilkenny to the drinkers. A few sandwiches were also eaten, and Jones, Jenny and McNally scribbled notes of conversations, but nothing appeared useful or important.

As the cardigan party stepped up for pint number two, the first of the questions about the Englishness of Carl and Tom were asked, and Tom happily gave them the answers. He also made sure they knew Wee Joe was coming back and their presence was a temporary thing. This seemed to placate them.

The steady stream of customers tested the note-taking and listening ability of the surveillance team, and McNally decided he would roll up his sleeves and take on two cameras, leaving the team with two each and Mr Singh also manning the as-yet-unused GPS monitors. But the usefulness of the information was limited. Jones had picked up references to today's events, but they were accompanied by eye-rolls and frustration rather than adding any further detail. It was clear this was a community fed up with the skirmishes, rather than wanting to fuel them further.

That was until around 9pm when the first familiar face appeared from the darkness into the front bar.

"Sweet Jesus," McNally exclaimed. "Stewart McIlhinney on camera three. The fecking weasel. I can't believe he'd show his face in here."

"This is his manor, though, isn't it?" Jones said. "Unless someone tipped him off about this operation. We'll soon learn."

"Has he ever met Carl or Tom?" Jenny asked, momentarily ducking away from her screen to see him walk in.

"Nope," Jones clarified. "That's why they've been kept in the background. Hold on, why isn't his arm in that jacket? Is he injured?"

The team watched on as Stewart McIlhinney took off his Harrington-style jacket and hung it on the coat stand to reveal his right arm in a sling and his forearm heavily strapped.

"He was the bloody gunman! He was shooting at a car containing his own brother before Wendy shot him! I don't believe it," Jenny was now standing behind McNally and watching him closely.

"Well, that could explain why he didn't just shoot him. Maybe he wanted to give him half a chance. I can't believe the big man ordered Stewart to kill his own brother. That's incredible," Jones added.

"Shhhhhh," Mr Singh interrupted. "Let's listen to this."

Stewart approached the bar, and the surveillance team held their collective breaths.

"A pint of Harp and a packet of dry roast, please," he called over to Carl.

"Right away, mate," Carl responded.

"You're English?"

"Yeah, we're at the Uni, studying hospitality. Only here for a few weeks before Wee Joe is back," Carl explained perfectly.

"How much do I owe you?"

"35p for the nuts. It's a free bar for a little while," Carl walked away. Stewart McIlhinney didn't respond.

The team watched as one of the cardigan-wearing men approached him and shook his hand and offered condolences for his loss.

"Yeah, thanks. We don't really know what happened yet, but it might be a case of Andrew being in the wrong place at the wrong time. We are all so raw," Stewart explained to maroon cardigan.

"What?" Jenny screamed at the screen. "You were throwing lit milk bottles at his car, that you'd packed full of gas cylinders and petrol cans! Are you having a laugh?"

"Calm down, Jen," Jones whispered.

Behind Stewart, another three men entered the bar. All three were in their mid- to late-twenties and made a bee-line straight to him. There were more condolences, shaking of hands, and hugs.

"Do we know any of these?" Jones asked. McNally shook his head and stared at the screen.

"We can take screen grabs of the monitors for reference." Mr Singh pushed a few buttons and an unseen printer burst into life under the table.

"Hold fire a second. They're discussing today." Jones pushed a button next to his monitor, and the conversation was relayed to the rest of the room.

"I saw everything, Stewie," one man muttered. "There was a

huge black fella, never seen him before in my life. He gave Andrew a real going over in the café. He was then put into a yellow car and after a while, something set it off. There was a hell of an explosion. Nobody saw your wee man after that. There was gunfire and then the minibus took the Peelers away."

"My God," Stewart responded. "What an awful way to die. We have to find out who did it."

"Some girl was on the scene, running around shooting in the air and saying they weren't police or something. Who the hell was it? You're the police, aren't you, Stewie? Can't you find out?" The man asked.

"I won't be able to get anywhere near the investigation. It'll be a clash of interests. But I'll be leaving the RUC soon, anyway. I was a fool to think a Catholic could join and have equal status. They've hated me from the word go," Stewart continued.

"I hate to say I told you so, at such tragic times. But..." The man put his arms around Stewart's shoulders and the surveillance team heard him whisper, "we'll get the bastards, every last one of them. You know we will." Stewart smiled in response.

"He really believes his brother is dead, doesn't he?" Jenny said, disbelievingly.

"I can't believe that no-one saw him being taken away by the minibus," Jones responded, standing behind her. "I guess there's a possibility that the minibus shielded him from view. But I think it's far more likely that Stewart has told the big man that Andrew's dead. He would have then carried out his orders."

McNally tapped on the screen as another face walked into the pub. "Mickey bloody Reilly. This could be all of our Christmases at once. Hold on to your hats!" McNally hushed the team, but not before Jenny let out an enthusiastic 'Bingo!'

Reilly appeared to be limping slightly as he pushed open the double doors to the pub and looked around. He was the first to seem impressed by the pub's modernisation project and ambled over to a quiet table and set his jacket down before walking to the bar.

"Evening," Tom greeted him.

"Am I too late for the free bar?" Mickey asked.

Tom looked at his watch. "You've another three quarters of an hour yet, mate. What can I get you?"

"Pint of Kilkenny and a Bushmills chaser." Mickey then looked around the bar as if orientating himself. He soon spotted Stewart, before going over and shaking hands with the cardigan wearing group.

Jones watched as Mickey started looking up at the ceiling and the architraves. Did he know there were cameras and microphones practically everywhere? It seemed unlikely.

"Good job you've made of the old place," Mickey said to Carl. Carl was caught on the back foot. He was midway through serving someone else and counted to ten in his head before answering. He could hear Wendy's words in his head telling him not to screw up.

"Well," Carl finally responded. "The brewery knew modernisation was overdue, I think. But I'm pleased you like it. Wee Joe will have a whole new lease of life when he's back."

"Grand. When's he back?" Mickey asked.

"Oh, about a fortnight, I think. Not long," Carl replied.

"It was well deserved," came the response. Mickey walked away and settled down with his drinks at the small table. He downed the Bushmills in one, and then bowed his head, as if contemplating life. He seemed tired. Jones furiously made notes of his demeanour whilst Mr Singh started capturing more screen grabs of other useful-looking customers.

Stewart, with his hastily consumed first pint now history, had been passed his second by one of his younger friends, before he slowly walked over to Mickey Reilly.

"This'll be interesting," Jenny piped up. McNally put his fingers to his lips.

"My condolences for your loss, young Stewart." Mickey barely looked up when speaking.

"Thanks. Can we talk?" Stewart responded.

"Not here," he answered. Mickey pointed outside. He took a long swig of his pint and nodded towards Tom and Carl behind the bar. "You never know who's listening. Have you got a smoke? Want to take the air?"

"Sure," Stewart replied. "I need to have a slash first. Give me two minutes."

"Bloody hell, what microphones do we have outside?" McNally shouted.

"Leave this to me," Mr Singh nodded at McNally. "Carl, Tom, this is Mr Singh. Start offering the free food around to those in the bar area. Try to get the larger Kilkenny-drinking man to have a samosa. Stewart too."

"I'm not sure free food is the answer here, Mr Singh. No disrespect," Jenny looked around at her colleagues, baffled, as Mr Singh held up his hand.

"Patience, team. Patience," were his only words in response.

Carl picked up the two trays of samosas and began offering them around the bar. One tray deliberately to the back of the bar area, with a foil-like liner in the bowl. The other, with a white doily base, to those around the bar itself, including Mickey.

"These are my friends' traditional Indian recipe. They're a little hot. I hear the Irish don't like their spicy food, but please give them a try," Carl called out to the bar.

"Little fella," Mickey put his hand on Carl's shoulder, "I was in India and Malaya during the Second World War, and I can assure you, I can stomach extremely hot food. I hope this lives up to your billing."

"What's that?" Stewart asked, returning from the gents.

"I hope he's washed his hands," Jones chimed in.

"I can confirm he washed his hands. He was actually very thorough." Jenny wasn't laughing. Monitoring the male toilets wasn't on her bucket list.

"They're hot samosas. Our new English barman has been passing them around. Take one." Mickey passed one to Stewart McIlhinney before they strolled outside towards two picnic benches, within a mere spitting distance from the Function Room and the surveillance team.

"Okay," Jones said. "What now? You want me to hide around the side of the building? Listen in?"

Mr Singh switched both the GPS monitors on, and two blue dots appeared on the screen. The location was immediately shown as the small grassy area outside the pub, which Wee Joe jokingly called a beer garden.

"We knew their location, we watched them walk out there," Jenny whispered, sounding unimpressed.

Mr Singh then walked over to a small shoe-boxed sized contraption and appeared to look for a frequency. He then patched the shoe-box gadget into the soundboard.

Mickey swallowed half of the samosa in one huge bite and Stewart followed suit. There was a shrug of indifference between the two of them.

"Look," said Stewart, "I honestly have no idea if he's dead or not. But I didn't see him leave in their minibus and the Metro was ripped to pieces. He could very well have been in there."

The voices came through, as clear as a bell, from the speakers in the Function Room.

"What in the name of Mother Mary are you using as the microphone for this conversation?" McNally, eyes widened, uttered in a barely a whisper.

"It's the samosa," Mr Singh smiled. "There's a transmitter hidden in the centre. It'll keep receiving until it passes through their system."

"Until they shite it out? You, my friend, are a fecking genius,"

McNally stood up and kissed Mr Singh on the forehead. "But everyone hush now. Write all this down, Jones."

"Who was it? Who was there?" Mickey was keeping his voice low.

"They're sneaky beakies, probably MI5. I know three of them. Declan McNally, he's a trainer from Thiepval. He's been running the show because the RUC has been so short on numbers, and they don't entirely trust the top brass. The others are trainees. One's called Jones. His first name is unknown. The other is Jenny Richmond. There was a third until recently, Isadora Brown, but she was shot a few days back in Deramore Park, Belfast. I'm guessing that was your doing?"

"Aye, she was a nosey wee bitch. We had to send them a warning. Why? Are you going to arrest me?" Reilly laughed. "What do you know about these Jones and Richmond characters?"

"BASTARD!" Jenny shouted. "He's murdering scum, and we have that on tape now. Surely we can simply take him? I'd like to..."

"I know what you'd like to do. I'd like to do worse, Miss Richmond, but we need to follow a process. We will ensure Isadora's murderer is punished," McNally patted her on the shoulder as the team continued to look wide-eyed at the screens. Jenny bit her tongue.

"There's no record of Jones or Richmond on the police database or our paper records," Stewart McIlhinney continued. "We don't have data on the MI5 folk. I think the big black lad was a bodyguard for Sam Jacobs and his wee sister."

"The still living and breathing, Sam Jacobs?" Mickey confirmed.

"Yeah. Back in Thiepval Barracks, I'm guessing. It's like Fort Knox there."

"Feck's sake." Mickey paused and there was the sound of liquid passing the transmitter.

"We can hear him digesting. That's just plain weird," Jenny announced. "Clever, but weird."

"Stewart, I realise it was a heartless request. But you were asked to silence Andrew. We can't say yet whether you've been successful. If he's not dead and is now briefing MI5, the whole thing could be finished. The entire system could come crashing down. Between Sam Jacobs and your brother, the key to millions of pounds of investments and the lives of our gangs across the globe are hanging by a thread."

"I know," Stewart whispered. "I'm sorry, Mickey."

"What?" Jones shouted. "Gangs across globe? Millions of pounds? What the bloody hell is he talking about? Surely that's an exaggeration?"

"What do you want me to do?" Stewart sounded extremely worried.

"We'll need an audience. We'll need to ask whether there's a way of using what remaining influence we have to limit the damage. You also need to pray that your cover isn't blown at the RUC. We don't need any more liabilities to deal with." Mickey took another swig of beer.

"My cover is secure, Mickey. Our contact knows we have his balls in a vice. If he gets the smallest clue that I'm blown, he'll get me out. We'll just have to wait and see about Sejanus." Stewart was breathing heavily. The transmitter was picking up the increased heart rate of the RUC mole.

"Sejanus?" Jones said, back in the Function Room. "What the hell is he talking about? What is that?"

"Sssshhhhhh!!" McNally responded. "Keep quiet and we'll learn more, you dope."

"Stewart. I'm warning you," Mickey Reilly began. "This is the last chance saloon for everything. My only son is already in prison. In the next 24 hours, you'll either be locked up or dead, too, unless this MI5 mob is called off. Either that, or we'll need to start targeting them, like that Isadora girl."

"Please, we've got to stop the killings. Every death brings them closer. Philip Bradley could have been managed, and George was just a wee scrote. Martha was paid off. She was away. None of this needed to happen." McIlhinney appeared to be appealing to Reilly's better nature.

"Who do you think you are? Shut your fecking mouth! You're alive because of your current usefulness. That's all. You are in no position to talk down to me or doubt my methods. We don't make deals with snakes. We cut off their heads. You are no different. Don't forget that. Now, get out of my sight and do as you're told."

There was silence. Within ten seconds, Stewart McIlhinney was back at the bar. The conversation was over. Reilly had no better nature. That was clear.

"There's a lot of information there. Lots to think about. Who is Mickey's only son? An audience with who? Who is Sejanus? Does that sound familiar to anyone?" McNally muttered, almost to himself, as he watched Jones continue to speed-write the verbatim notes.

"Hang about, I can hear an engaged tone from a telephone. Where is that coming from?" Jenny looked at Mr Singh, who shrugged his shoulders.

"Does Mickey have a mobile phone?" Jones ran over to the front of the Function Room and tried to peer through the tiniest of cracks in the black backing paper on the windows. "Damn, can't see a bloody thing,"

"Carl, I need you to do some glass collecting in the beer garden. Do it now. We need to know if the chap on the patio table is on a mobile call. Don't reply. Just cough if you've heard this." Mr Singh could see on the monitors that Carl had stopped and was listening, but he was relieved to hear him cough in response.

The surveillance team watched as Carl Kelly disappeared from behind the bar to the garden. He returned moments later with a single empty pint glass in his hand.

"Tom, no need to collect glasses in the garden. It's all clear out there. There's just a gent out there looking through a black contacts book and about to make a mobile call," Carl over-explained to Tom.

"Good lad, Carl. You're both doing a fantastic job out there. Just keep it basic, though." Mr Singh released the red transmit button on the soundboard, just as the engaged tone sounded again through the speakers.

"Who is he trying to reach?" Jenny asked.

"I think I might know." Jones had run back to his chair and was now writing furiously on his pad again. Whilst keeping half an eye on the screens.

"But Mickey Reilly is the big man? He killed Bradley, Martha, and George? Is that the view of the team? McNally?" Jenny was looking around the team looking for answers, but only Mr Singh was staring back, and he didn't have a clue.

"I say we wait for the Andrew McIlhinney interview. We have time," McNally finally responded. "I think the smart money is on Mickey Reilly, but who the hell is he ringing and seeking an audience with?"

"I agree, for what it's worth," Jones put down his pencil and looked over at McNally, just as the speakers kicked into life again.

"Hello, this is Mickey." Whoever he was calling had clearly finished their earlier call and he had connected.

"We have a problem," he continued, brusquely and clearly furious. "I think we've been lied to, predictably, and I think our man is blown. Sejanus is also massive problem. I suggest you box things up and prepare for a quick holiday, should the need arise. I'll deal with Sejanus, somehow. This has to end before the whole empire crumbles."

The voice on the other end of the phone said one word, it was almost indecipherable. But sounded like "*understood*".

"Did you catch that?" McNally asked. "The other voice. I heard female."

"I'm not sure what I heard; it was so quiet. It could have been male or female." Mr Singh was speaking and half-listening. He was already looking for ways to enhance the recording from Mickey Reilly's call. Reilly himself was back at the bar, and from the bar camera, his anger had already passed.

There was a knock on the door of the Function Room door. Jones shot up and jogged over to see who it was. "It's me, Carl. Didn't you see me coming over?"

"Shit, sorry Carl," Jones opened the door and was presented with a tray of drinks. It was a near perfect order. Two whiskies, a vodka and orange and two pints of Harp Lager. Carl walked away into the empty beer garden.

"Two pints of Harp?" Jones queried.

"I assumed you'd be thirsty," Carl called back. "Don't worry, nobody saw me. No-one's in the garden."

"Bloody legend," Jenny called out as Jones brought the tray into the surveillance room.

"Bit risky though," Mr Singh responded as Carl made his way back through the pub. "Luckily, for us and him, I think he's got away with it."

In the bar, Stewart was now sitting with the cardigan group at the table near the window and Mickey was sipping a whiskey near the bar.

"How much time left of the free bar?" he asked Tom, who checked his watch.

"Less than ten minutes."

"Why don't you tell everyone? Ring the bell. Tell them there's an hour and ten minutes left."

"An hour and ten minutes?"

Mickey began counting fifty-pound notes out on the bar. A few locals looked over.

"Here's £350. Ballyramsey has had a tough day. Call it my contribution to community relations." Mickey downed his whiskey and walked over to the door. "Keep it nice and tidy for

Wee Joe. Tell him I'll see him soon and we'll make a block booking."

"Oh, wow! That's very generous and yes, I'll pass on the message." Tom smiled at Mickey and rang the bell.

"Free bar extended, an extra hour! Courtesy of..." Tom stopped and called over to Mickey. "What's your name?"

"It's courtesy of the big man." Mickey then left and shut the pub door loudly.

"Okay," Jenny smashed her fist down on the table in celebration. "Unless he wants to put it in neon flashing letters over the door, that couldn't be any clearer. We have our big man. That's worth another drink. Let's nick him for murdering Isadora too."

"He didn't say *he* was the big man, Jenny," Jones countered. "He said it was courtesy of... let's not get ahead of ourselves. That money might not even be his. But I think we can safely assume that Michael Doyle and Mickey Reilly are the same person. Sejanus is a mystery though, isn't it?"

Forty-Two

Jube Spencer had extricated Marie Bristow from the confines of Knock Road to a café between Lombard Street and Rosemary Street in the city centre. Rooney's was close to finishing for the day when Jube ordered a pot of tea and a round of sandwiches for the pair. Marie, who had been busily working on a violent street robbery outside Woolworth's, was caught off guard by Jube's call and eyed him suspiciously as he pulled out his leather notebook.

"We've been handed a gilt-edged opportunity to interview one of only two witnesses to the killing of Philip Bradley, but this has to be off the books." Jube spoke as Marie tucked into her prawn sandwich.

"Why off the books? Are you sure this isn't just a typical MI5 attempt to keep the RUC out of the spotlight?"

"What if I told you that your boss was going to be overseeing the interview? Would that make a difference?"

"You're joking? Eric has agreed to an off the books interview?" Marie nearly spat out her sandwich.

"No, never in a month of Sundays. I'm talking about Orla

Massey. We'll interview the suspect in the hospital common room, with a standard issue tape recorder." Jube conjured up one of his most alluring smiles, but Marie wasn't buying it.

"What kind of idiot are you? I love Orla to bits, but she's off sick. She's broken her pelvis. She's high on painkillers. Anyway, whilst this kind of clandestine interview may be okay for the sneaky beakies, it could easily end my career. I won't do it."

"I understand your reluctance. But there's more to this than meets the eye. We have evidence that Rogers might be involved in this whole debacle, hence keeping it off the books."

"What? How?" Marie responded, suddenly interested but staying professional.

"One end of the spectrum is that Rogers might have been paid to turn a wee blind eye to certain illegal activities. The other end is that he's been paid over many years by organised crime gangs across UK and Ireland to purposely ruin or divert investigations. We're working on both possibilities. But this is absolutely hush-hush."

Marie Bristow smiled.

"I've always known he was a shitehawk and I've never liked him, but this is beyond my wildest dreams. Why aren't you tackling this through police internal affairs?"

"Now, now, Marie," Jube shook his head. "Why would we do that? The minute they were on the scene, the investigation and our intelligence gathering operation will be as dead as the proverbial dodo. You know that, surely?"

"Yeah. But those are the proper channels. That's what my training says." Marie sipped her tea thoughtfully.

"Well, I may have wasted my time here. I'm sorry, Marie. I didn't realise you were a box ticker. This is a much bigger opportunity than you think. Maybe I'm barking up the wrong tree." Jube gathered his notebook and put his pen back in the top pocket of his blazer.

"Hold on," said Marie grabbing Jube's arm. "For clarity, is this interview to find out who murdered George McCool, Philip Bradley and Martha Maddison, or to bring Eric Rogers down?"

"It's to work out who the big man is and whether he's responsible for the murders. However, this may supply tantalising detail on Eric's misdemeanours. Which I think we'll all enjoy. Am I wrong?"

"No. You're dead on, I'd love to bring that bastard down." She stopped again and gazed for a few seconds out of Rooney's front window, before making her decision. "Alright, Mr Spencer, you have your woman. I'm in. On one condition, though."

"Which is?"

"That if this goes pear-shaped, you'll do your damnedest to keep me out of the firing line and protect my career." Marie took the opportunity to finish another one quarter of the prawn sandwich whilst Jube considered his answer.

"I'll go further than that. If we bring in the big man, solve the murders and finger Eric Rogers, I'll talk to your Chief Constable and I'll ask him to consider a promotion. And if this all falls to dust; the clandestine interview never took place." Jube lowered his voice slightly, with the waitress getting close with the broom.

"Look, we are all beyond respectful for the way you've dealt with Isadora's murder. Her death casts such a long shadow. But the fact that you were there and able to pinpoint what she was doing and why makes us even more grateful for your help and understanding. You're one of us now," Jube concluded.

"You've a great wee team at the YCU, Jube. They're all class and so welcoming. And we have grieved together and helped each other."

Marie looked out of the window again. Perhaps letting a moment of emotion pass, Jube remained silent and let her compose her thoughts.

"The whole episode hasn't left my thoughts. Not for a single second. The awfulness of the trap we fell into. Jenny, Jones and McNally do genuinely make me feel like one of the team. Thank you, you're very kind, Jube Spencer," she half-smiled. "But you haven't told me who we're interviewing yet. One of the big man's henchman?"

"Andrew McIlhinney. The fella with the teardrop tattoo. He's the brother of your PC Stewart McIlhinney. Your mole? Remember?"

"Yeah, I remember. I've spent the last week trying to keep him away from any active investigation whilst you got your ducks in a row. You took your bloody time!"

"Actually, we were just keeping the RUC at arm's length whilst we learned more about Eric Rogers. The radio silence was deliberate. I'm sorry."

"You didn't trust me?" Marie looked alarmed.

"We didn't trust anyone at Knock Road until we had more intelligence from GCHQ. Don't take it personally. I've already told you; you're one of us. This was just an operational necessity."

Marie nodded. "That makes sense, I guess. It's difficult to trust us when our boss might be corrupt."

One of Rooney's waitresses was sweeping the floor near the main window, and it was clear they were nearing closing time. Jube bundled up his cheese and pickle sandwich, which he'd barely touched, into a large napkin and headed towards the door. Marie went in the opposite direction.

"I've paid, Marie. It's sorted," Jube called over.

"I'm getting Orla some lemon meringue pie. It's her favourite. I'll only be a second."

Whilst Jube waited outside the front door in the pitch black, he contacted McNally on the handheld.

"Andrew McIlhinney is under observation at City Hospital under lock and key. Clive put one of his best men on the door. After some persuasion, Marie Bristow will assist in an off-the-books interview. We are all systems go," Jube reported. "What news your end?"

"I really don't know where to begin. We'll need to compare

notes afterwards. But the Bradley's Site Manager at Mainstay Barns, Mickey Reilly, is the main suspect for the murders. He's already confessed to killing Isadora. We'll run a check on fingerprints we picked up from his pint glass, but we have a working assumption that Mickey Reilly is the new name of a former British Army veteran called Michael Doyle. His prints were on the bullets from Eden Vale. But there's a still a hell of a lot of confusion about other intel we've picked up."

"Confusion? Like what?" Jube pressed.

"Two things. Firstly, there are plenty of people around here that think Andrew McIlhinney died in the explosion at Ballyramsey. That's a story put about by his own brother, Stewart, who was, incidentally, the shooter in the window of the social club. You can definitely use that in his interview. His own brother was trying to kill him. But Mickey Reilly isn't entirely convinced of Andrew's death."

"Right, that's phenomenal intelligence, Declan." Jube pulled out his leather notebook full of his perfectly handwritten notes. He added to these and circled key points.

"Next?"

"Have you ever heard of the name, Sejanus?" McNally asked.

"He was an ambitious traitor. The power behind the throne, so to speak."

"I'm not sure I follow," McNally admitted.

"Do you not know your Roman Classical History, McNally? Sejanus was the commander of the Praetorian Guard under Roman Emperor Tiberius. He was basically the right-hand man of the Emperor until he was executed for treason. He was trying to manipulate his way to the top. He wanted to be Emperor himself. But what has this got to do with anything?"

"Impressive knowledge. It's something I heard tonight, maybe a codename. Were the Praetorian Guard like the police?" McNally asked.

"In some ways, yes. Look, I need to interview Andrew McIlhinney. I'll update you later and we can discuss Roman History all you want."

"Grand," McNally responded, deep in thought, before ending the call.

Forty-Three

It had been a long night in Ballyramsey and whilst the temperature had now cooled to 14 degrees; the pub seemed to trap all the day's humidity and sweat inside when the long maroon curtains were pulled after closing time. That, and the heady mix of alcohol and nicotine odours, made the place smell ripe.

With the locals gone and all intelligence gathered, the surveillance team had silently made their way into the main bar and began dismantling the scene. Aside from Mr Singh, who was working on clearing down the Function Room itself. The rest were locating the cameras, listening devices and other QD gadgetry.

Carl and Tom were the only YCU members momentarily sitting down. They'd undertaken a full shift behind the bar and were rewarded with a few pints of beer before joining the clear down. There was also a huge collective relief that Carl had managed to pull off his role without doing anything cataclysmically silly.

Jones, on top of a step ladder pulling the leads down from the pub's ceiling, was unnaturally quiet. Jenny knew he was trying to put together the pieces of intel from tonight's successful operation, and he was in download mode. They'd discuss it later and, for now, she'd leave him be.

McNally, on a pause from coiling up electrical leads, was sitting at one of the bar tables reading through everyone's notes and trying to understand how far they'd got. He desperately wanted to be in that interview room in City Hospital, but he knew that with Massey, Jube, and Bristow in the room, everything would be in order.

Wendy was back at Thiepval and was heading to bed. She'd opted against returning to the pub, as Andrew McIlhinney's Palace Barracks guard had taken several hours to show up. She also had tomorrow to think about. The parents of Sam and Emma Jacobs were due to arrive. They'd be interviewed by one of Bristow's team with a safeguarding qualification. Wendy knew serious questions would be asked about the trip to Ballyramsey, which could very easily have ended in tragedy. Somehow, though, all avenues of blame led back to Eric Rogers, who simply didn't have any clue what he was dealing with in communities like Ballyramsey, or more likely, had turned a blind eye to it. Whilst Jube sanctioned the operation, the lack of intel on the social club was the key issue.

With the clock ticking round to 12.30am, Bristow and Jube Spencer were now preparing themselves for the interview in a hospital common room. The room itself was surrounded by windows, but the grey vertical blinds would ensure confidentiality, and it was lockable from the inside. There were large brightly coloured plastic chairs positioned around the room, as well as a large Thorn EMI Television that looked like it had seen much better days. The small kids' play area in the corner of the room, with crayons and felt-tip pens, plus the collection of rudimentary drawings blue-tacked to the wall, dumbed down the feeling of a vital interview setting. But this was the only appropriate room for the interview and Jube had even had to bribe the Matron with a good bottle of Chablis for the meeting to go ahead at all.

Bristow had given Massey's two protection officers, who had been stationed at her door, the night off, but she knew she'd be questioned about that tomorrow, back at Knock Road. She'd need to have some story lined up, but it was all about the here and now and getting answers from Andrew McIlhinney and keeping his brother out of the loop.

Orla Massey was wheeled into in the room by a tired-looking hospital orderly. Massey had applied makeup for the first time since the explosion and was wearing a smart navy blouse. Her legs were covered by a large blue blanket as the surgical pins at the top of her legs and the plaster wouldn't allow for trousers currently. However, she looked the part. She was back on manoeuvres and felt good about it.

"Before we crack on," Jube started. "I've hastily pulled together two briefing packs from my hand-written notes. You'll note I've highlighted a few areas of interest on page two. If you can take a few moments to just digest all that before we start, that would be grand."

"Secondly. We need to work out fairly swiftly whether Andrew McIlhinney is actually more helpful as, point one, a suspect who is criminally prosecutable, or as a witness-come-super-grass who we may need to protect. Point two, we also need to work out whether he is more valuable, dead or alive."

"What do you mean? Is MI5 thinking of having him killed? Do you have James Bond on speed dial?" Massey said.

"My apologies. Look at the circled notes on page three. During the Ballyramsey surveillance operation of last night, which Sergeant Bristow is now fully up-to-speed on, we gained some useful insights. One is a strong local rumour of Andrew McIlhinney's death."

"Oh, I see." Massey was now scanning the notes. "And his own brother tried to kill him yesterday? That's pretty incredible. You see that, Bristow?"

"Yeah, all of this comes as a surprise to me. Stewart is a

complete wet weekend at work. He's a nervous wee pet. Trying to shoot and then firebomb your own brother doesn't seem his mentality at all."

"That's what fear does, I guess. The big man's influence." Massey was chewing the end of a pencil, and speed reading the rest of the notes.

There was a knock on the door, Jube strolled over to answer and the same jaded hospital orderly wheeled Andrew McIlhinney into the room. Jube smiled at the orderly and locked the door. Andrew was in the same blood-splattered green t-shirt and navy-blue bomber jacket, faded blue jeans and black Puma trainers as earlier. He had two thin butterfly stitches under his right eye and a small amount of gauze hanging out of his left nostril. He looked exhausted, and the bruises underneath his eyes from the broken nose didn't help.

Andrew stepped out of the wheelchair and took a seat opposite Bristow and Jube Spencer, barely acknowledging any of them.

"How are you doing? What's the prognosis on your concussion?" Jube asked.

"I may as well be dead," he responded. "I mean, I'm a dead man walking. But, health-wise, your man battered me. The concussion has gone, but I look like I've done six rounds with Mike Tyson."

"You're happy to be interviewed?" Jube continued.

"This ain't a formal interview, I know that. I need to know what your plans are with me first and who are you two? I know her," he pointed at Orla Massey in the corner of the room. "We all know her, Jesus!"

"My name is Jube Spencer, and this is Sergeant Marie Bristow from Knock Road RUC. Orla Massey is observing this interview. But you're right, this isn't a formal interview and I'm not a policeman. You are here of your own free will, but I suggest you comply."

"What are you going to do with me? Release me, and they'll kill me. You know that?"

"I understand your predicament, Andrew. But the plan depends on the quality of the information you give us," Jube explained.

"And whether it stacks up," Bristow added, then changed the subject. "We are going to record this interview for our information, but this could be used later to determine future courses of action. Do you understand?"

"Sure," McIlhinney replied. He shrugged his shoulders. Bristow pressed play and record on the portable tape player as Jube laid out his notes in front of him.

Andrew's right leg bounced up and down energetically, perhaps nervously.

"Let's start with something simple," Jube started. "Tell us what orders you had yesterday, when you met my team in Ballyramsey."

"To capture Sam Jacobs and bring him to an address in Derry."

"Who gave you the car? The yellow Austin Metro?" Jube continued.

"No-one. I was called and told the keys were at the Ballyramsey Social Club and the car was parked in a garage around the back. There was a wee brown envelope with my name on it, behind the bar."

"You weren't aware that the car was packed with cylinders and petrol cannisters designed to create an explosion?"

"No, Sir, I wasn't. I had no clue. I was unaware that they wanted me to die, too. That was a fecking surprise." McIlhinney added a small sarcastic tone to his last comment, but continued to stare at Jube, who was asking all the questions.

"Let's try a more challenging question. Who wanted Sam Jacobs dead and why?"

"Oh god. You know they'll kill my parents? They're sick. If

they find out what I'm telling you now. Everything is over for me and my family."

"Be brave, Andrew," Massey interrupted. "You have very little left to lose here. They wanted you dead yesterday. We are trying to prevent further deaths, believe me. Including yours."

"The big man. He had the politician killed in Ballycastle. We moved the body to the seafront. We then heard the English kid was in the wardrobe and heard everything. There were some very sensitive things discussed, which could bring the operation down. That's what I was told."

"Who told you Sam was in the wardrobe?" Jube pushed.

"The big man has moles in the RUC, in the Garda, and fecking everywhere."

"We know about your brother, Andrew," Bristow jumped in. "The mole in Knock Road is Stewart. Let's not shy away from that."

"Stewie's not the only one. But yeah, he briefed the big man about Sam being in the wardrobe. Sam was bloody lucky, so he was."

"Okay, take a deep breath, Andrew. We're going to go for a huge question now. Imagine you're on Bullseye and this is for the car or speedboat. Got it?"

"Go on right ahead," Andrew's head was now bowed.

"Who's the big man, Andrew?" Jube asked matter-of-factly, as if asking him about his favourite breakfast cereal.

"I've no idea. I seriously have no clue. You need to believe me." The lad looked imploringly at both Jube and Bristow.

"I don't believe you," Jube replied. "Shall I give you a name and see where we go from there?"

Andrew McIlhinney's leg shook wildly, and he took a boxer's stance in his seat, as if psyching himself up for the next few minutes of questioning.

"Yeah, whatever, go on," McIlhinney said.

"Mickey Reilly," Jube said, watching the lad's reaction.

"Oh, I see what you've done there. You've jumbled things up a little," McIlhinney replied. Massey shot Jube a confused look.

"No, no. Mickey's not the big man and neither was Mac, before he retired, like. Mickey and Mac were the big man's fixers. Enforcers, if you like. They're big men in stature; I'll give you that. But they're not in charge."

"Eamonn MacMillan? We have him in custody." Bristow clarified. "He and Mickey Reilly were the fixers? The front?"

"Yeah, course. Mac stepped down about six months ago. He only does minor jobs now, just to earn some pennies. But there were other fixers before him. I met one once. I can't remember his name. Colyn, or something." Andrew stopped and thought, before moving on. "Look, there's no way the big man would do that shit himself. My god. That would be insane."

"So, there's a team of fixers?" Massey asked. "Not just Mickey Reilly?"

"There's a team. The operation is much bigger than you think. It's fair to say the big man liked his fixers to be similar. Broad, muscular and pretty fecking fearless. Loyalty is a big thing as well. The fixer gave us the orders from the big man and paid us our wages."

Jube paused briefly and rifled through his notes. Willing himself to look unflustered but annoyed that he'd got the chain of command wrong. Jube looked over at Massey, who was also writing.

"So, who killed Philip Bradley and George McCool? Can we clear that up?" Massey asked, without lifting her head from her note-taking.

"Alright. Mickey killed them both. He was fishing in Lough na Cranagh. He's pretty much always up there. He'd asked me to babysit Philip, run errands, and keep him out of trouble. Phil was a massive coke fiend and had an eye for the women. I got the call and rushed up to the house. He wore that Batman suit, he was injured and wanted me to patch him up. Take him to the hospital or something."

"Go on," Jube said.

"Well, something changed. Mickey shows up, goes to the telephone in the house and calls the big man. Then Philip is dead. We paid off the tart and the rest you know."

"The tart?" Bristow asked.

"Yeah, Martha Maddison, we later found out from Stewie. I think she was a local prostitute. I was asked to track her down. But I couldn't find her anywhere. She vanished off the face of the earth."

"The big man didn't order her killing?" Jube clarified.

"As far as I'm aware, and as God is my witness, Mickey didn't kill Martha Maddison. There was no need to. She had been no trouble, we had heard nothing, and she'd been paid off. Only a couple of thousand. But I was just asked to find her." McIlhinney seemed suddenly buoyed by the conversation.

"Next thing I hear, she dead on the Bradley's yacht in Bangor and rumours of one million pound in a suitcase. Believe me, that wasn't my doing and Mickey looked surprised as I was when I told him to switch on the news. Can I get a drink or something?"

Bristow walked to the other side of the room and filled four NHS plastic cups with water from the sink in the room, then carefully carried them back in two hands. She gave Andrew his first before handing one each to Massey and Jube.

"What was Philip's role with the big man?" Jube took a quick swig of water and continued the questioning.

"Well, that's kinda weird. The big man has contacts all over Ireland, north and south of the border. But for some reason, he wanted contacts in Westminster. He had affiliates in London, Manchester, Birmingham, and Glasgow. I even went to Cardiff once. It's like an enormous empire."

"I'm lost," Jube explained. "What was Philip doing for this empire, as you call it?"

"I don't think he was doing anything except spending money, snorting his coke, and banging his women. Then, in political circles, he was a family man and even my ma and da had time for him, and he was a protestant unionist. They normally called those people the Hun. He was seen as alright, normal-ish."

"But his spending and all, I think that got out of hand. Then, Mickey was ordered to kill him. End of story. I know no more. The big man wanted him dead," McIlhinney continued.

"Did you hear the phone call between Mickey and the big man, when he arrived at the house in Ballycastle?" Bristow asked, looking up.

"Yeah, it was short and sweet. He said, Philip's in bed with this woman dressed as Wonder Woman, mask and all. He described her, short strawberry blonde and pale. Then bang! We then had a body to clear up."

"George McCool?" Jube continued.

"I saw that happen, too. Mickey shot him in the head at the old pub in Ballyramsey. It came from out of nowhere. The big man had found out that George had sold pictures of the scene to the newspaper. It was just a question of disloyalty. We were then asked to dispose of the body, and Stewie knew somewhere up near the old Control Tower at Ballyhalbert. I liked wee George. That was a shite thing to do."

"Just as a point of reference," Massey began. "There's a good 10-15-year prison sentence for what you've admitted to so far. So, whilst this is useful information, as I'm sure Jube will agree, you'll need to produce 24 carat gold intelligence to prevent you from spending your days in HM Maghaberry."

Andrew looked down at his feet. His leg shook again. It was as if he was summoning up the courage for what came next.

"You know what would be really interesting?" Jube scanned his notebook.

"What? I'm trying?" McIlhinney stuttered.

"If you could tell us a lot more about the big man's set up.

What does he trade on? Drugs? People trafficking? Where does the money come from?"

"Oh Jesus. I mean, I know bits and pieces, people I've met and wee jobs I've been given. But I don't have the inside track. I'm not one of the major players."

"So, who is?" Massey jumped in.

"There are about seventy shareholders. They're spread across Ireland, the UK, Spain, Italy, and America. There's one in Gibraltar, I think. The money flows into multiple offshore accounts. The shareholders all have nicknames. I just can't think of them, but they'll come to me. They're foreign sounding names."

"How do you know all this? For a small player, this seems a pretty high level of detail," Jube listened as Massey fired another question. She was now moving out of observer zone. But her line of question was, as always, brilliant.

"This is second-hand information. I got drunk with Mickey's son one night in Belfast. We were seriously smashed. It all came out. You've met his son, I believe? Ethan Smyth? He and Mac were the ones you nicked over at Eden Vale."

"Ethan is Mickey's son? Well, I guess that scans. He suggested several times in interview that he was utterly bulletproof. He told you all this? Drunk? Why?" Jube grabbed the reins back.

"Why the hell not? I'm not stupid. I have ambitions. I wanted to be a shareholder one day. I thought by understanding the process, I'd have a little advantage." For the first time, Andrew smiled.

"You still haven't told us about the empire. What did they trade on?"

Andrew looked Jube in the face, his leg stopped shaking and he settled himself deeper in his seat.

"Okay, okay. This is deal time. I can tell you what I think was traded and how. But that's going to need some protection for me."

Jube looked at Bristow and Massey, before realising that he was the only one in the room who had that that level of authority.

"As a freebie. I'll tell you that most of the shareholders have paramilitary pasts. Mostly provos. But one or two ex-loyalist big names have crept in recently. Those links may have come from Philip Bradley. I got the feeling that they saw organised crime as the next career move. It started with weapons and ammunition, and now it's drugs and money laundering. That's the clever bit. Right, that's the end of the freebie two-minute introduction," McIlhinney smiled again. The young man had changed from a nervous lad, keen to help and a little naïve, to a more professional criminal. The patter was there, Jube thought. 'Do I really want to give this fella a deal?'

"Before we talk deals," Massey leapt in again. "Maybe we ought to open your eyes a little?" Jube knew where this was going and needed to wrestle back control of the interview. Bristow had been on her best behaviour, but she was only a sergeant. Jube needed to control things. He interrupted Massey and jumped on her line of questioning.

"The big man asked your brother to kill you yesterday. He was at the window, he was firing at you, and he threw the firebomb into the boot of the Metro that nearly killed you." Jube almost spat the words at Andrew.

"You're lying. Stewie would never do that to me."

"Really? What if I told you we have a recording of Stewart admitting to being the man in the window? Oh, and then he told a crowded pub you were killed. Most of them believed him. We have that on tape, too."

"No. That can't be right. They think I'm dead? I don't believe you." Andrew violently shook his head.

"Don't you? You don't think Stewart's head was turned by the big man. Maybe the offer of money and a bit of attention. He's actually a sad little bastard, your brother. I should know, I've been working with him. He's all fart and no shite." Bristow finally joined the party.

Jube circled the word recordings in his notebook, as he didn't actually know whether the recordings existed. It was informed guesswork based on his faith in Mr Singh.

"So, we could all just pretend you're dead?" Bristow continued. "We wouldn't need to worry about a deal then. We'd figure this stuff out, anyway."

"You wouldn't figure it out. I'll give you the lot if you give me immunity from prosecution. Treat me like Black, McGrady, Kirkpatrick from the supergrass trials. Give me a new name, move my family away from here. In return, I'll give you access to all seventy of the shareholders. I may not know their names, but I know enough," he continued.

Jube tapped his pencil on the table and screwed his face up. He was feeling forced into a corner and there was something about Andrew that didn't feel right.

"I need to piss," McIlhinney chirped. "You can talk about it then. Talk to your bosses, whatever. Just find me a deal." Bristow followed McIlhinney as he headed for the locked door. The Palace Barracks security post was waiting outside and would escort him to the toilet. Jube needed some time to think.

With Andrew McIlhinney taking an awfully long time to relieve himself in the hospital lavatories, Jube had all the time he needed, and Marie Bristow also took the opportunity to recharge her police radio in the makeshift interview room. She hated the chunkiness of the radio and was one of many who had preferred the old-fashioned transistors that were more lightweight, but much less reliable. Soon enough, with the rise of mobile phones, she knew she'd be on call 24/7. There would be no hiding place anymore.

However, with the set almost dead, she decided to check the radio was still working and switched it on.

"Romeo Uniform 7-4, are you receiving? This is Watchman, Repeat Romeo Uniform 7-4, are you receiving?"

"Oh my god," Bristow, panicking, hurried back to the radio and quickly picked it up.

"This is Romeo Uniform 7-4, Watchman, I'm receiving. What's the craic, Watchman? I'm off duty and half asleep," she lied.

"Who's Watchman?" Jube asked Orla.

"It's the control centre for Special Branch. If they're trying to get hold of Bristow, then the shit has really hit the fan," Massey explained.

"Romeo Uniform 7-4 reports of a disturbance at the home of Tango Foxtrot 5-5. He's requesting attendance by a senior officer."

"Tango Foxtrot 5-5 is Eric Rogers," Massey whispered to Jube. "He lives over in Cultra, near Holywood. Massive swanky house overlooking the sea. Right opposite the Royal North of Ireland Yacht Club."

"Of course, he does," Jube said sarcastically. "He wouldn't have a wee bungalow, would he?"

"Why can't Special Branch attend?" Bristow responded to Watchman, clearly frustrated.

"They are at a major incident at Crossmaglen. You were asked for by name, Sarge. Over."

"Show me as attending the scene, Watchman. Await my updates."

"Romeo Uniform 9-6 is already on the scene, of his own volition. He was not radioed for support. But there's been radio silence for twenty minutes." The radio was tinny, and reception was fading in and out. But Bristow knew Uniform 9-6 was Stewart McIlhinney.

"I'm going to have to go, but I've no car here," Bristow replied. "I walked here with Jube, and remember, I'm in an off-the-books interview during my off-duty hours. This might get messy."

Jube picked up his handheld. "Is anyone receiving? We have a bit of an issue here. Marie Bristow has been asked to attend Eric's house for a reported disturbance, but we have no transport." For a few seconds, there was silence.

"McNally here. Myself, Jones and Richmond and the QD

team are still packing up in Ballyramsey. Wendy might be free?" There was a pause.

"I'm too drunk to help, sorry," Wendy finally replied. "It's best to be honest, I think. I found a bottle of Pernod in the briefing room and, well, it's been a long day."

"That's my bottle, Wendy. But I'll come and pick Marie up," Virginia chimed in. "I have the blue Mondeo. I'll be there in twenty minutes. Is there any reason you're not using an RUC panda to pick you up?"

"It's a long story, Virginia. Just trust me on this," Bristow responded.

"Righto, no problem. I'm on my way," Virginia signed off.

With the clock ticking, Andrew McIlhinney now appeared back at the door with his guard. He had a rather self-satisfied look on his face, Jube thought. Almost as if he felt he had the upper hand now. As the door was secured again and the guard settled back into his seat next to the door outside, Andrew checked on progress.

"So, ladies and gent. Do we have a deal?"

"Things have changed a little since you went to powder your nose. Maybe you'd like to hear about the current developments?" Bristow explained.

"Sure, but there'll be no more freebies. So, this better not be a tactic."

"Your brother, who is off sick with a bullet-wound sustained when he was trying to kill you, is currently outside Eric Rogers' house. There are reports of a disturbance. Care to shed any light on that?" Bristow continued.

"He's a silly bastard," Andrew snapped back. "That's all I'm going to say. You had your freebies. But if you're telling me the truth about Stewie trying to kill me, why should I be bothered, anyway? If he gets killed, well, that's his problem."

Andrew crossed his arms like a sulking child, and his leg started shaking again.

Jube Spencer was flicking frantically between two pages of notes and suddenly looked up, clearly trying to resolve something in his mind. Massey saw he was troubled.

"What's are you thinking, Jube? More theories?" she asked.

"Hold on. Just hold on, one moment," he replied.

Jube strolled back to the locked door and opened it slightly. "Are you armed?" he asked the guard outside.

"I am, Sir."

"Take Mr McIlhinney to the canteen, get him some food. Don't listen to any of his nonsense. Then lock him back in his room until I come and find you. I reckon I'll be about an hour." Jube walked back to his interview room chair.

"Sergeant Bristow, can I suggest you wait in the car park for Virginia Curry to arrive? Orla, please rest, I'll be back soon. We need to pause this interview. I have a theory I need to test."

"If you insist," Massey responded, rolling her eyes. "But I hate secrets. Can't you talk to me first?"

"I just have an inkling. That's all. Might be nothing." Jube stood up, straightened his tie, looked over to Massey and repeated. "Get some rest, Orla. Please."

The guard, with the door still open, let Bristow out first and then grabbed Andrew to escort him away. Jube was throwing his notes into a leather bag and preparing to leave the scene, too.

"What the hell...? Where is everyone going? What about our deal?" Andrew McIlhinney protested as he was led away. "You need me!" he shouted.

"Maybe..." Jube muttered and headed out of the door.

Forty-Four

"Something feels wrong," Jones announced. Carl handed him a pint of lager and asked, "Does that make things all better?"

"Normally it would, Carl. But I just have this terrible feeling we should be back and supporting Virginia," he replied. "She shouldn't be dealing with that alone."

"He's got a point, you know," Jenny agreed as she eyeballed a vodka and orange that Carl had presented. "The problem is there are no vehicles here. Wendy's taken the Land Rover back to Belfast and is now drinking Pernod, probably to excess, and we need the minibus to get home with the equipment."

"Is there anything we can borrow in the garages around the back?" Jenny asked, before looking over at Jones and smiling.

"What?" Jones replied, taking a small sip of his pint. "What's funny?"

"The hearse!" Jenny laughed again. "We borrowed that bloody hearse from a pub in Stratford, remember?" Jones smiled. "Oh yeah, it still had the curtains in the back. We hid in there to stake out Stephen Finch."

"Okay, okay," Jones grinned. "Let's check the back. Maybe Wee Joe has something usable out there. But I'm not sure I can deal with another funeral car."

The team filed out of the pub towards a collection of three small garages in the garden of the Hunter's Arms. The outbuilding looked barely touched for years. Weeds were growing in front of the doors and there was a musty smell that seemed to come from the garage on the right. McNally pulled open the door and discovered bags full of mouldy bread and rolls. Behind them, in a large bin bag, were packets of iced gems and cakes.

"Looks like Wee Joe had a christening or birthday party lined up before he got the message to vanish for a few weeks," McNally said, throwing the mouldy items outside. "I wonder how his wee holiday is going?"

"This isn't going to get us to Virginia any quicker," Jenny intervened. "Let's get the middle one open."

Jones and McNally grabbed the handle of the centre garage and pulled with all their strength. Jenny dislodged a large weed that was blocking the movement of the garage door, and after some heaving, the door gave way. Inside appeared to be an Aladdin's cave of Irish beer merchandise, some of it untouched since the late 1970s. Jones found Phoenix tankards, Satzenbrau bar trays, Perry's beer mats and countless bottles of Harp Lancer, that seemed to be a higher percentage. Jones and McNally were instantly fascinated, but Jenny persuaded them away.

"Focus!" she called over. They sheepishly moved away from the loot.

The final garage showed more promise but was locked, but not for long. McNally, using a random piece of wire found in the centre garage, soon had the door open and, sitting rusting inside, was a light blue Fiat cabriolet.

"What is that thing?" Jenny asked, squeezing between the passenger side and the wall to get a better look. "I mean... I realise it's a car. But it looks a little boxy."

"It's a Fiat Ritmo," McNally answered. "I drove one for a while, it was alright. I seem to remember I wrote it off by driving into the back of a stationary crane after a heavy night near Dublin. This looks like it's from the early 1980s. But judging by the spiders' webs and the smell of mildew, this hasn't been out in a while."

"And there's no roof either?" Jenny added.

"Don't be daft, Jenny. Of course, there's a roof. It's simply a convertible, it'll be tucked away at the back somewhere. Oh, hold on, scratch that," Jones corrected himself after peering around the car. "There's no roof. Jenny was right. It's been cut off." There were a few stifled laughs.

"Okay, leave this to me." McNally found the bonnet catch and checked for signs of life in the old vehicle. The engine was thick with dust and McNally sneezed loudly. "Jones, can you see if there's any petrol in it?"

"That's an affirmative. There's a half a tank," Jones confirmed after checking the dials.

McNally fiddled and adjusted the car for over twenty minutes whilst Jenny sat in the driving seat occasionally turning the ignition key and checking for signs of life. Jones, with no car maintenance skills and no driving licence, watched on with his hands on his hips. McNally then used his hot-wiring skills to get the car started. There was a plume of black smoke that engulfed the garage and Jenny carefully drove the vehicle out of the garage.

"Right," Jenny shouted. "Thanks to McNally's genius, I guess we'll head to Rogers' gaff in Cultra. Is there anything else you need from us? Are you coming too?" Jones slotted into the passenger seat.

"I think we're grand," McNally replied. "I'll join you in the minibus once we're sorted here. Make sure you're in contact and let me know what's going down..." But McNally was interrupted as Mr Singh ran out into the garden, looking excited.

"I have news. Using a little fingerprint scanner, I've borrowed,

I've matched Michael Doyle's prints to Mickey Reilly's. It's not foolproof, but I'm 97.3% sure they're the same person. It's confirmed."

"That's fabulous news! But borrowed? From whom?" McNally replied.

"That's not important." Mr Singh dodged the question. "They won't miss it and it gives us the intelligence we need. Doesn't it?"

"It's a result, Mr Singh. Top work." McNally slapped Mr Singh on the back as they waited for the pair to leave for Cultra.

Jones was delighted to spot that the radio cassette player was in full working condition. Wee Joe's had left his Van Morrison and Christy Moore tape collection in the glove compartment.

"Right, on that new piece of news, away with you both," McNally called out. "I can't imagine this is anything other than Rogers' getting jumpy. But we certainly need you on the ground there. You'd best let Jube know you're en route."

Jones was already on the case. With his handheld in transmit mode, he reached the old spook and gave an estimated time of arrival. There was relief in Jube's voice.

As Jenny took a right out of the main village road and, for a few seconds, enjoying the feel of the cold air blowing through the car after a night trapped in a hot room, the drizzle started. It only lasted around fifteen minutes, but by the time the Fiat had reached the main road, Jones and Jenny looked like they'd been jet-washed.

In the meantime, Virginia had picked up Marie Bristow and they were making good time. Virginia, resplendent in an orange summer dress and brown Clarks sandals, had wasted no time whatsoever in dispelling the myth about older drivers. She navigated the roads between Belfast and Cultra like a rally champion, on one occasion overtaking three cars on a blind corner and missing an oncoming ambulance by mere inches. She barely turned a hair. Bristow was as white as a ghost.

"These Mondeos have some oomph about them, if you really put your foot down," Virginia explained, her dangly earrings jolting backwards and forwards as she weaved expertly through the country roads.

"So, I see," Bristow managed to reply, gripping onto the car's interior like her life depended on it.

They sped through the outskirts of Holywood and into the opulence of Cultra, stopping only briefly to view an ordinance survey map of the area. But they needn't have bothered, as Eric Rogers' very modern house stood out on the lavish beachfront like a turd in a punchbowl.

"My god," Virginia said as she pulled up next to the kerb. "That house matches his personality. It's just awful and pretentious. What's it called?"

"Autumn House. Yeah, it's pretty clinical and doesn't match the townhouses on either side. I'd better look. I wonder if that's Stewart's car?" Bristow looked over at a red Ford Fiesta. "More importantly, what the hell is he doing here? He's signed off work and, unless all our intel is wrong, he doesn't know his cover is blown."

"He told the control centre he was here?" Virginia asked.

"Yes, he clearly still has use of his police radio. He's shown as dealing with this disturbance. But hasn't communicated for some time. It makes little sense to me." Bristow spoke as she rifled through her kit bag, checking her firearm and that her radio was fully charged.

"Marie, this stinks a bit. Take this handheld. Press transmit if you need support. I'll be out here if you need me." Virginia passed the YCU handheld to Bristow and she stepped out and slammed the door. She grabbed her service torch and focused it on the unlit steps leading to Rogers' door. It was eerily quiet.

Autumn House stuck out awkwardly between two traditional seaside townhouses. Contemporary homes are often distinguished by clean lines, geometric shapes, wide open floor plans, and thoughtful, intentional décor. Marie liked interior décor and had half an eye on upgrading her house in Ballymacash. But this was a very different proposition. All the joy seemed to have been stripped out and just the basics remained, with nothing that screamed 'welcome home'. Bristow's torch picked out vast windows, dark wood panels and plain stone tiles. There was no front garden or foliage, just shingle covering every conceivable patch of open space and a basic stone pathway. Eric's black Mercedes, a perk of the job, was sitting under a carport and an automatic light switched on as she stepped closer to the front door.

Looking around the doorway, she made out a thick rope bell-pull, which she yanked and heard a pleasing loud bell sound reverberate around the inside of the house. An internal light came on and she saw the silhouette of a figure walk to greet her. It was Eric Rogers himself. He opened the door, just a few inches to observe his visitor, and then, spotting Bristow's familiar face, he opened it wide.

"Ah, Sergeant Bristow. Thanks for attending in the wee small hours. But I'm afraid you may have had a wasted trip."

"Morning, Sir. We had reports of a disturbance and PC Stewart McIlhinney taking the call. Is this correct?"

"You're correct. But it was a false alarm. He's gone back to his bed now, too. Kind of him to attend when he was off sick." Rogers was standing, purposely blocking Bristow's view into the house, in his white and blue flannelette pyjamas.

"Was there a disturbance then? What made you make the call?"

"I thought I saw a figure in the back garden. But I was mistaken. Maybe it was a Sika deer? We're beginning to see more of them around these parts. Sorry that you've made an unnecessary trip out here."

"Well, Sir, you know the drill, I'd better take a look around." Bristow took a step forward into the house and Rogers grudgingly let her walk inside. He shut the door behind her.

The inside of the house was almost brutally minimalist. There were white walls, black furniture and the occasional small black and white prints or photographs of seascapes. There were no family photos, no signs of family life, no nostalgia and absolutely no mess. However, as Rogers showed her around, starting with the kitchen, she noticed the sign of a small fresh wound on the back of his head.

She then followed him to the empty bedrooms, all pristine but bereft of warmth or love, and then finally the down a long corridor which, she guessed, led to the living room and dining room. Automatic lights illuminated the way and Rogers said nothing as he opened doors and silently urged her to follow.

"Nothing to see, Sergeant Bristow," he reassured her before they finally emerged into an impressive living room. Impressive in terms of the incredible view, firstly over the large but sparse garden and then, in the distance, the beach and angry Irish Sea. Floodlights shone brightly and Bristow wondered whether anyone could ever tire of the scenery.

"Is this where you saw the figure, Sir?"

"Yes, just over at the back. Follow me," Rogers slid back some patio doors and led Bristow down a dimly lit path past a row of tall conifers.

It was halfway down the path that Marie Bristow starting to feel oddly uncomfortable. She had a feeling that she was being watched and thought she heard other people close by. Her intuition was hastily proved right when a large figure jumped out from the gloom and pistol-whipped her across the back of her head, and she fell to the ground. She had no time to react, no way of defending herself, and the pain was instantly immense.

The last thing she was aware of was the coolness of the concrete path and the sound of Rogers' exclaiming "Oh dear," loudly before she lost consciousness and her kitbag smashed onto the ground behind her.

Outside, Virginia was listening to BBC World Service on the

car stereo. It was a story about the ongoing war in Bosnia and America's recent bombing raids aimed at ending the ongoing turmoil in the Balkans. The sound of the explosions from the story and the correspondent explaining the tragedy unfolding almost masked the sudden white noise coming from Virginia's handheld. But something piqued her interest and she held it up to her ear.

"Put her back in the garden room," Rogers said. Virginia recognised the voice straightaway and was quickly on edge. Something was wrong and Marie Bristow had never been taught to push the *all channels* button on the handheld to alert colleagues to an emergency or danger. This couldn't have been deliberate.

Virginia thought about her own predicament. She was not an operative. She had never been engaged in any type of real time operation. But she had taught her YCU trainees for many years to use their instincts and draw on their common sense. Common sense was something Virginia Curry had in abundance. Therefore, she made two quick decisions. Firstly, she released the handbrake on the Mondeo and let it slowly reverse down the hill, ensuring a bit of distance between herself and the scene. She didn't want anyone inside to think Bristow had a partner waiting for her in the car. Secondly, she switched the channel of the handheld and raised Declan McNally.

"McNally," she whispered, "it's Virginia. I'm at Cultra, outside Eric Rogers' house. I think something terrible is happening. Can you hear the conversation on the open channel?"

"I'm hearing everything loud and clear. It's gone totally quiet. Virginia, are you safe?"

"Yes, I'm outside the property. I'm tucked away out of sight."

"Okay, I'll ensure everyone stays off the open channel. Sit tight. Jones and Jenny are heading your way, if their car makes it. I'll contact them now."

"Shouldn't we get hold of the RUC? Who can we trust?" Virginia asked breathlessly.

"I'm afraid we have no idea; we're going to have to keep this in-house at the moment. I'm so sorry you've been dragged into this." McNally sounded concerned.

"Oh, I don't mind. I'm just worried about poor Marie. We were getting along famously. I do hope she's okay. But I'll sign off for now. I'll keep my eyes open."

Virginia immediately switched back to the open channel. The white noise was still evident, but there was still background mumbling and indecipherable chatter. She ducked down in the driver's seat and listened hard.

Back in Ballyramsey, Mr Singh and the QD lads had stopped packing away the last remaining surveillance equipment from the earlier operation. Mr Singh found a lead from one of his many storage boxes and attached it to his handheld. He then switched on the last remaining sound board and speaker to amplify the sound and de-tuned the white noise.

"Just put her on the sofa," Rogers said. "She'll regain consciousness soon. Check her bag Stewart, look for her radio and gun."

"Good heavens," Mr Singh exclaimed. "There's at least two of them. This isn't good at all."

"What's the plan?" Stewart McIlhinney replied.

"Cable tie her to the sofa, wait for her to wake up and find out what MI5 know. I think she'll be co-operative with a sawn-off shotgun pointed at her," another voice said.

"Who's that?" Mr Singh asked. McNally shrugged his shoulders.

"I've got a terrible feeling it's Mickey Reilly," McNally had his head against the speaker. "It's his odd hybrid accent. Marie is in a great deal of danger."

"I tried to stop her from coming in. As you asked. This is our issue. It has nothing to do with Sergeant Bristow. Can't we just bundle her up and leave her somewhere?" Rogers sounded concerned.

"No, no, Eric. You know better than that. She can name us all.

She's been in your house. We'll extract as much information out of her as possible and then we'll have to kill her." There was that bitter voice again.

The fixer, Mickey Reilly, had some more clearing up to do.

Forty-Five

The floodlights illuminating the back garden at Autumn House were set to automatic and they unnerved Stewart McIlhinney every time they switched themselves on.

"Stewart, catch yourself on. It's the fecking conifers swaying near the sensors. Focus." Mickey nudged the youngster. "Anyway, we have much bigger issues to deal with. We came here to sort out the sudden interest in our activities from the law." He turned to Eric.

"Eric, the big man has been paying you for nearly ten years now. You deal with the terrorism, the paramilitaries, and your regular day-to-day crimes. We get on with the major stuff behind the scenes, you ensure we are not bothered. You get a nice little cut. Then you can buy lovely houses like this, can't you?"

"Yes, I'm aware," Eric replied.

"So, what went so catastrophically wrong? Why are we now being hunted? Why is the entire empire in jeopardy?" Mickey walked around the Garden Room like an angry headteacher.

"Nothing has gone wrong. I've kept my end of the deal. MI5 is the issue; I have no control over them. They have effectively gone around me to get answers for the Philip Bradley and George McCool murders. You screwed up by going on this pointless, vindictive killing spree."

"I screwed up? Are you insane? Have you got some kind of death wish?" He picked up the sawn-off shotgun from the sofa beside the unconscious Bristow and pointed it at Rogers. The pyjamaed man immediately recoiled.

"Sit down next to your fecking Sergeant, Eric. Tie him up, Stewart."

Stewart grabbed another two cable ties and pulled Rogers' hands behind his back, before securing him to the wooden arm of the sofa with another tie.

"There really is no need for this," Rogers stammered as McIlhinney manhandled him into position. "I'm still part of your empire and part of the solution."

"You were saying, Eric. How else have I screwed up?" The gun was now pointed inches from his head and suddenly Rogers looked like a vulnerable older man in pyjamas, totally out of his depth.

"I've given you the dirt on twenty-four leading policemen across the UK who have a responsibility for organised crime. These are CID leads, superintendents, and commissioners. Every single one has been blackmailed. And where there's been no dirt, we've made it up. Remember Paul Taverner in Edinburgh and Bob Flowers in Manchester? You threatened to send their families fake reports of child abuse, dalliances with prostitutes or even necrophilia. Just to get your way. Now the big man and his shareholders are living handsomely as those blackmailed senior officers avert their eyes from your empire's ongoing behaviour."

"True. But they've still had their successes," Mickey smiled sarcastically.

"Yeah, your competitors. Anyone that dared enter your territory, we moved the police chess pieces around and they were soon identified and imprisoned. Then, the empire continued. You and a team of fixers. It's been an incredible success."

"Until you wobbled, Eric. Did it get too close to home? Worried that you might lose your promotion?"

"How many more times? This is MI5, not me. Remember, I even blew up one of my own senior officers using confiscated Semtex to keep things sweet in Northern Ireland. For the empire."

"And yet she survived. You couldn't even do that properly. At least I pulled the trigger when it came to it. That Isadora Brown, she was becoming a pain."

"Again, that was insanity," Rogers nervously replied. "Brown was already incapacitated. That was just blood lust. She wasn't doing you any harm. From what I understand, she wasn't even working on the same investigation."

"Are you still criticising my approach? Are you insane? It would not concern me one iota if I blew your head off with this gun. You're worthless now, Rogers. Shut up, old man," Reilly shouted, within an inch of Rogers' face.

The automatic light in the garden came on again. Stewart turned and stared into the bleakness of the early morning Cultra gloom. There was nothing there.

"There's no-one out there, lad. Stop this," Mickey put the gun down again, on an armchair a few metres from Eric and his sergeant. The tension dropped for a moment. Rogers caught his breath.

"Where's the family, Eric? I half-expected to have to put the frighteners on your wife and daughter tonight. It's actually been a bit of a relief. I don't like threatening women. Present company accepted."

"They are all in Norfolk. My daughter is off to university. They took the dog too. I'm guessing your dislike of hurting women didn't include Isadora, Martha Maddison or the Sergeant here? They're fair game?"

"I don't normally kill women, but policewomen and spooks don't count. They've opted for the career, they knew the risks and I'm one of those risks. So, yeah, fair game. Yeah, Isadora Brown didn't adapt to the risks, did she? But I didn't kill Martha Maddison. Full stop."

Mickey perched himself on the edge of the armchair and stared at Bristow, waiting for her to regain consciousness.

"So, who did?" Stewart piped up.

"I don't know. Hold up. Did you assume I killed her too?" Mickey snapped back.

"Yeah, kind of," Stewart admitted, taking a few steps back towards the door.

"Jesus, I'm not a monster. I just have a job to do. I don't enjoy it. Like, I'm guessing Bristow here has a family. Yourself, Eric, I know you're married with an older kid. I don't want to deprive people of their mothers and fathers. But a job is a job." Mickey suddenly sounded oddly laid back about his role as a fixer and an assassin.

Bristow moaned, and the three men turned to look at her. Her black trouser suit had been muddied by Stewart and Rogers dragging her up the path and her make-up had smudged under both eyes. Her bobbed hair was caked with blood around the back, and it had smeared onto Rogers' expensive-looking furniture.

As soon as consciousness arrived, she remembered her predicament. She had both hands tied together tightly, and then a loop had been placed between her hands and around the arm of the sofa. Her legs were undone, but she was going nowhere. She was in pain, uncomfortable, and already in survival mode.

She saw her gun and police radio, with the battery unclipped, on the windowsill of the Garden Room and other items scattered nearby. She saw the handheld and the red LED glowing. Why hadn't they spotted that? She also noted that Eric Rogers had also been cable tied to the furniture.

"Welcome back," Mickey said, almost softly. "How's the head?"

"I've felt better," Bristow stared up at Mickey Reilly with real hatred in her eyes.

"We have a few questions for you," he continued. "I guess you could say there's a strong pass or fail element to the questions."

Forty-Six

Jenny had made incredible time speeding through the deserted rural roads and half empty main carriageways in a car with no roof. Jones had passed the time listening to an old mix tape that he'd found at the bottom of his rucksack. It contained the likes of Stone Roses, Teenage Fanclub, Primal Scream, Supergrass, Jesus and Mary Chain and even some Boo Radleys. Jenny, who had grown up on Motown and the Philadelphia sound, was getting used to some of Jones' favourites and found the energy of the distorted melodies and shoutable choruses infectious. However, Jones' need for loud music had prevented them from hearing the chatter on the handheld.

It took a Jones turning the cassette tape over for the muttered conversations in Autumn House to finally cut through in the Fiat, with the outside elements also making life difficult.

"Wait," she called over to Jones. "Can't you hear that?"

They both listened intently to the open channel and realised the situation. Jones changed the channel and spoke to McNally.

"You took your time," McNally answered. "What have you two been doing? We've been trying to reach you for a good forty-five minutes."

"Jones was his playing music too loud. Apologies. Fill us in," Jenny shouted.

"We believe Sergeant Bristow has been lured to Autumn House, Eric Rogers' home, under false pretences. She's in danger. Eric, Mickey Reilly, and Stewart McIlhinney are there too. Reilly has talked about murdering Isadora and he's given a rather fulsome explanation of Eric Rogers' role in the organised crime empire. He's been helping them blackmail senior police leaders across the UK."

"Blimey. That's bigger than we thought. So, what do you need from us?" Jones spoke over the sound of the Fiat bravely accelerating through the darkness.

"You're going to have to get Bristow out of there. I'll reach Jube and we'll plan some reinforcements. But we are unclear of how many of the Knock Road mob are involved in this. Are you fully equipped?" McNally queried.

"Equipped but soaked to the skin. We slung two equipment packs in the boot. Can anyone get us a plan of Autumn House? So, we know what we're dealing with?" Jones asked.

"I can do that," Mr Singh answered, listening in. "Give me ten minutes."

"Keep the line clear, Jones," McNally underlined. "Don't put any more over-rated modern rock onto that knackered stereo and concentrate on the job, in hand. That's an order."

"Over-rated? Are you..." Jones began. "Roger, over and out," Jenny shouted in anticipation of Jones' next sentence, before grabbing the handheld and switching it back to the open channel. "Focus, Jones. For Pete's sake!" Jenny shouted, as she rounded a rural corner at top speed.

Back in Belfast, Jube Spencer was jogging. He hadn't run in over eight years. He operated with guile and physical exertion was unbecoming. But this was different. Jube tucked his old school tie into his shirt and jogged to Queen's University, where he was amongst the alumni. He knew full-well that in the early hours of the morning, hardly anyone would take any notice of an ageing spook gently jogging through the half light of the city.

He paced down Fitzwilliam Street, overtaking a slow-moving milk float, before crossing over onto University Road and was there in no time at all. As he passed a bus shelter, he checked his reflection and restyled his hair, ensured his shirt was smoothed and untucked his tie. One clasp on his leather bag had come undone and he rectified that, too.

He dashed onto the university grounds, past an avenue of well-manicured trees and bushes, before jumping up the steps towards the entrance hall, where he knocked loudly on the glass door. It took around twenty seconds for an elderly man in a smart green security uniform to spot Jube and open the front door.

"Mr Spencer, dear God! It's almost 3am. Can this not wait?"

"I'm sorry, Henry, this really couldn't be avoided. But I'll be in and out in less than five minutes. I promise."

Henry, clearly suffering with his left leg, swiftly opened the door. He led Jube to the University's impressive first floor library facility and flicked a switch that saw the room light up in seconds. The fluorescent tubes made both of them wince slightly.

The old man had often found himself dealing with Jube Spencer's late-night visits and was aware of the spook's important role in Belfast, even though it had never been properly disclosed or explained. Somehow it didn't need to be. Henry simply assumed Jube was some kind of top-level government official and Spencer had no need to add further detail. The word 'spy' was superfluous. He was *important*.

Likewise, Jube, as a Queen's University old boy, knew exactly what he was looking for and headed straight over to the normally very comprehensive history section.

"Anything you're looking for in particular?" Henry called over in his gentle Belfast accent.

"Roman history, Henry. Should be around here," Jube ran his

finger along the Dewey decimalised books before pulling out a tatty copy of Boardman's Oxford History of the Roman World.

"My word. There are hardly any academic books on Roman History here at all. Have they scrapped the Ancient History degrees? Are they restocking?"

"There's been some thefts. It's all a bit of a mystery, really. The Vice Chancellor has even talked about putting shop-style security tags on every book to prevent them from being stolen. But it seems so awful."

Jube was only partially listening.

"I see. That's distressing. You couldn't rustle me up a cup of tea, could you Henners, old chap?"

"You've got some cheek. But I wouldn't want you trying the vending machine. It tastes like pond water. I'll brew up some Nambarrie for you. You still take one sugar?"

"You're a gent, Henry. One sugar and well stewed please."

Jube checked that the old man had made his way back to the night porter's office before dashing over to the row of offices adjoining the library. He slid his set of stainless-steel lock-picks from their leather pouch and used them to deftly break into the larger of the offices. He then squeezed his ample torso behind the desk in the Head Librarian's Office and booted up the computer before gaining access to the University's Management Information System. He then spent five frantic minutes checking the records of former students and attendance statistics. He was looking for one name and he found it. He allowed himself a little contended smile.

He hurriedly closed down the computer, wiping the keyboard clean with his monogrammed handkerchief and locked the door behind him. Jube then walked calmly back to the Ancient History section of the library and settled into a plastic chair, spreading the History of the Roman World book open wide on the table in front of him.

Henry re-appeared moments later, gamefully making his way through the library with two overfilled cups of tea. When Jube saw him approach, he sped over to relieve him of one. Jube took a quick but delicate swig off the top of the cup.

"Oh, that hit the spot. Thank you so much. I'll have to come here at 3am more often for tea like this."

"Well, I'll admit, it's broken my shift up a little. And it's always good to see a friendly face. What is it you're looking for, if you don't mind me asking, Mr Spencer?"

"I'm looking into Tiberius, the Roman Emperor. Have you heard of him?"

"No, I'll have to pass on that one. What's so interesting and urgent about him?" Henry took a big gulp of his tea, having settled into the seat opposite Jube.

"Righto, Tiberius was perhaps Emperor Augustus' last, desperate choice for a successor, and that's a long story in itself. But when he took the reins, it was clear Tiberius wasn't really interested in being emperor, which would be bad enough, but he was also very paranoid."

"Ah, I see," Henry said, nodding sagely.

"What's more, he actually let a subordinate, called Sejanus, a soldier, social climber and schemer, run things for him." Jube flicked through the History of the Roman World book and wrote a few notes in his pocketbook.

After a pause, Henry, who was hunting around in his pockets for some biscuits, turned to Jube and said, "I don't really follow, sorry old son. The last book I read was by Alan Titchmarsh. But I'm a good listener. Who was your man, Sejanus...?"

"Well, Henners, I think this is the guts of my case. Sejanus was a back-seat driver and people saw this as treason against the emperor. This led to treason trials with pretty flimsy evidence and multiple executions, including Sejanus himself. He wanted to be the emperor, but everyone hated him and used conspiracy theories against him to have him executed."

"And your case is a bit like that?" Henry asked, already looking a little lost in the conversation.

"Well, there's certainly a back-seat driver, who they are code-naming Sejanus. There are several traitors, most of whom have been killed already, and there are some unanswered questions that I don't think Roman History is going to help with."

"So, what happened with Tiberius?" Henry continued, politely trying to sound interested.

"Good question. When Tiberius finally died, of natural causes, apparently, the people were delighted and raised the chant 'To the Tiber with Tiberius!'. Caligula arrived as a relief, but then pretty much anyone would have seemed better than the late, unlamented Tiberius. But then we know how Caligula turned out, don't we?" Jube smiled.

"Do we?" Henry shrugged. "I'm not sure..."

"Not to worry, Henners," Jube interrupted. "That has nothing whatsoever to do with my case." Jube picked up the book and walked back to some of the empty Roman History shelves.

"I saw a really dirty film called Caligula once. I'm sure Helen Mirren was in it. Is any of it based on fact?" Henry smirked.

Jube couldn't help but laugh as all his theorising seemed sadly lost on Henry. Who, to be fair, had the scantest details of Jube's highly complicated case. However, he had just found two Garibaldi biscuits in his pocket and for that, Jube would have forgiven him anything. Having returned from the book racks, they munched in silence together as Jube tried to pull the last pieces of the puzzle together. But speed was the essence.

Jube then walked slowly behind the old man to the front entrance, thanked him for his above par hospitality, and disappeared into the early morning chill. Henry had just four hours left of his shift and was now a biscuit down.

Forty-Seven

Jenny guided the roofless Fiat to a halt right behind Virginia's blue Mondeo. She had been given a rough layout of Autumn House by Mr Singh en route, who had found the developer's drawings on the local council's planning database, held on a clunky Winchester disk that he'd accessed remarkably easily. The house had a bizarre design and there were definitely weak spots they could exploit.

They both exited the vehicle, each with a fully stocked equipment rucksack, and quietly settled into Virginia's car for a few moments to assess the situation.

"Goodness me," Virginia exclaimed. "You're both so wet, you're actually steaming."

"Apologies, can you turn the heaters on full blast? Is there anything we've missed?" Jenny asked, as she slipped into the passenger seat. Virginia adjusted the controls.

"Marie is clearly still struggling from whatever that awful man did to her. But I'm wondering whether she might be gilding the lily to buy a little time," Virginia explained.

"Gilding the what?" Jones questioned.

"Exaggerating things a bit, sorry. One of my mother's expressions. I think she's doing remarkably well in the circumstances. It must be hell in there."

The three of them fell silent as the open channel of the handheld sprang into life again.

"Could I have a glass of water, do you think?" Bristow mumbled. "My head is absolutely banging, and I can't even think straight."

"Stewart, get Sergeant Bristow a glass of water, but this will be her last piece of theatre before the shotgun gets involved," Mickey Reilly calmly responded.

"Right, we're going to have to get in there. Shall we review our approach?" Jenny was taking the lead with gusto, with Virginia watching on.

"Yes, Jen. We are going to access the property via the beach front, through the back garden and then get sight of the scene from what we think is a dining room or some kind of annexe." Jones was almost delineating the route with wild gesticulations.

"Be very careful," Virginia said. "I can't lose anymore of you."

"You won't lose us. But we do need to get on with it," Jenny responded and jumped out of the car, closing the door behind her stealthily. She'd left a large wet patch on the passenger seat. They both then headed towards the beach. Neither showed any signs of tiredness after the operation at Ballyramsey and with the time getting close to 4am.

The pair walked up the hill, turned right down a short passageway running alongside Autumn House, and were soon marching purposefully along a greensward next to the beach. Their shoes squelched as they walked and Jones felt the coldness of the sea air hit him and he glanced over at Jenny, who was gritting her teeth.

"This is where knowing you so well is a bad thing," Jenny said, as she caught him looking over.

"What do mean?"

"Jones, if you were anyone else, this would just be a mission. But now I'm just as worried about you as I am myself."

"Is that a bad thing? I'm worried about you too, it's only natural. Are you having doubts about working with me?"

"Of course not, Jones. I love working with you. I love our uniqueness. But it adds a bit of an extra element, doesn't it? It scares the shit out of me. Taking your boyfriend into a mission where either of us could be killed."

"Fair enough. We'd best not think about it too much then. Let's just get Bristow back. Yeah?"

"Why do you spend your life being grey and overthinking absolutely everything, until we go into battle, and suddenly you're black and white?" Jenny zipped open her rucksack and grabbed the gun.

"I'm terrible at this emotional stuff," Jones replied, and also fetched his firearm from his bag. Jenny kissed the end of his nose and smiled.

"You're just my pet weirdo," she grinned and pointed towards the back gate to Autumn House. "Let's have a squiz. See what we can make out from the gate."

"I've got some of Mr Singh's questionable Russian binoculars. They should be able to see through this gloom." Jones swung them around his neck, and they traipsed through the grass and shingle mix towards the back gate. However, as soon as they got within a few metres of the garden, the automatic security lights came on and Jones put his finger over his lips.

"I can hear something," he whispered. "Is that a door opening?"

They knelt next to the gate and Jones used his binoculars to try to see past the row of conifers towards the back of the house.

"What can you see?" she asked.

"It's Stewart McIlhinney. I can just make out part of the back window through these." Jones handed the binoculars to Jenny.

Jones switched on the handheld and turned the volume right

down to listen into the conversation. But it was too quiet and turning the volume up too loud would risk being heard. Instead, he switched channels.

"Mr Singh, it's Jones, what can you hear?"

"Not much," he replied, enjoying being part of the action. "I think the automatic lights are spooking Stewart. Apparently, he keeps coming outside to check."

"What about Bristow? Is she okay?" Jones asked.

"She pretending to feel nauseous. But I don't think they're buying it. Reilly keeps asking how much we know. She's saying nothing. She's holding firm."

"Okay, Mr Singh. Over and out."

The sound of movement seemed to get louder and closer, before Jones grabbed the binoculars back from Jenny.

"Jen, What the hell are you looking at? Bloody McIlhinney is literally next to the conifers. How did you miss him?"

"I was looking for a way in. I'm not interested in him yet. Follow me. Quietly."

Jenny walked past the gate and towards the end of the row of conifers.

"There's a row of conifers that's at least four trees deep there. If we slide in-between the first two, we won't be seen or heard by those in the back room. But the automatic lights will come on and that'll freak McIlhinney out. Which is a nice bonus." Jenny dived into the conifer row on her hands and knees. Jones followed. The pair made quick progress until they found themselves in line with the back of the house, but where the conifer row thinned out significantly.

Jones grabbed his binoculars again.

"My word. I can see straight into the room. I can see Mickey Reilly. He's standing up next to the patio doors, with a sawn-off shotgun in his hand. I can see Eric Rogers in awful pyjamas. He looks like he's tied to the chair. Bristow is out of view."

"I think I've got a plan." Jenny responded.

"Right. Care to explain?"

"What if I go back to the gate, shoot Stewart McIlhinney from there? Then I'll run back into this row of conifers and see if we can spook Mickey Reilly out from the back room?"

"Spook him? I would think shooting Stewart will bring Reilly outside anyway. What am I doing, Jen?"

"Maybe you can get inside and untie Bristow?" Jenny's brain was working at 100mph.

"That's my job?"

"Yeah, I'm doing the shooting. I'm the marksman now, or markswoman." Jenny then threw a handful of soil from the ground underneath the conifers onto the path. The automatic lights burst into life again and Stewart made his way down the path suspiciously. Jenny prepared to head back towards the gate.

"You're going? We've agreed to this plan then?" Jones whispered.

"I've agreed the plan. Keep up."

Jenny crawled back to the gate and waited for the automatic lights to go off again. There was complete silence amongst the first threats of daylight. Jones could hear his heart beating in his head and the feelings of anxiety up and down his body. But this was why he was employed. This was his job.

After around five long minutes in the darkness, Jones heard Jenny squeeze the trigger and Stewart went down. She'd aimed for his injured arm. Jones guessed the whiteness of the sling made that the easiest target. Jones wasn't expecting the second shot, that burst through his left kneecap and left the young man screaming in agony and as planned, Mickey Reilly then ran outside down towards the gate with his shotgun held in front of him. Stewart was crying out for help.

Jenny had already crawled back up the gap in the row of conifers.

"Whoever is out there," Mickey shouted. "You are a dead man. I will kill you."

"Sexist bastard," Jenny whispered. "Off you go, Jones, I'll cover you."

Mickey stood still and seemed to be listening for movement. His eyes were trained on the back gates, the direction of the shots. Jenny had already disappeared back amongst the conifers in the garden of Autumn House, possibly the least obvious direction of travel for any shooter. Running away along the shoreline was the more obvious escape route. But Jenny wasn't trying to escape.

Jones broke cover silently and crawled on his belly across the concrete path and into the house through the patio doors. With his grandfather's Swiss Army Knife already poised in his hand, he stole a look back down the path and saw Mickey still staring out at the shore through the gate.

In the blink of an eye, Jones got up and locked the patio door from inside, having slowly and silently slid the door shut.

It was then that Eric Rogers saw him. The two locked stares. Rogers' was a look of surprise and terror all rolled into one.

"You?" Rogers said, with shock written all over his face.

Jones considered the situation carefully, he knew Rogers was an egotistical bastard and would want to make some kind of clever comment in his typical demeaning or sarcastic style. He could even have shouted over to Mickey and given the game away. Jones wasn't ready for that. Instead, he punched Rogers repeatedly in the face as hard as he could muster - until he looked unlikely to speak.

Being tied up, Rogers was helpless and simply slumped forward, his cable ties stopping him from falling onto the floor. Jones punched him so violently that he injured his own wrist, knuckles and maybe a finger or two. He knew that this was against every protocol, to hit a defenceless man, but something felt good about doing it.

The floodlights then switched off again, which meant Mickey wasn't moving, and Jones felt that nagging sensation that something horrific was about to happen. He tried to put that to the back of his mind and calmly smiled over at Bristow, who was urging him to set her free. He crawled behind the sofa, shielded by the dwarf wall inside the room, confident he would not be seen from Mickey's position should the lights come back on. He sliced the cable ties off Bristow with his pen knife.

"Are you okay?" Jones asked Bristow.

"My head is in pieces. But I'll be alright. How did you know what was going on?"

"Your handheld. It must have switched on when you fell. Did you not realise?"

"No. You could hear everything? We need to arrest Mickey Reilly. I need to get out of here." Bristow was shaking her hands to get the feeling back in them. She had slotted back quickly into professional mode, her comfortable autopilot.

"Of course. Let's deal with Mickey first," Jones reminded her. "He's still out there. God knows his next move."

It was then that the floodlights came on again and seconds later, the glass in the patio doors exploded, as Mickey blasted them with his sawn-off shotgun.

There was a grunt of annoyance from the fixer, and he walked briskly towards the smashed doors.

"Jenny?" Jones shouted from behind the wall of the Garden Room.

There was the sound of two shots being fired in quick succession, the thud of bullet into flesh and then silence. Jones closed his eyes hard and prayed this was Jenny taking Reilly down and nothing else. He could feel the first sharp pangs of anxiety but this disappeared when Bristow kicked him, gently.

"What's happened out there, Jones?" she asked.

"Stay down," he replied.

He carefully peered his head over the wall and saw Reilly on the ground. Jenny had struck him in the leg and, by the looks of things, the forearm. Jones ran over to him and kicked the sawn-off shotgun away.

Lights from adjoining properties were suddenly switched on.

All the neighbours had probably been woken up. The community knew something was going down.

"Jones," Bristow called over. "Can someone get an ambulance for Stewart? And backup to get Eric Rogers to the custody suite at Knock Road." But Jones didn't move, he stared down at the injured man as he writhed on the floor. Bristow joined him.

"Mickey Reilly, I'm arresting you for the murders of Isadora Brown, Philip Bradley and George McCool and the attempted murder of Andrew McIlhinney..." she began.

There was soon the sound of an ambulance drawing up outside and Virginia Curry suddenly appeared. She ran through the back gate to check on Stewart McIlhinney. Jenny then emerged from inside the conifers. Mickey stared over at her, his face grimacing from the pain of the bullet wounds.

"Bastard!" Jenny shouted.

She bent down and pointed her gun at Reilly's face, the muzzle at his temple. But the fixer didn't move. He just stared upwards and smiled, though with the pain of his wounds still evident.

"It was you? You stupid little bitch. You'll regret this," he snarled. Jenny's finger was on the trigger and she had a look of determination on her face. Bristow shot a look at Jones and he held up his hand in response.

"Okay, Jenny. It's over," Jones calmly said. "This needs to stop now."

"You're damn right," she replied. "With the contents of his tiny brain all over the lawn."

"You killed Isadora. A woman, sitting in a wheelchair in a car, waiting for her colleague," she spat. "You deserve this, you coward. You deserve to be executed in cold blood, just like you did to her. You're scum, nothing more."

Jenny gritted her teeth and stared at Reilly.

"Jenny," Virginia called over. "She wouldn't want this. Would she?"

Jones walked over and grabbed hold of Jenny, holding the arm pointing the gun.

"She's right. This isn't the way. We've done what we set out to do," he whispered and squeezed her arm gently.

"Yeah, walk away, little girl. You've not got the balls. Anyway, our tentacles stretch much further than you think. We'll find you," he smirked as Jenny composed herself. "Walk away now, but I suggest you don't sleep too deeply."

"Whatever," Jenny replied, put the gun down and aimed a kick at Reilly's head. Once and then again, much harder. He made a quiet whimpering noise and closed his eyes. It was a poor second to blowing his brains out but made her feel better.

"Sorry, everyone, I lost myself then." Jenny held her hands up and looked around at Virginia, Bristow, and Jones. He could see Jenny was still trying to balance her emotions. She was angry and upset, but once again, she had been an inspiration.

"Sorry, Marie, did I interrupt you? You'd best arrest Rogers, too." Jenny called over. Some form of normality was resuming, and the paramedics were now beginning to enter the property from the front.

"I think he'll need another five minutes," Bristow called back. "Jones shut him up temporarily. He's out cold. But we can soon get him back to Knock Road."

"I don't think so, Marie," Virginia called over from her position next to Stewart McIlhinney. "Rogers will need to go back to Palace Barracks. He won't be going anywhere near a police station. MI5 will want first crack." She spoke as she applied a tourniquet to the gunshot wound around McIlhinney's knee. Just then, her handheld sprang into life. She stood up as the paramedic team came and took over.

"Right, everyone," she called over. "Jube's on the handheld. He's on his way over with a couple of the Palace Barracks team. I'm not sure your day is quite over yet. He wants a word with you, Jones."

"I'll call him back," Jones responded. Jube could wait five minutes, he thought. Bristow needed his help. He ran and found her police kitbag next to the sofa and applied handcuffs to Reilly but left McIlhinney to be dealt with by the paramedic team. He looked in a bad way, and Jones could hear Virginia's soft and calming tones trying to comfort him as the paramedics did their job.

Reilly then opened his eyes again as Bristow restrained him.

"You don't know the half of it," he shouted groggily as Bristow turned him over to apply the handcuffs. "This empire won't fall. Believe me. This isn't even a paper cut."

Forty-Eight

With the time 09.15am in Thiepval, the sound of the coffee percolating in Briefing Room Alpha was the only noise in the room. Bristow had stitches applied to the back of her head by the paramedics. Jones had a large bag of frozen peas on his swollen hand, and Jenny looked like only her raging endorphins were keeping her awake. They had all enjoyed less than two hours' sleep and there was an obvious air of tiredness and fraught emotion.

McNally had arrived a few hours earlier and he'd left the QD team to unload the surveillance equipment from the back of the minibus. Carl and Tom had slightly over-indulged after their shift at the Hunter's Arms and were ordered to sleep it off once the vehicle was unloaded. They were still missing in action. However, Mr Singh was smiling broadly whilst sipping his water, knowing his operation and the microphones in the samosas, the PEA, had been pivotal.

Jube and Virginia walked into the room and settled down next to McNally.

"Good morning," McNally announced. "I'm sorry to call yous in so early. I realise everyone here is exhausted. Your work over the past forty-eight hours has been nothing short of remarkable. However, there is one last piece of the jigsaw, and Jube thinks he's cracked it."

Everyone stared at Jube, who was midway through a plain digestive biscuit.

"Morning folks," Jube began breezily. "We have two options here. You can all head to your quarters and catch up on your sleep, and we can engage the Palace Barracks team to finish this off. Clive Gentry has been fully briefed, and he has suddenly found some spare resource to finish this."

"I bet he has! Absolutely no way," Jones interrupted. "We want to see this through. It's that simple."

Jube nodded. He looked impressed at the motivation of the team. That was exactly the reaction he was looking for.

Wendy then arrived, wearing a black bobble hat to cover her bed hair and a long grey hooded jumper that went past her knees. Her platformed Doc Martens completed the look.

"Do I smell coffee? Have I missed anything major?" she mumbled.

"Be a dear and sort coffee for the team, Wendy," Virginia smiled. "They've all had quite the night of it." Wendy wanted to roll her eyes but had a nagging feeling that she'd slept through something extremely important, so she swallowed hard, with the taste of last night's Pernod still fresh in her mouth and began to serve the coffee to those assembled.

Jube stood up and walked over to the whiteboard in the corner of the room. He dusted the biscuit crumbs off his jacket as he did so.

"Did anyone here study Roman History at school?" he looked over the team. There was silence. This wasn't the opening remark anyone was expecting.

"Okay, okay. What about classics? Who has a fair understanding of classical literature?" Again, the team was silent.

"I wouldn't call it study. But I did a project on Roman History in my third year at school," Jones offered. "I can be a bit geeky about it. Does that help?"

"Possibly," Jube responded, taking a cup of coffee from the bleary-eyed Wendy. "I've already had a couple of chats with Orla Massey about this, and she's equally in the dark about the Roman Empire. It's all very disappointing. Anyway, let's plough on."

"We've all heard the name Sejanus over the past few days and last night I visited my old University library to get a quick refresher," Jube continued, sipping his coffee.

Jenny looked at Jones, non-plussed, wondering how Jube had found time to nip to the library in the middle of this investigation and last night's furore.

"Where do I start? Well, the Emperor Tiberius wasn't keen on being in charge, so Sejanus filled the void. He was a soldier and wanted to make a name for himself. He wanted to be the emperor himself one day. However, the people didn't want Sejanus, so they mocked up some treason charges against him and he, along with others, were executed. Following me so far?"

"Yes," Jones replied. "That's all pretty basic stuff. The Romans needed someone to blame, and Sejanus took the hit."

The rest of the team looked far less comfortable with this information.

"I'll admit, I don't know the first thing about Roman History. But if this has anything to do with the rows of library books sitting in glass cabinets in Mainstay Barns, then I'm with you. Continue," Jenny said, wearily.

"The what?" Jube's ears pricked up.

"Jones and I attended Mainstay Barns three days ago. Saoirse has a vast collection of books about Roman Emperors sitting behind lockable glass cabinet doors. Only they weren't locked. They were filled with library stamps, with some stamped very recently," Jenny explained.

"The odd thing," Jones jumped in. "Is that the books weren't ordered properly. You'd have thought they'd have been stored chronologically. But she'd stored them alphabetically. And there were so many missing volumes."

"Sweet Jesus," Jube exclaimed, downing the rest of his coffee in one. "Then I'm very confident we have our answer, or at least the vast majority of it." He slapped the table in delight.

"Do we?" McNally said. "Please explain. Is Sejanus and the big man the same person?"

"No, Declan. You're barking up entirely the wrong tree. Sejanus is the ambitious, scheming traitor, at least on paper. The big man is Tiberius, the reluctant leader. I would also bet you a great deal of money that those books are effectively ledgers for the shareholders in the empire."

"Shareholders?" Jenny repeated.

"Yes, those who are paid by the big man for distinct elements of the organised crime syndicate. I bet every shareholder has a Roman nickname to avoid identification," Jube carefully explained. "This is fairly common in organised crime. But Roman Emperors is a new one on me."

"Is Eric Rogers one of them?" Bristow asked.

"He admitted himself that he'd been paid by the big man and so, I guess, he's one of the shareholders and will be listed in those books back at Mainstay Barns. But something will have triggered that relationship. The big man may have some dirt on him. We may never know."

"So, what are we all doing here?" McNally said, suddenly looking frustrated. "Why aren't we interviewing Eric Rogers or sussing out the big man?"

"Because I know who the big man is. I also know who killed Martha Maddison, also known as Caragh Reid. I'm also confident I can tell you who they've codenamed Sejanus."

Jube then turned around the whiteboard to reveal his working. There were coloured post-it notes, arrows explaining relationships and one name in the middle of the board in thick black dry-wipe pen.

Suddenly there was a knock on the Briefing Room door, which Wendy went to answer. Two soldiers were standing outside the door, both with impressive British Army moustaches.

"Mr Spencer, you have visitors at the front gate. I believe you're expecting them?"

"Thanks gentleman, could you please place them in Briefing Room Beta? Could I also request that once the interview takes place, we have guards at the door of the room?"

"No bother at all, Mr Spencer. Leave that with us," one replied. The briefing room door was closed as they left.

"I have also been speaking to the Chief Constable of the RUC this morning, as part of our hybrid arrangement. As a footnote, he is dealing with the fallout from the Knock Road controversy as we speak. Clearing up Eric's significant messes." Jube looked over at Marie Bristow.

"That's great, but it's all too fecking late," she whispered to Jenny.

"But with his help, I have secured several search warrants for properties in Bangor, Millisle, and further afield. There are police officers ready outside to execute those warrants." Jube looked at his notes again.

"Mr Singh, could you please take the minibus and bring back all the Roman History books from Mainstay Barns? Check every room, every nook and cranny. I want any evidence whatsoever of shareholder activity." Mr Singh nodded and left the room.

"Wendy, can you wake up Carl and Tom, and take them to Bangor Marina and do the same with The Mainstay yacht. Tear it to pieces. I want any evidence collated, and paperwork filed, and I want it back here urgently. I've made the Chief Constable aware we want first dibs." Jube had the bit between his teeth now. McNally's ingenuity had previously taken centre stage, but he now had to bring a global organised crime leader to justice. This was Jube's realm, and everyone knew it.

Jube then turned his attention to McNally and Bristow.

"Could you go to Belfast City Hospital and get Andrew McIlhinney? Suggest to him that a deal is still on the table, but it'll need to take place here, at Thiepval. Please apologise to Orla for my vanishing act last night and explain that I'll visit her later with an update." McNally, still stunned by this morning's revelations, nodded at Bristow and they left for the car park.

"Jenny and Jones, I'd like you in the interview room with me. I'll explain more in a second. Virginia, I need a favour from you, too."

Just then, the two soldiers walked past the double doors of the Briefing Room. There, resplendent in a bright yellow short summer dress, was Saoirse Bradley, flanked by her two young children. Jube dashed out of the room to greet her.

"Huge apologies for the early start, Mrs Bradley. My name is Jube Spencer and I'm helping the RUC with the investigation of the murder of your husband. I'm delighted to say we have some answers for you."

"It's terribly inconvenient, as we were about to leave for our summer house in the Algarve. Will this take long?" She replied, with her two boys following close behind.

"I'm afraid we may need to monopolise your time, rather," Jube smiled. "Can I also introduce Virginia Curry? She has kindly offered to look after your children whilst we chat through these issues."

Virginia hadn't volunteered her services at all, but she was savvy enough to realise the gravity of the issue and the unique circumstances with the RUC rudderless and Knock Road under full lockdown, with Internal Affairs crawling over the place. She'd guessed Thiepval would be the base for all the interviews.

The two boys, both around 8 to 10 years old, disappeared into the adjoining room with Virginia, who was mulling over how to keep the children entertained.

"You know Jones and Jenny?" Jube asked.

"Absolutely," Saoirse responded, half smiling.

Jube, Jenny, and Jones sat opposite Saoirse Bradley. Jube unpacked his leather notebook with Jenny and Jones hastily locating some A4 paper and a biro each.

"Mrs Bradley," Jube began. "Last night we arrested Mickey Reilly for the murder of Philip Bradley, your husband, a young man called George McCool, and a colleague of ours, Isadora Brown. He is heavily involved in an organised crime gang, which we believe has an international reach."

Saoirse looked at Jube with interest. He had expected tears or some form of explosive emotion. None were forthcoming.

"Mickey is a trusted member of the family. He is not involved in organised crime. He's an excellent project manager. He's also a war veteran with a heart of gold," she responded, her hands running through her short, cropped hair with nervous anxiety.

"I'm very sorry. But Mickey Reilly has been recorded admitting the murders and therefore there is no doubt. In those recordings, he often refers to being the fixer for the leader of the so called empire, the big man."

"This is utter nonsense. The empire? The big man? Organised crime? What planet are yous living on? And who is this so-called big man?" Saoirse snapped back.

"Oh, that's easy," Jube replied. "That's *you*, Saoirse. You're the big man."

Saoirse laughed loudly and shook her head in bewilderment.

"Ah, so the big man is a wee woman? That's madness. You believe I'm the leader of an international organised crime network? Have you lost control of your senses? I'm a young mother, a widow, and a Primary School classroom assistant."

"All of that is true, but you're also a reluctant leader. For someone who has almost all the Reid family inheritance, you've been getting other people to do your dirty work, and just sitting back and letting the profits roll in. All nicely laundered and stored in offshore bank accounts," Jube continued.

"This is madness," she responded.

"But the bit I like best, Mrs Bradley," Jube continued, ignoring her protests, "is your fascination with Roman History. The daughter of a feared terrorist, but with her degree in Ancient History, majoring on the Roman Empire. The University librarian appears to be missing nearly seventy books, all either taken out in your name, or stolen. I wonder why that would be?"

"Bang me up for stealing university books. It's a fair cop. I like to study," Saoirse smirked and held out her wrists. "I'll pay the overdue fines!"

Disregarding her sarcasm, Jube carried on. "As we speak, members of our team are at Mainstay Barns and The Mainstay yacht retrieving all the Roman History books that link your shareholders to the empire plus any other titbits of information. I'll give you this, Saoirse. You've been bloody clever."

"This is all fascinating. But I think I'd like to leave now. Bring me my children and we'll be on our way. This isn't a police station. You have no powers of arrest and I know my rights. I know who you all are."

"I don't think so. We also know that you've been paying Eric Rogers to keep a blind eye on your activities in Northern Ireland, as well as a number of other high-profile police officers across the UK and Ireland. We have almost everything." Jube explained.

"This is insanity. Can you hear yourself? I ordered the killing of my own husband, did I? I robbed my sons of their father? For what reason?"

"You knew Philip was having affairs. You knew he was wasting the family inheritance on drugs and extravagances. You also knew that if anyone was going to give you away, it would be him. Because, underneath it all, he had morals. One day the bubble was going to burst and so you asked Mickey to kill him." Jube was on a roll now.

"You also knew that Mickey, somewhat stupidly, let something slip in the bedroom at Ballycastle when Sam Jacobs was hiding in the wardrobe. And for that, Sam needed to die too. Along with

George McCool, who sold photos of the scene to the newspaper. The ultimate betrayal. Only Sam survived, despite your best efforts." Jube had prepared himself incredibly well for this interview, and Jones and Jenny watched on in awe. This was a masterclass.

"Mickey's decision, to kill one of our own officers, in what can only be described as a pointless assassination, I'm guessing that was his own idea as that appears to be without any kind of logic whatsoever. That's not your style." Jones registered the merest of flickers in Saoirse's eyes, but nothing else. She was holding firm.

"But who is Sejanus?" Jones piped up. "Who is the traitor? The team member who had ambitions and desire? Someone who perhaps knew you didn't want the leadership and the criminal lifestyle?"

"I have no idea what you're talking about. But I think I need a lawyer," Saoirse quietly said. "You're even making up words now. Sejanus? What are you on?"

"You'll be offered a lawyer when you have your formal police interview. This is something different. We are dealing with national security. So, with that in mind, tell me, am I right that you were shipping drugs around the UK and using international connections to people smuggle?"

"I did nothing of the sort." Saoirse shook her head indignantly.

"Of course, you knew full well that you'd never be caught, as you had the senior police officers in your back pocket? Like Eric Rogers? That's quite a scheme."

"I think you're delusional, Mr Spencer. I'm not sure where you're getting this from, but I'll give you credit for creativity. Look, I need to speak to my travel agent. I need to cancel our flight tickets to Portugal. The boys will be devastated. Maybe we can take a wee pause on this?" Saoirse seemed a touch too laid back, bearing in mind the accusations that had been levelled at her.

"Of course, it has been a long night for us too, so a comfort break is absolutely fine," Jube agreed.

Jube, Jenny and Jones left the room, shutting the door and nodding politely at the two soldiers on guard.

"That was weird. She seemed really cool," Jones started, as they walked into the other Briefing Room. "Have we got any means of hearing her conversation in that room? Is that allowed?"

"That's a grey area," Jube smiled, and reached behind the heating console and switched on a small amp. "This microphone has been a godsend in the past. There's a recording function too. We should be able to pick up everything. Ethical or not."

"Tell me it isn't true?" Saoirse was half shouting down her mobile phone. "Mickey's been arrested? Where is he? What about Andrew? What do they know?"

There was then silence as she listened to the response before she continued.

"I'm here at the Barracks in Lisburn. They're throwing everything at me. They know far too much for comfort. They are now raiding my home, is that allowed? I see... They have a warrant? Jesus Christ."

"Who is she talking to?" Jones asked.

"My guess is that they have a solicitor on call. Probably a fairly iffy one. There are a few names I could mention, but they're all pretty slippery characters. But what's more interesting is that she mentioned Andrew. That's a very useful confirmation of my other suspicions," Jube added.

"I need a plan," Saoirse shouted down the phone. "This is what I pay you for. You have about ten minutes to conjure one up, as you'll be implicated here too. I'll get very chatty, believe you me!"

"She's losing the plot. McNally and Bristow will be back any minute with Andrew McIlhinney. Her goose will be well and truly cooked then." Jube beamed. "Keep listening, you two. I'm off to get a cup of tea and another digestive."

"If it's being recorded, can I go in on my own?" Jenny asked. "Or is that against protocol?"

"Be my guest," Jube called back from the tea urn. "This isn't a formal interview. Just don't reveal anything new. Stick to the script to date. Be her wee pal, if you like. She needs that."

Jenny walked past the two soldiers and settled back into her seat.

"Do you want anything to drink, Saoirse? Maybe water? Or tea?"

"I'm fine. I just need to get this over with and take my boys home," Saoirse barked. "I thought better of you, Jenny. This is all shite, you know that?"

"No, it isn't. You need to accept it's over. Your boys are the victims now. They've lost their father and they're on the verge of losing their mum to a hefty prison sentence. That's a tragedy. You've got to salvage what you can for them," Jenny smiled sympathetically.

"Ah, you're good, Jenny. Emotional blackmail, it's an easy card to play." Saoirse played with her hair again and was clearly thinking hard.

"Tell you what," she started. "If you've really got all this sewn up, and if I'm the big man, or whatever, why did I make peace with my sister Caragh? Wouldn't I want this all to myself? I offered to go back into the family firm, to professionalise the Reid family business. You didn't know that, did you?" Saoirse looked indignant for moment, as if she'd just revealed a huge gamechanger.

But Jenny simply bit her lip. The team were already well aware of the olive branch. But if Saoirse already knew Caragh was the body on The Mainstay yacht, she was playing it remarkably straight.

"You've made peace with Caragh? That's not what you said before. Tell me about that," Jenny responded, playing into Saoirse's hands and opting to swerve any mention of Caragh's tragic murder. Saoirse had now been tripped up by one lie. Would there be more?

"Jenny, I'm not this criminal mastermind... the big man. I'm just a mother, a sister and a widow. I wanted peace and to bring my family back together. I'd do anything for my family. Surely you see that?" Saoirse looked imploringly at Jenny.

Elsewhere in the YCU, Andrew McIlhinney was being led into Briefing Room Alpha by Bristow and McNally. Jones, seeing them arrive, positioned himself opposite the soldiers guarding Saoirse. He wanted to look at Andrew's body language. Jube followed the three into the Briefing Room and, after fiddling with the volume on the microphone, settled into one of the chairs with his tea and biscuit.

Andrew appeared half asleep and already shell-shocked before the interview had even started. He sipped at the plastic cup of water on the table and his leg started jolting up and down. Marie Bristow started proceedings.

"Before we start, Andrew, we just thought we'd make you aware that two things have happened since our interview last night. Firstly, your brother was shot and seriously injured at an incident at the home of Eric Rogers last night. Secondly, I arrested Stewart and Mickey Reilly last night on a range of charges, including murder."

Jube saw Andrew's eyes widen and shoulders rise with anxiety, before intervening.

"Actually, Andrew, there's a third element. Saoirse Bradley is sitting in the adjoining interview room as we speak." Andrew pointedly didn't look at Jube as he mentally unpacked that last revelation.

"So, to be clear, there is only one deal on the table now. Be totally honest with us, give us the entire story and we'll see if we can protect you and your family. Leave anything vital unsaid and the notion of you being a supergrass is dead. You'll be a very old man when you leave prison, if they don't get to you first. Over to you, Andrew," Jube concluded.

"Saoirse is next door?" Andrew suddenly looked unnerved. His leg shook violently.

"Aye, she's next door. Her kids are here too. This is the endgame, Andrew." McNally delivered the last line as if handing down a sentence.

He shouted a series of loud expletives before placing his head on the table for a few moments. Such was his despair that Jube and McNally exchanged glances as they wondered whether he already needed time out. They were looking at a broken man.

But Andrew pulled himself back from the brink and raised his head and ran his hands through his mass of brown hair.

"So, you know then?" Andrew looked up at Bristow, Jube and McNally. "You know everything?" Jube thought tears might be next, instead his leg jerked up and down like a piston on an engine.

"Right, I'm ready for this. I'm ready for your endgame. I'll give you everything, on the proviso that my parents are safe and I want to be out of reach. I want supergrass status."

Jube nodded at McNally and Bristow. He was clearly still thinking through the connotations. He'd need to line up the supergrass approach with the RUC and speak to Clive too, but it was do-able as there was the merest chink of a paramilitary element, thanks to the Reid family connection. If Andrew could open up that line of enquiry – supergrass status was possible. He'd just have to be careful that he didn't incriminate himself so spectacularly that he'd be denied any deal.

Spencer walked over to the console in order to record the interview and pushed two buttons. One, he intentionally selected, the record function. The second one, the intercom button, was a mistake. But it was a work of accidental genius.

"Saoirse Bradley is the big man. She's been paying the shareholders via offshore bank accounts in the Cayman Islands and the Turks and Caicos Islands." As Andrew spoke, his voice was mistakenly transmitted into the room next door. As he did so, Saoirse recognised instantly who was speaking and closed her eyes in a gesture of defeat. Jenny saw the moment the penny dropped. But Andrew hadn't even started yet.

"Her property portfolio was the method of laundering the funds. Her shareholders were selling a property worth, say, £25k and she'd buy it for £250k. The price was artificially raised. Which then paid them for the drugs, people trafficking, even arms sales. That's why she has property all over the world and her accounts appear clean. It's a bulletproof approach."

"Interesting. Carry on, Andrew," McNally urged.

"Every shareholder has the nickname of a Roman Emperor. It was Saoirse's big thing. She loved the connection to the Roman Empire." Andrew McIlhinney took another sip of water. He was calmer now and articulated himself carefully.

"There is a date stamp in each Roman reference book in Mainstay Barns. Like you'd get in a library. That references the last payment. There is a Rolodex in the spare bedroom on the yacht which details the payments to the police officers. It lists the policeman as locations, as if it was towns and cities where the yacht has sailed to. But these are transaction dates or dates of our last communication." Andrew rubbed a stray tear away from his left eye and stared at Bristow.

"Tell us about the shareholders, Andrew," Bristow said.

"These are some of the biggest names in global organised crime. Trajan is a fella in Derry, Mick Carmichael, one of the biggest gang leaders in Ireland; Hadrian is Phil McClelland, an arms dealer from Dublin and a really dangerous man, Antoninus Pius is Danny Fisher a major drug dealer from White City in West London and one of Saoirse's biggest shareholders."

Jube, who was speed-writing names in his notepad, was almost giddy from the Who's Who of global crime lords Andrew was listing. But still he continued.

"Marcus Aurelius was Louis Stewart, a drug runner in Glasgow; Lucius Verus is an American people smuggler from Detroit; Commodus is Michelle Argus, a people trafficker based in Gibraltar; Jamie Travers, you'll know him, he's Gorian and probably the best-known arms trader in the Caribbean, based in Anguilla. I know where she keeps all the ledgers. I know how they're paid, and I know how to get hold of them."

It was all Jube could do to stop his mouth falling open in shock. If what Andrew was saying was true, he thought, this was possibly the single biggest link to global organised crime ever discovered. But the spook continued to nod sagely and simply listened and took his notes.

Jones walked into the second Briefing Room and sat next to Jenny; Saoirse didn't look up. He could hear the intercom from the corridor. He mouthed 'bloody hell' at Jenny and watched as Saoirse's world fell to pieces.

"How do you know all this, Andrew?" Jube pushed.

"I'm the accountant. I pay the suppliers, the shareholders and all the bent police officers who turn a blind eye. I wanted a legit job in finance, but life got in the way. I'm not the idiot people think I am. I'm not some kind of henchman." Andrew looked to the heavens briefly.

"Also, I have been in a relationship with Saoirse for three years now. We planned to move away from the Mainstay Barns with the kids and start again. It was a real relationship with proper plans." This revelation made Jube wince and momentarily look over at McNally and Bristow. He wasn't expecting that.

"So, she ordered the killing of her husband for the sake of your fledgling relationship?" Jube clarified. "There must be more to it, surely?"

"Oh aye, there was much more. But Philip made it easy for us by effectively signing his own death warrant," Andrew explained. "The silly wee bastard went over to Eric Rogers at the RUC station in Knock Road and made a full confession about the empire. He told Rogers everything. He wanted to clear his conscience. He thought the family could make a fresh start. But Rogers simply telephoned Mickey and within 48 hours Philip was dead. Whatever happened in that house in Ballycastle just sealed the deal."

"Philip confessed to Eric Rogers to ease his conscience, and that led to his murder?" Bristow remarked, as if scarcely believing it. "Holy mother of God. Rogers was complicit in the murder?"

"Yeah. You know what else he confessed to? He told Eric that he was having an affair with Caragh Reid. Fecking Saoirse's own flesh and blood, the arsehole. You see, Caragh went to Philip to discuss ending the feud. She saw him as the softer way in, where the peace deal might be better received. He was supposed to lay the foundations."

Jenny watched Saoirse's face turn crimson and expected a torrent of emotion. Instead, she just started shaking her head.

"I'm not having that," she cried. "This can't be real." But Andrew still hadn't finished.

"Phil and Caragh ended up together, for maybe eight months. I never told Saoirse. I'm not sure she ever found out. It would kill her."

"My own sister and my husband!" Saoirse screamed in the other room and banged her fists on the table. "Behind my back! The cheating bastard deserved to die. But Caragh, I just don't believe it. I just..." she stared at the intercom with tears falling down her face and with a look of confusion.

"But you killed him, you ordered his death," Jones said, quietly.

"I didn't have a choice," Saoirse whispered, looking at Jones. "Phil was going to bring the whole thing down. It would have ruined everything. When I heard about the confession, I knew that was the only option, but I knew nothing about Caragh. Honest to God." Saoirse looked at Jones pleadingly, as if this single detail made all the difference.

"Andrew was going to be my future, our future. But I was willing to let Caragh back in. I still am." Jones glanced at Jenny, knowing that emotional explosion, the news of her sister's awful death, was yet to come.

"So, who was Sejanus, Saoirse?" Jones asked.

"Andrew was Sejanus. But I never called him that. I loved him.

Or I thought I loved him," she corrected herself. "Eric Rogers has a rescue dog called Sejanus, a huge fecking thing. I explained to Mickey the Roman origins of the name. It kind of stuck with Andrew."

"Once Mickey realised Andrew and I were an item, he wanted him dead and out of the way. He saw him as a risk. He thought Andrew was desperate to be the big man, to run the empire. Like Sejanus. Mickey wanted the business protected. He made the link to Sejanus himself."

"So, was Andrew a traitor? Did he want to be the big man and steal your crown?" Jones pushed.

"Maybe. But maybe I wanted that too. Would I have given it to him willingly? I really don't know. Ultimately. I had more money than I knew what to do with. I was tired of the lies; the deceit and I wanted my kids to grow up differently. Juggling all the players across the globe, keeping people happy. It was never-ending. I just wanted to be a better person for my children."

"Isn't that also what Philip wanted?" Jones pointed out. "To be a better person for the children and to clear his conscience. But he still ended up dead."

Saoirse didn't respond. She bowed her head as if she'd run out of steam. But the interview next door wasn't finished.

"That just leaves one thing, Martha Maddison." Jube stared at Andrew McIlhinney in the other room. He guessed what was coming. Jube and McNally had already joined the dots, but they needed to hear it.

"When I saw Wonder Woman in Ballycastle, I had no idea who it was. I just assumed it was one of Phil's druggie tarts. We paid her off, just a couple of thousand. That's the truth." Jube believed him.

"But then, from nowhere, Saoirse had this mad idea that she wanted to bond the family again. She wanted peace with the Reids. They had lunch together at that posh hotel in Newcastle, Slieve Donard, and I followed them. I wanted to know what the craic was. That was the first time I'd ever seen Caragh Reid, and I knew straightaway she was Wonder Woman."

"No," Saoirse shouted. "NO!" she repeated, and she sobbed uncontrollably. Her head was resting on the table and her usually immaculate pixie blonde hair was being pulled and grabbed as Saoirse became more hysterical. "Turn it off, Jenny, please. I don't need to hear this." But Jenny didn't move.

"Do you know what Andrew's going to say?" Jones asked calmly.

"Is Caragh dead? Was my wee sister the body on The Mainstay? Did that bastard...?" Saoirse tailed off as Andrew started speaking again in the room next door.

"Caragh was really beautiful," said Andrew "A lot quieter than Saoirse had made out. I had been told she was the aggressor, that she had tried to prevent Saoirse from getting the family inheritance. But I didn't see any of that. They were hugging. There were tears of joy. It was a family reunited."

"Did Caragh start working with Saoirse as part of the Empire?" Bristow asked.

"It was baby steps. But who do you think brought the wee girl over from England, the Jacobs girl? That was all Saoirse's idea. It was like a proper test of loyalty for Caragh. She grabbed her from the swimming baths over in Surrey. I had a feeling she was going to be back in the family firm permanently. But I couldn't have that, could I?" Andrew paused.

"Why not, Andrew? Why didn't you want Saoirse and Caragh happy?" McNally asked.

"Because Saoirse was so close to handing the empire to me. I knew everything. I could make it work. All of her contacts all over the world trusted me. I was the go-to fella." Andrew collected his thoughts again.

"You see, she was sick to death with it all and she just had to say the word. I was ready. Then, suddenly, Caragh was back. She'd want her in the thick of it, wouldn't she?" Andrew looked over at

McNally, then Jube, looking for some kind of positive reinforcement. But nothing was forthcoming.

"So, I spoke to Eric. I told him everything, the complete story. He agreed we needed her out of the way. So, he found her a new identity, Martha Maddison. He had a passport made up, using his contacts, and a whole new back story. We offered her a million pounds sterling to start a new life. God knows, we had that kind of money on tap, and we bought her a ferry ticket. It took months of planning."

"What? She didn't want it? She didn't want to go?" Jube stared over at Andrew.

"Quite the opposite. She was fed up with the tribalism in Northern Ireland. She was a virtual recluse, with no real family aside from Saoirse, and her half of the inheritance had basically gone. She'd even sold the family business to another gang in West Belfast, the McQuiods. I think it became a protection racket. A shadow of what Kenny Reid had built up."

"What did you do, Andrew?" McNally asked, knowing Jube would have had this wrapped up in his head eons ago.

"So, I watched her coming out of City Hospital. I assumed she'd told Massey something incriminating, and I didn't trust her. So, when we met on The Mainstay, I strangled her. She was too much of a risk. I couldn't lose Saoirse, the empire, the money. There had to be finality. I couldn't have Saoirse wondering where she was and then her coming back, out of the blue again."

Saoirse, still listening in the other room in disbelief. She was now emotionally wrecked. The tears poured down her face and Jenny had moved to comfort her.

"I've lost everything and for what? What about my kids, Jenny? What will happen to them? If I go down, they'll go into care."

"I have no idea, Saoirse. These are not questions I can answer. You should have considered all this before. But I have one for you.

Did you order the killing of Isadora Brown? My colleague?" Jenny looked at her, emotionless.

"No, that was not my doing. I swear to God. Mickey was insane. He hated the police, the security services, and authority figures. He despised Brits and never felt that he fitted in after the war. He thought your colleague had made too many connections. He wanted to send a warning. But killing your friend was not an order from me," she replied. "That was his own doing."

Jenny looked at Saoirse but somehow felt empty. This gave her an answer, but she felt absolutely nothing from knowing it.

Jones walked out of Briefing Room Beta and knocked on the door. Jube moved to answer it. As Jones looked in, he could see Andrew was in much the same shape as Saoirse, broken and exhausted.

"Can I have a word please, Jube?" Jube got up, followed Jones into the corridor,

"Saoirse will confess to everything. I think we offer her an approach to keep her children safe. Andrew and Saoirse's evidence will bring down hundreds of criminal networks across the globe and end the careers of countless crooked police officers. We just need to put *something* on the table."

"I see. She'll confess? That's good work, Jones. What did you two say that broke her?" Jube responded, clearly surprised by this turn of events.

"We didn't need to do anything. You pressed the intercom by mistake. She heard every word of Andrew's admission. Including his killing of her sister. She's effectively had a breakdown in there. We just let her talk."

Jube fell silent. Jones knew this should be a moment of celebration. Countless organised villains brought to justice through these two tired interviews. But something felt hopelessly wrong.

"I'll find a way of protecting the Bradley children and Andrew's family. Let's get them out of Thiepval and into a high security prison on the mainland. When this news hits the criminal fraternity, the bounty on their heads will be phenomenal. We have work to do." Jube turned around and headed back to the interview with Andrew.

"Both of them to high security prisons? Didn't Andrew want supergrass status? Wasn't that the deal?" Jones queried.

"Well, it's legally feasible for a murderer to be given supergrass status here. But it would be hugely controversial and the press would go ballistic. Think about the peace talks too. Would giving him a new name and a council flat in Cornwall serve the broader interests of justice and public safety? I don't know. It was premeditated murder, Jones. I'll talk to Clive."

"Yeah, I see." Jones responded.

Back in Briefing Room Beta, Jenny was still sitting next to Saoirse and handing her tissues. Jube had switched the intercom off, and there was an icy silence that was sapping Jenny's last remaining energy.

"It wasn't me, you know?" Saoirse finally said, in-between dabs with her tissue.

"What do you mean?" Jenny responded. "You've admitted it all."

"I know. I mean, it felt like I was living someone else's life. I said to Caragh, in our last conversation, that I need to move on from this lifestyle. I hated my father for what he did, and I just ended up being the same hateful person, and I was fooling myself that being so clever about it made it all okay."

Jenny just looked at Saoirse as if absorbing the information.

"But there was also part of me that was proud. I felt like a single parent with Philip away at Westminster. I was patronised by parents and teachers for being just a classroom assistant and I had all the dads from the village trying it on with me. I achieved in spite of everything." Saoirse wept again. "It was just the wrong type of achievement."

"I was this wee woman, but behind it all, I was the big man pulling the strings. And now it's all been destroyed by Andrew, a little man with delusions of grandeur, just because I wanted my family back together."

"Sejanus," Jenny responded.

"Traitors and idiots everywhere," she snapped back, before her face crumpled once more and the tears flowed.

"My boys," she whispered. "My poor boys."

Forty-Nine

Somewhere, in a small chapel in east London, a memorial stands.

It is composed of polished stones from England, Scotland, Wales and Northern Ireland and honours all members of the various branches of the Intelligence Services of the United Kingdom from 1909 onwards. No-one visits, unless they know of its existence, and very few do.

The memorial recognises members, past and present, of MI5 (Military Intelligence Section 5), the SIS (Secret Intelligence Service or MI6) and GCHQ (Government Communications Headquarters) and also those who worked in the Government Code and Cypher School during the 1939-1945 war at Bletchley Park. Nothing else like it exists in the UK and certainly nothing as a standalone object in remembrance of security services lives lost in Northern Ireland – of which there have been many.

Declan McNally found a way to put this right. Somewhere closer to Thiepval and individual to the YCU. But it took a special relationship to make it happen.

No-one carried Isadora Brown's body into the church, as that had been released to the family, and they had said goodbye with the respect, hopelessness and sadness reserved for a family's love. Virginia had been told that over four hundred mourners arrived at the funeral, including friends from the military training college in Sandhurst, where they'd nicknamed her 'the machine'. However, only one person from MI5 had attended the Roman Catholic Church of St Michael in Solihull, where the service took place. This was Sir Charles Curry, the former spy chief and the man responsible for Isadora's recruitment to YCU.

In Solihull, he'd sat anonymously at the back and wished he could have told the family who Isadora really was and the bravery she had shown. Instead, now, stepping up to the lectern at the Church of St Bernadette's in West Belfast, with the doors bolted shut and the curtains closed, he would make that speech.

Charles looked out at the front row of mourners and saw Virginia Curry seated next to Jenny Richmond, with Jones gripping tightly to Jenny's hand. Next to them were Declan McNally, Jube Spencer, Clive Gentry, Orla Massey and Marie Bristow. Behind them, the Quartermaster's Department of Mr Singh, Tom Marsh, Carl Kelly and Wendy Watson. All of them dressed in formal wear, but with Isadora's favourite colour, a light purple, clearly in evidence.

Finally, Jube has also put in a call to Jim Shiels from J2 plus the elder statesmen of Bobby Moses and Ray McQueen, who were serving just down the road at Palace Barracks, thanks to the deal they'd struck with Clive during the Wild Flowers mission. Bobby had even pretended to be Isadora's father in Bermuda and had been dumbstruck when he'd heard news of her death. Everyone felt the same numbness.

Charles, as always, was fantastically attired and well prepared, but was as solemn and emotional as anyone had ever seen him.

"Isadora Brown was the shining light of the YCU. Right from her first appearance in Thiepval, Virginia and I knew she would change the world. She arrived here after swapping from a military training college in Sandhurst and was a year older than the rest of the team. The report I received from her assessors at Sandhurst described her an unstoppable machine, but we soon realised that was just as much for her training ability as her analysis and problem-solving skills. She was, frankly, brilliant." Charles paused for breath.

"Isadora had ambition to be a marine or join the SBS, but she believed she wasn't cut out to be a soldier. But as I think we can all testify, although she was diminutive in size, she was a fierce competitor with an enormous academic ability to boot. She simply wanted to be the best." He stopped briefly as he noticed Jenny had broken down in the front row and Virginia had moved to comfort her.

"We saw her as not just the standout female candidate but the standout candidate, full stop. And that was significant praise when I initially didn't want female candidates. I admit that. Male security service entrants were still the significant majority across the whole service and why did that need fixing? How wrong could I be? We now have some of the best candidates in the world, male and female, and it was Isadora that smashed through that ceiling. What's more, she then proved she could do it from a wheelchair." A few of those assembled nodded and smiled at those words. It spoke volumes about the abundance of respect for this fallen officer.

"Finally, you may ask why we are here today? A zone of Belfast where the British security services, in all their guises, have never been welcomed and understandably so. However, this wonderful church was the last place Isadora visited, when she spoke to Father Peter O'Callaghan, who is seated just in front of me now. Father Peter is working with Mr McNally on a small memorial which will be kept in the crypt here at St Bernadette's. There'll be no names inscribed, just the words '*in remembrance of the lives lost and for those unspoken*'. This, of course, includes Isadora's friends who died at Limehall and Lennoxville, as well as any future colleagues here who make the ultimate sacrifice. Father Peter tells me you will always be welcome here to visit and that the memorial will remain unmentionable. It will be for those of any faith and none. Isadora made this happen and we treasure our memories of her and hold dear her achievements."

There was silence as Sir Charles stepped down from the lectern and resumed his seat next to Virginia. Jones then stood up to add some final words. As her closest friend in the team, Jenny had been asked initially, but she simply couldn't commit to delivering the words without emotionally crumbling. Jones wasn't entirely sure he could either.

"Isadora was our friend and an inspiration," he began. "We will miss her more than words. But she hated formality, sadness, and being at the centre of attention for too long. So, we have arranged a wake at The Bunch of Grapes, where we will say goodbye to Isadora in a manner she would heartily approve of. I'd like to thank Sir Charles for arranging the wake and for his generosity." Jones didn't know what else to say. He turned and faced the small gathering in the pews in front and made one final, simple announcement.

"The YCU did some research on the Brontë family a few weeks back, as their father was born close to here. So, I'd like to adapt a short quote from Charlotte Brontë," Jones coughed and felt the lump grow in his mouth.

"Goodbye Isadora, our second self and our best earthly companion."

With that, he silently paced back to Jenny in the front row and let the emotion flood out of him. His friends gathered around him and formed a huddle of love and care. There was not a dry eye in the church.

It wasn't until 3am the following morning, when the last of the stragglers left The Bunch of Grapes and the pub had been almost drunk dry, that Jones and Jenny noticed three full drinks left on the side of the bar.

"What on earth are they?" Jones asked, slurring badly and just avoiding falling over a stool in the middle of the lounge bar. "Tell you what, I'll taste them," he called over before finding a seat.

"No, no," Jenny responded, equally refreshed. "You've had enough. Let me," and Jenny took a sip of the first of three identical drinks. On tasting them, in turn, she turned to Jones.

"These are all gin and ginger. Look, they've even got the slice of lime in there. Isadora's favourite. Her tipple of choice."

"Oh dear," Jones said, staggering to his feet. "I've bought three rounds. Jim Shiels bought two. Charles bought the rest. I've been memorising our rounds since we started living in Thiepval. I think I accidentally forgot to remove Isadora's order. Still... that's quite fitting, really."

"You're a sentimental old thing, aren't you, Jones?" Jenny smiled. She flung her arms around Jones and, as the landlord appeared with a broom, they walked back to Thiepval, hand in hand.

A fortnight later

There was a cool breeze blowing over the parade ground at Thiepval, where the Young Communicators Unit members were enjoying one of their regular physical endurance exercises coordinated by the military. Delta, captained by Ailsa, and Echo, led by Niall, were competing to transfer equipment from one side of the field to the other in the quickest time. It was a test of speed, strength, and ingenuity. Jones and Jenny had been working with their respective teams to devise a strategy.

Jenny had opted to join Delta and was midway through transporting a series of telephone poles to be stacked in order. Jones, however, was still on the injured list. His wrist had been badly damaged from punching Eric Rogers in the face, and he'd broken two fingers. Wendy had taken his place in Echo to even up the numbers. McNally was stationed at one end, next to a few other spectators. He was supposed to be acting as an observer and marshal but was actually chatting to Jones.

They both watched fascinatedly as four soldiers, in a Regimental Sergeant Major style, supplied the vocal motivation and momentum to the teams. Jenny and Wendy looked exhausted. Ailsa had barely broken a sweat.

McNally casually lit one of his cigarillos. "It's exhausting just watching. You must be pleased to have swerved it?"

"It actually might have done me some good. I can't get The Mainstay case out my brain. Jube reckons the investigations could last well over a year to bring everyone involved in the empire to justice. There are 119 people in the frame, is that right?" Jones asked.

"That sounds about right, yeah. It's a huge piece of work to bring them all to justice. I dropped Jube off at Aldergrove last week. He had to fly back to his flat in London."

"He's gone?" Jones replied.

"He went back to clear out his flat. Clive's asked him to end his secondment to Balfron Tower and work back in Belfast permanently. So, he's still attached to the investigation," McNally explained.

"He'll dine off this success for years. It's a feather in all our caps. It was one of the largest organised crime rackets smashed in recent years. But difficult not to feel sorry for people like Eric's wife, their family, and the wee Bradley children," he added.

"And Isadora. I still can't believe it. I helped empty her room with Virginia the other day. It was heart-breaking and her parents think she died in a car crash in America. It's all too awful for words," Jones reflected. They both paused for a second.

They watched as Jenny stopped momentarily to wave over at a small group of newly arrived spectators. Jones turned and saw who it was. Marie Bristow was wheeling Orla Massey over towards them. They'd been invited to the event by Virginia Curry.

"Don't look at me like that, Jones," Massey smiled. "I have two weeks and I'll be walking again and out of this damned thing."

"That's fantastic news. I guess we'll never be free of you then? You'll soon be released back into the wild," McNally laughed.

"You'll never be free of me, Declan McNally. I'm like a friendly virus."

"Anyway," Bristow chimed in, grinning broadly. "I don't know whether any of you have met Acting Chief Superintendent Massey?"

"Oh, wow!" Jones exclaimed. "Promotion? That's phenomenal news. Well done!"

"Oh, you'd not heard? I thought it was common knowledge. But thank you," Massey couldn't help but smile. "My photo is now on every police dartboard in Northern Ireland!"

"I think you'll find it was already on every dart board." McNally laughed. "But bravo! I can't believe that our own wee Orla is the first female Chief Superintendent in RUC history. We are all extremely proud of you."

"Well, your wee Orla wonders whether they asked me because they wanted an unpopular broom to sweep out the deadwood in Knock Road. You know, Eric had eight other officers on the payroll of the empire, including the two guarding me at the hospital. No wonder he knew everything."

"Unpopular broom or not, it's a fresh start," Bristow added. "And we all need that."

"Agreed. Anyway, as much as I hate socialising, I'm going to have a wee housewarming party next week at my place in Sailortown. I'd like you all there. You kept me sane during the dark hours. But you all need to bring one tin of dead expensive cat food for Georgie, as he's the real hero. He deserves the best."

Just then, Jenny ran over with Wendy close behind. Jenny's team had finished transferring the last of the telephone poles and they were now working on lifting what looked like the engine of an articulated lorry. Wendy put her hands on her hips and panted.

"I've just got a second," Wendy began, dripping with sweat and regretting undertaking the exercise in a black Nirvana t-shirt with black leggings. "We're so far behind Delta and I'm absolutely knackered. I think I'm actually dragging them backwards. But I just wanted to come and say congratulations to Orla."

"It was well deserved! I'm beyond excited for you. Can we take you out to celebrate, maybe next week?" Jenny added. "Jones and I would love to take you to that new Italian in Holywood."

"Hold on a second, you two knew? Was I the last to know? Why didn't you tell me?" Jones said. They both ignored him.

"Yeah, I'm taking Jones back to Bermondsey to meet the family for the first time next week. So, we'll miss the housewarming. But we'll only be gone a few days." Jenny told the collective, and then ran off, back to the competition. Wendy hung around and leant on McNally as if she was about to topple over.

"You kept that bloody quiet," Wendy smiled. "Meeting the family is a big moment."

"I'm having nightmares about it already," he replied, looking genuinely concerned. "This is all new to me. What if they hate me? Her other boyfriend was rich and successful, and I've got to stick with the cover that I'm a trainee journalist."

Wendy, Massey, and Bristow all laughed. McNally shifted uncomfortably in his seat. He was well out of his depth in this type of conversation.

"If you can handle all this shite here at the YCU, then you can deal with Jenny's parents. Just smile lots and wear a good white shirt. Make sure it's a clean one," Massey advised.

"Just don't make an arse of yourself, Jones. That's my only advice," Wendy smiled. "Mr Singh has been using that as his mantra for years."

"Right, moving on," Massey jumped back in. "I've been asked to brief you on some suspicious activity coming into Larne port. We're thinking gun shipments under the radar. It's all early days, but it smells bad."

"Now that's interesting," McNally responded, grabbing two manila folders from Bristow.

"It'll be my first case as Acting Chief Superintendent. I could do with your help, and I need a new technical officer to be based at Knock Road. It would be a secondment." Massey looked at Wendy.

"Really?" Wendy turned, looking shocked. "Me? Well, that's certainly something to think about. I'll need to speak to Mr Singh."

"Already done," Massey responded. "He tells me he can just about cope with Carl and Tom to fill the void. But nothing is settled. It's totally in your hands. If you want it, you can start next week. Once the operation is finished, you're back here in the cut and thrust of the YCU. But your knowledge would be a huge plus with a fledgling Knock Road team."

Wendy looked at Jones for inspiration, who shrugged in response.

"I'll have a think," Wendy replied. "But I'm going to find it hard to say no. Do you have good coffee?"

"No, we don't have good anything. You'll get ogled, you'll be tested by rampant male stupidity, and you'll lose your bap a hundred times a day," Massey smiled. "But you'll learn."

Just then, a loud air horn was blown in the middle of the parade ground. Ailsa stood in the centre of a vast assortment of objects, looking mightily proud of herself. Delta had won easily. Jenny, looking fatigued but elated, sprinted back and threw her arms around Ailsa in celebration.

Jones, feeling a touch guilty for not fully concentrating on the exercise, walked over to the side of the pitch and screamed some last-ditch positivity from the side-lines.

"Come on Echo! Drinks on me if you get within five minutes of their time!" he shouted.

"Bit late for that," Jenny chuckled, strolling back from Ailsa. "But that just about sums you up," she added. "Grabbing a different victory after the initial defeat. Changing the rules."

"Yes. I'll take that," he grinned. "Any kind of victory works for me. It's about learning to accept a spectrum of different outcomes."

With that, Jones slapped Niall on the back and urged his team on. There was definitely something Echo could take away from this defeat, he thought.

The author would like to thank:

Vince McLoughlin, Alison Robinson, Jo Jacobius and Hayley Webster for beta reading, editing and dealing with my tantrums; Sumaira Wilson and Nikki East at SpellBound for continued support and innovation and to Colyn Cranney and Daisy Robinson for design and project initiation throughout the series. I actually started writing this book in 2002, so it has been a real labour of love!

About the Author

Richard W. Robinson is an author and former journalist who spent his early days freelancing or working in agency positions across the UK and Ireland. The Mainstay is the third of a current series of spy fiction novels, where we follow the missions of Jones and Richmond as they make their way through the early years of a career in espionage. The novels are works of fiction but reference historic events in 1994-1996, around the time of the peace talks in Northern Ireland. Outside the literary world, Richard lives in East Anglia, England, with his wife and two daughters. He is the CEO of a charity focused on ending the abuse of older people. He's a very committed cratedigger (vinyl collector) and a supporter of QPR and Ulster RFC. Follow The Topaz Files on social media for future release dates. The series so far: Topaz (book one); Wild Flowers (book two); The Mainstay (book three) and Deep Swimmers (book four) and Seen/Unseen (book five).

Coming Soon

Deep Swimmers: Topaz Files Four

Deep Swimmers follows Jones, an MI5 field officer, as he faces a personal crisis while investigating a chilling connection to a WWII-era secret.

Returning home to Suffolk due to his mother's sudden illness, Jones finds himself entangled in a shadowy conspiracy that links the tragic deaths of two individuals at Belfast's notorious Ashton Tower to a wider network of espionage and military secrets. We learn more about Sir Charles and Virginia Curry, meet Jones' family and explore the darkest memories of Northern Ireland in the 1940s.

At the heart of the investigation is Edward O'Callaghan, a former Irish rebel with deep ties to both the IRB and British intelligence, whose wartime connections might hold the key to understanding the deaths of the O'Dowds—two people who were far more than they seemed.

As Jones, Jenny and McNally delve deeper into the mystery, they uncover a web of deceit, betrayal, and long-buried history that stretches back to the darkest days of World War II.

Can Jones unravel the truth before those who wish to bury it succeed?

Seen/Unseen: Topaz Files Five

After years in the shadows, Maurice O'Shaughnessy—better known as *Mo The Blow*—is back. Once the IRB's most feared bomb-maker, he's spent a decade training mercenaries across the world. Now, he wants out. But turning supergrass comes at a price, and in Belfast, old ghosts never rest.

As MI5 and the RUC move to dismantle the IRB's hidden arsenal, a dangerous game of cat and mouse unfolds. At its centre is Dinah Finnerty, a young woman who has spent her life unseen—until now. With a past that ties her to some of the city's most ruthless players, Dinah is on a path that could shatter everything.

Jones, struggling with his own demons, is forced to confront the cost of unfinished business. Reunited with an old shipmate and haunted by the fate of Jube Spencer—presumed vanished—he follows the trail deep into Belfast's underworld, where the lines between truth and betrayal blur.

Some wars never end. Some secrets refuse to stay buried. And in the tunnels beneath the city, the past is waiting to explode.

Also By Richard Robinson

Topaz : Topaz Files One

It's the summer of 1995. The US Peace Envoy, Fred Martinson, begins to broker a peace deal for Northern Ireland. The world holds its breath as the first tentative steps are taken.

Jones, an 18-year-old from suburban England, has stumbled through education and yearns to be a football reporter. He is offered a place at Milton College, a former secretarial school with a clandestine partnership with GCHQ in seeking the communication stars of the future.

Before he knows it, Jones has been recruited, paired with Jenny Richmond, who is every bit his equal, and sent to Northern Ireland to undertake skills development and resilience testing with the Young Communicators Unit (YCU).

Training becomes a matter of life and death when a group of trainee spies learning on the job are betrayed to their death, and their most promising member, Isadora Brown, is taken hostage. MI5 and YCU are sent a video of her reading demands by a mysterious organisation called Red Line.

What if a group of young trainees were forced onto the frontline to deal with one of the most sensitive issues in UK history? What if political relations were so sensitive at the end of The Cold War, that only a group of deniable students could change history and keep superpowers from ruining the chances of a peace deal in Northern Ireland?

It's a race against the clock to find and free Isadora, and make sure the US peace talks aren't sent up in flames. **But who, exactly, is betraying who?**

Also by Richard Robinson

Wild Flowers: Topaz Files Two.

Jones, an inexperienced spy, finds himself frantically trapped on the General Eduardo, one of the largest container ships in the world.

With escape seemingly impossible, Jenny Richmond is the linchpin in a daring operation by the Topaz team, racing against time to recover the lethal cargo hijacked by the Russians and bound for clandestine camps in Belize. The team have to pull out all the stops to try to rescue Jones and retrieve the millions of pounds of armaments and ammunition on board stolen from the IRA by the Russians.

However, they are not the only team keeping tabs on the stolen arms, with Russia's own double agent, Joseph Armstrong, chasing the shipment too. He's offered a million dollar deal by a larger-than-life Zimbabwean farmer, Irvine Terre-Blanche, to renege on his Russian paymasters. But what does Terre-Blanche want it for?

What's at stake? Millions of pounds and the sinister secrets of corrupt government official. As the stakes soar, a band of retired spies joins the fray, seeking one last hurrah in this high-octane thriller of deception and betrayal.

This is a roller coaster espionage thriller which follows Jones and Richmond as they embark on a life-changing mission. **And what is the mysterious Wild Flowers Project?**

Printed in Great Britain
by Amazon

60735279R10306